COWBOY
Tough

JOANNE KENNEDY

Published by Sourcebooks Casablanca, an imprint of Sourcebooks, Inc.
P.O. Box 4410, Naperville, Illinois 60567-4410
(630) 961-3900
FAX: (630) 961-2168
www.sourcebooks.com

Printed and bound in Canada
WC 10 9 8 7 6 5 4 3 2 1

To my husband, Ken McCauley,
who taught me to believe in love.

Chapter 1

CAT CRANDALL KNEW ARTISTS WERE SUPPOSED TO suffer, but this was ridiculous.

Sure, Picasso lived in an unheated tenement and burned bundles of his own drawings for warmth. Modigliani died of tuberculosis in a sordid Parisian garret. And Van Gogh's painting of his room at Arles is famous for its grim, depressing atmosphere. But asking a group of vacationing watercolor painters to spend two weeks living in the Boyd Ranch Bunkhouse was going too far.

Windblown and dilapidated, its siding weathered to a soulless shade of gray, the building looked like a stack of kindling someone had dumped on the open prairie when they realized it wasn't worth burning. The front door was stuck shut, which was probably a good thing. Cat hated to even imagine what the interior looked like.

But she was going to have to face it sooner or later. Her students arrived tomorrow, and she didn't believe in running from trouble. Especially when she was in the middle of God's great open spaces, with nowhere to run to.

Putting her shoulder to the battered wooden door, she gave it a shove. It popped open so suddenly she staggered inside, grabbing the back of a chair for balance.

"Ouch." She turned her palm up and eyed the splinter jutting from her skin. Biting her lower lip, she pinched it out with her thumb and forefinger, wincing at the sharp pain. She winced again as she surveyed her surroundings.

She'd expected quaint and rustic; what she'd gotten was old and dirty. The plank floor was scuffed and studded with nail heads, and smudged windows revealed a desolate swath of yellowing prairie. The chair she'd grabbed, like its mismatched companion and a crooked table, looked like a thrift shop refugee from a war zone.

The place had advertised an "Authentic Wild West Experience," and she supposed that wasn't a lie; probably the old-time cowboys hadn't lived much better than this.

But when she'd signed on with Art Treks, she'd been hoping for the Tuscany experience, or maybe the Loire Valley experience. But while they'd hired her to "facilitate creative plein air watercolor workshops in exotic locations around the world," they'd failed to define "exotic." Or "the world."

For the next fourteen days, her world would be Wyoming. And this, evidently, was exotic.

"We call this one the Heifer House," said a deep voice from behind her.

She whirled to see the Wild West himself standing in the doorway, feet planted, arms loose in a gunfighter stance.

Well, that was exotic: a cowboy, decked out in full high plains regalia. Instead of six-guns, he was armed with a bottle of Windex and a dirty rag.

He nodded toward another wooden structure, visible through the smeared window. It tilted tipsily windward on the far side of a concave dirt crater.

"That's the Bull Barn, for the men." His mouth was

twisted into a sardonic smile, and she couldn't help smiling back. His outfit was ridiculous.

The jeans were all right. The striped shirt was loud, but not outrageous. It was the oversized cherry red glad rag knotted round his neck and the chaps bracketing his legs that made him look like an extra from *Paint Your Wagon*.

Shoving the rag in his back pocket, he lifted a thumb and forefinger to tug down the brim of his hat.

"Ma'am." He punctuated the greeting with a sharp nod.

Did he have to call her that? It made her feel about a zillion years old.

"I'm not a ma'am."

"Oh. Sorry, ma'am."

Was he trying to annoy her, or was he really that dumb? Cat looked him up and down and decided she didn't care as long as he wore those chaps. They might make him look like a cartoon cowboy from the funny papers, but they hugged his slim hips and emphasized his muscular thighs. The leather tie at the front reminded her of a bow on a very nice, very masculine birthday present, and it put his assets front and center, making it obvious that under the cowboy costume was a very real man—maybe even a real cowboy, if such a thing still existed. He was tanned and muscular, with a swoon-worthy smile and dark eyes that invited her to reach over and untie that bow.

Adjusting the tilt of her broad-brimmed sun hat, she looked away. She wasn't here to gawk at men; she was here to keep her clients comfortable while they learned to paint landscapes in watercolor. And that meant she needed to do something about the less-than-stellar accommodations.

If it was just her, she wouldn't care. Squalor was an artistic rite of passage, after all. But while Picasso and Van Gogh would have welcomed the suffering, she couldn't let her students stay in this bare-bones bunk-house. Neither could her fifteen-year-old niece Dora, who was arriving the next day. The kid had enough issues right now without adding splinters and pneumonia to the list. It might be August, but the website had warned that nights in Wyoming could be nippy.

Setting her fists on her hips, she tilted her chin up so she could meet the cowboy's eyes. "This is not what I expected." She was tempted to poke a finger in his chest, but now that they were eye to eye—or eye to shirt pocket—she realized he was bigger than she was. A lot bigger. "The website said 'rustic,' not 'sordid.' Are you in charge here?"

He grimaced. "If I was, d'you think I'd be wearing this monkey suit?"

She gave the monkey suit another once-over. "I don't know. They look like cowboy clothes to me, and you're a cowboy, right?"

"Not today." He lifted one hand in a mock salute. "Today I'm the window washer, Walmart greeter, and general step'n'fetch-it."

He rolled his shoulders as if he wanted to squirm out of his shirt, then reached up and tugged at the oversized red bandanna around his neck. Tearing it from his neck, he shoved it in his pocket along with the window-washing rag.

Maybe he wasn't a real cowboy after all. Those guys

were famous for being comfortable in their own skin, and he looked like he wanted to rip off his fancy clothes and run for the hills.

The notion of him shedding his clothes almost made her smile in spite of herself.

"Guess I'm part of the rusticity." He'd dropped the aw-shucks drawl, but his voice was still low, with a baritone timbre that seemed to vibrate at the base of her spine. "I'm trying to clean up the sordid stuff, though." He stepped forward and offered a rough, calloused hand. "Mack Boyd. I'll be your wrangler."

Cat tried not to react as his big hand swallowed her small one, but she couldn't help sneaking a quick look up and down. If she could get him out of the monkey suit, he might be a decent model for a portrait. She wondered how he felt about posing naked.

If he was willing, she might overlook the accommodations.

Maybe she should borrow that Windex and wipe the rampaging fantasies out of her mind. It wouldn't do for fifteen-year-old Dora to see her aunt going all googly-eyed over strange men with bows on their assets. And judging from the way his square jaw softened as he took in her sparkly one-shouldered tunic, he might be having the same kind of thoughts.

Then he squinted at her hat and his lips tightened in obvious disapproval.

She touched the brim self-consciously. Okay, it wasn't a cowboy hat. But it kept the sun off her face, and it was a hell of a lot prettier than the dirty old thing he was wearing. Especially since she'd stuck a few road-side flowers in the blue silk scarf wrapped around the crown. He might look like a Louis L'Amour hero, but she looked like a Renoir painting.

"I'd better get back to work," he said. "Feel free to explore, and let me know if you need anything." He turned and shot one of the grubby panes with Windex, giving her a chance to appreciate the fine slice of Wyoming scenery framed by the fringe on his chaps.

Throwing her hat on a chair, she tossed her head to get her hair out of her eyes and her mind out of the gutter. She was supposed to be checking out the bunkhouse, not the wrangler. Raking her fingers through her hair, she strode down a short hall to her left, glancing right and left to check out the rooms.

The website trumpeted "private rooms" with a shared "luxury bath," but by that standard, a box stall in a barn would be designated a first-class suite. The bedrooms were more like cubicles than rooms, with walls that ended a foot below the ceiling. Inside each one, a neatly made bed was accompanied by a worn wooden kitchen chair and a rickety dresser. A few tin lanterns and antique rodeo posters were scattered around in a failed effort to transform the thrift shop furnishings into Western chic.

Returning to the front room, she peered out the newly cleaned window at the rough dirt crater between the two bunkhouses. It looked like a mortar hole in no-man's-land.

"What's that?"

"The fire pit." He stood back from the window, then reached out to remove a final streak of cleaner. The move reminded her of an artist putting the final touches on a painting. "I'll have benches around it by the time your guests get here."

She sighed. "I suppose we gather 'round at night and sing cowboy songs?"

He grinned. "Don't knock it till you've tried it."

"I don't know any cowboy songs."

That wasn't quite true. Her dad had loved Westerns, and the eerie, threatening whistle from "The Good, the Bad and the Ugly" sounded in her head every time she looked at this guy. He might be wearing the biggest white hat she'd ever seen, but he was definitely not Roy Rogers.

"I'll teach 'em to you." His smile revealed strong teeth nearly as white as the hat. Momentarily dazzled, she looked away and muttered something about freshening up.

Backing into the bathroom, she closed the door and sat heavily on the side of the claw-footed tub with her feet splayed and her knees together. Resting her forearms on her thighs, she hung her head and let the sights and sounds of the last few hours swirl in her brain.

The hollow drone of the airplane landing in Denver. The hum of the highway under the wheels of her rental car. The featureless prairie stretching out on either side of the road, marked by an endless parade of telephone poles. The ranch itself, a cluster of broken-down buildings bleached gray by the sun.

It might be authentic, but even the waves of testosterone emanating from the cowboy window washer couldn't mask the place's air of seedy desperation.

At least the bathroom was quaint, with its old-style tile and porcelain fixtures, though the dried-flower arrangement on the back of the toilet looked as if it had been culled from the dead weeds out front. A decorative shelf above it held a selection of antique cosmetics, along with a chipped mug bearing a selection of pearl-topped hat pins. She briefly considered suicide by hat pin but decided death by puncture wound would hurt more than getting fired by the Art Treks corporation.

But they couldn't fire her. Not yet, anyway. The Boyd Dude Ranch had been the company's choice. She was just supposed to make it work.

Which meant they would fire her later.

Rising, she checked her hair in the mirror, tousling the dark waves, and pressed her lips together to refresh her lipstick. The mirror was foxed and dim, with spidery cracks radiating from the corners.

Squaring her shoulders, she gave herself an encouraging smile and stepped out to confront the cowboy again. He was cleaning the panes in the front window now.

"Who do I talk to about this?"

"About what?"

She gestured toward the bedrooms. "The accommodations."

"What's wrong with 'em?"

She heaved a theatrical sigh. "Where do I start?"

His dark eyes narrowed, and what was left of his easy grin flattened into a grim scowl. "I guess you can talk to my mother. She's up at the house."

Great. Not only did he dress like Yosemite Sam and talk like Slim Pickens, but he was a mama's boy, too. She jammed on her hat and headed for the door, then hesitated on the threshold. Maybe she should pocket one of those hat pins so she could stab the person who put together that website.

Hell, she didn't need a hat pin. All she needed to put a hole in the proprietor of the Boyd Dude Ranch were sharp words and a sharper tongue. And while she might look like a doe-eyed Disney princess and dress like a drunken flapper, she'd never had a problem expressing herself.

Chapter 2

A HEAVYSET WOMAN WAS FLAILING AROUND WITH A broom in the front hall of the house, hounding a herd of dust bunnies over the doorsill. In her blue-striped housedress and white apron, she fit right in with the dude ranch decor—although the dress, unlike the ranch, looked reasonably new. And clean.

Cat cleared her throat. As the woman whirled to face her, dust bunnies swarmed around her feet in a broom-created eddy, then skittered for freedom.

"Why, you must be Miss Crandall." The woman propped the broom against the wall and crossed the porch in two long strides to grasp both Cat's hands in a surprisingly powerful welcome. She had the cute, dark-haired country charm of Patsy Cline—if Patsy had been six feet tall with the muscles of a stevedore.

"Welcome to the Boyd Dude Ranch." The woman's dark eyes crinkled at the corners. "I'm Madeleine Boyd. You can call me Maddie."

"Thank you." *Don't let her soften you up. Of course she's friendly; she's trying to rip you off.* "I had some questions about the accommodations."

Maddie gave her a knowing smile. "I suppose they're not what you're used to?"

"Not at all. The bunkhouse…"

"We call 'em the Heifer House and the Bull Barn." Madeleine smiled, which made her eyes squinny up and her cheeks go plump. If an enormous middle-aged woman could be adorable, that's what she was. "Don't worry. People don't come here to sit around in their rooms. They come for the campfires and the camaraderie. And let me tell you, we deliver on that."

Great. They were probably going to sing "Kumbaya." Or "Cattle Call." Cat wondered if the cowboy could yodel. He'd probably do it if his mother told him to.

"The website's misleading." Cat put on her best hair pin voice. "I saw pictures of the house that led me to believe…"

"If anyone wants to stay in the house they're welcome to," Madeleine said briskly. "But I think you should try the bunkhouse. Roughing it really adds to the Wyoming experience." She gave a sharp nod, as if the whole matter had been decided. "We have a fire pit out there, and a chuck wagon. Believe me, there's nothing better than supper under the stars. You've never seen stars like we've got here in Wyoming."

Cat suspected they were the same stars she'd seen in Chicago. She started to say so, but Mrs. Boyd laid a motherly hand on her arm and met her eyes so honestly Cat felt her will to fight flattening like a possum under a semitruck.

"All right," she said. "We'll try it."

It wasn't like she had a choice. She could hardly ask her students to stay at the Day's Inn out on the highway. And there was no other option for miles.

"Good." The woman's eyes sparkled. "Just so you know, your hostess—that's me—is a champion chuck-wagon chef. You haven't lived till you've tried my biscuits. Did you see the wagon? It's a bona fide piece of Wyoming history."

Cat remembered seeing some sort of wheeled vehicle parked by the Heifer House, but it had looked as broken-down as the bunkhouse itself. She'd figured it was a covered wagon that had been abandoned in despair by starving pioneers.

She must have looked as doubtful as she felt, because the woman amped up the spunky attitude and gave her a broad grin. "Give it a chance, hon. Let the West work its magic. I've never had a complaint about the place. Not once."

Cat was tempted to ask if they'd ever had anyone stay there before, but she simply shrugged. "It's just so important," she said. "It's my first workshop for the company, and I need a success. With good feedback from the clients, they'll keep me on. Otherwise…"

She let her voice trail off. She didn't want to think about *otherwise*.

"You don't make a living from your artwork?" Madeleine lifted her brows in almost comical surprise.

"No." Cat felt a familiar stab of dissatisfaction and a twinge of annoyance with herself. She always felt like a failure when she compared her youthful aspirations with her current status in the art world. "Not yet."

Maybe not ever. Her watercolor landscapes weren't edgy or bold or groundbreaking. They were beautiful, or at least Cat thought so, but beauty was apparently passé.

In fact, she was surprised she'd been hired by Art Treks, even for a trial period. One of her college friends worked for the company, and evidently he'd gone to bat for her in a big way. Most of the other teachers were well-known, with how-to articles in national maga-zines and big-city gallery representation. Cat, with her advertising background, could hardly have been their first choice.

She shook off the familiar, almost obsessive interior monologue of ambition and self-deprecation to turn back to what mattered.

"I'm concerned about my clients. They paid a lot of money for this trip. The wrangler—he's your son, right?"

"Right." The woman puffed out her ample chest. "And the best dang cowboy in Wyoming. Did you see those chaps?"

Despite her bad mood, the thought of the chaps made Cat smile. "Uh-huh. Impressive."

"He *won* those. Fort Worth, 2003." The woman nattered on, clearly proud of her son. "He's a bareback rider, you know. I've been trying to get him to quit for years, and this dude ranch thing finally got him to join the family business. He's so excited about the conversion—guiding tours is just his cup of tea."

Cat tried to picture the window-washing wrangler drinking tea.

She failed.

Up until now, Maddie Boyd had seemed utterly genuine, but the smile on her face as she talked about her son seemed forced.

"Never had any complaints about *him*, either," she said.

Of course not. Nobody would dare to confront this imposing woman about anything.

Madeleine Boyd was a human steamroller.

"You go on out," Maddie said. "Mack'll take you around the place. You ride horseback?"

"Sure," Cat said.

"Good. He'll help you find the spots you want to

paint." She made a shooing gesture. "Go on, now. You tell him to give you our best Boyd Ranch welcome. Tell him his mother said for him to do it right."

—∿∿—

Madeleine watched from the porch as Cat Crandall set off for the bunkhouse. The artist stayed in there for maybe ten minutes, then came out dressed in a man's shirt and jeans.

Good. The girl had some sense. Mack would never have let her ride with all those dangling beads and sparkles, spooking the horse and getting caught on stuff. She still had that hat on, though—a garden-party affair with a silk scarf wrapped around it. Hardly a cowboy hat, but at least it would shade that pale skin from the sun.

Somehow, she and Mack needed to charm this woman into the artistic experience of a lifetime at the Boyd Dude Ranch. A rave review would earn them a permanent contract with Art Treks, and a permanent contract meant full bunks for at least three months out of the year. These artsy folks were willing to pay a premium for the scenery Madeleine woke up to every morning, and she had no problem taking their money.

She'd been hoping to bond with the leader of the tour, but it was clear the girl was from another species. *Feminus Cosmopolitus*, or something; an exotic city bird with plumage to match. That meant the bonding was going to be up to Mack. Hopefully he'd turn on the considerable cowboy charm he'd inherited from his father—her first husband.

The good one.

The bad one was the reason they were in this mess.

But there was no point dwelling on the past. Mack's charm had worked on women before, and he knew everything depended on Cat Crandall's satisfaction.

It wouldn't be easy for him. He'd been anything but charming since he'd come home, and she could hardly blame him. He'd given up the rodeo season and come home to help her out of the mess she'd made. The look of betrayal on his face when he discovered how desperate they were had broken her heart—or at least, it would have if she'd had a heart to break. Her second husband had shattered that organ into so many pieces she doubted there were any left that were big enough to crack.

Chapter 3

MACK HEFTED A BALE OF STRAW ONTO A WHEELBARROW. A few loose wisps lofted up on impact, dancing with dust motes in a shaft of late afternoon sunlight. There was no wind today, not so much as a breeze, and they quickly drifted down and settled on the dusty barn floor.

"Trapped," he muttered. "Doomed to dude ranching."

His dog Tippy trotted in with her distinctive sideways gait. Collapsing in a square of sunshine, she let her tongue flop out of the side of her mouth and grinned.

"Probably shouldn't talk about traps around you, huh?" He ran a careless hand over the dog's sleek black head. He'd found her three years earlier, lying by the side of a dusty dirt road. She'd evidently had a fight with a coyote trap and lost—lost a leg, in fact—but she'd hung onto a sunny disposition that never failed to cheer him up.

Lately, he'd caught himself talking to the dog more and more. It was odd, because he'd never been much of a talker. Now that he was off the road and back on the ranch, he supposed he missed the rollicking camaraderie of the other cowboys.

He'd always known he'd have to return home someday. But he'd figured on running cattle, and it had been a shock to discover he was wrangling dudes instead. With that jerk his mother had married running the ranch, things had gone from bad to worse. The ranch had already been struggling; now they were dead broke. The evil stepfather had taken off with some floozy from Jackson Hole, and Maddie Boyd had stepped out of her ranch wife role to run the place.

He'd always known his mother could do more than housekeep and cook. Hell, she could ride as well as anyone he knew, and heft hay as well as the hired man. That ill-advised second marriage was the only time she'd shown a weakness, but that mistake was in the past and she was back to being her strong, capable self.

Still, she had no more idea how to run a dude ranch than Mack did. They were both playing by ear, and his mother was calling the tune.

Tippy sighed and rested her chin on the barn floor.

"Yeah, I know," he said. "It's not like I have a right to argue."

He knew he'd been a lousy son all these years, dedicating himself to his sport to the exclusion of everything else. Even after his father died, he'd stayed on the road, letting his mother run the place with the help of the ranch hands.

It was the biggest mistake he'd ever made. He'd never expected his mother to make a fool of herself over a man with oily good looks and a soul as black as an Angus bull. Never expected her to remarry barely a year after his father's death.

Parking the wheelbarrow, he reached up to pat the neck of a piebald mule who was foraging for the remnants of his breakfast in the first stall. "Got our first dude," he said. "Or should I call her a dudette?"

The mule seemed to consider this, then resumed the hunt for hay. At least the animal pretended to listen to him. Mack's mother didn't listen to anybody, and the only hand left on the ranch was Silent Hank. Mack had never heard the man say more than two words at a time, so you never knew if he was paying attention or not.

It was a rhetorical question anyway. Their guest would probably punch him if he called her a dudette. She seemed like a bad-tempered bit of city smarts, but she'd caught his interest the moment she turned in the bunkhouse doorway and hit him with those eyes. Dark blue, really dark, but with sparkles at the surface. It was like looking into a deep river struck by sunlight. Dark lashes, too, all set in a pale face. And that sharp-tongued mouth, deceptively lush and sweet.

"Plain air workshops." He shook some straw over the floor of an empty stall and pushed the wheelbarrow back to its spot at the back of the barn, steering it around the now-sleeping dog. "What the hell is 'plain air,' anyway? Don't they have any plain air back where she comes from?" He slapped dust off his thighs. "Only got fancy air in Chicago. Probably fancy people, too."

"*Plein air*," said a voice from the doorway, pronouncing it "plenn." "It means painting outdoors, in the open air. It's French. Painting outdoors is painting *en plein air*."

He turned to see the dudette herself haloed by sunshine in the barn's wide doorway. She was all wild hair and delicate curves, but those tempting lips were now pursed in disapproval.

He could hardly blame her. He'd shed the monkey suit, stripping down to a white T-shirt that clung to his chest, damp with sweat. Straw dusted his hair and shoulders and prickled the back of his neck. And she'd caught him swearing up, down, and sideways about fancy people.

Maybe he could just pretend he hadn't said that stuff.

"So." He cleared his throat. "You teach people to paint 'on plenn air'?" He pronounced the words carefully.

"That's right. So they can be fancy, too."

Evidently she wasn't into pretending. He hoisted another bale onto the barrow, trying to figure out a way to backpedal. She'd shed her sparkly clothes and dangling jewelry, opting for an oversized white shirt that probably belonged to some big-city boyfriend. She was still wearing tight jeans and that crazy hat, but he was relieved to see boots on her feet instead of the little sissy shoes she'd been wearing before.

"You don't look fancy," he said.

"Girls *like* to look fancy."

Shoot. Could he open his mouth just one time without shoving his foot in it?

"I meant that as a compliment. I don't like fancy women."

"Yeah, I got that."

"Sorry. This dude ranch thing is all new to me. It's—different."

That was the understatement of the century. Dude ranching was more than different; it was a disaster. He'd always felt awkward with tourists who thought a working cowboy was some kind of anachronism. They'd go on about how he was "a dying breed," living "a vanishing way of life." It made him feel like a bug under glass, or some zoo animal.

But he had a feeling this woman saw him as something more than a curiosity. He'd caught a light in her

eyes back at the bunkhouse, a faint glimmering of something sexual. Those blue, blue eyes went straight to his
gut. Or was that his heart? Whatever it was, something
was building inside him like an oncoming storm, a high-
pressure system that was pushing his common sense
and self-preservation into the next county. He'd have to
avoid looking her in the eye.

He let his gaze drift down to the collar of her shirt and
slide down the front, but he couldn't help picturing the
buttons slipping undone, one by one. The shirt might be
loose, but it was well-worn, and he could see the outline
of a white lace bra underneath.

She took a step back. Had she read his mind?

With as much strength of will as he'd ever brought to
a bronc ride, he fixed his gaze on the barn door just over
her left shoulder. There were essential questions he'd
have to leave unanswered, even though they'd torture him
the rest of the day. Front clasp or back? White or ivory?

And what the hell was her name? Some kind of animal...

"Kitty, right?"

She rolled her eyes. "Cat. Short for Catherine." She
drew herself up to her full height. It wasn't much, but it
was all attitude. "I am definitely not a Kitty."

"Right. Catherine. I like Kitty, though." He grinned,
playing the easygoing cowboy. Easterners usually liked
that kind of thing. He ought to talk slower, put on a
drawl. Play the dumb lummox to put her at ease.

"Kitty Crandall." He looked up at the beamed ceiling and tapped his chin, pantomiming thought. "Sounds
like—never mind."

Sounds like a stripper name.

Maybe he really was a lummox. He'd damn near said

that out loud, mostly because he was distracted by the thought of that bra. He could picture her in that slanted ray of sun in her next-to-nothings, all smooth, soft skin, and gentle curves…

What the hell was wrong with him? Sure, the woman was hot top to bottom, from her plump lips to her small rounded breasts, from her sloping hips to her delicate little feet. She looked like one of those sexy little Japanese cartoon characters, all big eyes and shiny hair. But he was looking at her goggle-eyed as a teenager who'd never seen a woman before.

She set one hand on her hip and shifted her weight. The other hand plucked at the collar of her shirt. Her eyes dared him to keep looking. "Do I look like a Kitty to you?"

"You don't look like a very happy kitty."

She folded her arms across her chest. The gesture made him look down, but as soon as he hit the swell of her breasts he flicked his gaze back up to her eyes.

Look her in the eyes. Not the breasts. Not the breasts. The eyes. No, don't. Don't look at anything. She's looking back.

How was he supposed to work the cowboy charm without making eye contact?

Jokes. Make a joke. Smile. Do something.

Quit staring.

"I talked to your mom." Her dry tone sure didn't match the sweetness of her face. "She says this dude ranch gig is a dream come true for you."

"She has a tendency to exaggerate."

"So you're not a natural-born dude wrangler?"

He spread his arms in surrender. "I'm whatever you

want me to be. Right now I'm Mr. Clean, getting the
place ready for our close-up."

"There won't be many close-ups. We'll mostly be
doing landscapes. Unless you'd—oh, never mind." She
waved a hand in airy dismissal.

"No, really. What do you need me to do?

She peeked at him from under her lashes, a devilish
smile tilting her lips. Tapping her chin with one finger,
she looked him up and down in a way that made his
blood rush through his veins.

A cloud passed in front of the sun, and the patch of
light by the barn door suddenly disappeared, waking
Tippy to rise and stretch. The barn chilled a little and
it seemed as if Cat did too, her brows lowering, her
smile dimming.

"So can we do something about that bunkhouse?"

"Hey, we just fixed that up. Were you expecting five-
star digs or something?"

"Or something."

He supposed the bunkhouse was a little bare-bones,
but hadn't she read the website? It said *authentic cowboy
experience*, and the bunkhouse was a palace compared
to some of the places he'd stayed in. She ought to try
sharing a room with five dusty bronc riders at a Motel
6. Better yet, she should try a bedroll on the hard, cold
ground. That was the real cowboy experience.

He bit back that response and tried to think of something positive. "You won't be disappointed in the views.
Lots to paint here."

"That's true." Her stance softened as she stared out
the door at the sunlit grass and bright blue sky, drinking
in the landscape like she was starving for scenery. She

probably was, being from Chicago. He couldn't imagine spending his life hemmed in by skyscrapers, with the hum of humanity drowning out every bit of birdsong. No open space, no animals—just concrete and traffic. It would harden anybody. Maybe he should give her a break.

"Sorry," he said. "You didn't exactly catch me at my best. I thought this thing started tomorrow."

"It does. Your mother said I could come a day early and scout locations. In fact, she said I'd have a guided tour, and I think she figured you'd be the guide." She shrugged. "But if you want, I could go on my own. I'd just need you to remind me how to saddle the horse."

"You ride?"

"I've ridden ponies at birthday parties. How hard can it be?" She scanned the row of placid, hay-munching horses. "They don't look like Seabiscuit or anything."

"No, they're not. But they're from a kid's camp. They get kind of stubborn, getting kicked around and stuff."

His mother had bought every one of the ranch's barn-sour and bedraggled animals from nearby Sunnyside Cowboy Camp, where horses spent every summer getting their training obliterated by the hands and heels of dozens of children. The one thing they were good at was scraping off inexperienced riders.

He pictured Cat in the backcountry, unhorsed and on foot in her baggy shirt and oversized hat. She could fall into a ravine, stumble over a tree root, break those pretty delicate bones.

"I'll take you," he said. "You shouldn't ever ride alone."

"You do it."

"That's different. I'm a…" He stopped himself. He'd

almost said, "I'm a man." That would have set her off. "I'm a professional."

She shrugged. "Whatever. When do you want to go?"

He took off his hat and ran his fingers through his hair, then slapped the Stetson back on his head. In his experience, women came in two types: the ones that annoyed him, and the ones that jacked up his hormones and made a fool of him.

He'd expected this woman to be the first kind, not the second. But maybe he'd been wrong.

She was both.

Chapter 4

CAT WAS WEARING HER FAVORITE PAINTING SHIRT. IT was worn and comfortable—and now that she was backlit by sunlight, she realized it was practically transparent. The way the wrangler's gaze slid all over the front of it made her wish she'd chosen something else to wear. It had seemed okay in Chicago, but it was probably pretty racy for Wyoming.

Heck, a flour sack was probably racy in Wyoming. The guy had seemed to enjoy the view at first, but now he'd gotten control of those wandering eyes and seemed determined to look at the ground, the sky, the barn wall—anything but her.

She was doing a fair amount of looking herself. He'd changed out of those distracting chaps, but the jeans, worn in all the right places, were even worse. With the torn shirt displaying his biceps and the beard stubbling his chin, he looked like an ad for men's cologne.

Cowboy, it would be called. Or *Leather*. Or maybe something more descriptive, like *Sex on a Stick*.

Her thoughts broke—shattered, really—when the animal in the first stall stretched his neck toward her and let out a tremendous gasping shriek. It sounded like somebody was strangling a grizzly bear with his bare hands, along with a horse, a goat, and a whole flock of chickens. The chorus ended with a startlingly human sound.

"*Awwwwww.*"

"Holy crap." She staggered backward. "Is he okay?"

"Sure. He's half horse, half donkey. You just heard the donkey part."

Cat felt her lips twitching and finally let herself smile. Now that he'd shed the ridiculous cowboy costume, the guy obviously wasn't pretending to be anything other than himself. She doubted that he could.

After all the posturing and preening that took place in her world, it was refreshing. He was hot, in a rugged, natural way that had nothing to do with gym memberships and everything to do with hard work. He'd hefted that bale of hay like it was a box of Kleenex. Plus he did windows. It didn't get much better than that.

The mule sniffed the air in front of Cat's face and huffed out a straw-scented breath. He was a ridiculous-looking animal, like something from the Sunday funnies. Against a ground of dirty white, his coat was splattered with huge, irregular brown polka dots, as if someone had draped melted Salvador Dalí watches all over his body. "So is he yours?"

"Yup." He reached up and tugged one of the mule's long ears through his hand. The gesture was so gentle and assured she was sure he'd done it a thousand times. "But Mom loves him. Calls him her grand-mule."

The black dog sleeping by the door perked up and stared at Mack, watching him pet the mule, then rose and trotted over with a weirdly syncopated gait.

"Hey, your dog only has three legs."

He stared down at the black lab with his eyes widened in mock horror. "Oh my gosh. Wonder what happened to the other one!"

Cat smacked his arm. "Seriously. What happened?"

"Coyote trap, I think. Don't know. The leg was gone when I found her." His voice took on a defensive tone. "She gets along just fine, though. Runs just as fast as a normal dog. She's okay as long as she keeps moving. I call her Tippy."

"What is this, the last resort for wayward animals?"

"There's nothing wrong with the animals." He scrubbed Tippy's flat head with his fist, and the animal gave him a grin. Her tongue lolled off to the side as she panted, giving her expression a slightly lunatic cast. "They've just had it a little rough, that's all. It's not their fault."

Cat wasn't sure, but she was starting to suspect he'd had a rough start himself. "Grand-mule, huh? I take it you don't have any kids."

"I do, actually. A girl." Again, she caught a wounded look in his eyes. "My ex hardly ever lets her come up here, though, so Mom's got to make do with what she can get. And what she can get is Rembrandt."

"Your mule's name is Rembrandt?"

"It is now." He came up beside her and leaned against the stall door. The mule, obviously an attention-hound, shoved its big nose between them and exhaled a long, hay-scented breath down the collar of Cat's shirt. "I figure that'll make you like him."

"I'm pretty much getting paid to like him. I guess you are too."

He slumped his broad shoulders and stared down at the scarred floor of the barn. "Not really. We're not exactly flush around here." He shifted his shoulders, as if his shirt was suddenly too tight. "If I'd made it to Cheyenne…"

"Cheyenne?"

"Cheyenne Frontier Days. Big outdoor rodeo. Big money if you win."

He shifted his gaze as if he'd said more than he intended. In the dusty shaft of daylight that was filtered through the window at the back of the stall, he looked like something out of a Wyeth painting—a rugged counterpart to Helga. She really did want to paint him, naked or not.

He shoved off the stall and strode to a cooler just inside the barn door. It looked like something from an old general store, with a Coca-Cola logo on the side and a sliding glass lid.

"Beer?" He held up a can of Coors.

Cat started to shake her head, then shrugged and took one. She was on the job, but part of that job was making nice with the natives. Lewis and Clark had accepted peace offerings from the Mandans, so she could probably hoist a beer with this cowboy. Besides, she didn't have students coming until tomorrow, and there wasn't a thing she could do about this dude ranch disaster, drunk or sober.

He popped the top and handed her the can, then opened one for himself. Tilting her head back, she savored the cold, refreshing draught a little too enthusiastically. She wiped her mouth with the back of her hand as beer dribbled down her chin.

Mack handed her the bandanna out of his pocket. He was apparently accustomed to drooling woman, and no wonder. Leaning against the wall beside her, he looked moody and tragic and hard, like the hero of an old-fashioned Western.

She sipped the cold beer and contemplated the land

stretching from the doorway. It was a wide canvas of russet and gold, broken by rocky outcroppings and the listing silhouettes of the two bunkhouses. The open ground was edged with crooked trees and spires of pine. Clouds streaked the sky like careless slanted brushstrokes, wispy white over the deepest blue she'd ever seen.

She might be disappointed in the accommodations, but the landscape was way beyond her expectations. So much land, so much sky.

She had a sudden urge to spread her arms and take off running, like a kid cut loose from school. It must be the beer. She took another swallow as a few crickets started up a hesitant orchestral accompaniment—or were those cicadas? The only insects in Chicago were roaches and houseflies, and she did her best to avoid both. This was nice, though. The soft rhythm seeped into her senses and stilled the panic that had plagued her since she'd arrived.

She looked up to see Mack watching her with a gaze that was surprisingly gentle, almost pitying. There was a breath, a heartbeat, where she felt an almost uncontrollable urge to step toward him. She knew, just knew, he'd meet her halfway and something would start between them—something like a kiss, or maybe more.

She needed a distraction—something that would re-establish the casual, bantering tone they'd had before. Because standing beside him and sharing the landscape suddenly seemed far too intimate.

Chapter 5

CAT BIT HER LIP AND GAZED OUT AT THE ROCKY PLAINS stretching into the distance. The leaning fence posts and drooping barbed wire surrounding the pasture looked far too fragile to hold the rugged land. Men like Mack had pounded those posts into the rocky ground, strung that wire, and tried to cut the endless open spaces into something they could tame.

She watched his biceps swell as he folded his arms over his chest. Cautiously, she brought one hand up to dab at the corners of her lips. No drool. So far, so good.

"So." She tried to think of a topic of conversation. Something they had in common. "Um—so."

Rodeo. He said he did rodeo. Men liked to talk about themselves, right?

"You do the—you're in the—what was that about rodeo?"

"I ride broncs." He lifted one eyebrow. "Mack Boyd?"

She gave him a blank stare.

"Guess you don't follow that stuff where you're from."

"No, we don't. We're too busy breathing our fancy air."

He had the decency to duck his head. "Sorry about that." He kicked a few strands of loose straw into a pile with the toe of his boot. "I've been riding broncs most of my life. Doing all right, too. But my mom—her husband left and there's been some... trouble."

"Your dad left?"

"Nope. My dad's—gone." He kicked the pile of straw and it scattered, one piece flipping onto the toe of Cat's boot. "This is her second husband. *Was*, I mean." He swept his foot through the scattered straw. "So I'm a dude ranch wrangler now."

"And a window washer."

He grinned. "And a window washer."

"Yeah, I'm in the middle of a career change too," she said. "Guess I'm getting my midlife crisis over with early."

She stared out at the landscape and thought how much things had changed, and how they'd change even more if everything went right with this trip.

—∿∿—

A week ago, Cat had been sitting at a conference table at the Trainer and Crock advertising agency, battling boredom and watching the bubbles rise in her Diet Pepsi. She'd survived the stultifying boredom of those meetings every week for six years and dutifully executed the projects they planned there.

But two weeks of leave for her sister's funeral had changed everything.

It was her first day back, and she smothered a yawn as she trailed her finger through the frost on her Diet Pepsi and watched her boss Ted hold forth from the head of the conference table. The rising bubbles made her think of what the minister had said at Edie's funeral. Something about souls rising to heaven. Her sister's soul. A bubble. *Pop*.

Gone.

"You've seen these bears Charmin has, right?" Ted

pointed to the substantial derriere of a grinning teddy bear. "They're adorable, right? They make the customer see the product in a positive light."

Ted was the company's art director, and he'd grown old in the service of advertising. Everything about him was flat—his voice, his face, even his skinny behind. He was so dedicated to his craft that he had dwindled down to two dimensions, like the cartoon characters he featured in his ad campaigns.

"That's how you sell toilet paper," he continued. "Cuteness. I was thinking maybe we could do a baby."

"A baby." Cat grimaced. Ted always wanted babies. At the age of fifty-nine, he'd evidently developed the biological clock of a thirty-year-old woman. Her own clock ticked steadily but softly, background noise in a life dedicated—for now—to her career. When the ticking threatened to grow louder, she smothered her maternal instincts by doting on her niece.

Who no longer had a mother. Who had endured the funeral with her thin shoulders painfully straight and her sharp, fragile face pale and expressionless. Dora had been a troubled child before her mother had died, a teenager with issues. Cat had told herself it was normal, but now that Edie was gone it was her problem, normal or not.

"Yeah, I'm thinking a baby, Cat," Ted continued. "Or maybe a kitten. It plays with the roll, you know? Gets all tangled up in it. Then it falls asleep, because it's so soft. Softness, that's our theme. Softness and cuteness."

Cat slid down in her chair, rolling her gaze toward the ceiling. *Cute* was Trainer and Crock's stock-in-trade. *Cute* was the watchword in their office, the magic trick that sold everything from floral delivery to flashlights.

Cute was starting to make her teeth hurt.

"Can't you put me on a campaign for chainsaws or shotguns or something?" she muttered.

"What was that?" Ted slid his half-glasses down his nose and shot her a stern look. She straightened in her chair and drew a happy face on the sketchbook in front of her.

She added fangs to the face, then devil horns.

"Nothing," she said. "Nothing. Just thinking out loud."

Later that night, she spent half an hour staring at a pathetic shred of ivy that had managed to root itself in the brick wall outside her apartment window. Her drafting table was littered with graphite sticks and colored pencils, the floor behind it buried under a chaotic layer of discarded sketches.

Her efforts to create the Fluff Enuff Toilet Paper baby had resulted in fifteen or twenty sketches of what appeared to be a demonic imp from hell. No matter how hard she tried, the baby sported an evil leer and wielded the roll of toilet paper like a weapon.

So she'd moved on, tried a kitten. That had gone well until she began to add detail to the face. Despite her best efforts, the eyes took on a ferocious glint, and the little animal's salient feature was its very small, very sharp teeth.

Clearly, cute wasn't going to work for her. She needed a new concept. Leaning back in her drafting chair, she stared at the resolute sprig of ivy as it struggled to conquer the unforgiving brick.

Sometimes, making a living as an artist seemed to

require the same kind of tenacity. But her roots hadn't been tough enough to take hold.

Tough. That's what was needed here. Not cuteness. *Toughness*.

The next morning, she staggered into Ted's office bleary-eyed and dazed, tossing a folder full of drawings on his desk.

"I pulled an all-nighter, Ted, but I think I've got a real winner here." She cleared her throat, suddenly doubting what she'd done. It had looked terrific the night before, but in the clear light of day she wasn't so sure of herself.

"Let's take a look." He opened the folder with a flourish and stared down at her first renderings of the Fluff Enuff pit bull. The animal was snake-hipped and broad-shouldered, and his face was set in a permanent snarl inspired by John Wayne in *The Green Berets*. He was presenting a roll of toilet paper to the viewer with a gesture that demanded obedience. Across the bottom of the page, a line of text bracketed by crossed rifles read "Fluff Enuff Kicks Butt."

Ted sat in silence for a few too many beats.

"Great, huh?" she said hesitantly. "I know it's not what you asked for, but I thought we needed to set ourselves apart from the competition."

"Where's my *baby*?" Ted looked absolutely bereft, as if she'd snatched his beloved firstborn from his arms.

"I thought this was better. Toilet paper has to be tough. Think about it, Ted. Toilet paper takes a lot of abuse."

"I really don't want to think about that. And I don't think our customers do, either."

"You don't want the buying public to think Fluff Enuff is sissy toilet paper, do you? You want them to know it's *tough*." She punched a fist through the air. "Fluff Enuff can take it."

"Didn't you do any babies?"

She rummaged through the portfolio, pulling out a sheaf of papers and slapping them on his desk. As he flipped through them, Ted's face became grave.

"These are terrible," he said.

If she'd learned nothing else in art school, she'd learned to take criticism. Art teachers rarely told students what to do—they just sent you off to do it so they could rip your efforts to shreds later. But four years of shred-ripping hadn't prepared her for this kind of failure.

Because it *was* failure, no matter how well she'd drawn the pit bull character. She'd had a job to do, and she hadn't been able to do it.

"They look like devil babies." Ted turned the page. "And look at this kitten. It wants to rip my lungs out."

He tapped his pencil on the desktop, eyeing her over the tops of his glasses.

"Burnout," he said.

Cat nodded, scanning the conference room for a Kleenex. Ted shoved a sample roll of Fluff Enuff her way, and she tore off a couple of squares. It was incredibly soft, which only made it harder to hold off the tears.

What she had was a lot worse than burnout. Watching her sister fight the cancer she'd discovered too late had made her reevaluate her whole life, and she'd come to the conclusion there were more important things in life than a career. Dora, for starters.

She'd asked for a leave of absence from Trainer and Crock and taken the job with Art Treks so she and her niece could spend some time together. She'd be instructing workshops, but more important, she'd be seeing the world with Dora—and they'd both be painting, so Dora could exercise the talent she'd inherited from her mother. If the trip went well, Cat would continue to travel with the company, taking Dora along whenever she could. And she'd be able to leave Ted and his babies behind forever.

She looked straight through Ted, through the window behind his desk, and saw herself painting. Painting a temple in Tibet. Painting a meadow in Tuscany. Painting the idyllic Yorkshire Dales.

"It's good you're taking this time off," Ted said. He gave her a sharp sideways look. "You coming back?"

"Yes. I mean, I'm planning to. If this…" She waved at the drawings. "If this doesn't get me fired."

"We won't fire you, Cat. But I know you're not happy here. And since your sister passed, I know you must be rethinking things. It's only natural."

She sniffed and wiped her nose with the square of Fluff Enuff. "She was so talented, Ted. And all she left behind was two sketchbooks and her student paintings. And Dora, Dora will never know how talented her mother was. What she could have done. Her paintings—they mattered. They made you see things differently."

He nodded gravely. "This job isn't enough for you, is it?"

She felt a spasm of remorse. "It's enough. It's fine." She began stuffing the drawings into her portfolio. "I'm sorry about the pit bull. I'll knuckle down and give you a baby before I go. I promise."

They both laughed at the double entendre.

"Your work here matters, you know," he said. "Millions of people are touched by what you do."

"I know. But I want to make people do more than clip a coupon," she said. "I want to make them think. I want—something."

He plucked a number-two pencil from behind his ear and tapped it on the desk. "So did I, once," he said. "But once I married Joyce, had the kids, it turned out this was enough."

"I don't think it's going to turn out that way for me," she said. The picture of the homicidal kitten fluttered to the floor, and she hastened to shove it into the case.

Ted smiled, his kind eyes creasing at the corners. "You never know," he said. "You just never know."

―――

When Cat blinked out of her reverie, the cowboy was still talking. She wondered how long she'd been trucking down Memory Lane. He didn't seem to have noticed her departure from the conversation.

"I thought I'd be wrangling cattle, not artists," he was saying. "Kind of a surprise."

She gave him a bright smile, wondering what she'd missed while she was daydreaming. "Well, we're probably better behaved than cows."

"Doubt it. Cattle are very—accepting. They live in the moment. Take whatever comes."

"Zen and the Art of Cowboying," she said.

"Kind of." He chuckled, clearly getting the reference. If it turned out there were brains under all that brawn, he was going to be hard to resist.

Standing in the doorway, they fell silent and scanned

the land stretching off to the horizon. The silence between them should have been uncomfortable, but somehow, she didn't mind. Maybe the cowboy himself was kind of Zen, too. There were apparently a lot of changes swirling around him—leaving the rodeo, turning the ranch into a tourist spot—and yet there was a solid stillness to him she'd never had in her own life.

Finally he spoke. "It must be a nice change for you. From the city, I mean."

She shrugged.

"I can't imagine living with all those people around, no green things, everybody in such a hurry..." He scanned her from head to foot, but this time the assessment wasn't quite as insulting, maybe because she was getting to know him, or maybe because he seemed to be truly seeing her this time. "You don't look like the type for that kind of life."

"Maybe not," she said. "It was the life I always wanted, but it didn't really work out, so maybe you're right."

Deep down she knew the problem wasn't whether she was a city mouse or a country mouse. The problem was the gap between what she'd dreamed of and what she'd managed to accomplish. She'd steered herself by the wrong star, and now she was so far off course she didn't know how to find her way home.

She looked at the man beside her. He'd had to leave his own dreams behind for the sake of his family. Now he was setting a new course, reaching for new goals.

Maybe she needed to do the same.

But Dora had to come first.

Chapter 6

MACK STRODE DOWN THE AISLE BETWEEN TWO ROWS of stalls, stroking a muzzle here, fondling a forelock there as the animals stretched their necks to greet him. His easy familiarity with the animals and their eagerness for his touch reminded Cat of a star on the red carpet accepting the adulation of his fans.

She envied his confidence. She loved animals, but she wasn't particularly good with them. She'd never had pets as a child, and though she handled them carefully, she seemed to make them nervous.

Reaching up, she stroked the velvety muzzle hanging over the nearest stall door. The horse nodded his head, so she supposed she'd done it right.

"Ready to saddle up?"

"Sure." She set her shoulders back and shifted her weight to one hip. She was supposed to be the leader on this trip. She needed to appear confident and in charge so she'd have some semblance of authority over the group—and over the wrangler.

She had a feeling that last bit was going to be a challenge.

"Which one?"

"We'll let you ride Rembrandt."

"The mule?" Her voice cracked. She couldn't help it. The animal was huge. And loud. And kind of scary.

But if she didn't step up and succeed with this trip,

she'd be spending the rest of her life drawing babies and kittens. She might never make it to France or Italy.

"So are there any particular tips you want to give me?" she asked. "I heard mules are stubborn."

"Nope. They're not stubborn, just smart. If he balks, it means you're trying to do something stupid."

Great. Evidently the mule was the real brains behind this operation.

"Here." He slid the bit into the animal's mouth, slipped the headstall over his ears, and handed her the reins.

"He'll take care of you. Trust me." He caught her disbelieving glance. "Or trust him." He flashed a grin. "He's probably more trustworthy."

As she backed out of the stall leading the mule, she was aware of Mack's gaze taking a long, lingering journey around her backside.

"You'd be a fifteen, I think," he muttered.

She had no idea how to respond, so she fell back on humor and dropped a flippant curtsy. "Out of ten? Thank you."

He looked startled. "Saddle size."

Turning abruptly, he headed down the aisle and disappeared, Tippy at his heels.

Score. She'd made him blush.

When he returned, he had a Western saddle propped on one hip. The brim of his hat shaded his face, drawing her eyes to the broad chest and narrow hips, the muscular arms, and big, square hands. Despite the weight of the saddle, he walked with a swinging, casual gait.

She and Tippy watched him slide a bulky saddle blanket over the mule's back, then toss the saddle effortlessly on top and tug the cinch under the animal's belly. He started a complicated knotting process with a leather strap and a D-ring, and she held out a hand to stop him.

"Can you show me how to do that?"

"You won't need to. It's what I'm here for." He tied off the knot, giving Rembrandt a quick nudge in the belly with his knee.

"I have eight students coming. I think it would be best if I knew how to help you saddle up."

"We'll have to go over it later, then." He nodded toward the barn door. Long shadows slanted from the tree line and the sun hung low in the sky. "Right now we'd better get going. You two get acquainted while I saddle up."

Alone with the mule, she eyed the saddle perched high on his back. Maybe she should ask Mack to let her ride one of the chubby little horses in the other stalls, because this animal was *huge*. He'd been all concerned about the size of her seat, but had he looked at the rest of her?

It didn't matter. It was important to take charge of this situation, show the animal—and the man—who was boss. She'd ride an elephant if she had to.

Shoving her foot in the stirrup, she gave a mighty hop. She'd seen enough Westerns to know how to swing her leg over the saddle, but in movies the animal stood still.

Not this animal. Rembrandt laid his ears back and moved one small step to the right, as if he was doing the hokeypokey. Her leg slid off his hip and she fell back to earth, left foot still stuck in the stirrup.

The mule snorted and headed for the barn door, oblivious to the desperate hopping woman clinging to the saddle horn. Saying good-bye to leadership and dignity, she lurched gamely after him. She was sure she looked ridiculous, bouncing around, mad as a trapped chicken and making trapped-chicken-like sounds. Her arm was stretched to the limit, her thigh aching, and they hadn't even gotten started.

"Stay." She used her strictest leader-of-the-pack dog-training voice, but apparently mules weren't pack animals. Well, actually, they were—but not in the I'm-the-boss-so-you-better-mind-me sense.

Pinning his big rabbit ears back, Rembrandt let out a loud hee-haw that just about burst her eardrums. She pulled her foot out of the stirrup and staggered away, covering her ears.

Mack emerged from the tack room. How could he say mules weren't stubborn? She wasn't doing anything stupid. She was just trying to ride the damn animal like she was supposed to.

She could see Mack's mouth moving, but it wasn't until he grabbed her wrists and pulled her hands away from her ears that she could hear what he was saying.

"He's trying to tell you we don't mount up in the barn," he said.

Oh. So she *was* stupid.

"You'll get your head knocked off if he bucks," he continued.

"He *bucks*?"

"Everybody bucks." He tightened his grip on her wrists and smiled. "At least a little bit. It just depends how much you rile 'em up."

She looked up at him, feeling impossibly vulnerable. She shouldn't let him manhandle her like this, should she? There was a part of her that was enjoying it, but that wasn't the part of herself she should listen to—was it?

No. It was the part of herself she needed to smother into submission. But her body was softening, and so was her brain—shutting down the sensible sections of her consciousness and opening up the ones that said *It's okay. He's hot. Just once. Just one time.*

She knew better. In the past, one time had always led to twice, and twice led to heartache. The men she'd met in Chicago were always on the make—for women, for money, for pleasure. But never for commitment, or love.

And they weren't even real men. Not when you compared them to this guy. If most men were uncaring and selfish, what would this ultra-masculine cowboy be? Selfish to the umpteenth power, no doubt.

And strong. He wasn't just gripping her with his hands; he was holding her with his eyes too, reading her face, watching her battle her urges as if he was taking in a boxing match. And judging from the amusement that sparkled in his dark eyes, he knew which side was winning.

She needed to get a grip. She was stuck in the middle of nowhere on a dilapidated ranch with some guy she didn't know and his crazy mother. The violin sound track from *Psycho* started screeching in her head and she tried to remember the self-defense workshop she'd taken before moving to the city.

Step down hard on his instep. No, that wouldn't work. He was wearing heavy work boots, and he probably wouldn't even notice.

Turn around and run. Yeah, right. Where was she going to run? It was twenty miles to the nearest town, and even that was nothing but a couple of gas pumps, a convenience store, and a boarded-up schoolhouse.

Kick him in the...

Could she actually *do* that? And what would happen when he did? She'd be back to running again, and there was absolutely nowhere to go.

Besides, she didn't really want to do any of those things. He was so different from her, so big and tough and *real*. She'd lost a stare-down with a leopard at the Brookfield Zoo once and felt the same thing: the dangerous heat of a predator's heart hidden behind a hard stare.

She'd never been good with animals, and she'd never had much luck with men either. But for some reason, she couldn't take her eyes off him. She didn't want to fight it. She didn't want to run, either.

She just wanted to stay there, looking into his eyes, for as long as he'd let her.

Mack looked down into two big Bambi eyes wide with fear. When a horse went rigid like this, you held on and waited for it to give to pressure. He loosed his hold on Cat's arms, but he didn't let her go.

And slowly, surely, he felt the resistance drain out of her.

Rembrandt leaned down and nipped at his belt loop, probably wondering why he was all saddled up if they were just going to stand around and stare at each other.

"Stay," he said to the mule.

Tippy slammed her butt obediently to the floor, but the mule just gave him the stink-eye.

He looked back at Cat and repeated the command, softer this time, as he tugged her closer. "Stay."

She felt so good, soft in all the right places, firm in the others, with her body snug against his and her breath coming quick and tight. She smelled like flowers, and the sweet scent mingled with the familiar ones of straw and hay and horses in a heady, feminine stew.

Suddenly, he was happy to be right here, right now. Forget rodeo season. Forget his stepdad, his mom, his family troubles. Right now, home was a good place to be.

Holding this woman shouldn't feel right. The two of them weren't just strangers; they were two different species. But when he clasped his arms around her, he felt a hot, wanting energy flowing between them that sure as hell made them something more than friends.

"Stay," he said again, and he meant it. And he proved it by dipping his head and kissing her, the way he'd wanted to kiss her from the first moment he'd seen her.

Chapter 7

STUPID. PLAIN, DAMN STUPID.

Mack cussed himself even as he pulled Cat closer. How was he going to explain to his mother when the Boyd Dude Ranch's first and only customer kneed him in the groin and took off screaming for the hills? Or worse yet, accused him of assault?

All day, he'd felt like his life was slipping out from under him, leaving no solid place to stand. He'd had a meeting with the bank and discovered his mother's second husband had spent the past two years tossing money away with one hand while he cooked the books with the other. Now the ranch was mortgaged and bills were coming due faster than they could pay them.

The worst part was that Mack suspected Ollie wasn't done wreaking havoc on their lives. He hadn't even signed the divorce papers yet, because they couldn't find him. That meant everything was still up in the air, like a set of juggler's balls that might plummet to earth at any moment.

It was natural to want to hang onto something, but this woman was the wrong thing to grab for. Her body was poised to run like a wild horse dodging a rope, and he was sure she was about to scream, to slap him, to push him away and run.

But then those pretty, pillowy lips opened and she kissed him back. His brain and body flooded with relief—relief and a hot rush of need. For one blissful moment, he forgot everything but the way it felt to warm himself in the heat of a woman. It was like the two of them were the center of the universe, with the world spinning crazily around them on its newly tilted axis.

When she pulled away, she didn't scream or run. She just stood there, bringing her fingers to her lips as if she could cool the heat with a touch.

But nothing could cool that heat.

Tippy whined from her position on the barn floor. She was still "staying."

"You can go now. Go on up to the house and hang out with Mom," he said.

Cat looked startled.

"I meant the dog."

Damn, she probably thought he was some kind of cowboy Casanova, jumping women the moment they arrived. But the truth was, he was more than cautious around women; he was downright cagey. When the other guys prowled the bars and beer tents for buckle bunnies, he kept to himself.

Marriage had taught him women were more trouble than they were worth. At the start of their relationship, his ex had been starstruck and starry-eyed. She'd showed him off to her friends as if she'd lassoed the prize pony at the fair. But the minute they married, she resented every minute he spent on the road. She didn't care if he was shackled to a desk nine to five, working construction, or selling his soul; she just wanted him tied up and tamed, coming home to some McMansion she could show off to her friends.

Of course, he'd wanted to be home more too, once

their daughter was born. From the first time he'd laid eyes on Vivian's tip-tilted nose and tiny fingers, he'd stopped seeing rodeo as an adventure and started seeing it as a job. A man had to provide for his family, and he could do that better through rodeo than anything else. But his ex had never understood the shift in his priorities.

Maybe Cat was different. She'd come out here to a place she'd never seen and plunged into an unknown world. While that meant she was a greenhorn, it also meant she had some courage. If she was the kind of woman who wanted adventure, he was more than willing to provide it.

She was still standing there, pressing her fingers to her lips, but her eyes had gone from scared to speculative. Finally, she turned and set her hand on Rembrandt's saddle. "So I should mount up outside?"

He shook his head to get his thoughts back on track. Apparently they were going to pretend the kiss had never happened. That was probably lucky for him, since it would cut down on the running, the screaming, and the possible lawsuits. He ought to be relieved, but pretending it hadn't happened would put it in the past, and he didn't want it to be over.

He'd play her game, he decided, but he'd play it his way. Reaching out, he touched her arm—just a friendly touch, to remind her that they'd shared something.

"Just lead him out and wait, okay? I'll get Spanky and we'll head out together."

She grinned. "You named your horse Spanky?"

"The horses are from a kids' camp. Their names tend to be a little on the cute side."

By the time he led Spanky outside, Rembrandt was cropping grass while Cat stared off into the distance as if mesmerized by the open plains. The reins hung loose in her hand, forgotten in her absorption with the landscape. Mack felt a stab of sympathy for her city-girl past, but she needed to get a grip. On the reins, and on the responsibility of handling a thousand-pound animal.

"Don't let him eat when he's tacked up." At the sound of his voice, Rembrandt looked up, annoyed. "You need to stay in charge."

He reached over to show her how to hold the reins. As their fingers touched, he felt that shared heat again and glanced at her face, wondering if she felt it too. But she was concentrating almost fiercely on the mule, her brows drawn into a determined "V."

"Don't let him tug." He formed her fingers around the leather just below the mule's jaw.

The mule didn't tug but Cat did—tugged her hand away from his and shot him a warning look that reminded him she held the future of the Boyd Ranch in her hands as surely as she held the mule's reins. No matter how sizzling hot that kiss had felt, he needed to be careful. Just because the running and screaming hadn't happened the first time didn't mean he was in the clear.

He watched her gather the reins in her hand, grab the saddle horn, and stick one foot in the stirrup. Her boots were going to be a problem. They were designed for style, not practicality, and the tips were so rakishly tilted they must strain her calf muscles with every step.

She gave a mighty hop and hauled herself up the mule's side, struggling to hoist the other leg over the saddle. No way was she going to make it. Without thinking, he palmed her butt and gave her a shove. He was a little worried he'd overdone it and she'd slide down the other side, but she caught the far stirrup and straightened out just in time.

She eyed him from the saddle with a strict school-teacher squint. "If we're going to work together, we're going to have to set some ground rules."

He leaned one elbow on the mule's withers and tried to look attentive, but behind his back he flexed the fingers of his other hand in a vain effort to hang on to the warmth of her pleasantly rounded backside. It would be nice if the ground rules included some more palming her butt and kissing in the barn, but he didn't think that was what she had in mind.

"First of all, no touching." She was trying to be harsh, but with her big eyes and small stature, she reminded him of a kitten spitting and showing its claws. "None. We're here for the students, not for—well—*that*."

"That?"

"You know what I'm talking about."

"I do?" He knew he shouldn't tease her, but he just couldn't help himself. And women liked it when you flirted a little, right? "No, really. What?"

"*That*."

"Oh, *that*." He let the smile fade as he shoved his hat up so he could meet her eyes. "I'm not sure I want to give *that* up."

"Well, you're going to have to," she said. "My niece is coming on this trip, and I don't want her to see anything inappropriate. She has—issues."

As far as Mack could see, all women had issues. And

he had a feeling this one had more than most. But then again, so did he.

Maybe they had something in common after all.

———*—

Cat looked down at Mack and tried to smother the rush of arousal that was still flowing from the spot where he'd touched her. Apparently the clear country air was making her crazy. It was hardly "plain," with its heady scents of sage and earth and straw.

But the real problem was the cowboy himself. In his ragged shirt and worn jeans, he looked as much a part of the landscape as the gnarled trees and the weathered barn. Tough, elemental, and real.

"Never mind." She waved one hand carelessly, as if the rest of the rules were obvious. "Just keep it professional. Obviously that's a challenge for you, but please try to be serious."

"I am serious." There was a defensive note in his voice that made her think she might have struck a nerve. "You don't succeed in my line of work unless you're pretty damn serious about it."

"I'm sure that's true," she said. "But I'm not a bucking bronco; I'm a woman."

"I know," he said. "I'm serious about that too."

Chapter 8

CAT WAS DOING HER BEST TO LOOK COLD AND PRO-
fessional. It wasn't an easy look to master when you
were five foot two and looked like a Disney princess.
To add to the challenge, she was mounted on an animal
that felt about the size of one of those giant equestrian
statues they put in city parks. She remembered seeing
one where the horse was rearing up on its hind legs and
she gripped the saddle horn a little tighter.

Mack edged away and circled his horse right, then
left. Pivoting on its back legs, it raised a showy cloud of
dust, then burst out of the spin into a smooth, fluid trot.
Mack allowed it a few strides before he slid to a stop—
raising more dust—and looked back at her.

"You know how to make him go, right?"

She nodded and twitched her leg against the mule's
side, breathing a sigh of relief when the animal lurched
forward. She followed Mack's lead, admiring the way
he managed to sit ramrod straight, yet stay relaxed. His
torso moved with the horse as if they were some kind of
compound creature. She watched him covertly, trying
to emulate his easy movements as he swung his mount
toward the ranch house and prodded it into that easy,
swinging trot.

The discovery that her destination was Wyoming had
put an abrupt halt to her dreams of handsome Italians
and debonair Frenchmen, but maybe cowboys were

just as good. Or at least they would be if Dora wasn't coming. Once her niece arrived, she'd have to get her hormonal yearnings under control.

They rode in silence, with only the chattering of the birds to keep them company. Cat felt awkward and unbalanced in the saddle, and evidently Rembrandt had caught her fear. He started when a stone skittered out from under the horse's hooves and shied at a fence-snagged tumbleweed that twitched in a passing breeze.

"Try and relax," Mack said. "You're making him nervous."

She let the mule fall behind so they could ride in single file. The animal settled down, plodding sedately in what appeared to be the tracks of a hundred horses before him, and she turned her attention to the landscape. Since she didn't know much about rock formations, trees, or flowers, she'd keep her conversation with her students to art topics. She could compare the views to paintings by Bierstadt and Moran, noting the problems in perspective formed by the jagged canyon and distant mountains, and discuss color and composition...

Mack turned in the saddle and looked back at her. "You okay?"

"Fine. You know anything about what we're looking at?"

"Pretty much everything. I was born here."

"So what are those?" She pointed toward some purple flowers that bobbed by the side of the trail.

"Flowers."

"No, I mean what are they called?"

He shrugged. "Cattle won't eat 'em, so it doesn't really matter."

It was lucky she'd brought a field guide along. She'd have to look everything up, but at least she could title the paintings if a student chose wildflowers for a subject.

The sun dropped toward the horizon as they rode, throwing long shadows over the pasture grass. Mare's tail clouds whipped the skyline, suggesting a high wind on the distant peaks. Gradually, they turned gold, then pink as the sun sank. Replicating the otherworldly quality of the light here wouldn't be easy. She thought about color—alizarin crimson and cerulean blue, sap green and yellow ochre. It was easy to push the cowboy to the edge of her consciousness, she told herself. She was here to paint.

He drew rein at the top of the rise and she did the same. A broad panorama was spread before them as if God had shaken out a multicolored blanket. This was the kind of view that would give her clients a hundred lessons in light and aerial perspective. The land rolled gently into the distance, hill upon hill, a rumpled patchwork of greens and golds that faded into the distance. A thin purple border of mountains marked the horizon, and off to the east a scattering of spindly pines thickened, swelling to a dark wave that lapped at the side of a rocky mesa.

She'd become a painter from an urge to save fleeting moments like this one, and there was a lot worth saving in the scene before her. Maybe Wyoming wasn't a penance after all.

She slapped her shirt pocket and cursed silently. She'd been so flustered by all that had happened that she'd left her camera in her luggage. Now all she could do was try to imprint the scene on her memory.

Mack dismounted. "Get down if you want."

She stayed in the saddle. Enjoying the view from horseback made her understand why King Richard offered his kingdom for a horse. She felt like the ruler of the sun-soaked plains and the deep blue distance.

Resting his arm on his saddle, Mack leaned on his horse's hip, gazing out at the landscape as if he couldn't drink in enough of it. He looked like the quintessential cowboy—an image from a country song, or maybe a movie, with his craggy profile outlined against the pine-clad mountains.

She wouldn't mind ruling him, too.

Gripping the saddle horn a little tighter, she squeezed her eyes shut and cleared her mind of all the long-buried longings the cowboy's kiss had brought to life. This trip was about Dora. Painting, and Dora.

No cowboys allowed.

———⁓⁓⁓———

The rest of the ride passed mostly in silence. Mack pointed out a few of the more scenic overlooks and what he thought were the prettiest places, and Cat seemed too busy drinking in the scenery to talk.

He wasn't sure if it was a friendly silence or a hostile one, but it worked for him. He wasn't much of a talker anyway. And when he talked to women, he always seemed to say the wrong thing.

As they headed back to the ranch, Mack paused to watch a couple of dust clouds rise on the distant road.

"Lot of traffic today," he said.

Cat laughed. "Two cars?"

"That's a lot."

By the time they got back to the ranch, she was learning to move in concert with Rembrandt's easy, rocking gait. Tippy raced out of the house at a lopsided run, then paused to circle a silver SUV that was parked in the turnout near the barn.

"I thought you weren't expecting students till tomorrow," Mack said.

"I wasn't. Somebody's early."

It figured. She'd hoped to have some time to herself to do some sketching and jot down notes on the scenes they'd seen from the ridge—preserving what she should have captured with her camera—but instead she was going to have to make nice with a client.

Oh well. Maybe she'd make a new friend. It was always nice to talk to another artist, and at least she wouldn't have to spend the evening making awkward conversation with the reluctant dude wrangler and his matchmaking mother.

"Just pull Rembrandt up to the gate." Mack pointed toward a corral beside the barn. "I'll take care of him."

Cat pulled up at the gate and dismounted, wincing as her thigh and calf muscles stretched to their limit. She tossed the reins and silently thanked the universe and all its powers when they draped gracefully over the top rail. She might not care what Mack thought of her, but a nagging sense of embarrassment nibbled at the edge of her consciousness, making it extra important to maintain her dignity.

She paused to pet Tippy's sleek head while she pondered the new arrival. He certainly had plenty of dignity. Tall and blond, he stood beside the SUV with one foot on the running board, surveying his surroundings like a duke dismounting from a phaeton. He was dressed impeccably in crisply creased khakis, a green polo shirt, and hiking boots that were just worn enough not to be gauche. Blond hair swept back from his high forehead in graceful waves.

Cat was painfully conscious of her own grubby duds as she stepped up and shook his hand. "Hi."

"Trevor Maines." His grip wasn't weak so much as languid. "You must be our Cat."

Our Cat. What was she, a pet? Maybe he had a leash and a litter box in the back of that truck. And there was nobody with him, so was he using the royal "we" when he called her "*our*" Cat?

Maybe "dignity" was the wrong word. The guy was a snob.

She squelched an urge to meow. "That's me."

He looked down his nose at her the way a scientist might regard a particularly commonplace insect. As his gaze flicked from her face to the surrounding landscape, his nose wrinkled slightly. The scene had struck her as stunningly beautiful moments before, but now she noticed the ragged grass surrounding the barn and the distinct odor of cowflops mingling with the scent of sage.

What was this aristocratic stranger going to say when he saw the bunkhouse? Anxiety clawed at her stomach, putting a final kibosh on the serenity she'd enjoyed on the ride.

"Trevor Maines." Cat flipped through her mental files. Maines had been a late addition—the final registration. He was from California. Some kind of photographer. Fashion work. That was it. And that explained the casual perfection of his hair and clothes. It was probably also the reason behind his erect posture and the upward tilt of his patrician nose.

She tried and failed to brush a streak of dirt off her jeans and decided she needed reinforcements. This guy was as sophisticated as Mack was down-to-earth, and she couldn't imagine the two of them getting along.

Fortunately, there was one person on the ranch who could handle just about anyone.

"Let's head on up to the house," she said. "I'll introduce you to our hostess."

Hopefully, the steamrolling skills of Maddie Boyd would prove as effective on Maines as they had on Cat herself. Maybe she could find a way to get Madeleine to show him the bunkhouse.

Let her explain to this guy the quaint charm of sleeping with the spiders.

Chapter 9

MACK STRODE INTO THE BARN WITH REMBRANDT'S saddle propped on his hip and the bridle draped over one shoulder. Tippy trotted beside him, gazing up at his face with a good-natured grin. The way her tongue dangled out the side of her mouth made him smile in spite of the way he'd screwed up the whole afternoon.

"Women," he said to the dog. "They're the problem."

She put her tongue back in her mouth and looked worried.

"Not you," he said. "Human women."

His mother. The artist. The mere thought of his ex-wife. They all had him spinning in circles. His mother bossed him like he was still a little kid. His ex was a nightmare. The artist...

Well, the artist hadn't really done anything wrong. In fact, she'd done just about everything right. She'd been quiet and appreciative on their ride. She might not be a top hand, but she did her best with the animals.

And that kiss—she'd kissed him like she meant it. The effect she had on him was something new, something instantaneous and irresistible. It wasn't just a sexual attraction; it was something more.

The problem was, he didn't know how to follow up on something like that. What was the proper etiquette after you'd kissed a stranger with the kind of passion that was usually reserved for lifelong lovers?

He had no idea. Saying he was sorry would make it seem like he regretted the kiss, and he didn't. Pretending it hadn't happened seemed equally rude. Maybe he should just do it again, but she hadn't exactly asked for an instant replay.

"We'll make the best of it—right, Tippy?" He bent and ruffled the thick fur on her shoulders. "We'll get along with Miss Crandall somehow."

"Good luck with that," said a voice from the shadows. "I've been trying to get along with her since I was born."

Shoot. Another ambush in the barn. He was going to have to quit talking to the animals, or at least check for humans first.

He turned to see a slim figure hovering by one of the stalls. It was a young girl, slight as a fairy, with pale skin and a halo of frizzy blonde hair. She had one hand on Bucky's muzzle and was using the other to scratch the horse under his whiskered chin.

"Who the heck are you?" Mack squinted into the dimness. The kid wasn't more than about fifteen years old, and she might weigh ninety pounds if you handed her a ten-pound brick. Judging from the relaxed way Bucky was letting his eyes drift shut, she was a horse lover—but the frown on her fine-boned face told him she wasn't too keen on the rest of the world.

She glanced at Mack, then returned her attention to the horse. "Aren't you supposed to say 'Howdy, pardner' or something like that? I thought you'd talk in cowboy lingo."

"Yeah, I'll have to work on that."

She was about a year younger than his daughter Viv,

and apparently she carried the same teenaged chip on her shoulder Viv had at that age.

A family counselor had told Mack that adolescent rudeness was a protective shield. Viv hadn't wanted to express her feelings about the divorce so she'd tried to push her parents away. In Mack's case, she'd succeeded—mostly because her mother was pulling her away from him just as hard. He and Viv got along pretty well now, but cutting through her resentment had taken time and patience.

"Just don't go yelling 'yee-haw,' okay?" The little blonde gave the horse a final pat and followed Mack into the tack room. "I don't think I can handle any of that John Wayne stuff. I'm more into Clint."

She narrowed her eyes and set her narrow jaw, taking on a Dirty Harry squint. "*Go ahead, punk. Make my day.*"

"Pretty good." He grinned as he hung the bridle up, then grabbed a plastic bucket of grooming supplies with an *S* scrawled on the side in black Sharpie marker. Handing it to the girl, he grabbed another one marked with an *R*.

"You know how to groom a horse?"

"Yes." She turned sulky. "I know a lot about horses. I do dressage."

"Well, my horses don't need to dress up. I just keep 'em clean."

"That's not what dressage is." She tossed her golden frizz and scowled. "It's…"

"A joke. Just a joke, hon."

"I knew that."

He tried to hide his grin. This kid might be disagreeable, but she definitely had spunk. He strode out to the corral gate, where Rembrandt and Spanky were blinking in the sunshine.

"You can take care of Spanky, here. I'll do the mule. Saddle goes in there." He cocked a thumb toward the barn.

"What am I, the help?"

"Hope so." He gave her his most winning cowboy grin and got a bemused smile in return. Turning his attention to Rembrandt, he watched out of the corner of his eye as the girl unsaddled the horse like an expert.

When she returned from the barn and started rubbing a curry comb over Spanky's dusty coat, he gave her a nod of approval. "You must be Dora."

The squint returned. "How'd you know? Did Aunt Cat tell you about me?"

"Yeah, but she didn't say you were coming today."

If he could befriend the kid, it would probably score points with Cat. Besides, it seemed like she needed a friend. He watched her switch to the finishing brush, knocking it on her hip with each stroke to get rid of the dust.

"How'd you get here, anyway?" he asked.

Her lips flattened into a thin line. "Shuttle."

"All the way from the airport?"

"Uh-huh."

He could almost feel the wall going up. Probing would only make her add more bricks, so he let it go— for now.

"Does Cat know you're here?"

She shrugged. "I'll find her in a minute."

He should probably send Dora up to the house to find her aunt, but she seemed totally absorbed in brushing the horse. Cat had said the girl had issues, and dealing with animals always calmed him down. Maybe it would do the same for Dora.

"So your mother was Cat's sister?"

"Yeah. She died."

Shoot. This went way beyond "issues." He didn't know what to say, but Dora saved him by yammering on.

"Aunt Cat likes to *think* she's my mom now. Like she can replace her or something. That's why she took me on this trip. We're supposed to *bond*." She brushed harder at the horse's smooth coat, cleaning off dirt that wasn't there and blinking fast. "Like that's going to happen. My mom didn't even like her most of the time."

Mack swallowed and tried to think of something soothing to say. This was evidently his day to be tested by women, and he'd failed every trial so far.

He stopped his own work and watched her trade the brush for a hoof pick. She ran her hand down the horse's leg and Spanky obediently lifted his foot.

"You're good with horses."

He was rewarded with a luminous smile that made the girl's pale face almost pretty. "It's easy to be good at things you like to do." The smile dimmed so fast it was like a shade being drawn over a lighted window. "What sucks is being good at stuff you don't want to do. Stuff you never want to do again."

"Like what?"

"Art." She lowered her brows, and Mack could swear a tiny thundercloud was forming above her bright halo of hair. "I *hate* art. And that's all I'm going to be doing for *two whole weeks*." She said the last words like she was pronouncing a life sentence at hard labor. "You're our guide, right? The wrangler?"

Mack nodded. He was tempted to say he wasn't looking forward to the two weeks either, but grown-ups were
supposed to set an example, so he kept his mouth shut.

"Maybe I could help you with the horses. Like, work
for you. Instead of painting."

He could feel the solid barn floor beneath him turning
into a quagmire. She was trying to get him to take sides.
Viv did the same thing, setting her mother against her
father to distract them from her own misbehavior.

"Maybe you'd better ask your aunt."

"Why? It's not like she's my mother or anything."
She straightened, absently rubbing the small of her back
as she tossed the pick into the bucket. "No matter what
she'd like to think."

———∿∿∿———

To Cat's relief, Maddie welcomed Trevor Maines
with her customary enthusiasm. Taking a cue from
his lord-of-the-manor attitude, she declared it was
time for afternoon tea and began bustling around the
kitchen as if the king of England had arrived. Cat took
the opportunity to mumble a polite excuse about getting organized and hightail it for the relative safety of
the bunkhouse.

She'd chosen the smallest room in the Heifer House
for her own, a windowless cubicle at the end of the hall
furthest from the bathroom. It was the approximate size
and shape of a grave, which left barely room for herself
and her luggage. For the moment, the cave-like solitude
suited her.

Tugging a string that dangled from the bare bulb
screwed into the ceiling, she knelt by the bed and fussed

over her art supplies. She needed to have two of every-thing. Dora would be arriving tomorrow, and Cat had no doubt she'd conveniently forget her own brushes and paints. The girl had been strangely resistant to painting ever since her mother died.

Cat hoped she'd be able to figure out why on this trip. Figure out why and fix it. Underneath the hard shell Dora had donned at her mother's funeral was a sweet, talented girl. And Cat aimed to bring that girl back into the light.

She put everything back into the canvas bag she'd bought just for the trip. The brushes fit into neat slots, graduated by size. The paints themselves went into a plastic-lined compartment, and there was a removable zipper pouch for sketching pencils, charcoal, and erasers.

She loved art supplies the way some women loved fashion or food. There were so many possibilities wait-ing inside the tubes of bright color, and the blank paper was just waiting to take the paint.

The sketchbook went in last, and reluctantly. She'd noticed a rustic cabin behind the house, set in a copse of trees at the end of a picturesquely winding path. It would be lit by the lowering sun right now, with long, crisp shadows stretching from the sagebrush. She'd love to do a quick watercolor sketch of the place, but she needed to check on Trevor Maines and see if Madeleine Boyd had stolen his free will yet.

She hoped so.

Strolling up the steps to the ranch house, she was careful not to even look toward the barn. She had trouble enough without ogling the cowboy again. She mounted the steps and edged the door open.

"Anybody home?" She hoped her voice sounded more playful than she felt.

"In here." Madeleine sounded chipper enough.

Trevor was laughing as she entered, his head flung back so that his blond hair flowed over the back of the chair. The laughter sounded forced and artificial, and when he slanted his gaze her way she caught a hard gleam in his eyes that had nothing to do with humor.

What was it about this man that made her so uneasy? For some reason he set off alarm bells in her head.

"It looks like Mrs. Boyd made you comfortable," she said.

"Oh, yes. We're old friends now." He shifted his feet, which were resting on a fringed footstool constructed mostly of cattle horns. Like much of Maddie's furniture, it looked like a relic of the nineteenth-century west of cattle barons and entrepreneurial British nobility. The website said the original Boyd was a duke from Scotland whose father had sent him to America after he'd killed a rival in a duel.

She tried to picture Mack fighting a Scottish duel, but she only got as far as the kilt before her thoughts wandered off on a rocky and forbidden track.

Or maybe not so rocky. The kiss had been awkward, but she had to admit the cowboy was growing on her. There'd been a companionable silence during their ride that felt somehow soothing, and he'd let her look at the landscape as long as she wanted. Most nonartists got impatient with her gawking, but Mack had a stillness about him that let her relax and enjoy the view. She enjoyed looking at him too, but she'd been serious about the "no touching" rule. There was no way she could indulge herself in a wild cowboy fling once Dora arrived.

Still, she wasn't sorry she'd taken a quick sample of what the Wild West had to offer.

"You have to try this shortbread." Trevor gestured toward a plate of buttery cookies dusted with sugar. "It melts in your mouth."

"No thanks." She forced a smile and turned to Madeleine. She'd hoped the woman would show Trevor to the bunkhouse, but evidently that job was reserved for Cat. "I'm sure you'd like to see your room before dinner."

"Oh, I've seen it," he said. "Quite nice. The rustic decor's a bit, well, *forced*, you know? Rather juvenile. But it'll do."

Cat felt like she'd just cleared the biggest hurdle in a boot camp obstacle course. Maybe she'd been wrong about the bunkhouse. If it was okay with Trevor Maines, surely it wouldn't be a problem for anyone else.

"The bucking horse motif is a bit over-the-top," he said with a languid wave of his hand. "That bedspread, those curtains."

Bucking horse motif? Cat blinked. She'd checked out the Bull Barn, and it hadn't had any kind of curtains at all. The bedspreads had been plain blue-ticked cotton.

"I thought Mr. Maines would be more comfortable in the house, so I put him in Mack's old room," Maddie explained.

"I take it the photographs are of your son?" Trevor asked.

"That's right." She tapped him playfully on the knee. "So you look out. Those bucking horses might get in your blood. They sure got into his."

"I can't wait to meet him," Trevor said, his bored tone belying the words. "He sounds so… rustic."

Cat felt something in her spark and flare. "From what I hear, he's a very successful bronc rider," she said. "It takes a lot of skill to get that far."

"Well, well, well." Trevor flashed her a wicked smile and she heard the alarm bells again. "I think we've found the teacher's pet." The smile bent down into a sneer. "I hope that won't affect the quality of our instruction."

"Of course not." Cat laced her hands in her lap, trying to look prim and teacher-like. Was it that obvious that she had a crush on the cowboy? She forced a smile. "I promise, the teacher's pet will be the one who's the best artist. I'm sure Mr. Boyd is hardly Leonardo da Vinci."

Trevor tossed his hair and laughed. The sound made her grit her teeth, and she wondered how many times she'd have to endure it on this trip. A hundred spiteful retorts rose in her throat, but she only laughed along halfheartedly, hating herself for not standing up for Mack. She'd always believed in standing up for your friends, and while Mack wasn't exactly a friend, he was something.

Really something.

And she'd better make sure he didn't become anything more.

Chapter 10

CAT RETURNED TO THE BUNKHOUSE TO FIND MACK AT the fire pit, constructing a dense nest of kindling. A slim figure stood beside him, holding a few sticks and twigs.

A very familiar slim figure.

It couldn't be.

"Dora? What are you doing here?" Cat struggled to make her brain work. "You can't be here yet. You land tomorrow."

Dora flicked her a tight smile, along with a fluttering finger wave loaded with adolescent irony.

Cat set her fists on her hips. "How did you get here?"

"Interstate 25."

Her tone made Cat's heart sink. Her niece sounded as sour as she had the day of her mother's funeral, when she'd refused to look at the casket or shed a single tear. She'd always been a sweet child, funny and loving, but on the day her mother died she'd turned into an angry little ghost of her former self. Cat had worried that her niece would burst into emotional flames at any moment—although at this point, a crying spell would be a good thing.

Cat had hoped it was only the freshness of Dora's grief that had turned her into a grim-faced zombie, but it looked like nothing in her niece's attitude had changed. Who could say how long it would take a fifteen-year-old girl to get over the death of her mother? Trying to help her grieving niece was like navigating an unknown country without a map.

At least Cat was making an effort. Her brother-in-law, Dora's father, was so lost without his wife and playmate that he could barely spare a glance for their only child. Couldn't he see Dora was the one part of Edie that was left?

Cat turned over the notion that had been fermenting in the back of her mind ever since the funeral. Maybe Dora's dad wasn't capable of caring for a teenaged girl. Maybe she should be with her Aunt Cat all the time.

She pictured the two of them living in Chicago. Painting together, going to museums. Shopping for school clothes. She hadn't spent nearly enough time with Edie, and she was determined to do better with the little family she had left—which was standing here in front of her.

Dora bent down and poked a stick of kindling into the bottom of the pile. A few logs collapsed and fell to one side. Mack touched her shirtsleeve.

"Leave it alone. It's fine."

To Cat's amazement, Dora gave Mack the same tight little sideways smile she'd always given her mother when she'd admonished her for some misstep. Cat had been hoping to dig that smile out from under Dora's grief on this trip. She'd figured a change of scenery would help, but Dora wasn't smiling at the scenery. She was smiling at the rakish cowboy who'd kissed Cat senseless within hours of her arrival.

Things were getting complicated.

Raking her hair back from her face, Cat bunched the wavy mass in her fist while she glanced from Mack to

Dora and back again. Dora was supposed to arrive on the airport shuttle van tomorrow, along with Trevor and five other students who were scheduled to arrive on various flights between nine and noon. The shuttle had been scheduled weeks ago as part of a carefully thought-out plan that was apparently already in tatters.

"How did you get here?" she asked again.

"I took the shuttle."

"The shuttle? By yourself?" Cat was trying not to screech, but she couldn't help herself. "The airport's three hours away. It must have cost you a hundred dollars! Dora, your dad said you were only supposed to use the credit card for emergencies. You can't…"

"Dad doesn't care." She grimaced. "He didn't even care about the money the airline charged to send me a day early."

"He sent you a day early?"

Dora shrugged. "He had to go to Costa Rica. He's buying a beach house."

And that mattered more than his only daughter. Who had lost her mother only six months ago, and was clearly troubled. Cat had told herself to give Ross a break. He was healing too. But right now, what she wanted to break was his bones. Every one of them.

"The shuttle wasn't *that* expensive," Dora said. "Would you rather I rode with that guy?"

"What guy?"

"That Trevor guy. I met him at the gate. He said he'd take me here, but I said no."

"What?"

Dora rolled her eyes. "I saw his art supplies, put two and two together. We were going to sit together on the plane, but... I don't know, he's kind of weird." She quirked a mischievous smile. "But he rented a Lexus. That's way better than one of those skanky airport vans."

"I don't care if he rented a Cinderella carriage and flying monkeys."

"So you're glad I took the shuttle." Dora looked triumphant.

"Well, you can't go getting into cars with strange men."

The crunch of gravel made her look up to see Trevor approaching from the house.

"I beg your pardon," he said.

"I don't mean that kind of strange." Actually, she did. The guy gave her the creeps, and the fact that he'd talked to Dora at the airport set off warning bells in her head. But Dora had said that *she* saw *his* art supplies. So he hadn't instigated the conversation.

Still, it made Cat uncomfortable. "I meant that she doesn't know you."

"We got to know each other."

Cat literally bit her tongue to keep from responding. There wasn't a thing she could do about it now. And Dora was here, safe and sound and apparently unmolested.

"So where have you been since you got here?" she asked her niece.

"Helping Mack."

"She's got a great touch with animals," Mack said.

"I told you, if you'll just show me how, I'll be happy to help with the horses," Cat said. "Dora's here to paint."

"No shit?" The thundercloud was forming over Dora's head again. "I thought I was here to relax. Get away. Have some *girl time* with my Aunt Cat."

Dora looked angelic—tiny, balletic, and blonde—but

she seemed to have developed a mouth like a sailor and the rebellious spirit of a spoiled princess since her mother's death. Ross said she'd been suspended from school once for fighting, and once for cussing out a teacher. But this probably wasn't a good time to wash her mouth out with soap.

"We'll have fun, hon. We will. But it's also a great chance for you to get some painting done. Some new subjects."

Dora had always been a talented artist, but since her mother's illness, her paintings had taken on a dark tone. When she painted at all, she churned out abstracts, tortured scribbles in dark blues and blacks. Her work was incredible, especially for her age. But hanging one of her pictures on the wall was a sure way to suck all the air out of a room.

"I told you, I don't want to paint. I'm going to help Mack with the horses."

"But…"

"They make me happy, okay? And Mack treats me like I'm normal."

"You *are* normal." That wasn't quite true; Cat thought Dora was exceptional in many ways, good and bad. "I'm just worried about you, hon."

"I'm not the one who died, okay?" Dora's brittle veneer cracked for half a second, but she quickly straightened her shoulders and shot Cat a scathing glare. "I'm sick of people worrying about me." She kicked a stone into the fire, which was starting to eat its way up the carefully stacked wood. "Just leave me alone."

—∿∿—

Dinner was everything Maddie had promised and more. Mack arranged log benches around the fire pit as promised, and the casual atmosphere and gorgeous setting made everything taste better.

Not that Maddie needed help coaxing flavor out of food. Two Dutch ovens nestled in the coals. Lifting the lid on one of them released a curl of swooningly fragrant steam and revealed a cozy cluster of biscuits, browned to golden perfection on top and light as spun sugar on the inside. Another bubbled over with glistening chunks of what proved to be venison floating in a rich sauce along with potatoes and carrots. Cat felt like she was eating Bambi's mother, but the meat was full of flavor. Corn, steamed in its husks, completed the meal. Dessert was apple cobbler cooked in a skillet over the coals.

Tippy spent mealtime circling the benches, staring pleadingly at each diner in turn. Dora chattered animatedly with Mack and Maddie, and even with the hired hand—a tall, quiet man who'd sat on the far side of the fire and eaten in near-total silence. But she ignored Cat, and when Maddie began loading the quaint enamel plates and cooking pots into wicker laundry baskets for the trip back to the house, the girl jumped up to help, chattering as if she'd known these people all her life.

Cat watched her niece trot up to the house, followed by Maddie and Trevor. She started after her niece and was stopped by a strong hand on her shoulder.

"Let her go," Mack said.

She tried to shake him off, but the hand just got heavier. There was nothing sexual in his touch this time. It was just firm. Decisive. Somehow, that was sexier than if he'd caressed her.

"Seriously. Let her go. I have a daughter the same age. If you act needy, you're done for."

"I'm not needy."

"You need her to like you. It's pretty obvious."

She toed a line in the dirt with the toe of her boot. "I just want her to be happy."

"Right now, making you miserable is what makes her happy."

"Thanks a lot."

"It's about the only thing she has power over right now."

That was true, and pretty perceptive for a cowboy.

"I know it's hard," he said. "We took my daughter to a counselor when things got bad with the divorce." He settled onto one of the benches. "He gave us a lot of tips on dealing with exactly this kind of thing."

"Did counseling help?" she asked.

"A little." He shrugged. "It's all theory. Not much of it seemed to work with Viv, but Dora seems more normal."

If Dora was normal, Cat hated to think what his daughter was like. "So what kind of advice did he give you?"

"Be there for her. Care about her. But pretend you don't."

She scraped up a little hillock of sand with the side of her boot, then tapped it down with the toe. "I'm not that good an actress."

"I noticed." He grinned, resting his elbows on his knees and clasping his hands together. The firelight made his tanned skin glow like gold. His eyes were bright with reflected flames. "Your heart's pretty close to the surface."

She felt her face warm, and it wasn't from the heat of the flames. Her heart had been close to the surface back in the barn—close enough to catch fire. But she'd laid down the law, and she was going to follow the rules she'd set for both of them.

No touching.

"She's your sister's daughter, right?" he asked.

Cat swallowed and nodded. She pictured Dora's sharp little face, then let the image soften and melt in her mind, the features becoming Edie's. It had barely been six months since Edie's death, and yet she could only find her through Dora.

"She was. Edie—Edie's gone." She sank down beside him, carefully keeping a hand's breadth of space between them. "We were close. Our parents were kind of distant, and we had to take care of each other. Dora's so much like Edie. I love her like crazy. Probably too much."

"Girls that age need somebody to love 'em." He grinned. "God knows it's not easy. Viv drives me nuts."

"No kidding. The other night I had a dream where a pack of ravenous wolves brought Dora down like a deer in a nature documentary. When I woke up I was hardly even sorry. I still feel terrible about that."

He smiled, poking a chunk of unburned wood into the center of the fire with a stick. A quick blue flame rose and danced. "That annoying, huh?"

"That frustrating."

"Tell me about her mom."

She shouldn't confide in this man. But what did it really matter? She shouldn't have kissed him either, but the whole thing would be over when she went back to Chicago. And there was nothing wrong with talking.

He nudged her again. "Earth to Cat. Your sister?"

She hadn't talked about Edie since the funeral. She'd gone home to her empty apartment with nothing but a photo of Edie that her brother-in-law had mounted in a silver frame. She talked to the picture now and then. One night she'd clutched it to her chest and let herself cry. But other than that she kept her grief quiet.

Of course, no one had ever offered to listen before. She felt her heart opening and was helpless to stop herself from spilling out her story.

"She was two years older than me. We both went to the Academy, both majored in visual arts. But we were so different." She looked up at the sky, where the silver of twilight was fading to black and stars were beginning to wink out of the darkness. "I was the workhorse, studying hard, developing my craft. Edie was a natural."

She smiled up at the sky, remembering how fearlessly her sister had wielded a brush, how boldly she'd attacked blank canvas. "She had so much talent. She'd sketch the simplest thing—an old shoe, a pigeon—and it would be *the* shoe, *the* pigeon. She caught the essence of things like no one I'd ever seen."

"And you think Dora's just as talented."

"I do. Trouble is, she's just as unmotivated. Edie was too busy living to paint. Boys. Parties. Crazy stunts, you know? She barely graduated. And then she married the richest boy in town and partied some more. And then she got cancer."

"But first she had Dora."

"Thank God. There's so much of Edie in Dora. But she's all we have left. My sister had a few sketchbooks, most of them half-full, and she did a Christmas card every year. That's all the art she did after she got married."

"Too bad."

"Yeah, but Dora inherited her talent, and I think she's got the drive to use it. She just needs a little guidance."

"And that's your job."

Cat thought she caught a little sarcasm in Mack's voice, but she let it pass.

"That's my job," she echoed. "To make sure she doesn't get lost like her mother. To help her make a mark on the world."

Mack set his hand on the edge of the bench behind her. If she sat back, changed her position the slightest bit, he'd have his arm around her. She'd be able to lean against him, just for a minute.

But Dora might come out any moment. She edged away. He didn't seem to mind, picking up a stick and poking at the fire. Maybe she'd only imagined he was making a move.

"Your sister made a mark on you," he said. "That's about all we can hope for. To matter to the people we love."

"But she could have made such a difference." Cat felt her lower lip tremble and sucked in a deep breath. "The world should have seen what she could do. I'm not letting that happen to Dora."

"Sounds like a big job."

"Not really." Cat looked up and watched the stars shimmer as the sky darkened. "She's my second chance."

Chapter 11

MACK WATCHED CAT AS SHE WATCHED THE STARS. HER head was tilted back, and those dark blue eyes were sparkling with reflected light.

She caught him looking. "What?"

"I'm just thinking—you take a lot of responsibility for other people. Does someone take care of you?"

"Sure. I have a boyfriend." Even in the dim light, he could see the flush spreading over her face. "That sounds funny at our age, doesn't it? Boyfriend."

"So how come you don't marry him? You're what—twenty-five?

"Twenty-eight. And that's kind of personal, don't you think?" Her eyes darted from his face to the fire and back again. She was hiding something, he was sure. There was something fishy about her relationship with this boyfriend. Mack wondered if she'd made him up. "It's just—he's—I don't know. I should. He's amazing."

Yeah, right. Mack was pretty sure she wasn't stuttering from the depth of her feelings. "Amazing, huh?"

She nodded eagerly. "He's a painter. A real artist."

"You're a real artist."

She laughed. "How would you know?"

"I looked you up. Online. Your work's terrific."

She looked flattered, surprised, and uncomfortable all at once. And changed the subject back to the boyfriend as quick as she could.

"Well, his work's hung in museums all over the world. MoMA bought one of his pieces last year."

"Your momma?"

"No, MoMA."

Her lips quirked up in a grin and he wondered if she knew he was egging her on. He might not have visited a lot of museums, but he knew what MoMA was.

"The Museum of Modern Art. In New York."

"Oh. I guess that would be a pretty big deal. So would I have heard of this guy?"

"Maybe. Ames Whitaker?"

"Doesn't ring a bell."

"Well, it would if you were into art. *TIME* magazine called him 'America's most promising young abstract expressionist.'"

"So what else about him is amazing?"

She plucked a sprig of blue flax from beside the bench and spun it in her fingers. She'd stuck several of them in her hat, but the petals had dropped off, leaving a few weedy stalks sticking up like antennae.

"You need more than that?" She lifted her chin. "He's a major talent. Unique. And he's—different. It's like he lives on another plane than the rest of us, really. Sometimes I tease him about living in a dream world."

Mack knew the type. Guys who thought they were special. He'd seen it too often in rodeo—the big stars taking advantage of their status, using a woman until some other pretty face came along.

"Are there ravenous wolves in this dream world of his?"

She laughed. "No."

"Well, they introduced them to Yellowstone. Maybe we can set some loose on Ames Whosiswhat."

"It's Whitaker." She laughed. "Jealous?"

"No. But I'm still wondering who takes care of you."

She shot him a narrow-eyed glare. "I take care of myself."

"Hmm." Mack thought a moment, wondering how far he should go. Cat deserved better than this Ames guy—that was obvious.

He might as well be honest with her. She'd be gone in two weeks. Maybe he could teach her something more than how to ride horseback.

"Sounds like this guy's a total bust in bed."

"I didn't say that." She was really blushing now, and picking furiously at the poor flower. Two soft petals fluttered to the ground. "It's just that… well… it's a different kind of relationship. There's more to it than that."

"I guess. Like name-dropping. Doesn't do you much good when you're around normal people, though. I never heard of him."

He didn't know why he felt compelled to counsel this woman on her love life. Or why it twisted his heart into a knot to hear her talk about another man. He barely knew her.

Sure, he'd kissed her, but he'd kissed women before. He'd kissed Alex, and look how that had turned out. He'd gotten Viv out of the deal, and he'd never regret that. But he'd also gotten massive credit card debt and a mortgage for a house he didn't live in.

But Cat didn't seem like the money-grubbing type. In fact, he wondered how she could survive in Chicago. He'd always figured living in the city would be like living among that pack of wolves they'd been joking about.

After his divorce, he'd begun to think it was women

who were the wolves. Now the pang of jealousy he felt when Cat talked about her boyfriend told him he was falling prey to another one.

She rose and walked away, heading up the path to the house without a word. He ought to feel lucky, like the deer would if a wolf snapping at his heels suddenly veered off in another direction.

But he'd been enjoying the chase, and that pang of jealousy turned into a different kind of pang as he watched her go.

He'd made up his mind when he'd returned to concentrate on the ranch, and on his family. He wasn't looking for a woman, that was for sure.

So why did he feel so lonely watching her leave?

By the time Mack finished the evening chores, the fire had dwindled to a flicker he could barely see from the barn. He headed down to the bunkhouse to kick a little dirt over it and caught Cat sitting silently on one of the benches, staring into the flames.

"How'd it go with your niece?"

She shrugged. There was a definite chill in the air, and it wasn't just because the fire was flickering out. He'd probably earned the cold shoulder with his comments about her boyfriend. He didn't know why he'd said that stuff. It had just pissed him off, her going on about how Honey Bumpkiss lived in a different world. She deserved better than that.

He suspected the guy wasn't any more talented than Cat herself. The paintings of hers he'd found online had been amazing. And she'd been swept away by the beauty of the landscape on their brief ride. He'd had to tap her on the shoulder twice, waking her up while she drank in the scenery.

But instead of putting whatever vision she'd absorbed into a painting, she was worrying about Dora, worrying about this Whitaker character, worrying about her students.

Worrying about him and what he was going to say next. Or do.

He needed to get a grip and make up for his previous clumsiness. Guiding a bunch of tenderfoots through the ranch's vast backcountry wasn't going to be an easy task. They needed to be a team.

"I'll do what I can to help with Dora." He sat down beside her. "It seems like this might be a tough time for her."

"What's not a tough time when you're fifteen?" Cat said. She seemed to be asking the sky, not him, so he didn't answer. The next question was addressed to him.

"So how old's your daughter? And where is she?"

"She's sixteen. Lives with my ex in Colorado." He grabbed a stick and leaned forward, poking at the fire. It didn't need poking; he just didn't want to have to look at Cat while he answered.

"Do you see her much?"

He shook his head. "She's supposed to spend most of the summer with me, but Alex—my ex—always has some reason she can't make it."

"How long have you been divorced?"

"Five years. Alex doesn't like the way I live. 'The rodeo lifestyle,' she calls it. She doesn't seem to understand it's my job."

"Doesn't it keep you from having a stable place for your daughter?"

He swallowed an angry retort. "This place is pretty stable."

She nodded. "But you didn't live here. When you were married, I mean."

"No. Alex didn't want me to rodeo, but she wasn't cut out to be a ranch wife, either. Soon as we were married, she turned into a freakin' Kardashian. All she wants to do is dress up and go to parties. And shop. Shopping is her life—she'll tell you so. I don't know if you've noticed, but this isn't exactly retail heaven."

"I don't know." She surprised him with a smile. "I saw some great sunglasses for sale at the Kum 'n' Go. And the prairie dog figurines were to die for." She stretched her legs toward the fire. "Doesn't Viv like to come here? Dora seems to love it."

He shrugged. "Alex is trying to turn Viv into a little clone of herself." He sighed again, more heavily this time. "I don't mean to be nasty. I loved Alex once. It's just that we have nothing in common. Money matters so much to her."

"It doesn't to you?"

"I want to have enough. But I don't need a whole lot of stuff. Just the basics—enough to keep the people I love happy and safe." He leaned back and looked up at the stars. "She's got Viv convinced that she needs stuff to be happy, though, so it's kind of a catch-22."

"Can't you insist Viv comes for the summer? It's a crucial time, I think. Girls that age are deciding who they'll be the rest of their lives."

"Alex says Viv wants to go to modeling camp."

"I'll bet you're thrilled about that. Can't you say no?"

"That would just feed into Alex's goal of turning Viv against me. She's got her almost all the time. And when I do have Viv, she spends half her time texting on the cell phone Alex made me buy her. What the hell does a sixteen-year-old need with a cell phone?"

Cat smiled. "You don't know much about sixteen-year-olds, do you?"

"I was one."

"Yeah, in the Dark Ages." She cocked her head. "How old are you, anyway?"

"Thirty-five." There was another reason things couldn't work out between them. He was older than her. Seven years older. Not a lifetime, but enough to make a difference.

Enough about him. He tilted his head toward the bunkhouse, where Dora slept. "So did you notice Trevor and Dora at dinner?"

"What? They didn't even talk to each other."

"I know. There's something fishy going on there. It just doesn't feel right."

Cat looked thoughtful. "Same with me. I felt like she was lying about something. Like who instigated the connection at the airport. We need to watch him."

We. He was getting somewhere. "You bet." He rose, brushing off his jeans. "You need to get some rest. Sorry to keep you awake with my sordid past."

"It's okay." She stood and staggered a little. "Wow. I'm a little stiff."

"Saddle soreness takes a while to set in." He reached out to steady her, gripping her elbow. "Might be a little tough getting out of bed in the morning."

He looked her in the eye, but he made sure she felt his gaze right down to her toes. "I just want apologize for— for everything." He still had no idea what he'd done, but that should cover it.

She apparently was at least considering accepting his apology, because she let him keep hanging onto her arm. She'd gone still, like a wary animal testing the air.

"I like the way you care about your niece, the way you look out for people." He kept his voice low since they were so close to the bunkhouse. "And I want you to know someone's looking out for you."

He put his other arm around her shoulders and drew her close. She looked up at him, her eyes troubled and maybe a little scared. Something in his heart melted and he bent his head to kiss her, but she put her hands on his chest and pushed him away.

"No, Mack." She said it gently, but it still hurt. "Not with Dora around."

"Dora's asleep."

"I don't know that for sure. And I can't take any chances." She stepped away.

"Life's all about taking chances," he said. "You can't play it safe all the time."

"No, but I can do my best." She walked away, heading for the Heifer House. "Good night, Mack."

Chapter 12

MORNING CAME WAY TOO SOON FOR CAT. SHE'D STARED up at the ceiling half the night, wondering why she'd felt compelled to lie to Mack. Ames wasn't her boyfriend. Sure, she'd dated him—once. They hadn't even made it to the main course before realizing they were better as friends. Ames should have been exactly what she wanted in a man, but for some reason the idea of touching him left her completely cold.

Unlike the cowboy, who heated her up like a spark striking tinder. When he'd boosted her into the saddle, she'd thought she was going to melt right off the mule. The ride, the ranch, the worries about the bunkhouse, and her clients—they'd all receded as a series of images flashed through her brain.

Images of sliding down into his arms. Images of being carried off to the barn. Images of the two of them literally rolling in the hay in various states of undress.

It was ridiculous. She'd just met the man. So she'd brought out Ames in self-defense, figuring there was some kind of Code of the West that forbade poaching another guy's gal.

No such luck. Maybe the Code only counted if the other guy was a cowboy too. And Ames was certainly no cowboy.

She'd finally fallen into a restless sleep, but she'd dreamed all night—dark, flickering dreams where she and Mack made love again and again under a starry Van Gogh sky. She'd woken up exhausted before dawn, and stayed in the rickety bed worrying about her sanity for almost an hour before she got up.

What the hell was she thinking? This man was wrong for her in so many ways. He was as different from her as night from day, the Mutt to her Jeff.

Worse yet, he was a business associate. The one thing they had in common—besides an ill-advised lust for each other—was a burning desire to make this trip a success. Which meant they needed to ignore all the other burning desires that threatened to send the whole project up in flames.

She needed to make the most of this day, not lie around mooning about cowboys. For her, work was always the solution to the problem. That was probably why Ames was the closest thing she'd had to a boyfriend in years. It hadn't taken her long to figure out that city socializing wasn't for her. She went to a few openings and kept up some professional relationships with drinks after work. But she much preferred the company of Alizarin Crimson and Cerulean Blue to most of the men she met.

She loved losing herself in a painting, surrendering to the hypnotic flow of pigment in water. That was one reason the noise and bustle of the city had never bothered her—she'd spent her evenings absorbed in the workings of her brush, the sweep of charcoal on rough paper. Days had belonged to Trainer and Crock, but nights had been filled with glowing, fanciful paintings, always of natural subjects—trees and clouds, water and sky, all painted from photographs and vacation memories.

Here, she had nature all around her. And time was

wasting while she worried about a man she'd be leaving in two weeks—a man she'd never see again after this trip.

She bounced out of bed and took the world's shortest shower, smoothing her hair with her fingers and dabbing sunscreen on her nose, chin, and cheekbones. She edged open the door to Dora's room, summoning up the courage to suggest they go out and look for subjects together. The rest of the students would be arriving later, so they'd have some of that girl time Dora was so scornful about. Maybe she'd be a little easier to get along with this morning.

But the girl mumbled something, scowled in her sleep, and turned toward the wall. It might be best to let sleeping Doras lie.

Grabbing her collapsible easel and a portable plastic palette, Cat headed outside. She'd just do a few quick watercolor sketches, demos for her students. The ranch might not be the height of dude luxury, but it was certainly picturesque. The house glowed in the pink sheen of sunrise, one lighted window marking the kitchen. Maddie was probably already toiling over breakfast. The barn glowed too; Mack was already at work. As she watched, he passed the barn doors with a pitchfork slung over his shoulder. Maybe she should talk to him about posing for a portrait. That would certainly break the ice.

Yeah, right. She'd gone over every hard curve and solid plane of his body last night in her dreams. The last thing she needed to do was trace the same lines this morning with a pencil. They'd be stamped on her mind's eye indelibly and she'd never get focused on the trip.

She reminded herself of her rules. This trip was about Dora. Not cowboys. And certainly not sex.

So why couldn't she stop thinking about cowboys and sex?

The sky was turning from pink to pewter, but the sun still lit the face of the barn. It warmed the red paint and sharpened the shadows that defined the rough wood. Behind and above, clouds blended and blurred. Cat doubted she could improve on it any, but she could preserve it. She had just set up in front of the barbed wire fence when Mack strode out of the barn.

"Sorry it's not better weather." He stood behind her as she stroked the top third of her paper with a water-soaked hake brush, edging around the barn's roofline. Dipping first into blue, then just touching a dab of burnt umber, she laid in the darkest part of the sky, doing her best to ignore him. She hated it when people watched her work, but she'd better get used to it if she was going to teach.

"How do you know what colors to use?"

She shrugged. "Four years of art school. Lots of mistakes."

He apparently figured out from her terse answer that she didn't want to talk, and as she dabbed color on the paper and watched her painting emerge, she finally forgot he was there. Eventually he gave up and returned to the barn. The loose, devil-may-care grace of his walk was a distraction, and the sight of his backside was even worse, but once he was out of sight she managed to get back in the zone.

She was adding finishing touches when he spoke from behind her.

"Lunchtime."

He was close, too close, and she jumped and spun to face him. Paint flew from the brush and slashed a stripe of alizarin crimson across the front of his pale blue shirt.

He pulled the shirt from his body so he could see the damage and shook his head ruefully. The paint looked like blood spatter from some grisly crime. "Another one bites the dust. I go through clothes like a horse goes through hay."

She grabbed a sponge from her supplies, dipped it in her water bottle, and dabbed at his chest, but that only spread the rich pigment, staining a wider area. She dabbed harder, biting her lip.

She was so intent on getting the stains out that it took her a second to notice how close they were standing, how warm his chest was under her hands, and how his eyes sparkled over a bemused smile. Once she did notice, she probably looked like an idiot, staring up at him with her mouth half-open.

Apparently she looked like an idiot who wanted to be kissed, because he ducked his head and next thing she knew she was being thoroughly and profoundly seduced under the shady brim of his cowboy hat.

She splayed one hand over his chest to push him away, but her body seemed to be caught in some inexorable flow of energy moving from his lips to hers. It was like the river she'd seen storming through the bottom of the canyon the day before. Even from high above they'd heard it, rushing forward, pounding over rocks. The same water that fell in gentle rain and nourished the prairie flowers had carved that canyon, working its will with a steady strength that found a way through every obstacle.

She felt all her own hard edges being worn away just as steadily. Tension hummed in her veins, but she was tumbling like a round rock in strong current. Mack had her sealed to his body with one hand around her shoulders and the other cupping her seat. He shifted, hoisting her up on tiptoe, and she couldn't help clinging to him as he made a low noise in his throat and deepened the kiss.

She was going to faint. She was going to fall. Yesterday's kiss had been casual, a chance encounter. This was very, very deliberate. It was the kind of kiss that made you forget your name. Forget your promises. Forget what you were here for...

Dora. She was here for Dora. And Dora could be watching right now.

She moved her hand back to his chest and braced herself, summoning the will to shove him away. He tightened his grip for a second, then let her go and staggered backward.

She stumbled a little herself, then caught her balance. He looked as shell-shocked as she felt, as if the kiss had surprised him too. She wiped her lips with the back of her hand, mostly to hide the fact that they were swollen and trembling with—lust? Emotion? What the hell *was* that? And what was she going to do about it?

She opened her mouth to speak and nothing came out. She stood there, gasping like a fish, for what seemed like an eternity before she could eke out one word.

"Stop."

"I did." He was breathing hard, his chest heaving like he'd just run a marathon.

She cleared her throat and stroked a lock of hair out of her face. What did you say to a man like this? How did you stop a river's flow when all you wanted to do was ride it, floating like a leaf on the surface, twirling in the eddies and shooting down the falls?

COWBOY TOUGH   93

"This is a professional relationship." Her own voice sounded foreign to her, breathless and a little shrill.

"Professional?" His eyes glinted with their usual humor, but his voice was husky. "Well, that explains a lot."

He seemed to realize he'd crossed a line before he'd even finished the joke. Raising both hands like a holdup victim, he started backing away. "Wait. Sorry. I didn't mean…"

"It doesn't matter." Cat grabbed her hat from the top of the easel and clamped it on her head, fooling with the brim as though the world depended on a rakish angle. She cocked it right, then left. Then right again.

"I told you—no touching. What if Dora had seen that? What if Trevor did?" To her own horror, she felt tears heating her eyes. Turning away, she stalked off, all stiffness and dignity.

The trouble with dignity was that it demanded you tilt your nose in the air, and then you couldn't see where you were going. Her toe hit a hillock and she stumbled, flailing her arms and losing what little poise she had left. Glancing back, she expected to see him grinning over her misstep, but he was standing just as she'd first seen him, his arms loose in that gunfighter stance.

Only this time his hands were empty, and he looked a little lost as he watched her go.

———※※———

"Darn it; they stopped." Madeleine turned from the window and beckoned to Hank Slay, who'd been watching her from the doorway like a sad and silent watchdog. "Mack was kissing the daylights out of that woman."

The hired man shoved his lanky body off the wall

and came over to the window. He'd been a hand on the ranch most of his life, working for two generations of Boyds. He was the only one who'd stuck by her throughout Ollie's tenure, patiently fending off her second husband's inexpert orders with stubborn silence. But despite the fact that he'd lived on the place for twenty years, Madeleine felt like she barely knew him. He wasn't much for fraternizing with the womenfolk.

The womenfolk. She'd heard him refer to her that way. Despite the fact that she was just one woman, Hank seemed to regard her as an entire alien race. She didn't know what had happened in his past to make him so spooked about females, but it must have been one of those traumatic experiences that stayed with you all your life, like the wounds soldiers suffered in war. Whenever he had to face her, he'd clutch his hat in front of his chest in both hands, as if it was the steering wheel of a race car going a million miles an hour. His knuckles would go white as he spun it right and left, left and right as if he could steer himself right out of the room.

But since the Ollie incident, he seemed to have transferred his loyalty to her. She'd assumed he'd take to following Mack around, but he shadowed her instead, lurking in corners and hovering outside the back door, scaring the daylights out of her whenever she turned and saw him standing there with his hat in his hands. She'd taken to talking to him in a running monologue, though she wasn't sure if he understood a word she was saying. He never responded. It was like talking to a dog or a cat—one-sided, but somehow still satisfying.

"I hope to hell he knows what he's doing," she said.

Hank spun the hat to the left.

"Everything depends on this first bunch of customers," she said. "Our reputation's at stake. Plus I need to make back the money that son-of-a-bitch husband of mine stole."

He didn't respond, but she just kept talking—partly to see if she could get a rise out of him. "Oh, I know you think a woman can't do it. But you mark my words, I'll make this dude ranch thing pay. Make it pay enough to make up for my stupid mistake."

She blinked fast, keeping her eyes fixed on Mack and the painter lady so Hank wouldn't see that she was tearing up. She wasn't a crier. She was a ranch wife, tough and resilient.

And Ollie Kress was hardly worth crying over. It was obvious her ex wasn't the man she'd believed him to be. He didn't love her like she'd thought, either. She'd just been a means to an end, a foolish woman willing to hand over all her assets, and her body too. That was the part she regretted most. Thinking of Ollie's hands on her, of the way he'd used her, made her want to crawl out to the barn and die. It shamed her just to think of how foolish she'd been.

It was easy enough to make excuses for herself. Her grief for Mack's father had been deep and wide, a cold, dark river she couldn't seem to cross. Life without him on the ranch had been unbearably lonely, and Ollie had offered her a distraction.

But in the end, she'd just heaped a heavy dollop of shame on top of her sorrow.

She twisted her hands in her apron, pretending she needed to wipe them clean. She wouldn't let anyone catch her wringing her hands over Ollie. Not even Hank.

It was just anger that made her do it, anyway. Not hurt. Not heartbreak. Anger.

"I know it's been hard on you." She shot Hank a sideways glance, knowing that if she looked at him directly he'd shy away and disappear. "Here you've been relying on me, and I let you down. I'll pay you, you know. All I owe you, plus interest."

Hank shoved his hands in his pockets and rolled the toe of his boot over a pebble that had somehow escaped the wrath of her broom. He rolled it over and back, over and back, until she was half-mesmerized by the repetition. Maybe he thought he was shifting gears in that race car. Who knew what went through the man's head?

"Well." She rushed to fill the silence. That was the problem with Hank. His quiet ways set her to babbling. "If my son wants to seduce that woman into thinking this is the right place for the Art Treks, that's fine with me." She turned and strode out to the porch, not caring if Hank followed her or not. "God knows the bunkhouse didn't impress her."

"She's good for him," Hank said. "You ought to get her to stay."

She spun and faced him.

"Why, Hank." She struggled to find her voice. He'd shocked the talk right out of her. She watched him redden and turn away and realized she needed to act casual, pretend this was all normal. It was like taming a wild animal. Don't make eye contact. Don't get too close.

"You think she's right for him?" She kept her tone casual.

"She's strong."

She leaned against the door frame, staring up at the

rafters that lined the porch roof. "Well, I don't know," she said. "If she was a horsewoman, maybe, or some kind of sexpot, I'd figure she was more his type. But that woman sits a horse like she's perched in a church pew."

A faint smile creased Hank's face, but he kept his eyes on the floor. "That ex of his was no horsewoman," he said.

"Got a point there." Madeleine pictured Alex as she'd last seen her, dressed in a black broomstick skirt and fringed suede jacket. She'd been draped with so much Navajo jewelry she looked like she was leaking turquoise and silver from her pores. "You know, I knew she was wrong for him. But I wanted him to marry her anyway." She pulled a metal bar from a nail in one of the porch posts and used it to ring out a summons to the table on the old-fashioned triangle that had hung there for generations. Spinning on her heel, she walked briskly back to the kitchen, knowing Hank would follow. "Not because I'm one of those women that wants grandkids so bad. I'd never sacrifice my boy's happiness for something *I* want, you know. But if it took a woman like that to tie him to home, I was all for it. Anything to keep him off those broncs."

"Broncs won't hurt him." Hank spat over the porch rail before he shoved off the wall and followed her into the house. She supposed she should be grateful he'd done it outside. Far as she knew, the man wasn't housebroken. "No bucking horse'll hurt you like a woman will."

Madeleine turned and pinned him with her eyes. "Is that what you think?" She dismissed the notion with a toss of her head. "Mack wouldn't want a woman that didn't have any spunk."

"She stands up real straight. She's got some fight in her." He thumbed toward the door, indicating the artist woman. "That's a good sign. She's strong on her own, so she won't need to take anything from him."

Madeleine straightened her own spine. Hank probably saw her as she saw herself, as a woman without a backbone. A woman who'd been walked all over by a man.

Well, she'd prove that wrong. Nobody was taking this place away from her—not Ollie, not the bank, not anybody. She might only be a Boyd by marriage, but she loved this ranch like she'd been born to it. And she'd fight for it like a man if she had to.

She took a calico apron from a hook on the wall and tied it around her waist. Glancing over at Hank, she paused, then unhooked another one and tossed it to him. He clutched it in his fist for a moment, staring at it like it was a snake.

"Put it on," Maddie said. "I need you to chop some onions."

He shrugged and tied it on as if he'd done it all his life, looking up at her while his hands fumbled with the bow behind his back. She felt something oddly intimate when their eyes met. Hank was quiet, but so watchful. Sometimes she wondered if he knew exactly what she was thinking.

The faintest trace of a smile crossed his lean face, and for a moment he looked almost handsome.

"You see?" he said. "You stand up straight too." He stroked the apron over his thighs like a girl adjusting her prom gown, and the creases in his face smoothed into their customary noncommittal expression. "Show me where you keep those onions."

Chapter 13

LUNCH WAS AN ORDEAL. THERE WAS NO WAY FOR CAT to avoid sitting right across from Mack; it was almost as if Maddie engineered the seating arrangement for maximum awkwardness. The two of them avoided each other's eyes, but every moment seemed fraught with innuendo. She couldn't tell if she was just paranoid, or if everyone was conscious of the tension between her and the wrangler.

Not that Cat had any idea what that tension meant. After kissing her like he was starving and she was lunch, he'd come to the table with his eyes averted and kept his attention solely on the food. He met her gaze only once, and she wasn't sure if it was arousal or annoyance that glinted in his eyes.

Between him and Hank, there was a whole lot of quiet at the dinner table. Dora was quiet as well, casting quick, resentful glances toward Cat. Only Madeleine managed to keep up a running conversation, answering her own questions when Cat's words stuck in her throat. So it was a relief to hear the crunch of gravel as the airport shuttle pulled into the drive.

Shoving her chair back, Cat practically ran to the door, bouncing down the steps with a welcoming smile that hopefully masked her nerves. She didn't know much about her students besides their names. Edward Delaney and his wife Emma, their daughter Abby, and

Charles Brodell. With Trevor, that made five clients to educate and entertain.

She glanced at Mack. He leaned against the porch railing in a graceful slouch that radiated cowboy cool, but his eyes were fixed on the van as intently as hers, waiting for their future to spill out the side door. With his square jaw set, his strong cheekbones, and those dark eyes, he looked like a bird of prey waiting for a mouse to come out of a hole.

A faint scratching noise from the interior of the van turned to panicked scrabbling, then pounding. Mack strode down the steps and grabbed the door handle, hauling it open to reveal the shadowed interior. Cat almost held her breath as she waited for her students to emerge. Whoever came out of that van would be her responsibility for the next two weeks.

A blue-veined leg that terminated in a very sensible shoe poked out the door and felt around for the running board. It was followed by an equally sensible-looking woman with wire-rimmed glasses and white hair as wispy as her fragile build. She was dressed in splashy floral capri pants and a T-shirt that read "I'd Rather Be Painting" in loose, flowing script.

"I couldn't find the door handle," she said. "They ought to put it where a body can—oh, look!" She stared at Mack, who had shed his hat for lunch and looked remarkably virile in a white T-shirt and jeans. "Abby, look. A cowboy!"

The next woman to emerge was as large as the other was delicate, with broad shoulders and an almost masculine build. Standing with her shoulders hunched and her legs slightly bowed, she looked like a pugnacious bear who'd been awakened too soon from hibernation.

She was a good twenty years younger than the first woman, so Cat had to assume that this was Abby Delaney and the other woman was her mother, Emma. The dad must be a pretty big guy, because Abby's size sure didn't come from the maternal genes.

"You're right, Mom." The big woman shot Mack an accusatory gaze. "One of those men that breaks the spirits of wild mustangs and ropes helpless baby cows."

Someone protested from the depths of the van. "You ladies just don't know a thing about real men." The voice was shaky and thin—a perfect match for the old gentleman who stepped out next. Maybe Abby Delaney got her build from the postman.

"How could I?" Mrs. Delaney smacked him on the arm. It wasn't a hard smack. Cat thought you could almost call it a love tap, but there was a lot of spunk in it. "I've been married to you for forty-nine years."

Ed Delaney hobbled over and stood with Mack. "Women," he said with a conspiratorial wink. "Can't live with 'em, can't shoot 'em."

"*I* could shoot 'em." Mack gave the elderly couple a slow once-over, then slid his gaze to Cat. He'd obviously calculated their age and come up with the same number she had. Seventy. At least.

This trip was going to be a challenge.

"Don't know what it is that stops me from shooting 'em sometimes." Mack strode to the back of the van, where the driver was unloading luggage. He drew his wallet from his pocket, counting out bills for a tip.

Cat shook hands all around, introducing herself and

welcoming her guests to the Art Trek. She struggled to focus on each person in turn, resisting the urge to peer past them into the back of the van, where her last customer was slowly making his way up from the third-row seat.

Very slowly.

As he emerged, Cat took an involuntary step back. He was so big he had trouble maneuvering around the seats, and once he eased out of the door she wondered how he'd ever gotten back there in the first place. When he thumped to the ground and straightened, she realized he was even taller than Mack. With his shaved head and the tattooed sleeve running up his arm, he looked like an ex-con, or maybe a biker.

"Uh, hi." Cat put out her hand, but she almost whipped it back when he reached for it. The back of his hand was tattooed to look like the head of a lizard, with its tongue flicking out along the middle finger. The creature's talons grasped his muscular forearms as the tail wound up his biceps to curl around several disturbing images—a skull with snakes spilling out of its eye sockets and a knife that seemed to spurt blood from a tattooed wound. It was possibly the best-drawn tattoo Cat had ever seen, but also the most disturbing. The realism made the lizard seem eerily alive, with glittering eyes that followed the viewer.

But he shook her hand with surprising gentleness, his eyes meeting hers only briefly before they skittered away and lit on the ranch house. He seemed to be probing the shadows, and she had the impression that he was looking for danger. Maybe he really was an ex-con. Maybe he was on the run.

Well, at least then he wouldn't mind the accommodations. He'd feel right at home in the cell-like rooms of the Bull Barn.

"So have you all met?" Cat winced as she asked the question. Of course they'd met. They'd just spent three hours in a cramped van together.

"Well, we're family," Abby said, gesturing to Ed and Abby. "And that driver was a nice guy. Him?" She angled a thumb toward the man with the lizard tattoo. "He didn't say a word the whole way."

To Cat's surprise, the big man hunched his shoulders and winced. "Sorry."

"Be nice, Abby," Emma said. The response had the feel of a reflex. Cat suspected Emma had to remind Abby to be nice pretty often. The younger woman seemed to be the exact opposite of her parents—heavyset while they were frail, rude while they were sweetly polite, grumpy while they seemed unflaggingly cheerful. Even Cat's postman theory didn't account for the contrast. Maybe the daughter was adopted.

Madeleine Boyd was beaming from the front door, waving the group inside. As each new guest approached, she extended both hands in greeting and leaned in to bestow dramatic air-kisses, closing her eyes as if each gesture was the most heartfelt smooch in history. Whatever her faults, Madeleine seemed to genuinely love welcoming people to her home. When Charles approached, her eyes widened at the sight of the lizard tattoo, but she recovered quickly and gave him the same warm greeting as the others.

Cat was the last to enter the house. Somehow, Maddie had managed to clear the lunch mess and lay out an elegant afternoon tea again. She wondered how the woman had transformed the dining area so quickly, but then she saw Hank standing at the sink, elbow-deep in suds. Maddie seemed more than capable of handling the crowd, so Cat slipped out and joined Mack, who was sorting the luggage into heaps that seemed to have no rhyme or reason. Dora was already hefting a bag of art supplies.

"What's with the old folks?" Dora asked. "I thought this company was called 'Art Treks.' We're not going to be doing much 'trekking' with them along." She lowered her voice to a stage whisper. "Art Wrecks, I'd call it."

"No kidding." Mack took a suitcase in each hand and shot Cat a furious glare. "Somebody's going to break a hip. And I'm not sure my insurance covers geriatric pack trips. You could have warned me, Cat."

"I didn't know," Cat said. "There's no screening. The company processes the applications, and I doubt they turn anyone down if the check clears."

"I guess not." Dora laughed. "It looks like a nursing home picnic."

"Abby and Charles are young."

"And weird," Dora said. "That lady looks like a bear. And the lizard man is just scary."

"Be careful, okay?" Cat tried to keep her tone light. "Someone could hear you."

She felt like she'd scored a major victory when Dora shrugged and didn't talk back.

"So what's the plan?" Mack didn't look happy. It was hard to believe this was the same man who had kissed her like his life depended on it just an hour before.

"Well, the first hurdle is the bunkhouse. I'm going to try to avoid that until after dinner. Maybe you could give them a tour of the ranch when they're done with tea?"

Mack nodded.

"Make it a good one. Wear them out. Then, if dinner's as good as last night, I'm hoping they just fall into bed without analyzing the mattress," she said.

Mack pulled off his hat and ran his hand through that thick, dark hair. At the phrase "falling into bed," his eyes lit on hers and his lips curved into a faint smile.

Now *that* was the man who had kissed her. She wished her various female parts weren't so happy to see him again. She felt that current tugging at her heart again, pulling them together.

"So where do you want these?" Dora asked, hoisting a canvas easel case over her shoulder and picking up a pochade box. "Bunkhouse or barn?"

Mack's smile faded. "Bunkhouse," he said.

At the same moment, Cat blurted out, "Barn."

He shrugged. "Barn, then." He hefted a suitcase in each hand and turned to face Cat. "Your students, your rules." He flashed her a smile, but it didn't come close to the warmth of that look they'd shared. "And I promise to follow all of them."

Cat watched him go, the muscles in his arms bulging with the weight of the suitcases. She was starting to regret all the rules she'd posed.

Especially the one about "no touching."

Chapter 14

CAT STOOD AT THE DOOR OF THE BUNKHOUSE AND stretched, giving the rising sun a happy salute that was part yoga, part pure joy. Mack's ranch tour the day before had been a success, mostly because he'd taken the time to demonstrate some roping techniques and let everyone try their skill on a dummy calf made out of a pair of horns and a hay bale. That had worked up an appetite, and Maddie's formula of great food and campfire camaraderie had worked its magic again. Cat didn't think any of the students had noticed the Spartan living conditions in the bunkhouses. They'd been too tired and full of good food to do anything but fall into bed.

And now, it was a new day—the first real day of painting. Eight saddle horses were lined up against the corral fence, stamping and blowing in the cool morning air. Three others were laden with art supplies, their bodies crisscrossed with a complex network of knotted rope and leather straps.

Mack assigned each student a mount, offering tips on each horse's personality. Tippy tagged along, offering each participant her trademark tongue-lolling grin. She reminded Cat of a dim but cheerful water boy psyching up the team.

Mack, however, didn't seem so cheerful. Boosting Abby and the Delaneys onto their mounts was no easy task, and his patient grin was worn to a thin line by the time Cat climbed aboard the mule as assigned.

He hung behind as the group proceeded down the trail, signaling Cat to leave the group and stay with him. Her heart thrummed a little faster. This would be the first time they'd been alone since yesterday. He was mounted on a tall chestnut horse Cat hadn't seen before, a handsome animal with a wide white blaze and four white socks, and he looked like he belonged on a "Welcome to Wyoming" postcard.

Resting her forearms on the saddle horn, she watched the riders pass two by two, like an orderly parade of animals headed for the ark. Dora looked like she'd been born in a saddle, and Emma was watching her carefully to see how to hold the reins just so. Abby rode a little stiffly, while her father grinned from ear to ear and swiveled his head to take in every detail of the experience. Charles, big as he was, looked comfortable in the saddle. Trevor, of course, had insisted he could only ride "hunt seat." He'd shortened his stirrups until his knees ended up clenched at the horse's withers. It didn't look to Cat like he was liable to catch anything he was hunting.

Her heart sank when Mack shot her a scowl. "I'm not sure we should go on with this," he said once the group was out of earshot.

"We don't have a choice."

"It would be different if they were experienced." He cast a worried glance up the trail as the last horse rounded a curve that took the group behind a rocky outcropping. "Lots of old hands ride. But Ed and Emma are so stiff. If they fall, they'll break."

"Then we'd better make sure they don't fall." Cat

shrugged. "I think you're underestimating them. They're very enthusiastic about this trip, and I'm sure they'll be careful. Besides, they signed a waiver."

He grimaced but nudged his horse forward. She started to follow, but the sound of pounding hooves made them both pull up their mounts.

Up ahead, a horseman rounded the curve at top speed and hurtled toward them at a furious gallop. Cat barely recognized the old man crouched over the horse's neck. Ed was grinning from ear to ear and thumping the horse's sides with his heels.

"Stop!" she hollered, steering her own mount off the trail. "Whoa!"

The old man thundered past on his panicked buckskin, then spun a quick circle. Cat was relieved to see the guy was grinning.

"Yee-haw! This baby can really run!" The horse crow-hopped a little while his rider clutched the saddle horn. "I'm a regular rodeo rider here!"

Mack didn't speak, just shot the old man a quelling look and rode on. When they caught up to the group, Cat noticed he'd turned an interesting shade of purple.

"Um, I think it's time to talk about some rules," she said. "Can you all hold up a minute?"

Ed's mount had sidestepped into the sagebrush, where he was tossing his head and testing the bit.

"Mr. Delaney, can you steer Bucky back to the group?"

"I sure can. Watch me!" The old man tapped the skinny horse with his heels and trotted neatly back into the line. Looking at Cat's disapproving face, he frowned. "I suppose you're not going to let us have any fun."

"We're here to paint, Edward," Emma said sternly.

"Now cut out your shenanigans. You're upsetting Mr. Boyd."

"We need to discuss the rules." Cat held the mule's reins loosely with what she hoped was a careless air of authority. "No running the horses."

"Oops," said Ed with an unrepentant grin.

"We walk at all times," she continued, struggling to hold a straight face. "And be careful."

"Watch your surroundings." She was relieved to hear Mack chiming in. "Horses can shy at all sorts of things, and accidents can happen in a heartbeat. Stay together, and keep an eye on each other. Cat knows the way, so she's going to lead with Rembrandt. Charles, I'd like you to ride drag."

Charles's panicked glance slid right, then left, as if he was hoping to discover another "Charles" in the group. "Um, I don't... I'm not..."

Abby let out a surprisingly girlish giggle.

"Not that kind of drag," Mack said. "Sorry, cowboy talk. It means take up the rear, just behind Spanky, there, and whistle if anything happens. Can you whistle?"

The normally quiet Charles contorted his face and let loose an earsplitting siren. The beleaguered buckskin broke from the group again and carried a delighted Mr. Delaney rocketing past the group.

"Maybe something a little more subtle," Mack said.

With the crisis averted—at least temporarily—they set off, the horses plodding sleepily along, the riders enjoying the view. Frothy clouds floated in a sea of placid blue, promising fine weather. Cat smiled as a slight breeze lifted the hair on the back of her neck. There was something to be said for this Zen thing; living in moments like this was pure pleasure.

The following week brought more Zen moments than Cat could count, and new painting lessons every day. On Tuesday, they rode far out on the prairie to paint a view of the huge, slope-sided buttes that rose from the flatland. Wednesday they followed the river down into the canyon for a class on painting water. Thursday was devoted to perspective, using the buildings at the ranch; and Friday they returned to the buttes, climbing a dizzying hairpin trail to the top for a view of a sky so wide it felt limitless.

Through it all, Mack kept his promise. There was no touching. In fact, there was barely any looking or talking. Once or twice she caught him eyeing her from under the brim of his hat, but he'd looked quickly away the moment his eyes met hers.

She tried to tell herself that was a good thing. She needed to concentrate on Dora, and on her students. And Mack needed to focus on his wrangling duties. They didn't have time for any kind of nonsense, but the truth was she missed the nonsense.

In fact, nonsense was all she could think about. As his interest had faded, hers had become an obsession. She turned their stolen moments over in her head the way you'd finger a smooth, round rock, savoring the texture, admiring the way it fit in your palm.

Friday's dinner was Maddie's best yet: pork chops cooked to unbelievable tenderness in a Dutch oven along with onions and sliced potatoes. The group seemed to love their new rustic lifestyle, and Abby was even learning to do a little Dutch oven cooking of her own.

After the meal came the cowboy songs, with the quiet ranch hand strumming a guitar while Ed led the group in rousing renditions of "Home on the Range" and "Don't Fence Me In." Mack had led the singing the first night, surprising Cat with a resonant baritone, but he'd been happy to turn that duty over to Ed, who seemed to know every cowboy ballad ever written.

By the time she crawled into bed, Cat was sleepy enough that she thought she might conquer the absurd fantasies that danced through her mind every night. But they unspooled in her mind like a feature film the moment she closed her eyes.

Mack in the sunshine, kissing her like he had the day the students arrived. Mack in the firelight, the flames reflecting in his dark eyes as he took her in his arms. Mack in the dark, the feel of his hands on her body.

Mack. Mack. Mack.

If only she could stop remembering the way he sat in the saddle, moving in perfect synch with the horse, his posture as relaxed and easy as a man in a rocking chair. Trying to ignore him was like trying not to think of an elephant—the forbidden creature only loomed larger in your mind when you tried to exclude it.

She closed her eyes and pictured distant mountains, the sun sinking behind them in a blaze of glory. She added Mack on horseback silhouetted against the horizon, his figure dwindling as he galloped away. There. She'd sent him riding into the sunset like a movie cowboy. Now maybe he'd leave her alone.

She stared up at the ceiling and turned her thoughts to her work. What colors would she use to capture the late-afternoon light on the red rock of the mesa? How would she mix the unique blue-green color of the sagebrush? How would she show the way Mack's shirt skimmed over the muscular breadth of his shoulders?

Mack. She almost screamed with frustration. If it wasn't for him, Boyd Ranch would be her new happy place, replacing the imaginary beach she pictured whenever she needed to relax. It would be nice to find a place in the real world that made her tension ease and her heartbeat slow—but no matter how hard she tried, she'd catch a whiff of his scent, that combination of hay, wood smoke, and leather, and then he was back. It drove her crazy.

She turned over onto her left side, bunching the pillow under her head, then flopped onto her back. The silence drove her crazy too. She was used to the city, the endless hum of traffic, the staccato beeps of car horns, and the murmur of conversation from neighboring apartments, but here there was only the faint whisper of a breeze rattling the sagebrush. It was too damn quiet. How could people sleep?

Finally, there was a sound—a faint rustling, a stomp, and a flurry of thumps that might have been something stumbling. Something large and graceless. Cat remembered Mack saying something about bears living in the wooded area behind the bunkhouses. She pictured a big, mean one reeling past the Heifer House, looking for children to eat.

No. Wait. She knew better than that. She'd read *Night of the Grizzlies*. Bears didn't care if their victims were children or old ladies or stinky old hunters in moth-eaten sleeping bags.

They were just *hungry*.

Chapter 15

TOSSING OFF THE COVERS, CAT SLIPPED HER FEET INTO her unlaced Keds—not because she was planning to go outside, but because she might need to run if the bear came in. She sat up against the headboard with her knees pulled to her chest, huddled in her own embrace.

There were no more stumbles, no more stomps. If there had been a bear, it had given up and moved on. The glow of the fire faded and died. The night stretched before her, silent as before.

So why couldn't she sleep?

It was the infernal quiet. The only sound was a cricket who'd gotten his bow all rosined up and was fiddling out the rhythm part to some obscure Philip Glass composition. *Screech, screech, screech, screech.* He seemed determined to play it all night.

All. Night. Long.

Cat hugged her knees tighter and stared into the darkness. It seemed like the ranch took on a whole new dimension in the night. What had been gently waving grasses became sharp-edged knives jutting from the ground. The occasional calls of night birds became the shrill cries of lurking predators. Cat had never noticed before how much crickets sounded like the violins in *Psycho*.

Gathering her robe about her, she tied the sash tightly and stood. Supposedly, facing your fears rendered them toothless. The thing you feared would turned benign once you stared it down in the flesh. Hopefully that would be the case with whatever was out there in the wild Wyoming night.

As she stepped out into the night, she heard something swish through the tall grass off to her left. Did bears come this close to human habitation? She'd heard they were attracted to food, and there had been plenty of that here tonight. She could still smell the rich scent of Maddie's pork chops lingering on the air.

But animals were afraid of fire, weren't they? And the campfire was surprisingly active. She'd expected a heap of embers at best, but a lick of flame flickered from the center of the pit, dancing happily in the darkness.

Lowering herself onto one of the benches, she sighed and looked up at the stars. There wasn't much hope of sleeping tonight. She might as well enjoy the view.

Mack stared up at the ceiling, his mind churning. Watching Cat disappear into the Heifer House had started the nightly wheel of speculation spinning in his mind.

What did she wear to bed?

He'd pictured her in everything from Hello Kitty pajamas to sheer black lace. Frilly nighties to threadbare T-shirts.

Maybe she didn't wear anything. Maybe she slept in the...

Aw, hell, he needed to get a grip. How could he be thinking about frivolous things like women when his family was in such dire straits? The dude ranch project was the best chance they had to save themselves, but instead of doing his best to make it work, he was thinking about a woman.

The wrong woman. The one who could make the whole thing go south.

He shifted on the narrow cot. The limp layer of foam that covered the springs of his iron bedstead might be good enough for a hunting camp, where a man could down a few shots of whiskey before bed, but it wasn't going to cut it for people like Trevor Maines.

Or Cat. Maybe she couldn't sleep either. Maybe he should go check.

No. He'd managed to behave himself for five whole days. He couldn't blow it now.

But he would blow it. It was inevitable. When she'd been laying down the law, he'd had a chance—but lately he'd seen her watching him. And not like she was looking for riding instruction, either. She had one of those faces you could read like a book, and lately the book was all about the two of them. Together.

He turned over on his left side, then his right, trying to find a position where the bed didn't jab him in the kidney or poke him in the shoulder. After flopping around a while like a fish on dry land, he sat up and rubbed the back of his neck, listening to the wind rustling the sagebrush. There were crickets chirping, and the faint call of a horned owl—and...

And something else.

He straightened, listening intently. Someone was outside. He could hear the grass rustling, and then a faint crackling, as if someone was crinkling paper. The fire flared up briefly and died.

Somebody was up to something.

He squinted into the darkness and listened. More footsteps, stumbling over rocks. The creak of a door.

Grabbing his jeans, he stepped into them and pulled a T-shirt over his head in one quick motion. He was out the door quick as a panther, pulling it closed behind him and standing against it, shielded by its shadow.

—⁓—

Cat gazed up at the frothy spill of stars overhead, waiting for the deep calm of the night sky to wash over her. But she couldn't help straining for the sound of an intruder. Maybe not a bear. Maybe a human.

But there was nothing out there. Just crickets. Crickets and…

Breathing.

It was coming from behind her, as if someone was watching. Waiting.

She turned slowly, half expecting to feel the swipe of a mighty paw striking the side of her head, huge claws scraping her…

"Aaack!"

She leaped to her feet, grabbing a log from the fire—and found herself standing in a bogus martial arts crouch, brandishing a half-burned stick at Mack, whose chest heaved in hearty but silent laughter.

She dropped the stick and straightened, setting her fists on her hips. "What are you doing out here?" she hissed.

"Checking to see what *you're* doing out here," Mack said. "Could you maybe make a little more noise? I thought a herd of elephants was coming through."

"I *was* quiet! I thought I heard something. I couldn't sleep."

"Worrying about Dora?"

She bit her lip. It would be easy to just say yes. And it wouldn't be a lie. Dora was always in the back of her mind, like a faint and ever-present ache.

But she was going to be here for another week, so she might as well tell him what she was really worried about. She was probably being silly, and he could put her fears to rest.

"Are there really bears here?"

"Yes."

So much for putting her fears to rest. She pictured a reversed version of the Goldilocks story, with the bear trying each bed in turn—and taking a bite out of each occupant.

Too big, too small… mmm, just right.

"They wouldn't come right up to the buildings though, would they?"

He laughed. "Heck, one came right in the house once."

———

Mack knew he shouldn't scare Cat. She needed to report to the Art Treks company that the Boyd Dude Ranch was a paradise for artists, a safe, serene place where they could paint in peace.

But there she was, all wide-eyed and wondering, and he couldn't resist the juvenile temptation to scare a girl. Even if that girl had dashed his fondest dreams by turning up in baggy gray sweats.

"A bear got in the house while Mom and Dad were in Denver at the stock show. Damn thing busted the door down, tore the place apart looking for food. Broke a couple windows. Crapped all over the place, too. Must have been in there for hours."

She edged toward him until their thighs touched.

"It was kind of funny. There were two big paw prints on every mirror in the house." He put his hands up, one on each side of his face, like a mime in a glass box. "Right at eye level. He must have stood up and looked at himself."

Cat let out a shaky breath and he realized he might have scared her a little too much.

"Don't worry; it won't happen with this many people here, or with the fire burning."

She sat down beside him. "You sure?"

"Yep. Plus it's more likely to happen earlier in the year. They're pretty damn hungry when they come out of hibernation."

"Well, thanks. I feel better."

"Good. People usually do once they know more about things."

Mack watched Cat as she clutched her knees to her chest, tilting her head back to look up at the sky. Her pale profile stood against the black backdrop like a cutout silhouette.

"I love the sky at night," she said. "You ever see that Van Gogh painting *Starry Night*?"

He nodded, relieved she'd mentioned one of the two or three paintings he knew by name. Maybe later they could discuss the *Mona Lisa* or *American Gothic*. He needed to spread out those conversations, though, since they covered the sum total of his art knowledge and they still had a week to go.

"It's a great painting," he said. He remembered trees, wind, swirling stars.

"I think every artist has a starry night," she said dreamily. "A scene that speaks to her. The landscape that defines her."

"Like a horse you're meant to ride," he said without thinking. Oh, shoot. He sounded like a total yokel.

She gave him a long, appraising look. He waited for her to laugh, dismiss what he'd said, but she just nodded. "Exactly."

Tilting her head back to study the stars, she leaned closer. Maybe she liked yokels.

"That's why I'm so excited about this trip. If it works out, I can get out of advertising and travel and paint for a living. I'll end up going all over the world. Tuscany. Maybe Paris. The mountains of Tibet. I'm bound to find my starry night sooner or later." She smiled sleepily. "That probably sounds crazy to you."

"No crazier than rodeo. If you have a dream, you have to chase it wherever it leads." It felt like they were sharing something—something that mattered. He slid a sideways glance her way. "So. You want a tour of the heavens?"

She tried to respond, choked on her own breath, coughed, and spluttered. "No," she croaked out. "And that is the worst pickup line I've ever heard."

"That's not what I meant. You said you came out to look at the stars. I meant I'd tell you about them. Their names. Old stories that go with 'em."

"You know the constellations?"

"Sure." He kept up the hokey yokel act. It seemed to put her at ease. She probably needed a break from all the Chicago fanciness—especially the boyfriend. Amos Whittamer, or whatever.

"Okay," she said. "Give me the tour."

"Hang on." Jumping to his feet, he jogged into the bunkhouse. He'd done this on dates, and girls always liked it.

Not that this was a date. Those baggy sweats should make it easy for him to stick to the rules. But stargazing required a certain ritual, and that ritual required a blanket.

Whipping a puffy quilt off one of the empty beds, he carried it outside and shook it out over a patch of ground just outside the glow cast by the fire.

"Okay, come over here." He lowered himself down on the blanket and patted a spot beside him. "Tour bus is leaving."

She tossed him a suspicious glance and tightened her grip on her knees. "I'm fine right here."

"No you're not. You'll strain your neck. We're going to do some authentic cowboy stargazing here, and we've got to do it right."

She smiled and relented, just as he'd been hoping she would. Her strides were remarkably long for such a small woman. She was all feminine curves on the outside, but he suspected there was a strong frame under that delicate exterior. If she were a horse, she'd be an Arabian.

Not that he could tell in those sweats. Why didn't she just put a blanket over herself and be done with it?

He smoothed the quilt and stretched out, patting the space beside him. "Come on. This way the sky's just like a movie screen, see?"

She cast him a doubtful look and he thought he'd

lost her, but then she stretched out herself and lay staring at the sky, her hair puddling on the quilt. She wore a rapt expression, and he could suddenly picture her as a schoolgirl paying close attention to the teacher. Teacher's pet, no doubt.

No petting tonight. No touching.

The stars swirled for a moment and he wondered what it was that had made him dizzy, but then they paused and the world spun steadily on its axis again.

"You know the Big Dipper?"

She turned and gave him a disbelieving look. "We have stars in Chicago too, you know."

"Right."

"They're pink, and extra-sparkly."

"What?"

"Yup," she said. "Super *fancy*. In my world, God's last name is Swarovski."

He groaned. "Are you ever going to let me forget that 'fancy' comment?"

"Nope. So tell me about the stars."

"You know the Pole Star?"

"The one sailors steer by."

"And cowboys. That's our reference point, okay? All the constellations spread from there. So you see how you can follow the Pole Star to the lip of the Dipper? Follow that line and you'll see Hercules."

She squinted and nodded. Obviously she had no idea what he was talking about. He tilted his head closer to hers so he could see from her point of view and point.

"Right there."

Dang, her hair smelled good. What was that—strawberry shampoo or something? It seemed to cloud his mind. His arm wavered. What was he pointing to again?

"Hercules?" she prompted.

"Right. He was a cowboy, you know."

"Oh, I get it. The Augean stables."

"It's not just because he cleaned the stables."

"No?"

"No. It's because he did it by redirecting the river. A cowboy always finds the easy way to get the hard work done."

"Uh-huh." She turned her head and he felt her breath on the side of his neck. "Is that what you're doing now?"

"Well, if I have to be a tour guide, I might as well do it lying down." The moment he said it, he felt his face heat. Did that sound as suggestive to her as it did to him? He didn't dare look at her to find out, so he tried to judge by the feel of her breath on his skin. It was brushing his cheek now, so she was close enough to see that he was blushing.

He looked. He couldn't help it.

And she smiled.

He'd been right that first day, out in the barn. He *was* doomed—but dude ranching was the least of his troubles.

Chapter 16

CAT COULDN'T HELP SMILING. SHE'D MADE MACK BLUSH again. The big, tough, muscular cowboy was stumbling over his words like a schoolboy.

She'd probably stammer herself if she tried to speak. They were lying close together, their two bodies an island of warmth in the cool Wyoming night. Despite the knowledge that her students were sleeping in the bunkhouses just a few feet away, she felt like they were very much alone.

Anything could happen.

He made a random stab with his finger toward the east. "That's Pegasus. Pegasus was a quarter horse; did you know that?"

"No." She let herself relax and tilt toward him a little.

"Strong, agile, flies over the land. And look at his hindquarters. Look at…"

He paused and she turned to see what was wrong, only to meet his eyes mere inches from her own.

"Look at you," he said softly.

Something in that gentle tone seduced her. Without thinking, she closed her eyes.

And felt his kiss all the way down to her toes. He tasted faintly of toothpaste and smelled of saddle leather and something woodsy, a combination of pine and smoke. When he brought one hand up to cup the back of her head, he wrapped the other around her waist and she pressed into him. He felt solid as a rock.

He shifted slightly and she realized he really was hard as a rock, just like that. It should have made her pull away, but instead it sent a plume of warmth from the point of contact, filling her with a reckless hunger. She reached down and cupped his hips in her hands, pulling them toward her and pressing herself against him. God help her, she was actually *grinding* into this man she barely knew. Anyone could come out here and see them. Dora. Emma. Anybody.

It seemed to take Mack a while to realize she'd switched from grinding into him to pushing him away. When he let her go, the cool air sobered her like a splash of water to the face.

"Sorry." He blew out a short breath and stared off into the night. "I didn't mean for that to happen. It was—involuntary."

"Right. So you got me out here on a blanket under the stars to—what?"

He stared down at his hands and shook his head. "I have no idea." He turned and looked into her face. "You do something to me. It's stupid."

She rolled her eyes upward in a swooning gesture. "Oh, Romeo."

"Not stupid. I—well, maybe you make *me* stupid."

He reached out and touched the angle of her jaw. Who knew that was an erogenous zone? The touch was so gentle she couldn't help leaning toward him. "Can we start over?"

He answered with a kiss—one that was obviously not involuntary. It was a kiss calculated to conquer, and it worked. She felt herself falling, losing her grip on the world, on all her careful strategies and well-thought-out plans. Nothing existed but the sage-scented night, the faint shrill of crickets, and the scent and touch of this man. Light swirled in the darkness behind her lids, spinning in graceful curves and swoops of flame, with little rockets and flares going off when he touched her cheek, her neck, her breast—oh, God, he was touching her breast and she wanted that. More of that. She'd been wanting it for days.

She pressed into him and took the lead, letting her own hands wander down the muscles of his back, stroking the dip just above the back loop of his jeans. She let her fingertips slip under the rough fabric just enough to make him draw in a quick breath. His hand squeezed her breast, softly at first, then harder, and then they were flailing around like a couple of teenagers, gasping for air between kisses, clawing at each other's clothes. She slid her hands up under his shirt and dug her fingers into the muscles that ran up either side of his spine, then traced a curving path around his body to his chest. She ran the flat of her palm over his nipples and felt them harden at her touch.

He pushed her over and then they were grappling on the ground. He was on top again, tugging her shirt up. She felt the cool air hit the swells of her breasts and wished he'd take her bra off too. With his teeth. With his tongue.

He rolled and she spun on top of him, riding him, feeling his hardness between her legs. She threw her head back and resisted a ridiculous urge to howl at the moon.

This was crazy. She barely knew this guy. But the urge to pulse her hips against his was so strong she could hardly help herself.

Until the door of the bunkhouse creaked open.

Dora.

Nothing like an audience to quell an urge.

How could she have forgotten? She was supposed to be a good influence. Set a good example. Instead, she was rolling around on the ground with a man she barely knew.

She and Mack bounced apart, pawing at their clothes, smoothing their hair. Dora stood on the steps, squinting and blinking like a toddler awakened from a nap.

"What the hell," she said. "Are you two screwing or something?"

"No." Cat frantically smoothed her hair, struggling to regain her composure. "No. Mack was showing me the constellations and we—we…"

Dora smirked. "You want me to finish that sentence, since you're having so much trouble? How about 'we tore each other's clothes off and went at it like a couple of hamsters'?"

"We didn't. We…"

"I *saw* you." Dora sat down on a corner of the blanket, hugging her knees to her chest and looking happier than she had in a year. "What was that lecture you were giving me about strange men?"

"I'm not strange," Mack said. "Well, not really."

"Sure you're not." Dora's smirk widened.

"Well, you shouldn't be out here in the dark," Cat blustered. "It's dangerous. There are bears."

Dora gave Mack a sideways grin. "Amazing," she said. "I never knew bears wore cowboy boots."

—∿∿—

Mack raked his fingers through his hair, then realized it was probably making him look like a wild man and stopped. What he needed was a hat. His Stetson would perform the dual purpose of covering his hair and shading his eyes so these women couldn't tell what he was thinking.

But what *was* he thinking? He didn't even know himself.

"Sorry." He lurched to his feet and grabbed the stick he'd been using as a poker earlier, holding it out as if to defend himself. He didn't even know which female he was apologizing to. Maybe he should apologize to the whole species.

"There's nothing to apologize for." Dora giggled and turned to Cat. "Good job. He's way cuter than Ames."

"I'm not looking for cute."

"No, you're looking for trouble." Dora lapsed into a schoolyard singsong. "And I think you found it." She gave Mack a saucy grin and leaped to her feet to execute a shimmying curtsy. It made him feel old to watch her. Vivian had the same effect; the girls were like sparks flying up from a campfire, light as air.

Cat was watching her niece with a stunned, wide-eyed expression. Mack almost laughed. She'd wanted to make the girl happy, and they'd done it. Maybe he'd finally done something right.

"I'll leave you two lovebirds alone." Dora spun and tripped back up the steps to the bunkhouse. "I was just worried there was a bear out here. Didn't realize it was just you two doing the nasty."

The door closed behind her, leaving Cat looking shell-shocked and very, very sorry.

"That can't happen again," she said.

He poked at the flames, stirring them to dancing, flickering life. "Does this mean the rules are back in force?"

"I think they have to be."

She seemed genuinely sorry, which was nice but also meant she was serious. He sorted through the coals to avoid looking at her, fishing out a few shreds of paper that were scattered through the ashes. Since he didn't want to make eye contact with Cat, he fished them out of harm's way, flipping one over as if it mattered what it was.

Hmm. Maybe it did. It was a photograph, printed on plain paper. He flipped over another shred, and another. As he scraped them out of harm's way, Cat noticed what he was doing. She knelt down and delicately pincered one piece out of the ashes.

"It's… that's weird." She knelt and pulled out another piece, and another, laying them on one of the flat rocks that surrounded the fire pit. "It's Dora." She scowled down at the torn picture. There was just enough left of it to show Dora's smile, and one of her eyes. Cat glanced back at the bunkhouse. "I thought I heard something. That's why I came out. Why would she come out here and burn a picture of herself?"

"That wasn't you?"

"No." She shot him a glare. "Why would I burn pictures of my niece?"

"I know you wouldn't. It's just… I came out because I heard someone at the fire. I figured it was you."

She shook her head. "I figured it was you."

"It must have been Dora." Mack poked another piece of the torn photo into place. "Maybe she doesn't like the way she looks in it. My daughter Viv is worse than a supermodel. You can't take a snapshot without her going on about which is her best side and whether she'll look fat."

"Dora's not like that, though." She looked back at the cabin and he could practically hear gears turning in her head, but she sighed as she rose from the fire and tossed the pieces of the photo back into the flames. "I hope it's not—it seems like self-hate, doesn't it? Burning a picture of yourself?" She frowned down at the reassembled photo. It had been taken at an angle that accentuated the sharpness of Dora's chin and the hollows under her cheekbones. She looked almost grown up in the picture, and looking at it gave Cat a sense of unease.

She turned and looked at the bunkhouse door.

"Don't try to talk to her now," Mack said. "After what just happened… well, you can hardly start lecturing her about anything."

She shot him a reproachful scowl.

"Hey, it wasn't my fault," he said. "I just came out to check the fire."

She dismissed him with a wave. "It doesn't matter, Mack. You're right." She laced her hands in front of her and shifted nervously from one foot to another, like a nervous child. "You're definitely right. Look, you're great but…" She sighed. "But I need to concentrate on Dora. I mean, obviously…" She waved one hand toward the picture. "She has problems. And I can't help her if I'm… distracted."

She gave him a long look, and he wondered if she was thinking of kissing him good-bye. But her eyes hardened and she gave him a quick nod, as if he'd been dismissed, and slipped into the Heifer House.

He'd never been so sorry to be right in his life.

Chapter 17

THEY SET OUT THE NEXT DAY FOR HIDDEN LAKE, WHICH promised wildflowers, water, and a view of distant mountains. They trekked around the butte through a wooded area scattered with large boulders that sloped down to the lake—or so Mack said. There was a reason it was called Hidden Lake; not so much as a glint of water showed in the distance.

"How much further?" Trevor shifted uncomfortably in his saddle. "I thought you said this was a short ride."

Dora rolled her eyes. "I figured this trip would be too much for you senior citizens."

Trevor glared at her. "I am not a senior citizen," he said, biting his words off sharply. "I'm a grown-up. There's a difference."

He didn't sound like a grown-up. Evidently he'd never spent much time around teenagers, because he was rising to Dora's bait like a trout leaping for a fly. Come to think of it, he was a little like a teenager himself, with his grandiose posturing and "me-me-me" attitude.

Cat was distracted from her thoughts by a flicker of light through the dark pines. As they rounded a curve, the forest seemed to draw aside like a stage curtain to reveal an aspen grove whose pale green leaves fluttered in polite applause. The trees circled a placid, mirrorlike pool edged with a fringe of multicolored wildflowers.

One by one, the horses stepped into the sunlit clearing

and stopped as if they, too, were struck by the beauty of the scene.

"All right." Cat hated to break the spell, but there was work to do. She hopped down from the saddle. "Let's unpack."

Mack worked with silent efficiency, helping the students unload their gear with the help of Ed and the surprisingly industrious Dora. Cat staggered across the soggy ground laden with three heavy pochade boxes, her arms burning with effort.

Setting the boxes on the ground, she ran a hand through her hair. She felt sticky and hot, and the gesture probably left her looking like a madwoman, but what did it matter? It wasn't like she was here to seduce anyone. In fact, it might be a good idea to let her appearance go.

She felt something twitchy under her skin and glanced over at Dora, who was standing on tiptoe to reach a canvas portfolio strapped to the top of the load. Trevor was just a few steps away, watching the girl like a wolf watches sheep.

"What?" he said when she caught his eye. "She's okay. I'd help her if she needed it."

"I'm sure you would," Cat said. "But fortunately, she can take care of herself. And you never know when that might come in handy."

———

Mack watched Cat swing her easel off Rembrandt's back and extend the legs, spinning the brass screws tight. She looked competent and confident, as comfortable with her equipment as he was with a lasso and roping saddle.

Once the easels were arranged in a neat semicircle

and everyone had their supplies at hand, she gathered the students around her.

"Nature's not perfect," she said. "But for some reason, your mind will try to make it all neat and symmetrical. You've got to fool yourself into making something free and organic. To do that, you have to let your paints flow naturally."

She tilted the easel until it was almost flat, then dipped a big, soft brush into a clear jar of water she'd clipped to the easel and swept it across the bottom third of her paper. Next she uncovered a plastic palette box and dipped her brush into a puddle of blue paint so dark and intense Mack almost lifted a hand to stop her, afraid she'd ruin the painting. Nothing in nature was that deeply colored. To make matters worse, she dipped the same brush in a dab of dark brown, but as the paint flowed onto the wet paper, it plumed and flowed together in a convincing imitation of the luminous pool of water.

She lifted the panel from the easel and swung it first left, then right, letting the paint drift and flow. Shoving his hands in his pockets, Mack leaned back against a tree. Every time he'd looked at Cat today he'd sensed her tensing like a deer sighted by a hunter. But when she painted she seemed oblivious to everything around her.

As her brush darted from palette to paper, the painting transformed into a little world of her own creation. She moved differently when she painted, like a dancer, with no movement wasted.

"Now the trees," she said.

He wasn't sure if she was talking to her audience or herself as she picked up two spray bottles like a Wild West gunfighter and spritzed blue and yellow paint above the blue pool, letting it speckle and puddle on the paper. The colors flowed together, creating every imaginable shade of green. A miniature forest formed before his eyes.

"Reflections." The further her painting progressed, the less aware she seemed of her audience. She pulled an old-fashioned square razor blade from her pocket, slipping off the paper wrapping and then laying it against her painting. As she pulled it down from the water's edge with a quick squiggling motion, reflections of the trees appeared in the surface of the water.

"Highlights…"

Her small, graceful hand darted to the partitions in the pochade box, choosing a Q-tip this time. She dragged it horizontally across the surface of the water.

"And branches."

The pointed wooden end of her brush scraped random tree trunks and fallen logs at the edge of the forest, and the razor blade scratched out a few sunlit limbs.

"There." She stepped back. What looked like a pleasant but random design at close quarters resolved itself into a portrait of the lake before them, bordered with a realistic tangle of trees.

"I'll add detail once it's dry—the flowers, and maybe a few more highlights on the water. But this is how you let nature itself define your painting." She sounded drowsy and satisfied, and her movements were languid as if she'd just risen from bed after, well, after something he shouldn't be thinking about.

"Air and water are the core elements of nature, so what you get is actually much more realistic in appearance than a careful copy of the scene."

"That's wonderful," Emma said. "I saw something like that in *Artist's Magazine* once, but I've never seen anyone actually do it. It helps so much to see the whole process."

"You can't learn anything from those step-by-step tutorials in the magazines," Trevor said. "Buying those things is just throwing money away."

Cat looked at him, surprised. "You think so?"

"Definitely. I never read those rags."

"How did you hear about the workshop, then?" Cat's eyes narrowed. "That's the only place we advertise. I figured everybody here read *Artist's*."

"Not me." Trevor thumped his skinny chest. "I've learned everything I know from other painters. You know Zoltan Szabo? I've done three workshops with him." He smiled a smug, superior smile. "You might call me a bit of a protégé."

After the demonstration, Cat expected everyone to settle down to work on their own paintings, but Charles and Abby were the only ones who got any work done. Cat had to get up and break up a squirt bottle fight between Emma and Ed, and Dora was back to being her bratty high-maintenance self.

"You tell me to focus, and then you let this happen," she complained, waving toward Emma and Ed. "These people don't take their art seriously, so why should I?"

Cat had to agree that Emma and Ed weren't exactly model students. The squirt bottle fight had ended, but they were giggling maniacally as they flicked paint-loaded brushes onto each other's white smocks. Trevor had wandered over and sketched a reclining nude onto Ed's paper while the older man was occupied with the paint fight.

"Why don't we just go to one of those paintball places and be done with it?" Dora slammed her easel shut and stuffed paint tubes and brushes back into the oversized tackle box she used to hold her equipment. "I hate this stupid pond anyway. It's so—you know, so trite." Hitching the easel up under one skinny arm, she picked up the tackle box. "I'll go find something else to paint."

"Where?" Cat asked.

"I don't know." Dora waved a vague hand toward the trail. "Over there."

"All right. I'll check in a while and make sure you're okay."

"I'm fine." Dora flashed her a hostile glare. "Just leave me alone. I work better that way, and you want me to work, right?"

"I want you happy, Dora. It's not about me."

"Sure it's not." Dora flounced off into the trees. "And it's not about my mom either."

She set off up the trail, disappearing behind a screen of ragged pines.

Cat sighed and strolled over to check on the others, trying to act casual. No one needed to know how deeply Dora could hurt her.

Emma and Ed had fallen silent when Dora began her tirade. Now they were hard at work, bowing their heads over their paintings like chastened kindergartners. Charles was diligently working on a passable interpretation of the scene, but Trevor shifted his easel when she passed, as if he didn't want her to see his masterpiece. Ignoring him, she joined Mack, who was lounging on a nearby boulder. He was staring at the lake, absently rubbing Tippy's ears.

"You were smart to let her go," he said.

"I guess I'm learning." She slouched down beside him.

He bent over Tippy, rubbing her bony chest. The dog flung her head back in ecstasy. "Hey, what are you thinking about when you paint?" he asked.

"I don't know. I'm thinking about painting, I guess."

"It seems like you're in another world."

"I am. Everything else goes away. That's why I love it so much. Nothing feels better."

He edged closer until his shoulder touched hers. She was suddenly conscious of the warmth of the sunlit boulder.

"Nothing?" His face was inches away. She stared at the wildflowers at her feet, faking absorption and hoping he couldn't tell they were just a blur of festive color.

"Nothing." She realized what he was implying and felt heat creeping up her neck in a telltale blush.

"I guess I was right, then." He looked amused.

"About what?" She knew as soon as the question flew out of her mouth that she shouldn't have asked it.

"Arms Weimeraner must be a total bust," he said. "And I'm going to have to up my game."

Chapter 18

CAT STROLLED OVER TO TREVOR'S EASEL. SHE'D EXpected to see an amateur rendition of the lake scene, but he'd traded papers with Mr. Delaney and was hard at work developing his reclining nude. She was surprised at his ability. He'd handled the foreshortening really well, although the pose he'd chosen was a little derivative. It was a blatant rip-off of Manet's *Olympia*, but she was resting against a log instead of reclining on a chaise lounge.

She moved closer. He'd given his subject a slim build, with dark, cat-slanted blue eyes and dark hair curling around her face. The likeness was unmistakable.

Trevor Davis was painting her. Naked.

"Cat," Mrs. Delaney called. "I can't get these trees to look right."

Grateful for the interruption, she turned away from Trevor's easel and tried to concentrate on a demonstration of her patented pine tree squiggle while she wondered what the hell to do about Trevor. This wasn't a situation that had come up in the Art Treks teacher's manual.

If it had happened among her friends back home, she'd pass it off as a joke. Nudes were a common subject, and artists frequently posed for each other. She'd been half reclining in an exact copy of the *Olympia* pose earlier, when she'd been talking to Mack. That had been Trevor's inspiration.

But the guy made her uncomfortable. And she definitely didn't want Dora to see what he'd done.

As usual, she smothered her anxiety in work, coaching the Delaneys, helping Charles, and studiously avoiding Trevor. She finished her own painting too, but she wasn't happy with the results. The thought of Trevor watching her closely enough to put her in a painting made it impossible for her to concentrate.

"Hmm." Mack strolled over from where he'd been fiddling with the horses' fittings and admired Ed and Emma's work. Trevor stepped back as the cowboy arrived at his easel. Raising his brush theatrically, he smiled smugly as Mack examined the painting.

"Let me see this." Mack plucked the picture from the easel. Cat stood motionless, dizzy with embarrassment and dread.

It took a moment for the subject matter to register, but as he surveyed the painting Mack's expression darkened.

"You need to follow instructions better." He dropped the painting facedown on the ground and placed a booted foot on the back of the foam core-support. "You're supposed to be doing the lake."

He scuffed his heel deliberately, grinding the painting into the ground. Then he picked it up and placed it on the easel. Standing back like a connoisseur at a museum, he pondered the effects of his work. The portrait was destroyed, the figure smeared beyond recognition and streaked with dirt.

He turned and faced the rest of the class, who were staring at him with open mouths and wide eyes, and shot them a disarming grin. "Hey, I don't know much about art, but I know what I like." He shrugged. "And I didn't like that. Didn't like it at all. Anyway, it's about time to go, Cat."

Trevor stood frozen in place, his expression a combination of disbelief and rage. "Is this how you allow your clients to be treated? You allow your… your lackeys to destroy works of art?"

"That was no work of art, buddy." Mack stepped up to Trevor and Cat was struck by the difference between them. It wasn't just that Mack was bigger and taller. He had something more than size—an air of solidity that Trevor lacked. "And I'm no lackey. You can consider me the Art Treks bouncer."

Trevor backed away, busying himself with his supplies.

"Everybody pack up," Cat said. She consciously slowed her breathing to keep her voice from shaking. The picture was only a joke, after all. If Ames had done the portrait, she would have laughed.

But Trevor wasn't Ames.

"I'll go get Dora."

She strode toward the woods, grateful for an excuse to leave the group. As soon as she was out of sight, she sank down on a rock and put her head between her knees, feeling the dizziness fade and relief flood through her veins. She was fine. She really was. It had just been a joke.

So why did she feel so shaky?

She heard footsteps on the trail and lifted her head, which brought on another wave of dizziness. Mack knelt down in front of her.

"You okay?" He brushed a lock of hair from her eyes with a gentle finger and laid one hand on her thigh. It was a protective touch, not a sexual one, but it felt good. Too good.

She dashed away the tear that was dangling from one eyelash, trying to make the motion seem like a casual wave. "I'm fine."

"You want me to smack him around?"

"No." She sighed. "He's just a case of arrested development, you know? Never got past the sixth grade when it comes to girls."

"He's a creep."

"He's a client." She forced a smile. "I know you're the law here on the Boyd Dude Ranch, but you can't go assaulting my students, okay?"

He stiffened. "My first impulse was to stomp him into the ground, but I figured you'd act like this."

"Like what?" She stood. "Rational? In charge? What's done is done. Let's just start over, okay?"

He stared at her in disbelief. "So you're going to keep working with the guy?"

"What else am I going to do? It was a joke, Mack. Not a very good one, but still a joke. Art Treks isn't going to let me throw him out of the class."

"They should. It's sexual harassment."

"The world doesn't always work the way it should." She brushed her hair out of her eyes. "Just let it go, Mack."

She watched him struggle with that concept. Gradually, his fists unclenched and his brow cleared.

"I have to go find Dora. Could you help the old folks pack?"

Sighing, he turned away. "It's what I live for."

He jogged off down the trail. She knew she should be jogging in the other direction, looking for Dora, but she couldn't help watching him go any more than she could help thinking of the night before.

The authentic cowboy life was more of a challenge than she'd expected—mostly because of the authentic cowboy.

———

Cat caught sight of Dora in just ten minutes, but actually getting to her was going to be a challenge. She shaded her eyes with one hand and gazed up at the rock formation rearing above her, wondering how her niece had managed to get not only herself, but her supplies too, up on the flat rock that seemed to balance precariously on the top of the pile.

As she watched, Dora took a step back from her easel, touching the handle of her brush to her lower lip and cocking her head in a pose so like her mother's "thinking" pose that it made Cat's heart ache. Then the girl darted forward, dabbed at the painting, and dodged back again. She looked like an ethereal fencer from fairyland, feinting and retreating, stabbing her brush home like an épée.

Reluctantly, Cat stepped out of the trees, figuring Dora would see her and stop—but the performance continued. Her niece was so absorbed in her work she didn't even hear the pebbles bouncing off the rocks as Cat clambered up.

Dora was in the zone, and Cat knew just how she felt. She'd been the same way at that age, and she'd known, from the way time flew when she was painting, that she was meant to be an artist. When she was working, art *was* life. It was all that mattered, and everything else was just a way to get from one canvas to another. She painted not to make money, not to get famous, but to earn the right to paint some more.

It was obvious Dora had the same passion. So why did she insist that she hated art?

As Cat crested the edge of the flat-topped boulder that created the stage for Dora's dance, she deliberately kicked a good-sized stone. It shot off the rock and bounced away, ricocheting like a bullet.

Dora spun, her eyes wide as if she'd been awakened from sleep.

"Oh." She grimaced, and Cat wondered if she was that sorry to see her, or that unhappy at having her work interrupted.

"Sorry, hon. It's time to go…" Cat stepped up to Dora and caught sight of her painting. "Wow."

"It's shit." Dora moved toward the easel almost as if she was going to knock it down. Without thinking, Cat grabbed her arm. The two of them overbalanced, then caught each other, stumbling away from the edge of the rock. As they broke apart Cat put a hand to her chest, trying to still her thumping heart.

"Way to go. Kill me, why don't you?" Dora scowled. "But save the painting, right?"

"No. Dora, it's just… it surprised me." She looked back at the painting, at the way Dora had balanced light and dark, the way she'd blurred the distant hills to draw the viewer into the scene. It was an amazing piece that could hang in any gallery. Hard to believe it was the work of a fifteen-year-old.

She scanned the girl's face and tried to read the complex blend of emotions. Anger, embarrassment, fear, and grief. Mostly grief.

Cat knew Dora was still mourning her mother. She would probably mourn her all her life. But it seemed like grief was holding her in a tight-fisted grip that altered her whole personality. There was some facet of her mother's life or death that wouldn't let her move on.

Cat looked at the painting again, wondering if it held a hint. But all she saw was an echo of Edie's talent, along with a bright flash of something unique that was pure Dora.

She wasn't going to let that flash dim and die because of Edie's death. But she needed to proceed with caution.

"It's good, hon." She cocked her head to one side, masking her admiration with a critical squint. "It maybe needs some darker values on the lower left, to balance the sunset."

"I know. I was going to deepen this shadow here." Dora darted forward again, gesturing with her brush. "And maybe put some of that sap green here and here, so the trees pop."

Cat smothered the urge to say that *everything* in the painting popped. That Dora was as talented as her mother—maybe more so. She blinked back the sudden heat behind her eyes, and Dora shot her a wary look.

"What's the matter?"

"Nothing. It's just…" Cat waved a hand as if what she was feeling didn't matter, as if this whole scene hadn't brought her sister back to her. As if the emotions she was feeling hadn't left her as breathless as a punch in the chest.

"Don't be thinking I'm like Mom." Dora's brows lowered, and two red slashes of color flushed high on her cheekbones. "I'm just fooling around."

"But it's *good*, Dora." Cat took a step toward her. "You are like her, in the best possible way."

Dora's lips narrowed into a hard, thin line. "I'm not." She stepped forward, quick as a cat, and jerked off a strip of the tape that held the paper to the board. Tearing the painting from the easel, she held it up in front of her face and tore it in half, then half again. The portions fluttered to her feet.

"I'm *not* like her." She stamped her foot like a toddler, grinding a piece of the painting into the rock. "I'm not anything like her. I don't care if things are pretty or not. I don't *care*."

Cat darted to catch a shred of the painting as it caught on the breeze and flipped toward the edge of the rock. Dora grabbed her arm and pulled her back.

"Let it go. It's *shit*. I don't care about it. I don't care about painting, okay? I don't *care*."

Cat held onto Dora for a moment. The girl's slim body was pulsing with tension, trembling with emotion—but she stiffened almost immediately and pulled away.

"Come on." Blinking fast, she gathered up the brush she'd dropped and tossed it in the plastic tackle box that held her art supplies. She screwed the top on her water jar and shoved it in there too, along with a sponge and a few other brushes. Snapping the lid shut, she flipped the latches and stood up, brushing dust off her thighs as Cat slowly folded the easel and collapsed the legs.

"Let's just go." She snatched the easel from Cat and set off down the path.

"Dora, wait." Cat stood forlornly on the rock, wishing she knew what to say, wishing she knew what to do. "We need to talk."

"There's nothing to talk about." The girl set her sneakered feet and locked her knees to slide down a pebble-strewn slope, then leaped the last couple feet to the forest floor. "Come on. There are other students, remember? This project has to succeed. It's your *career*."

Cat winced at the echo of her own words. She'd told Dora this trip was important. But though the thought of failure was a grim one, her niece mattered more. Didn't Dora know that?

She paused, hoping her niece would stop if she didn't follow. Looking out at the woods below, she saw the scene as Dora had painted it—the dark trees, the lowering sky, and tracing through the midst of it a silver ribbon of a stream. The water flowed toward the glow of the setting sun like a thin thread of hope.

"Come *on*." Dora turned and walked backward a few steps, scowling.

Cat glanced back at the sunset one more time, then bent and picked up a shred of the ruined painting. Tucking it in her pocket, she followed her niece down the rock and into the dark wood.

Chapter 19

MACK WAS TYING THE LAST KNOT ON THE FINAL PACK when Cat returned to the group with Dora in tow. The girl's expression was stormy, and Cat looked pained and confused. He could tell they'd had a fight.

"Thought you were going to help with the horses," he said. He knew Dora was delicate, knew she was mourning her mother, but it still ticked him off to see the way she hurt her aunt. Cat was a good person—maybe too good. It seemed like the two of them didn't have much family left. So why was Dora trying to alienate the one relative she had left?

"I was. You should have had Charles whistle," Dora said. "You didn't have to send *her* to get me."

"I didn't send her. She was worried about you." He watched Cat scramble up onto Rembrandt's back, then mounted his own horse. "And Charles was busy. He was the one who ended up helping with the horses."

The trip back passed mostly in silence. The older folks were obviously tired, but Mack knew they also felt the strain between Cat and her niece. Even the cool coming of twilight and its accompanying breeze couldn't dissipate the tension between them.

He reined his horse off to the side of the trail. "Charles, you want to take the lead?"

Without a word, Charles edged out of the line and trotted his horse up to the front. Mack watched the slouching figures of the riders pass, hoping nobody fell asleep and tipped off their horse. Cat was last in line, and he fell into step beside her.

"What happened?" he asked.

She tightened her lips and shook her head. "Nothing."

"Yeah, right. Talk to me, Cat."

"We don't have time for that. We have to take care of them." She nodded toward the line ahead. "We can't just leave Charles to lead them."

"I'm sure Charles is capable of following the trail back to the barn," he said. "And the horses know it's dinnertime. You couldn't get them to go anywhere else. So tell me what happened. Maybe I can help."

She sighed. "I'm not sure anybody can help. She did a painting—a really good one, maybe a great one."

"That's good, right?" He gave her an encouraging smile. Maybe he'd misread the situation. If Dora had done a painting, she might be coming out of her shell. Maybe Cat was just tired.

"It was terrific. Beyond terrific. But when I said so she tore it up." Cat stared straight ahead, blinking fast. "She said she doesn't care about art. That she didn't want to be like her mother."

"She tore it up?"

Cat nodded.

He thought back to the night before—what they'd found in the fire. "She tore up that photo, too."

Cat nodded again. "I know."

"Does Dora look like her mother?"

"Some," she said. "Not a lot. They have the same eyes, the same chin. But Dora's paler, and her mother had darker hair. Not brunette, but more brown."

Mack rode a while in silence, wondering if he dared offer advice. He wanted to help, but Alex had always gotten mad when he tried to solve her problems. She always said he should just listen.

"I don't know what to do," Cat said.

Okay, that was *asking* for help.

"Is she eating?"

"What?"

"Is she eating? Because tearing up the picture, tearing up the painting—it seems like self-hate. Viv—my daughter—she had some problems with an eating disorder. That's why we took her to counseling. The shrink said she didn't like the girl she saw in the mirror."

Cat looked dubious. "I haven't noticed her not eating. But I haven't been paying that much attention to it. I'll watch. Thanks."

Maybe Cat was different from Alex. Maybe she didn't mind taking a man's advice. "On the art thing, maybe you shouldn't push her," he said. "Maybe she really doesn't want to do it."

"But she's meant to." Cat straightened in the saddle and adjusted her hands. She was turning into a halfway decent rider. "You didn't see it, Mack. It was amazing." She patted her pocket as if to assure herself something precious was stored there. "She's gifted. She has to use that talent."

Mack knew he was treading on dangerous ground. Cat cared deeply about the art thing. It was tied to herself, to her sister. He should bite his tongue and stay out of it. But despite her sour attitude, he liked Dora. He could see a spark of sunshine in that pretty face clouded by grief.

"You can't make her do it," he said as gently as he could.

"No. But I have to encourage her," she said. "If you have that kind of talent—and I'm talking a lot of talent, genius-level talent—you have to use it."

He cleared his throat, finding it suddenly swollen. He hated talking about himself, or his family problems. But he wanted to help.

"I wanted Viv to do sports," he said.

She nodded almost dismissively. "You're a man."

"It wasn't just that." He stared down at the saddle horn, remembering his daughter at ten, at twelve. "She was made for it—all long legs and high energy. But to her, athletics just emphasized the things she thought were flaws. I saw that cute adolescent awkwardness— like a colt with legs too long for its body, you know? But she felt clumsy."

"I guess that's normal for teenagers."

"Up to a point. But she blamed herself for every point the other team scored, every game her team lost. It fed that eating disorder, made her miserable. I couldn't make her into what I thought she should be."

He looked ahead, watching the riders bunch, then string out around a turn. "Everything got better once I quit insisting she go out for sports. She started eating again. We could talk. It took a while, but we're better now. She's better." He paused. "*I'm* better."

Cat bit her lip. "Creative people—people like Dora— get eaten up inside if they don't follow the urge."

He looked over at her. "And you know this because…"

"Because I feel it myself." She continued quickly, as if she was worried he'd get the wrong idea. "I'm not saying I'm a genius. Not by any means."

"But you're an artist. You're following the urge, right?"

"Not really. Not the way I want to." She snorted, a surprisingly unladylike noise. "My job is in advertising. Mostly graphic design. That's part of the reason I'm here—because this lets me do more painting. More *real* art."

The wind picked up as they emerged from the woods, sending dry leaves skittering down the path in front of the horses' hooves. A slip of white paper danced up from behind them, fluttering between the horses' legs. Mack's horse shied and pranced a little before he tightened the reins. Rembrandt, true to form, took the surprise right in stride.

The paper caught on a clump of sagebrush just ahead. As they passed, Mack let Cat ride ahead, then slipped from the saddle and grabbed the paper.

He looked down at it, trying to assess what he saw. It was only a part of a painting, but there was no mistaking the subject. Dora had been up on Battleship Rock, looking down at the Little Fork River. The painting caught the dark mystery of the pines, the ribbon of bright water winding through them like a silvered path.

Even he knew, from just this scrap of the painting, that she was good.

He caught up to Cat and handed it to her, pulling his horse to a stop at an angle so the mule would stop too. She set the scrap of paper on her thigh and smoothed it out, then took another from her pocket and matched them up. Her gaze flicked up to his and he nodded.

"It's good," he said. "I see what you mean. But…"

"But you're right," she finished. "She has to decide for herself."

She slid the two scraps of paper carefully into her shirt pocket. "It's just that I feel like I'm losing her and Edie too. Losing my sister all over again." She patted the pocket as if putting a blessing on the torn scraps of paper, and turned haunted eyes to meet his. "I know it's selfish. But I just can't let them go."

Chapter 20

CAT TRAILED BEHIND MACK, CHEWING THE BITTER remnants of her ambitions for Dora like a tough bite of jerky. Maybe she was transferring her own ambitions to Dora, trying to live vicariously through her niece. But she didn't think so. She really did see a creative spirit in Dora, and the girl's resistance to it couldn't be healthy.

I'm nothing like my mother. I don't care if things are pretty or not. I don't care how things look.

Maybe Mack was right, and Dora's resistance had something to do with self-hate. That would be easy to believe if Edie had been the kind of mother who dressed up her daughter and tried to make her into a mini-me. But Edie had always celebrated her daughter's uniqueness and encouraged her to be herself. She'd never been critical of Dora's appearance. She'd barely been critical of her behavior, even though Dora had been rude and defiant at times even when her mother was alive.

And she hadn't pushed her when it came to art. If anything, she'd done the opposite, encouraging Dora to open herself to new experiences, new hobbies.

So why would Dora be so hostile to her mother now? Sure, she was mad at her mom for dying, but her reaction seemed so extreme.

As the ranch house came into view, welcoming lights winked on and streamed from the windows. She and Mack had fallen far behind the group, and he gave his horse a poke with his heels, sat up straight, and made a quick kissing sound. His mount broke into a smooth trot, and Rembrandt pricked up his ears.

Copying Mack, she urged Rembrandt to keep up and enjoyed, briefly, the feeling of control as the mule obeyed her commands. But they caught up to the others quickly and the sight of Dora, riding ramrod straight in the saddle, looking neither left nor right, reminded her that the mule was about the only thing she could control.

Night fell fast on the high plains. Cat felt like she'd barely had time to put her gear away before Maddie clanged the old-fashioned triangle that called the hands to dinner at the wagon.

It was a creaky, crippled group that answered the call. Though they were clearly uncomfortable, Emma and Abby lowered themselves onto their respective benches with smothered grunts and groans. Ed opted to hold onto his dignity by pretending he preferred to stand until Charles, holding out the lizard-bedecked hand like a peace offering, helped the older man lower himself down without too much strain on his knees.

Only Dora seemed unaffected by the day's exertions. She watched the fire with the same absorption the average teen girl would have given to the latest installment of the *Twilight* saga. The only thing that diverted her attention was Mack. When he laughed, which he did often, her gaze flicked from the fire to his face and echoed his good humor. Right now, it was just nice to see the girl having a good time. Though Cat hadn't known Mack long, and her own interactions with him had been decidedly inappropriate for a couple of virtual strangers, she felt surprisingly willing to trust him around Dora. He was a father, after all. And his easy humor was charming the kid out of her funk.

Trevor Maines had apparently recovered from his encounter with Mack and was dominating the conversation with tales of his career in fashion photography.

"Oh, Rebecca Romijn is lovely." He flailed a careless hand in the air as if supermodels were a species he dealt with every day. "Difficult, of course, but aren't they all?"

Emma murmured pitying assent, as if she too had dealt with famous folks on a regular basis. Charles, on the other hand, was watching Trevor from under lowered brows, his eyes flat and lifeless, yet somehow threatening. Clearly Trevor had hit some kind of nerve with the big guy. Cat didn't know if the tattooed man had seen the portrait. She hoped not.

"But Heidi Klum—now she's a sweetheart."

Cat glanced at Mack. He looked like he was in pain, and his fingers were curled as if he was just waiting for an opportunity to strangle the other man. Dora caught Cat's eye, then flashed her gaze toward Trevor and rolled her eyes. Cat echoed the gesture and felt a warm flush beyond what the fire provided. There. They'd shared a moment. Maybe things were going to work out.

They had to. Dora needed some sort of female role model now that her mother was gone. Ross might eventually remarry, and hopefully he'd choose someone Dora could love too. But though she wasn't a big fan of her brother-in-law, Cat had to admit he had loved his wife deeply. So the only adult woman in Dora's life for the foreseeable future was Cat.

She thought of the burned photo they'd found the night before and worry clenched her heart like a fist. She needed to ask about it. Find out why she'd done that.

She drained her Coors—*Coors for courage*—and got up to toss it into the box Maddie had set out for recyclables. Casually, she strolled over and joined Mack and Dora.

"He's obsessed with models, isn't he?" She nodded toward Trevor.

"Sure is. It's ridiculous. I mean, what's their big talent? Making dumb faces and showing off." Dora tossed her hair, tilted her chin, and gave Mack the heavy-lidded, tight-lipped moue of a supermodel.

Cat laughed. "I think you've got it. Maybe that's your future career."

"I don't think so."

Cat clenched her fists in her lap, telling herself to tread carefully. This was the perfect opportunity to get to the bottom of the burned photo incident, but if she said the wrong thing she had no doubt Dora would shut her down.

"Don't you like the way you look?" she asked. She flashed a look at Mack, hoping he'd catch on to what she was doing.

Dora tilted her chin up and glared at Cat. "Why? Don't *you*?"

Well, that didn't take long. The storm clouds were lowering already.

"Of course I like the way you look."

"Oh, yeah, because I look like my mom. So you can keep on thinking I'm just like her, right?"

"No." Cat was trying to be understanding, but she couldn't help bristling a little at the accusation. "That's not it at all. For one thing, I don't think you look like your mother."

"You don't?" Dora sounded hurt now, and Cat thought maybe she should just give up. She couldn't do anything right when it came to her niece.

But this mattered too much. If Dora was disturbed enough to burn a photo of herself, who knew how deep her scars might be?

"I think you're a lot like your mother in the ways that matter," Cat said.

"But you don't like the way I look."

Cat braced herself against the drama. Soon they'd be hollering "Did too!" and "Did not!" at each other and stamping their feet like kids in a schoolyard.

"I'm just asking because girls your age sometimes don't have good self-esteem," she said patiently. "I just want to make sure you know you're beautiful."

Dora shrugged and stared moodily into the fire. In this light, she really was beautiful—or she would be if she'd smile.

"Whatever," she mumbled.

Cat edged closer. "I found your picture in the fire the other night," she said. "I was wondering why you'd burn a picture of yourself."

"My picture?" Dora gave her an incredulous stare.

"The one you burned," Mack said.

Cat shot him a grateful smile. She needed all the help she could get.

Dora glanced from Mack to Cat and back again. "I didn't burn anything. You guys are crazy." She hopped

to her feet and practically raced around the ring to where
Ed was sitting. "Hey, Mr. Delaney. Do you need help
getting up?"

The old man grinned. "You trying to get rid of me?"

"No." Dora shrugged. "I just thought, well, these
benches are kind of low."

Ed accepted her help. It seemed like there were two
Doras—the sweet, helpful child and the troubled teen.

"So tell me, Mr. Boyd," Ed said. "What time are we
heading out in the morning?"

"I thought we'd do breakfast at seven." Mack glanced
at his mother, who nodded approvingly. "I'll load up
while you folks eat, and we'll hit the trail around eight."

"Need some help?"

Ed had been an eager assistant on every trip, loading
easels and art supplies under Mack's supervision. At
first Cat figured he was just trying to escape the nagging of his wife and daughter, but he seemed to revel
in the male bonding. And Mack had been touchingly
solicitous of the older man's limitations, finding light
tasks Ed could perform without too much strain.

"I could help you load up," Ed said.

"Sure." Mack grinned. "I could use a sidekick."

Cat smiled to herself. Ed was probably more trouble
than help, but Mack wouldn't say so. He really was a
nice guy. If things were different...

But they weren't.

No stargazing, she reminded herself. *And no shirt-
cleaning either.* Emma asked her a question about mix-
ing colors and she refocused on her students, explaining
the virtues of sap green versus Hooker's green.

Trevor shoved himself to his feet and stretched with

a great deal of chest-thrusting and shoulder-rolling, as if he had muscles to show off. He let out a long, theatrical yawn, interrupting Cat and Emma's conversation.

"Well," he said. "I'm about ready to turn in."

"Carry this for me?" Maddie handed him a teetering stack of tin plates. Judging from the way he lusted for the lead role in every conversation, Trevor was hardly the sidekick type—but like everyone else, he seemed unable to resist Maddie's friendly but firm leadership.

"Me too." Emma rose from her bench with gallant assistance from Ed and turned to Dora. "Good night, sweetie. And good night to you, young man."

"See you tomorrow, Aunt Cat." Dora's lips tightened into a scheming smile. "I guess you and Mack need to finish up out here. Take your time, okay?" She grinned. "I feel like I'm going to sleep soundly. Really soundly. No getting up in the middle of the night for me—no matter what sounds I hear outside."

"Oh, me too," Emma said. "I sleep like the dead. So does Abby."

"Well, that's good." Dora was smiling madly now. "That's really good news, isn't it, Aunt Cat?"

Mack let out a soft chuckle. "Sure is, hon. Thanks."

Cat felt that fist close on her heart again, but this time her worry was for herself. She was going to be alone with Mack again—and she wanted to talk to him.

Just talk. Nothing more.

But the memory of that kiss, unplanned, unexpected, and most of all unfinished, hovered in the air between them, dancing like the flames in the fire pit and lighting the night with promise.

Chapter 21

MACK TRIED TO READ CAT'S FACE AND FAILED. HE never knew what women were thinking. He could sense the faintest signal from a horse, but the female mind was an eternal mystery.

He kicked dirt over the coals as she approached the fire, shuffling up a cloud of dust that was more appropriate to a raging grass fire than the dying embers of a fading campfire. The cloud drifted her way and settled on the white canvas shoes she was wearing.

She settled onto one of the benches and he wished he hadn't smothered the fire so soon. At least flames would give them something to watch. Something to talk about.

Maybe they could talk about the stars again. He felt his body stirring to life as he remembered their interrupted tour of the heavens. Tonight, the moon was floating serenely over the ranch, its face flat and inscrutable. Its pale light made the winding path that led away from the fire look somehow magical, as if it had been dusted with silver.

"Beautiful." Cat's tone was hushed, and he wondered if she was talking to him or just thinking aloud.

"Want to walk?" He held out a hand and time stopped while she hesitated. He'd felt the same tension when a horse took a half second to decide whether to trust its trainer or flee.

She glanced over at the bunkhouse as if she expected

to see Dora peering out the window. Didn't she realize the kid would be cheering them on?

He thought he'd lost her, but then he felt her hand steal into his. Barely daring to breathe, he started down the path. They passed the Bull House, then the barn, before she spoke.

"What's that?" She nodded toward the cabin that stood near the tree line. A tributary to the path they were walking veered toward it, creating a faint depression between clumps of sagebrush and spiky yuccas.

"It's a cabin," he said.

"Wow. Such an informative guide." The smile in her voice surprised him. "You're going to have to do better than that."

"It was the original claim shack," he said. "My great-great-granddad homesteaded there while he built the house. My dad used it as kind of a hideaway."

"It's cute. How come your mom didn't put Trevor there?"

"It's—it was my dad's space. And mine, after my mom remarried. I didn't get along with her second husband."

Understatement of the year. He'd hated Ollie with a deep, visceral hatred that made him question his own judgment. His mother had fallen for the man, and his mother was no fool. But something about him had made Mack mistrust him.

He should have listened to his instincts.

"What happened to your dad?"

"Accident." His throat tightened and the words came out hard. "They think he fell asleep at the wheel coming home from a sale. Had a heavy trailer on the back, and once he lost control…"

He hated thinking of that moment. Life could end in a heartbeat, when you least expected it. And it always seemed to end for the wrong people.

He needed to change the subject. "We were thinking about making it into an art studio if we get the contract with Art Treks."

"Contract?"

He nodded, realizing she didn't know how much this trip mattered to the future of the Boyd Ranch. "If this goes well, your company might sign on for a permanent reservation. It would give us some solidity—a predictable income, even if it's only for a few weeks."

She considered the cabin with her head tilted to one side. "It might work," she said. "You'd need to put in skylights. On the other side, so you'd get north light."

"You want to see the inside?"

"Sure."

They trudged up the path together. She rested against the cabin wall with her hands in her pockets, looking up at the moon while he fished out the key.

He opened the cabin door and flicked a switch. Faint yellow light beamed from a brass fixture that hung from the ceiling and brought the past back, lighting his father's place. The rickety table where he and his fellow ranchers had played poker. The small kitchen where he'd kept a fridge full of beer and a few frozen pizzas. The old television set, with its foil-wrapped rabbit ears. His father had created a man-cave before man-caves were even invented.

He paused. They were going to be alone in there, which would be a good thing if the air between them wasn't so loaded with stress and uncertainty. He needed to clear it.

"So where are we on the rules?" he asked.

She stared down at her feet. "I don't know. I think—we barely know each other. How do I know I can trust you?"

She probably couldn't. This whole mess with the ranch, the business with Ollie, had made him distrust himself. He'd left when his mother needed him most, just because he couldn't get along with her new husband. He'd known the guy was a jerk, and he'd walked away and left him in charge of the ranch. He'd risked his family's past, present, and future because he'd been too angry to see straight.

Angry about his mother remarrying so soon. Angry at seeing a man so clearly unworthy taking his father's place. Angry at his own powerlessness.

He wasn't worthy of this woman, and he knew it. But she made him want to try to do better. And for some reason, when he was with her anything seemed possible.

Anything.

"I think I do know you," he said. "I know you love the landscape here, and the open spaces. I know you're worried about your niece. I know you lost your sister, and you loved and admired her. I know you want your life to count for something."

She shrugged. "I told you all that."

He nodded, then shot her a sharp look that probed for the truth. "Did you ever tell Amos?"

"His name is Ames." Cat shifted uncomfortably. "And of course I did. He's known me for years."

"Does he care?" Mack tightened his grip on her hand. "Does he help?"

She looked away and he knew he'd hit a nerve.

He just hoped it was the right one.

—◦◦◦—

Cat looked down at Mack's hand clasping hers and felt tears prick at the back of her eyes. She didn't know if it was the situation, the setting, or the man himself, but somehow they'd become partners over the course of the past week. He was right; he knew her.

Except when it came to Ames. He didn't know anything about her relationship with Ames, because she'd lied about it. She was claiming she didn't trust him, but she was the one who'd lied.

He stroked back a lock of hair that had fallen over her eyes. "Do you care about him?"

She intended only to glance at him, but their eyes locked and held and she knew he read the truth, or some part of it.

"No," she whispered. "Not like I care about you." She took a deep breath. "I lied, Mack. I'm sorry. Ames isn't—we're not a couple."

"Don't apologize." He leaned in and brushed her lips with his. "That's the best news I've heard in a year."

The kiss they'd shared at the fire pit had been heated, hot, and just a bit domineering. If there had been any message in it at all, it had been strictly sexual.

But this one was lighter, gentler. Friendlier. And even sexier. Telling him how she felt, frankly and honestly, had been the right thing to do. They'd cleared the air and made room for a comfortable intimacy between them. The confusion was gone, and what shimmered between them now was warm and full of promise.

He reached over and flicked off the light.

No confusion there.

But something tingled at the back of her mind—an edgy, uncomfortable feeling. She remembered what he'd said about the contract. He needed her to give the ranch a rave review. His future depended on this trip as much as hers did.

That was a good thing, right? A common goal. He wasn't the kind of guy who would seduce a woman for the sake of financial success.

Was he?

"I shouldn't let this happen again." She couldn't help pushing her hips against him as she said the words.

"Yes, you should."

He kissed her again, deeper, warmer, heavier with lust but somehow shimmering with something more. Her misgivings faded, then disappeared. That tingling, troubling thought was gone.

In fact, she couldn't even remember what it was. Something about a contract…

To hell with contracts. To hell with jobs and careers and art and everything else. Everything but Dora.

Dora.

But Dora liked Mack. All that about sleeping soundly—she'd practically pushed the two of them together. Clearing her mind, Cat let herself fall into the kiss.

It retreated and advanced, ebbed and flowed, following some primal pattern. At the same moment, they drew away and looked into each other's eyes. There were no words spoken, but there was a question asked and answered, and they both knew everything had changed.

The light slanting from the windows was dim but somehow hard-edged, casting the edges of the old furniture in bold relief and highlighting each rung of the rough-hewn steps that led to a small, crude loft. *Stairway to heaven*, she thought. *Wonder what's up there*.

Apparently, she was going to find out.

Chapter 22

CAT REACHED THE LOFT ON A TIDE OF WARMTH AND feeling, her feet tripping up the steps easily, her weight supported by Mack's arm around her waist. She shivered when she reached the top, and it wasn't from the cool air. It was a good shiver—a shiver of anticipation.

She pushed away all her doubts like lace curtains blocking a bright window. Mack was a good man—grounded and respectful, kind and caring even if he didn't always communicate his feelings. He was strong, even aggressive, but there didn't seem to be a mean bone in his body.

And in this relationship, there would be no questions about the future, and no ugly breakup. Those only happened when one partner expected more than the other, and they both knew better than to expect anything between them to last. She was out of here in a week. Heading back to her world, and leaving him to his. That made a relationship practically risk-free.

Deep down, she felt a tug of warning. No relationship was without risk. But she smothered the foreboding and concentrated on the present.

Zen cowgirl. Live in the moment.

He tilted her backwards and she fell, unresisting, on the bed. Mack was smiling, his eyes lit with anticipation as he flicked on a small bedside light. He looked down at her.

"You," he said.

"You," she echoed. A laugh bubbled up in her chest and she let it out. It came out in a ridiculous schoolgirl-ish giggle, but she didn't care. She felt like a girl—like a girl sneaking off to be with a boy.

"This is going to be good," she muttered. She hadn't meant to say it out loud, but Mack just grinned.

"Yes, it is." He took her hand. "Very, very good."

They'd avoided looking at each other for days, and she was surprised at what she saw in his eyes—relief, of course, that they'd dispelled some of the tension between them, and the same sexual spark she'd seen under the stars. But there was something else there—something new and better. She felt as if they were something more than strangers coming together to satisfy their needs. They were friends, free of expectations, free of rules.

Their gazes locked and held, and she realized they'd never shared a held gaze. He'd never let her. Their ex-changes had always been guarded, cautious.

Not now. And with that protective cloak of uncer-tainty lifted, they shared something far more honest and real.

Maybe it was *too* honest and real. She could feel a connection humming between them, as if they were joined by a wire that was electrified and just a little too hot. Up until now, he'd been a cowboy, something ex-otic and a little dangerous, a dalliance in a far country. But now he was *Mack*. A man. And a lover, unless she shut him down right this minute.

That tight fist of fear tugged at her heart again. She had an impulse to crack a joke, laugh, cut the tension some-how. But all she could do was look, and let him look back.

He really did live in the moment—fully and without reservation. In life, that meant he was easygoing and adaptable. But in a relationship, it meant he was fully present. She felt like they were both naked, and they hadn't shed a single article of clothing.

Yet.

Impulsively, she kicked off her shoes and twisted in his arms, letting the soft parts of her body meet the hardness of his. Opening the top button of her shirt, she swept it over her head in one quick motion. If he looked at her breasts, maybe he'd stop probing her thoughts. Maybe he'd skim the surface instead of plumbing the depths with those dark, intense eyes.

A button snagged on a bobby pin and she tilted her head back, tugging her bun so her locks uncoiled down her back. She didn't know how it looked to him, but to her it felt graceful, quick, and wonderfully wanton.

She'd been right; the breasts changed everything. His eyes went suddenly soft, his gaze reverent. He reached for her as if he couldn't help himself, tucking a finger under the delicate strap of her bra and tracing it down to the lace that cupped the swell of her breast. She was glad she'd worn lace that day, ivory with a thread of gold running through it. In the light of the moon, it looked like a fairy garment spun of silk.

She leaned back on the pillows and let him look and touch. He stroked his finger gently along the edge of the fabric and set every nerve in her body to flickering. She felt like she'd come alive in a new way, waking from the sleepwalk of the everyday into a world of possibilities.

Sighing, she reached up and swept her fingers through the hank of dark hair that fell over his forehead.

Touching him like that made her feel tender, fond, and somehow protective of this strong man who was so obviously undone by soft skin and a scrap of lace.

While she stroked his hair, he found the clasp at the front of her bra and undid it, sweeping the halves to either side and cupping her flesh in his hands. She wasn't exactly Marilyn Monroe, but he made her feel soft and round and wonderfully feminine. He stroked his thumbs over her nipples and she arched her back, closing her eyes.

She opened them to find him watching her again. There was a faint note of triumph in his smile. He'd knocked down a few walls and he knew it.

It was time to play defense.

She knew this wasn't a fight. They didn't need to dominate each other or settle who was boss; that was something that wouldn't matter in the short time they'd be together. But she wanted to tussle with him, wrestle and tumble and *play*. Grabbing the collar of his shirt in both hands, she pulled. It was something she'd been wanting to do since the morning, when she'd noticed as she sponged off his shirt that it was fastened with snaps, not buttons.

It clicked open with a satisfying series of pops, revealing a tanned chest with a veil of dark hair fanned over hard swells of muscle.

"Mmm." She let out a wordless purr and lowered her head to run her mouth over the blade of his collarbone. Her left hand skimmed down the side of his face, swept past his neck, over his shoulder and chest. She stroked one flat nipple with her fingertips and was rewarded with a sharp intake of breath. Looking up, she saw his eyes weren't focused on hers anymore. They weren't focused at all. She'd won this round, stroked him into stunned silence.

Cat one, cowboy zero.

Well, that wasn't quite true. The cowboy had scored a few points himself, but she wasn't about to admit that—to him or to herself. She was enjoying herself too much to keep score.

It was about then she realized her pants were gone. Just gone, in some fabulous cowboy stealth move. How had he done that? The giggle burbled up again as she thanked God for matching lace panties. His admiration of the little bow that decorated each hip was giving her some time to regroup.

But once she was fully grouped, she realized the bows were gradually making their way down, down, down. Down her thighs, past her knees, over her calves, and off.

He was way ahead. It wasn't fair. Her clothes slipped off; his required a wrestling match.

It was time to get to work on that belt.

―――

Mack had heard artists were crazy, and now he knew it was true. This woman was a wild thing, beautiful and eager for him in a way that was somehow pure. There was no buckle-bunny agenda. With other women, he'd always felt like he was taking and they were giving. Like they were doing him a favor. He was always conscious, even in the throes of sex, that there was a price to pay.

But Cat wanted him in a simple, straightforward way that made them equals. This wasn't about promises and lies, expectations and bargains. It was about this moment, right now, and the sweet sensation of touching each other.

He paused in his mission—which was to hook her panties over the bedpost—and watched her tug at his jeans. The panties sailed off in some random direction. God only knew where they landed.

"It works better if you take off the boots first," he said as denim bunched around his ankles. She let out one of those little animal sounds that drove him crazy, a choked little laugh mixed in with a mew of frustration. He toed off one boot, then the other. She bent down to slip his jeans off, putting her face on a level with his lap.

They didn't have any secrets now. She knew exactly what he wanted, and how bad.

She pointed a finger and stroked it slowly down the length of him, making him twitch and throb. He couldn't help watching her face. She seemed fascinated by his body, transfixed.

"Yee-haw." She drew out the last syllable like it tasted good.

Resting her arms on his thighs, she kept stroking. He looked down at the pale seashell curve of her back, the tumbled curls spilling over her shoulders. He was savoring the little dimples just above her sweet round ass when sensation rippled through him and stole his breath.

Her mouth. She was using her mouth. That little tongue, those sweet lips. Dreams really did come true, even the sexy ones.

He leaned back and groaned, gathering her hair in one hand so he could see her face. Her eyes looked up at him, honest but somehow enigmatic, challenging even as she gave him everything he wanted.

"You have to stop." He closed his eyes and clamped his jaw. "I'm going to lose it."

Her eyes gleamed wickedly as she ran her tongue up the hard ridge on the underside of his shaft. But she only did it once before she scrambled up to straddle his lap. Warmth flooded him as she laced her arms around his neck and snuggled tight against him, her lips nibbling his jaw.

He set his hands on her hips, letting his fingers stroke the tempting dimples he'd been eyeing earlier. She pushed into him, then rose, her tongue flicking his ear, her soft mound against his hard body. She paused and rested her head on his shoulder, and the world stopped spinning. He hadn't been listening to the chirp of the crickets, the rustle of the trees that surrounded the cabin, but he missed them now in the hush that formed around them, bound by the circle of golden lamplight.

She lifted her head as if she caught the change too. When their eyes met, he swore there was a crackle, a jolt of electricity, and the crickets started up again. Expelling a soft sigh, she lowered herself onto him, slowly, deliberately, her eyes on his the whole way.

He was losing his grip on his sanity, his world, and his hard-won self-control when she rose again. She paused, and he knew by her smile that she'd caught his moment of weakness. This delicate, fragile-looking woman was triumphing over him and enjoying every minute.

He tightened his grip on her hips and held her there. He liked seeing her this way, but he wanted to see it for more than five minutes.

"Hold on," he whispered. "Slow, darlin'. Slow."

Her eyes softened, maybe at his tone, maybe at the

endearment. He'd figure that out later. But for now, the mood had changed and they weren't vying for control anymore—they were together, moving in a sweet, slow rhythm, watching each other's faces to gauge the pace. What had threatened to be a quick, hot gallop turned into a smooth long lope to the finish line. He took time to enjoy the view, caressing her breasts, tracing the curve of her waist, the swell of her belly, before regretfully rolling her over and pushing her away.

Her eyes widened, and he felt a quick surge of victory before he cupped his hand between her legs to soothe her.

"Slow down, honey. There's more."

Cat was whimpering. *Whimpering*, and pushing herself into Mack's hand like some kind of crazed nymphomaniac. And then purring, as he stroked and fondled, teased and touched.

In the back of her mind, she was struggling to sort things out. He was a cowboy. A simple man, in tune with nature and the land. She'd expected something quick and easy. Satisfying—she'd had no doubt of that—but simple. She'd expected to be ridden, mastered, spun in a few circles and pulled to a sliding, skidding stop.

Instead he was playing her, drawing out her pleasure like a musician stroking notes from a cello.

She felt herself rising in a slow crescendo of need. She forgot he was a stranger, forgot she was supposed to hold back, forgot her own name as she cried out and shattered at the last, perfect, sweet high note of the song.

—ᴍ—

Mack closed his eyes and drew in a breath, savoring the sweet honeyed scent of Cat's hair and the weight of her in his arms. She'd gone limp as her breathing slowed, tensing once or twice as aftershocks rocked her body. Her head rested in the hollow below his shoulder, and her breath teased his chest.

She blinked awake in minutes, looking slightly bewildered. He smiled and waited for her to catch her balance. The world might have stopped for him, but clearly it had spun for her. She clung to him and he knew he'd better enjoy it while it lasted. She wasn't the clinging type.

Sure enough, she was wriggling out of his arms in five breaths, rising to her knees in seven. He knew better than to hold her down. For one thing, she wouldn't stand for it. For another, he really wanted to know what happened next.

Hands. Hands happened next, sweeping through his hair, trailing down his face, tracing his lips, and teasing the curve between his neck and shoulder. She caressed his chest and walked her fingers down his ribs. Sweeping her hands back and forth and back again, she caressed, teased, and stroked, smiling all the while with an evil glint in her eye.

It wasn't long before he was back where he'd started, hanging onto a thin ledge of sanity with his fingernails scrabbling at the edge of the cliff.

Roughly, he pulled her on top of him. Her eyes flipped open, the lazy glow turning to a bright light as she eased him inside her and he marveled at the slick glide of wetness and warmth. Setting one hand on his chest, she lifted the other in the air like a bronc rider. She pulsed her hips and he felt his grip on the cliff sliding perilously close to the edge.

"Now this is more what I expected," she said.

With his hands on her hips, he slowed the pace. "What you expected?"

"From a cowboy," she said.

"We're smarter than we look." He braced an arm behind her back and rolled her over. "And way more complicated."

"I knew that," she said. "I… know… *you*…"

And then she was spinning again, he could tell, lost in the sensation, and he was whirling with her. Together they spun faster and faster until all their colors blended and they were one ecstatic spiral, spinning into space.

Chapter 23

THE NEXT DAY'S TRIP WAS MERCIFULLY SHORT. EVEN IN the wide-open spaces, Cat could feel the tension thrumming between her and Mack. It was a good tension, but the light of day had brought worries with it. She felt like the others could see what had happened just by looking at her. Every time she looked at Mack she blushed.

The war between wanting him and hanging onto her professionalism kept her from noticing her fatigue until she climbed the few steps to the porch. Suddenly her aches and pains leaped into high definition.

"Whoosh," Emma said from behind her. "I feel like that horse *dragged* me over the trail."

"I can't feel my ass," Abby moaned, rubbing her backside.

The sweet yeasty smell of baking bread hit them the moment they walked in the door, and everyone's step livened up a little. Maddie rose from the table, where she was sitting with a pretty teenaged girl about Dora's age.

"Welcome back!" Their hostess gestured toward the dining room, where a long table was set for a crowd. "I thought you might like to go civilized tonight and eat inside. We're having a ranch hand dinner in the kitchen—something to stick to your ribs and replace all those calories you worked off on horseback. It'll be ready in half an hour."

"Do you need any help?" Cat asked. They'd paid for

full amenities, but Mack's mother was starting to feel like family.

"Nope." Madeleine waved toward the girl beside her. "Viv's here to help out. Viv, honey, this is Cat Crandall. She's the artist I told you about. The one your dad likes so much."

Cat felt hot all over. She wanted nothing more than to flee the room, but the girl was looking at her with an amused half smile. Apparently she didn't mind her dad kissing strange women.

"Look out." She tossed her dark hair and laughed. "My dad's a hound dog."

Cat barely heard Madeleine introduce the rest of the guests. She was too busy trying to figure out what kind of relationship Mack had with his daughter. The girl had the same wry sense of humor as her dad, but she seemed more gossip girl than cowgirl, with long silky hair and stylish clothes. Mack had said she was turning into a clone of his ex-wife. If that was true, his ex-wife must be gorgeous.

She felt a stab of jealousy and found herself smoothing her hair. When Mack walked into the room with Ed and Charles, she deliberately messed it up and jerked her hand away. She wasn't trying to impress him, or even start a relationship. With his daughter here, he probably wasn't either. Not anymore.

When he caught sight of Viv, a half-dozen expressions flickered across his face—shock, confusion, startled pleasure, and then a radiant smile—the kind of smile every daughter wants from her father. As usual, his face advertised his emotions like a highway billboard.

At least Cat didn't have to worry about him lying to

her. And something about that smile tugged at her heart. Her own father had rarely smiled—rarely even looked at her. His expressions had been provoked by Headline News or Bill O'Reilly when they weren't totally obscured by the local paper, which he complained about with equal vigor. Mack seemed like the kind of father who did things with his daughter, who worried about her. Who loved her.

Maybe she should listen to his advice when they talked about Dora. Because looking at Viv, watching the two of them embrace, she felt a pang of envy. Maybe she wasn't a real parent, but Dora needed one. And Cat wanted that closeness, that bond.

She was going to have to try harder.

Dinner that night reminded Mack of a Norman Rockwell Thanksgiving. The students lined the table, with Cat at one end and Madeleine at the other. Dishes of chicken and dumplings, potatoes, buttered green beans laced with bacon, and baked beans made the rounds, passing from hand to hand.

And Viv was there. Mack hadn't had time to figure out why; he only knew her mother had dropped her off that afternoon and wouldn't be back for a week. Mack suspected the boyfriend had wanted Alex all to himself, but it didn't matter to him. What mattered was Viv.

And he hadn't just gotten Viv; he'd gotten *happy* Viv, who'd been a stranger for far too long. Normally his daughter sulked through her stays on the ranch as if she'd been sentenced to some kind of Gulag, but she and Dora had hit it off and that seemed to make all the difference. The two girls chattered nonstop, their heads tilted together like co-conspirators plotting a coup.

The students kept up a lively conversation too. The only quiet ones at the table were Hank and Trevor. Hank was Hank, working his way through his food, dogged as an old plow horse. He was a hardworking plow horse, so Mack had no complaints. Actually, the man's taciturn silences let Mack off the hook for his own quiet nature. All he had to do was sit beside the hired man to seem chatty and personable by comparison.

Trevor's silence was more unexpected. Normally, he seemed to fancy himself the life of the party, but tonight he was wary, glancing at Mack occasionally as if he expected to be sucker punched at any moment.

"So what brought you to the ranch?" Mack asked Viv. He toyed with his chicken as he spoke, pretending he wasn't hanging on every word his daughter said. He'd told Cat to pretend she didn't care, but he wasn't much good at following his own advice.

"Mom brought me. You missed her."

He didn't miss her a bit, but he wasn't about to tell his daughter that.

"She and her loser boyfriend dropped me off. They're on their way to Vegas."

"Vegas?"

Maybe Alex would get married again. He pictured his wife in a cheesy little chapel on the strip, wearing a sequined jumpsuit and saying "I do" in one of those Elvis-themed ceremonies.

Maybe not. If Alex remarried, she'd never elope. She'd done that the first time and spent half her married life regretting the gown she hadn't worn, the bouquet she hadn't thrown, the rehearsal dinner and reception and honeymoon she hadn't had. Every time they went to a wedding she pouted for weeks. Mack was sure she wouldn't miss out on all that attention the second time around.

"Is she still seeing that banker?" he asked.

"Nope." Viv stabbed viciously at an innocent dumpling. "It's Emilio now. I think he's a mobster."

Mack paused with a forkful of food halfway to his mouth. "Why?"

Vivian took her time chewing the dumpling while she thought about her answer. "He wears a pinkie ring."

Mack winced. Jewelry on men never made any sense to him. It was too easy to get stuff caught on a nail or snagged in a horse's mane. Besides, who would spend money on that stuff? Better to buy land, or at least a good horse. Something with real value.

"Do you like him?" He kept his expression carefully neutral. He tried not to be judgmental about the men Alex chose. His ex might trash him every chance she got, but he knew it was important for a girl to love her mother. It wasn't always easy to keep his thoughts to himself, but he did his best.

"I hate him," Viv said. She stabbed another dumpling. Hard.

Bells went off in Mack's head, but he stayed calm. "How come?"

Viv shrugged. "He's a creep."

She continued torturing her dumplings, clearly unaware that she'd just upped her dad's protective instincts to high alert.

"Did he ever touch you?" Mack asked.

"No. He's just a creep."

"Does he look at you?"

She rolled her eyes. "Well, yeah, Dad. He's around, you know? He has to look at me. I think he'd rather not, though." She splayed her hands in a "ta-da" gesture. "Hence the trip to Vegas, and my exile to the colonies."

He vowed to get in touch with Alex at the first opportunity and find out about this Emilio creep. "It's not exile. We'll have fun."

"Whatever, Dad."

The rest of the meal was spent in small talk, though the issue of Emilio festered in the back of his mind. By the time the meal was over, the guy had grown fangs and a barbed tail in his imagination.

Maddie cleared the table while the students fetched the day's paintings and propped them against the wall in the front parlor in preparation for their nightly review. Cat picked up the first painting—Emma Delaney's rendition of the lake—and glanced around the room.

"Dora?"

"Up here!" her niece hollered from upstairs. The two girls had pounded up the stairs like a couple of high-spirited ponies the minute the meal was over, taking the steps two at a time in their haste to get away from the grown-ups.

"We're doing the paintings now," Cat yelled.

Dora appeared in the doorway, her face flushed. "Viv wants to show me some stuff," she said. "We're talking."

"But you're supposed to…" Cat glanced up at Mack, who was slouched in the doorway. He gave a faint shake of his head. She slumped her shoulders. "Okay. Go ahead."

The girl didn't have to be asked twice. A cascade of giggles swept down from Viv's room almost immediately.

Mack hardly needed to listen while they rehashed the day's work. He could hear Cat saying something about color and value and hue. Man, he didn't even know what she was talking about. It was like they spoke different languages. He must be crazy to think they had anything in common. But last night...

Last night was over. A memory. And it would have to stay that way, with Viv here.

He strolled into the kitchen, figuring he'd help his mother with the cleanup. Someone in a frilly apron was at the sink, scrubbing dishes—but that someone wasn't Maddie.

It was Hank.

What the hell? As far as Mack knew, Hank had never said a word to his mom—or any other woman, for that matter.

As he stood dumbfounded in the doorway, his mother strode in from the dining room carrying a teetering stack of dishes.

"Here you go," she said. "Don't put those wine glasses in the dishwasher."

"Yes, ma'am."

To Mack's surprise, Madeleine giggled—*giggled!*—and smacked Hank on the arm. "Quit it," she said. "I told you not to call me that. You make me feel about eighty years old."

"Well, you're not old," Hank said. "Not old at all."

The giggle erupted again. Was Mack's mother *flirting*? With *Hank*?

Mack gripped the side of the door frame, feeling suddenly dizzy. Hank had always been more than a ranch hand; he was family. But judging from Maddie's shining eyes, he was becoming something more. That would take a lot of getting used to, but it would be a lot easier to deal with than her disastrous marriage to Ollie. In fact, Mack couldn't help wishing Hank had tied on that frilly apron a lot sooner.

He slipped out the back door. Standing on the top step, he looked out over the fire pit, past the Heifer House to the acres of land rolling beyond it and the low hills marking the horizon.

He'd spent most of his life leaving this place behind, watching it fade in a cloud of dust in the rearview mirror as he headed for some rodeo. But all along, the land had been the base that held him steady, the one thing he could depend on. Only after the disaster with Ollie had it occurred to him that there might be a day when the ranch wouldn't be there to catch him if he fell.

But they'd held onto it so far, despite the financial ruin brought on by Ollie's shenanigans. If this business with Art Treks worked out, and they could get a few more clients and sell some cow/calf pairs in the spring, the ranch might still be here for Viv someday.

Viv. He really ought to check on her. He stepped back into the house and shut the door quietly behind him. The low hum of voices came from the kitchen, but his attention was on the upstairs rooms, where his daughter was.

He wasn't sure Dora, with her bad attitude and deep-set scars, would have been his first choice as a friend for Viv. His daughter had reached a delicate détente with both him and Alex, but Dora, with her sarcastic attitude and scorn for authority, might tilt the balance back toward war.

Then again, maybe the girl's bereavement would remind Viv that she was lucky to have two parents—even
if they weren't together.

In any case, he knew from experience he didn't have
a choice about Viv's friends. And he shouldn't worry.
Somehow, despite the tumultuous ordeal of the divorce,
his daughter had grown into a young woman who knew
who she was and wasn't about to cave to any kind of
peer pressure.

Mack was proud of her. If only he could see more of
her, he'd be fine with the way things had turned out. Let
Alex have the house and everything in it; he just wanted
a good relationship with his daughter.

He climbed the stairs quietly, pausing halfway to
listen to the high piping voices of the girls. He wasn't
eavesdropping—not really. He just wanted to hear how
they were getting along. And see if they were talking
about Emilio.

"No! Eww—we're not doing that."

That was Dora. Now Viv joined in.

"Just go back to your room. We're not into that stuff."

And then a male voice.

"Oh, come on, girls. It'll be fun."

Mack stood motionless for half a second, dizzied by
the rage that leaped up like a flame in his chest. Trevor.
Trevor was in there with the girls, trying to get them
to… to do something.

And Mack was going to stop it.

Chapter 24

AS THE REST OF THE STUDENTS STUMBLED OFF TO THE bunkhouse, Cat had ducked into the kitchen and found Maddie drinking a cup of tea at the kitchen table. The tall, rawboned ranch hand sat across from her, sitting so stiffly Cat suspected he wasn't normally allowed on the furniture. He wasn't drinking tea or anything else; just sitting, with his hands in his lap and his heels resting on the chair rungs. He'd probably be more comfortable if someone gave him a set of reins to hold.

The kitchen was spotless, the counters gleaming, all signs of the enormous dinner absorbed into a haze of spray cleaner. Across the room, the dishwasher churned rhythmically.

"You need any help?" Cat asked.

"We're fine." Madeleine had her stocking feet propped up on the chair across from her, but she swung them to the floor and shoved the chair a couple inches toward Cat. "But come set a spell."

Cat thought maybe she should join her students and rest up for the next day, but Maddie's orders were hard to disobey. Besides, she kind of liked the woman.

"How are you doing with that little niece of yours?" Maddie sat back, folding her hands across her stomach.

"Oh, fine." Cat faked a smile, wondering if Mack had told his mother about her personal problems. She hadn't meant for any of that to be shared. "Why?"

"Just wondered. Noticed she acts up a little. Seems troubled."

Cat's temper flared. "She's fine."

Maddie shrugged. "If you say so."

Cat struggled to smooth herself down. There was no reason to go on the defensive. This woman knew children. She was a mother. A grandmother. And it hardly took a genius to figure out Dora had issues.

"She lost her mother. She's been having a hard time." Cat sighed. "I thought bringing her here would help."

"Well, maybe it will. She and Viv are getting on like a house on fire."

"They do seem to get along." Cat glanced at the ranch hand, who was watching the conversation like a tennis match. The man never seemed to speak, so why should she care if he listened? "Mack and his daughter seem to get along too."

Maddie sat up, suddenly animated. "Oh, yeah. Viv's a feisty one and she doesn't listen worth a damn, but her dad loves her and she loves him right back. You got any kids?"

"No."

Cat had always thought she'd have kids, but time was slipping away, even though she barely felt like a grown-up herself these days. Her life felt unsettled, as if she hadn't found her purpose yet. Maybe that was why she was so desperate to help Dora. With no kids of her own, she'd channeled all her maternal instinct to her niece.

"Don't you want to have a family?" Madeleine asked.

This was getting awfully personal. Cat glanced at the ranch hand again, but he was staring at the wall across from them, a little slack-jawed. Maybe the guy was slow or something. In any case, he wasn't likely to spread gossip.

Cat shook her head. "I've been mostly focused on my career."

"Thought this was your first trip."

"It is. The first trip of my second career. The first career's still going, but it's on life support."

"So how long are you going to focus on this one?" Maddie cupped her palms around her mug. "The clock's ticking, you know."

Cat didn't know why she felt like laughing instead of smacking the woman. "It's not really just about my career. It's my art I've been focused on. I doubt that will ever change."

She dug through her brain for the thoughts about dedication and creativity that had seemed so important a week ago. They must have moved to the bottom of the pile, underneath her worries about Dora, her new career, and her ridiculously randy feelings for a certain cowboy.

"Artists have to respect the creative urge," she said. "It can take some time to find your inspiration—your *Starry Night*. But you can't give up the quest."

"You got a starry night right outside." Maddie's dimples creased as she smiled. "Ask my son to show it to you sometime."

Cat smiled. "I don't mean that literally. I mean..." She paused. "Do you know Van Gogh's painting? *Starry Night*?"

"That the windy one with the trees?" the ranch hand asked.

Cat tried not to act surprised. "That's the one. Well, that painting has come to define Van Gogh's creative genius. I think every artist has to find their *Starry Night*—something that inspires them like nothing else. That's why I'm so excited to join Art Treks. It'll give me a chance to see the world, see if my *Starry Night* is out there somewhere."

She blushed. All of a sudden, the sentiment that had carried her so far sounded like pseudo-intellectual nonsense. It was a direct quote from Ames Whitaker—her pseudo-boyfriend.

There wasn't much left in her life that was real. Just Dora, and…

And Mack. Last night had been real. But she could hardly hinge her reality on a one-time fling with a cowboy.

Unless she made it a two-time fling.

"Maybe your *Starry Night*'s right here." Madeleine settled back, sipping her tea. The dimples flickered back to life as she set down her cup.

"I don't think so. I mean, this place is beautiful. The lake, the canyon—well, I know the students found it really inspiring. But I haven't caught that spark yet."

"Maybe you're looking for it wrong," Madeleine said. "Maybe what you need isn't a place. Maybe it's a person."

Cat heard footsteps on the stairs—loud, male footsteps. Mack was going up to see his daughter. She glanced at the door.

"Go on up," Maddie said. "See what they're up to."

Cat shoved her chair back from the table just as a flurry of footsteps and a deep, male shout erupted from upstairs. There were a couple loud bangs, as if furniture had fallen over.

Then the girls started to scream.

Chapter 25

CAT DASHED UP THE STAIRS AND INTO THE LIGHTED bedroom to see Trevor lying on the floor like a broken doll, his face streaked with blood. For a second, she wondered if he was even still alive. Mack was astride the man's body on his knees, pummeling him with one fist, then the other. Both girls hung on his arms, struggling to haul him off the apparently unconscious man.

"Dad." Viv tugged at his arm, then tugged again. "Dad. Stop."

Judging from the look in his eyes, Mack was lost in some bloody cloud of homicidal madness. But as he blinked at Viv, Cat felt his power ebb a little. There was still a steady, throbbing energy there, like a powerful engine idling at a stoplight, but the wild light in his eyes started to fade.

"Stop," Viv said. "It's all right." She let out something between a laugh and a sob. "Don't kill him, okay?"

"He—I heard him."

"It's okay, Dad." Viv put her arm around him and patted his back. Dora let go and backed away, her eyes wide.

Cat knelt beside Trevor and took his hand, fumbling for a pulse. His eyes were staring at the ceiling, and for a moment she thought he was dead. But then he blinked. Cat dropped his hand and he reached up to tentatively touch his face, wincing as he pressed the bruises blooming on his forehead, cheekbone, and chin.

"Trevor, I'm sorry," she said. "I'm so sorry. Let me get something to clean you up." She looked up at Mack, suddenly realizing all over again how big the man was, and how strong.

And how angry. He was still staring at Trevor, his chest heaving. It was obvious he could barely hold himself back from attacking the man again.

"What the hell is wrong with you?" Cat was almost crying. She had no idea what was going on, but she did know this trip was a disaster. So far she'd slept with their guide and allowed that same guide to beat up a client—twice. The place was a wreck and their host was homicidal.

She was doomed.

"There's nothing wrong with me." Mack's voice was low and menacing. Viv tightened her grip on his arm. "It's that little pervert. I heard him trying to get the girls to…" He sucked in a deep breath and Cat saw that his eyes were glistening. "I can't even say it."

Viv shook her head. Incredibly, it looked like she was suppressing a laugh. "Oh, no. Dad, what did you hear?"

Mack looked agonized. "Don't cover for him, Viv. I heard the whole thing."

"Tell me what you heard." The teenager sounded like the parent now, coaxing a story out.

"You told him to leave," Mack said. "You told him 'you weren't into that stuff.' And he was trying to talk you into it. He said it would be 'fun.' It makes me sick."

"Dad, he wanted to have a *pillow fight*," Viv said. "I mean, it's kind of weird, but it's not what you thought. And we said *no*. What do you think we are, stupid?"

"Pillow fight?" Mack looked down at the pillow,

which was lying on the floor with feathers spewing from the seam.

A little of the stuffing seemed to go out of him, too.

"Yes, a pillow fight," Viv said. "And we're not helpless. We told him no. If he hadn't left, I'd have kicked his ass."

That got a near-smile out of Mack. "You would have, wouldn't you?"

Viv nodded sharply. "Definitely."

Trevor was sitting up now, leaning against the side of the bed. Cat had found a box of Kleenex on the nightstand and was dabbing at the wounds on his face.

"Okay." Mack nodded reluctantly. "I might have overreacted."

Trevor shot him a glare. "*Overreacted?* Is that all you have to say?" He struggled to his feet and staggered toward the door. "You can say it to the police, that's who you can say it to."

"Trevor, wait." Cat followed him. "We need to get you cleaned up."

"I can clean up myself," he said. "At the police station."

"Just wait. I'm sure Mack will apologize, and…"

"Think again," Mack grumbled. "Pillow fight, my ass. Guy's a pervert."

Cat had to admit the whole scene was disturbing. But Trevor apparently hadn't laid a hand on either girl, and she had a feeling Mack was in trouble. Maines wasn't the type to let things go.

"I don't want an apology," Trevor said. Even with his bloodied face, he was trying to retain some dignity. "I want *you* in jail." He pointed toward Mack. "And I want *you* fired." That was for Cat. "You'll be hearing from my lawyer."

"Just wait," Cat said, glancing from one man to the other. She could feel the whole venture whirling away like the clouds in Van Gogh's painting, spinning out of control.

"I won't wait," Trevor said. "And if you think I'm going to spend one more hour at this fleabag redneck ranch, with this arrogant homicidal cowboy, you're wrong. I'll be contacting the police as soon as I get to town." He turned to Cat. "And I'll be contacting your company as well."

Mack made a valiant effort to calm himself as Trevor stormed down the stairs. Moments later, an engine fired up outside and a vehicle, presumably the Lexus SUV, took off in a spray of gravel.

"Good riddance," he muttered.

Things were awfully quiet now that the fight was over. He looked up to see Cat shooting him a hard glare. Viv and Dora seemed a little shell-shocked. At some silent adolescent signal, they leaped up in unison and hightailed it out of the room, leaving him alone with Cat.

The silence continued. Obviously, she expected him to say something.

"You wouldn't have wanted him to stay, would you? After he tried to coerce a couple of teenaged girls into a little bedtime *pillow fight*?"

"I didn't like the guy either," Cat said. "And the pillow fight thing is kind of creepy. But…"

"*Kind of* creepy?" He couldn't keep the edge out of his voice. "After the stunt he pulled with that painting? Dora could have seen that."

"It was just a nude."

"It was you."

"It had my face, that's all. It was an imitation of a famous painting, Mack. Just a joke. I was sitting in the same pose as Manet's *Olympia*."

He couldn't believe she was defending the guy. "Cat, he was picturing you. Thinking of—you. Naked."

He hoped she couldn't tell he was thinking about the same thing. He'd been thinking about it all day. He hadn't had much to do while the students painted, so he'd fallen into an X-rated reverie while he'd been sitting there watching her.

How could he help it? She'd been wearing a man's shirt again—a white dress shirt. It was splattered with paint and hung loosely on her body. It was hardly a sexually provocative outfit, but when a woman wore a man's shirt, it was usually something she'd scooped off the bed after sex. He'd wished it was *his* shirt, scooped off of *his* bed.

"Okay," she said. "I know the guy's weird. And I'm even glad he's gone. But that wasn't the way to handle it."

"He was in here with our daughters, Cat. Well, my daughter. Dora might just be your niece, but it's your job to protect her, just like I protect Viv. You should be glad I took care of it."

Her expression grew even stormier. "I do protect her. I don't need you to *take care* of anything."

"What would you have done?" he asked.

"I'd have asked him to leave."

"I saved you the trouble."

"I would have asked him to leave the *room*, not the ranch. And then I would have kept the girls away from him."

He folded his arms over his chest and the two of them traded glares in an Olympic-level stare-down. "So you care more about your career than the girls' safety."

"No. I just don't think the girls were in real danger."

"I think you're wrong. The guy has a problem."

"Well, where I'm from, we don't solve problems with our fists." She flushed. Maybe she realized she sounded like a prissy old preschool teacher.

"Where I'm from we don't have many other options. You know how long it's going to take him to find a cop?"

She shook her head.

"We don't have a police station on every corner around here. We solve our own problems. And we protect our own children."

He put a hand to his head. His fear for his daughter, his rage at Trevor, his worries about the ranch—it was all feeding into one hell of a thumper. And the way Cat was looking at him wasn't helping. She looked utterly repulsed.

He slouched down on the side of the bed. "I'm just telling you how things are around here, that's all."

"And I'm telling you there was a better way to handle it." She spun on her toes and stalked out of the room.

A moment later he rose from the bed and looked out the window to see her crossing the yard toward the Heifer House. Her stride was long and her fists were clenched at her sides. This was a very different woman from the one that had melted into him the night before.

Well, *that* would never happen again. He'd felt such a kinship between them, as if they were the same at heart despite their different lives. But he'd been wrong.

Viv was all that mattered to him. Not women, not

work, not even the ranch. He'd thought Cat felt the same way about Dora. He'd started to respect her, even admire her for her devotion to her niece. But she had her priorities screwed up. That career of hers mattered more than anything, even the girls' safety.

He'd just turned from the window when there was a tap on his door.

"Dad?" Viv slipped into the room. "I need to talk to you."

"Uh-oh."

"No, it's nothing bad." She laughed, and for a moment he was intensely grateful to have a happy, well-adjusted child.

"It's just... I want to trade places with Dora," she said.

He looked at her, uncomprehending. She wanted to be a screwed-up child who hated everyone? She wanted her mother dead? What the hell was she talking about?

"She's really unhappy, Dad."

"I know. But we can't do much about that, honey. She's had a terrible loss, and it's going to take her time to get over it."

"But we *can* do something about it." She danced from one foot to the other, clearly excited.

"I take it you have a plan," he said, smiling. Viv had always been tough on the outside and sweetly tender on the inside.

"She loves horses, right? And you know I hate that stuff."

He did know. Viv hated to get so much as a finger dirty, and she'd never really been an animal person. That apparently wasn't a genetic trait; it was nature, not nurture. He wished he'd done more nurturing when she'd been little. While he was off riding broncs at rodeos, he should have been in the corral at home teaching Viv to ride a pony.

But it was too late for that now.

"So she'd really love helping you with the horses. And I want to take the workshop."

"Since when do you care about art?"

"Since, like, over a year." She rolled her eyes. "Didn't Mom tell you? I joined the art club at school, and Mr. Swanson's been teaching us drawing and stuff like that. Did you see the pictures they painted today?" She tossed her hair back and looked at the ceiling, as if envisioning a fabulous future for herself. "If I could go back knowing how to do that, it would be so cool. I could enter something in the show at the Civic Center. If you get accepted, everybody in town sees it, and there's a big opening, with wine and stuff."

He scowled. "No wine."

"They don't give it to the students, Dad. I just mean it's classy and stuff."

Who was he raising here—Cat Junior?

"So Mom didn't tell you about my pictures?"

"Nope." A year. She'd been into art for a year, and he'd had no idea. His own daughter was becoming a stranger to him.

"Well, I'd way rather take the workshop than have to mess with the horses."

"I was hoping you and I could spend some time together," he said.

"We can. I'll come on all the trips. I just won't be, you know, getting all dirty and stuff. But Dora will. She'd love it. She hates painting, and she's so jealous

I get to be a cowgirl." She made a sour face. "I don't know why. She's pretty cool, but she actually *likes* that cowgirl sh—stuff."

"Amazing."

"Hold on." She dashed out of the room and he heard her thrashing around in her bedroom, obviously hunting for something. She was back in a flash, holding out a coil-bound notebook. "Here. Look."

He opened the book and turned the pages. It was filled with drawings—good drawings. Kind of silly and fanciful, full of fairies and fashion models and other girlie stuff, but well-drawn. He didn't know much about art, but he thought she was pretty good.

"Wow," he said.

She flushed with pleasure. Standing there all big-eyed and hopeful, with her hands behind her back and a shy smile lighting her face, she looked like a fairy herself.

He grinned. "Okay. But don't get in Cat's way."

"Thanks!" She flung her arms around his neck and gave him a resounding smack on the cheek. "I've got to tell Dora."

It wasn't until after she'd rocketed down the stairs that he realized he'd just okayed Dora's departure from the painting class.

Cat was not going to be happy.

Chapter 26

BY THE TIME CAT GOT BACK TO THE BUNKHOUSES, someone had lit a fire in the pit. It was puny compared to the one Mack had built the night before, but the flames still flickered a warm invitation in the cold night air. The students were huddled on the log benches, their arms wrapped around themselves for warmth. Summer nights at this altitude could be nippy.

It was strange, Cat thought. It didn't feel like they were on a mountain, but the high plains sat at seven thousand feet. She could feel the thin air sapping her strength on their longer treks and wondered how Ed and Emma managed.

As Cat approached, Ed tottered to the fire and poked it with a stick. "Don't know why this won't burn like it did last night," he fretted.

"I think it's nice, Mr. Delaney," Dora said.

Cat peered past the dancing flames to see her niece sitting with Viv on the far side of the fire. Evidently Dora liked Ed. Almost as much as she liked Mack, and Viv, and Maddie.

Actually, she seemed to like everyone except Cat. And Trevor, but nobody liked Trevor.

"So you say Mack beat up that fashionista man?" Emma clasped her hands and rocked backward on her bench. "I'd like to have seen that." She glanced around as if she was afraid someone had heard. Cat wondered if she should assure her that nobody in her book group or bridge club was liable to be prowling the Wyoming plains.

"Sounds to me like he needed whuppin'." Ed poked the fire again, sending up a fountain of sparks. "I'd have been happy to help with that."

"Me too," said Abby. "A man like that shouldn't be allowed around young people."

"Well, Cat's really pissed at Mack now," Dora said.

Cat resisted the urge to scold her for her language and ducked into the shadow of the Heifer House. This would be a good chance to judge the other students' responses, figure out how to handle the situation.

"She ought to thank him," Abby said. "The man painted a dirty picture of her today, up at the lake."

"He did?" Dora tilted her sharp chin up and straightened her shoulders. "Well, I'd have let Mack beat him up if I'd known that."

"Mack took it and tore it up," Ed said. "Ground it into the dirt. He's a gentleman, I'm telling you."

"Yeah." Viv stepped into the circle, looking pleased and flattered at the compliment to her father. "He's an old-fashioned kind of guy. He thinks women ought to be protected." She preened a little, then frowned. "It's a good thing he's not around when my boyfriends come over, though."

"I like him," Dora said. "I think Cat should hook up with him."

"*Ew*. That's my *dad* you're talking about."

"Well, get used to it. I think they already did it." Dora pitched a leaf into the fire and watched it flare up and burn. As the ashes rose and fluttered on the flames, Cat wondered if she was watching her new career go up in smoke. Not only had their outfitter beat up a student, but she'd also been outed for sleeping with him.

"Good for her," Emma said. "If I was twenty years younger..."

She winked and Ed gave up on the fire and strode over to where she was sitting. "You'd what, Emma Delaney?"

"I'd marry you all over again," she said. "But I'd get you a pair of those Wrangler jeans first."

"Well, it doesn't matter." Dora looked glum. "That little honeymoon's over for good. You should have seen the way Cat looked at him afterwards. I mean, he was protecting us, and she acted like he'd committed a crime or something."

Evidently assault wasn't a crime in Dora's book. Cat just hoped the police felt the same way.

"She's so *tense*." Dora sighed. "I wish she'd loosen up a little. I just want her to be happy. She's been so sad since—well, since some stuff happened." She looked down at her hands, obviously remembering her mother. Cat was touched that even from the depths of her own mourning, she realized Cat was grieving too.

"Well, you're part of the reason, missy." Ed stabbed his stick into the ground for emphasis. "You ought to treat the people who love you with more respect. Your auntie might not be here for you forever, you know."

Cat winced as the group fell suddenly silent.

"No kidding. I know—I kind of figured that out when my mom—never mind." Ducking her head, Dora covered her face with one hand for a moment, then rose and ran off toward the house. Viv jumped to her feet and followed.

"What'd I say?" Ed asked the group. It was clear he wasn't expecting an answer. "Young people today." He shoved the stick into the fire again, sending up a shower of sparks. "They just don't have any respect."

"And old people don't have any brains," Emma said.

"You think we ought to go after her?" Abby asked.

Emma turned and looked straight at Cat. Evidently she wasn't as well-hidden by the darkness as she'd thought. "Nope. Cat's here." She waved a hand in a shooing motion. "Go. Go on and get her. Maybe she'll talk to you now."

———

Cat caught up to Dora and Viv on the porch. Dora had slouched down on the top step and was sitting with her head in her hands while Viv patted her back.

"Dora," Cat said. "Honey, I'm so sorry."

Viv glanced up at Cat and whisked away into the house, leaving her alone with her niece. Cat was tempted to take her place and put her arm around Dora, but the girl had never been the touchy-feely type—with her, anyway—so she simply sat beside her. They were sitting together, staring off in the same direction, feeling the same pain.

It was a start.

"It's okay. It's just that I'd finally started to feel better." Dora sniffed. "Viv—she's really nice, and I'd kind of forgotten…"

She looked stricken as she realized what she'd said. "I mean, not forgotten. I'll never forget."

"Of course you won't."

"But things were starting to seem brighter, you know?

It was like I'd been walking around in a fog, and it lifted a little. And then Ed had to go bring it up. I know he didn't mean to. I'm not mad. I'm just..."

"Sad?"

Dora suddenly slammed the flat of her hand into the newel post. "No. I take it back. I *am* mad." She kicked it again. "I'm fucking furious."

Her vehemence was a little scary, but Cat pushed on. "You'll feel better again, hon. You just have to go on as best you can. I don't blame you for being mad." She edged closer to Dora. They were finally talking—really talking. Maybe she could find out what was going on in Dora's head when she'd torn up the photo the night before and destroyed her painting today.

"Your mom would have loved that painting."

Dora stared at the newel post as if it was the architect of all her troubles and smacked it again. "Well, I don't care what she would have liked. I really don't give a shit. She didn't give a shit about me, so why should I care what she thought?"

"Dora, that's not true!" Cat was shocked. Edie had loved Dora, and it had shown every day, in everything she did. There was no way Dora could have felt unloved.

So why was she so angry? Sure, anger was one of the stages of grief—but that was anger at the universe for taking your loved one away, not anger at the deceased herself.

"It *is* true. She didn't care. And I am never, ever going to be like her." Dora stormed off the porch, heading for the bunkhouse. Cat stood and followed her a few steps, then paused in a square of light and looked back at the house.

Viv was standing at her bedroom window, one hand

on the pane. She followed Dora a short distance with her gaze, then looked down at Cat. Sadly, she shook her head.

Was she telling Cat not to follow? Casting one last look at the departing Dora, Cat turned resolutely and climbed the steps to the house.

She needed to talk to Viv. Maybe Dora had confided in her.

But when she climbed the stairs, the door to the girl's bedroom was closed. She raised her fist to knock, but she just couldn't do it. This was Mack's daughter. Much as she wanted to know what kind of crazy thoughts were scampering through her niece's brain, she didn't really want to draw the Boyd family into her own personal drama.

There'd been enough drama here for one night.

She leaned against the wall, exhausted. She wished she had someone to talk to. To depend on.

She did, actually. She took a longing look at the closed door at the end of the hallway. Was Mack in there now that Trevor was gone? She took a step toward it, then paused.

She'd told him she could take care of herself, and she'd meant it. Maybe she shouldn't admit to her weakness. Maybe she should just go.

She stood like a statue, her fist raised, her mind racing with indecision. If only Mack was here. Seeing him with Viv had made her respect his advice, and she wished she could ask him what to do now.

She was tired of trying to do this alone. She remembered what he'd said—*I want you to know someone's looking after you.* Why had she pushed him away?

For the first time in her life, she wished she was the kind of woman who could let herself depend on a man.

—⁓—

Mack was a coward. That was the only explanation he could come up with.

Why else would a grown man be hiding in his childhood bedroom, sitting on the bed with its bucking horse bedspread, while the woman he—loved? No, *cared about*, that was it, he *cared about* Cat—was standing in the hallway looking for some sign of life.

He must care about her, because when he'd heard her arguing with Dora on the porch, he'd felt like his heart was going to break. Cat loved her niece, but she didn't have a clue how to handle her.

He knew from experience there was no way to force a teenaged girl to do something she didn't want to do. You had to let them go, let them grow up and make their own decisions. At a certain point, all you could do was watch them make a mess of things and try to protect them from the consequences.

He heard her shuffle her feet outside Viv's bedroom door. Then she heaved a heartbroken sigh.

Maybe Viv had gotten her tender heart from her father's side of the family, because he couldn't hear that without his own heart breaking a little. He pictured her out there, alone in the hallway, her slender shoulders slumped. He pictured the sorrow in those blue eyes, the sad pout of that pretty little mouth.

And he stood up and opened the door.

Chapter 27

MACK STOOD ON THE THRESHOLD OF HIS CHILDHOOD bedroom and wished he hadn't opened the door. He'd pictured Cat looking sad, but she just looked pissed off.

And no wonder. He'd beaten the crap out of one of her clients. He'd shown a side of himself that probably didn't fit into the rarefied world of gallery openings and cocktail parties. He'd accused her of failing to protect her niece. And then he'd made a promise that affected her niece without asking her.

Of course, she didn't know that last part yet. And looking at her clenched fists and belligerent stance, he wasn't about to tell her.

He wasn't going to apologize, either. Not for anything. Trevor Maines was a danger to the group. Mack had felt it the moment he met the man. He hadn't just been protecting his daughter; he'd been protecting Cat, too. And if Dora didn't want to paint, nobody was going to make her do it. If Cat wasn't comfortable with that, it was her problem, not his.

What *was* his problem was the way he felt about her. The two of them were a total mismatch. It was like Little Red Riding Hood cozying up to the Big Bad Wolf.

But he wanted her. Wanted her now, in his arms, wanted to wipe that scowl off her face and kiss her until she softened in his arms and forgot what she was so all-fired mad about.

Maybe she sensed what he was thinking, because she seemed to wilt as he watched her. The shoulders rounded, the scowl softened, and when he stepped back from the door she walked into the room as if he'd invited her.

"Hey." She didn't sound happy to see him, but she didn't sound mad, either.

She sounded numb.

He really couldn't blame her. She'd had a hell of a night. So had he, for that matter. Maybe she'd let him comfort her. At least then he'd have something to hang onto.

Because nothing felt solid anymore. The ranch was starting to feel like a roadside attraction he'd seen once on the way to a rodeo—"The Wonder Spot." The "spot" had been a rickety little house set back in some trees. It looked like a perfectly normal building from the outside, but when you stepped in the door it was like entering a fun-house mirror. The floors slanted, the walls tilted, and you lost your sense of which way was up and where the floor was.

He felt that way now, as if someone had altered the reality he'd always depended on. As if the ranch's subtle, soothing gravity had been replaced by a world with no laws and no safe place to stand. Not even here, in his old room. Still decorated with all the trappings of boyhood, it had always been his safe place.

Suddenly, he was acutely conscious of those trappings. This room might be full of happy memories, but it was hardly an appropriate place to entertain a woman. It had hardly been an appropriate place for his mother to install Trevor Maines either, but he hadn't had any say in that.

He looked around at the bedding, an old-fashioned print with tiny cowboys on bucking horses scattered amid hats, boots, and saddles. On the wall above it, 4-H prize ribbons vied for space with old photos of his boyhood triumphs. There was a photo of him with his first horse, the obliging and ever-patient Smoky. Another of him as a gangling teen, kneeling beside the high-dollar steer he'd raised for a long-ago state fair. On the opposite wall were rodeo photos, ranging from his first bronc ride to a more recent picture of him standing at the rail at Frontier Days with Bobby Mote and Kelly Timberman.

The furniture, as well as the decoration, was unabashedly masculine. And just inside the door, looking as dainty as a princess, was Cat.

She still looked pissed off. Without thinking, he stepped close and wrapped his fingers around her upper arms.

"I'm sorry," he said.

Where the hell had that come from?

"You are?" She looked skeptical.

"Probably not for any of the right things," he said. "I'm sorry you're angry with me. Sorry you had to see that side of me. Protecting Viv is—well, it's what I do."

She shrugged him off and scanned the room, taking in the old-fashioned decor. At least the place was clean.

"What happened, happened," she said. "It's over and done."

"I was protecting you too."

She stared at him a long time—a hard, cold stare. He returned her gaze as honestly as he could, willing her to understand, and gradually her stiff posture relaxed and her eyes went sweet and soft again.

"I know you don't need it," he said. "But it's what I do."

"You're right. I don't need it." She dropped her voice to a whisper. "I don't need it, but sometimes — sometimes I want it."

He wrapped his arms around her and she rested her head against his chest, tucking her hands into his back pockets. He held her a moment, then reached back with one hand and swung the bedroom door shut.

"Good," he said. "Let me show you what *I* want."

Cat couldn't believe she was here in Mack's childhood home, necking in the bedroom like a teenager. The ridiculous bucking horse decor was a not-so-subtle reminder that he'd been a boy here. A rough-and-tumble kid by the look of things, obsessed with horses and ranching even then.

Well, he wasn't a boy anymore. He'd proven that just moments ago, when he'd punched Trevor into unconsciousness.

She didn't like violence, or violent men. She went for brains, not brawn. But right now, pressed up against all that brawn, she was starting to rethink her priorities. Mack Boyd wasn't a master painter or a hotshot intellectual like Ames, but being with him made her dizzy and breathless and confused and weirdly, ecstatically happy — as long as she didn't ruin the feeling by thinking too hard.

Because feeling was better than thinking. She needed to shut out her problems with Dora and her worries about her career. She needed to just *be*, here with Mack.

Be here now. Zen cowgirl.

Hard as she tried, though, the thought that Viv was right next door kept her from surrendering to the moment.

"Viv," she said. "We can't…"

"It's an old house. Thick walls." He'd clearly thought this through, probably before opening the door. "We'll just have to be quiet," he whispered, running his hands up her arms and over her shoulders. "Very, very quiet."

Grabbing the collar of her shirt, he tugged her face to his and kissed her.

The touch of his lips set off something desperate in her, something primal and basic and real. Grabbing the hem of his T-shirt, she bunched it in her fists and yanked it up over his chest. She wanted his bare skin under her hands. She wanted to feel the flex of his muscles as he embraced her. She wanted to feel his skin warm under her touch.

She wanted everything, all over again. And again. And again.

The shirt was up and over his head in one breathless moment, and they kept on kissing while his fingers worked at the buttons on her shirt. He'd only made it halfway down the front before he shoved it off her shoulders, briefly trapping her in the fabric with her arms pinned to her side. She writhed and twisted, then shrugged it away. The cool cotton slid down over her hips and pooled at her feet, leaving her standing before him in just a bra and jeans.

She felt a quick flash of self-consciousness, a jolt of worry about her belly being a little soft, her breasts a little small. But when he looked down at her, his eyes ate her up. Clearly, he liked what he saw.

His rough hands slid around her waist, skimming up her rib cage and slipping into her bra, squeezing and teasing and making her crazy. His touch left a trail of sweet sensation in its wake as he slid one hand to her back and unhooked her bra with an expertise that could only come from experience.

"You've done that a few times before," she murmured, smiling into his neck.

"I have."

"Here?" she asked. "In this room?"

He paused and she wondered if he was going to lie.

"Yes."

She felt a whoosh of relief. She liked his frankness, the way he couldn't help but tell the truth. It was one of the things that separated him from all the other men she knew. With Mack, the truth deep inside things seemed to matter more than the surface.

"It was never like this, though." His whisper was hushed, almost reverent as his lips skimmed the curve between her shoulder and neck. "Never anything like this."

She glanced at the door. "Does that lock?"

In answer, he leaned over and pushed a button in the doorknob with a satisfying click.

They sank down on the side of the small bed as if they'd agreed on the timing, both of them fumbling with belt buckles, snaps, and zippers. And then they were naked, gloriously naked, facing each other in the dim light that glowed through the curtains. The moonlight was warmed by a yellow lamp at the corner of the eaves that lit the whole front yard, and the combination created an ethereal, enchanted space. She could see all of him. Not just his body, but his heart, shining in his eyes.

This was what she needed. Not protection, but feeling. Warmth. Love.

She chased that last thought away, wiping it out of her mind like a wayward streak of paint on an otherwise perfect canvas. Not love. Just lust. Sex.

They stretched out on the bed, facing each other, and he stroked her hair, letting his palm drift under her jaw and cup her chin so he could look into her eyes. There was a question there, and she answered it by pulling closer and closing her eyes. Love, lust, want, need—the words just didn't matter anymore. Neither did her job or her future.

She lifted her hands over her head and felt the current they'd created tug her away from reality. She was floating like a leaf on flowing water, riding swift, unstoppable waves as his hands ran over her body. He paused and she swirled in an eddy, then caught the current and the two of them were swept away.

His hands moved swiftly over her body, stroking the wings of her collarbones, smoothing her shoulders, shaping her breasts. Then his rough thumbs scraped her nipples and he kissed her, greedy and hard. Hands, lips, tongue—it all blended together as he moved down her body, his fingers tracing her ribs, trailing down her side, teasing with soft touches that almost, almost went where she wanted them.

And then he found the heart of her and set loose a flood of need and emotion she couldn't contain. She heard a small cry and didn't realize it had been her until he put his mouth over hers to stifle the sound.

"Shhhh."

"I can't help it. We have to stop. I'm going to…"

She broke off and bit her lip to keep from moaning as he kissed her again and stroked her center, immersing her in sensation and then lifting her slowly up, up, up— until she broke the surface and gasped. The air around her warmed and hummed. Incredibly, she kept on rising, floating impossibly high, flying on the invisible edge between dreams and reality.

Cat blinked her way back to reality to find herself resting against his chest. His heart pumped under her cheek, the sound seeming to fill the room with a slow, steady drumbeat.

Across the room, his face looked out at her from a half-dozen framed photos, years younger. Mack riding a wild horse. Mack with his buddies, grinning like the troublemaker he was. Mack with some kind of enormous cow on a leash.

She knew the pictures held clues to his past, to who he was, but it was a childhood so foreign to her he might as well have grown up in India. She should study them sometime, look for clues.

But what did that matter, really? He was whoever she wanted him to be. They wouldn't be together long enough for his past to matter. Or his future.

The thought made her suddenly sad, but she knew what would make her happy. Sitting up, she straddled him and reached for the nightstand, feeling for the drawer pull. Hopefully he had protection somewhere.

"Already got that." He held up a shiny square of foil and tore it open. He put it on with quick, efficient motions and she reminded herself he'd done this before—who knew how many times, with how many women in rodeo towns all across the West.

She felt herself shrink with the thought, as if she mattered less in the world if she didn't matter to him.

But that wasn't what this was about. She was making her own choice here, finding her own satisfaction. She wasn't like the women that hung around rodeos, hoping to bag a champion. She was herself, Cat Crandall, taking all the experiences life had to offer. Looking for beauty in every corner of the world, and finding it here, in the dark, in this man's bed.

Mack watched Cat's face, searching for any trace of doubt. He'd never expected to have this chance again. They'd spent the past few hours proving how incompatible they were, and here they were, blending like they were born to be together. It didn't make any sense, but he wasn't about to question her, or remind her that she'd written him off three times that day.

She smiled and those blue eyes glowed with a shimmering heat.

"Go," she said.

She straddled him and bent to kiss him as she rubbed herself against him. Her hair fell forward, creating a tangled curtain, and he watched her face as those blue eyes darkened, then turned soft and met his so honestly that it felt like the boundary between them blurred.

He'd expected heat from Cat since the day he'd first met her. He'd known she'd be incredible in bed. She had a light, bright energy about her that was full of promise, but he hadn't expected to bond on this level.

This obviously wasn't a one-night stand. It wasn't a two-night stand either. He didn't know how two people could create a relationship when they lived worlds apart. But somehow, he had to hold onto her beyond this brief summer romance.

Looking into her eyes, he felt like she could read his thoughts. She had to know he was falling for her. For a moment, she seemed to look through him, but then their gazes met and he knew, as surely as if she'd said it aloud, that she was falling too.

She eased herself down, letting him slide inside. Her gaze heated and her resistance seemed to melt as he reached up and framed her breasts with his big hands, moving his thumbs over the nipples as she moved with a sinuous grace. The two of them dipped and floated, rose to the sparkling surface and then dove into deep water, clinging together in a vast, blurry darkness where there was nothing but them, the two of them together, sharing breath and time and sensation.

Arching his back, he savored the sweet bliss of it, rocking slowly, then faster, feeling her clench in another climax as his heart lifted to join the stars that swirled in a dark perfect sky inside him.

When they'd finished, he held her, resting her head on his chest, and was thankful that she couldn't see his face. There was no way to hide what he was feeling. Who'd ever think two people so different could touch each other so deeply in such a short time? He felt like this woman was forever and everything. His life was in turmoil, and she was the knot at its center, the one thing in the world that held it together. The one thing he had to hold onto.

He knew the knot probably wouldn't hold. She'd leave, and he'd lose her. But he'd always want her, and always remember. His world had shifted forever onto a new axis, one that had him slipping and sliding and hanging on for dear life.

He looked up at the slanted rafters above the bed and thought back to that roadside attraction with its crazy angles and angled beams. The Wonder Spot.

Cat buried her face in his shoulder and smothered a laugh. "I never heard it called *that* before."

"What?"

She looked up at him with a playful smile. "You were talking in your sleep. I think you said 'Wonder Spot.'"

"Oh. Yeah." He thought about explaining it, but he didn't feel like he had to. He'd never had this kind of deep-down harmony with a woman—never wanted it, actually. But right now he felt like he could stay here forever, holding her in the quiet night.

"We're in the right place," he said, tightening his arms around her. "Right here. Right now."

She snuggled closer. "Yeah," she said. "I know what you mean."

Chapter 28

CAT WOKE TO THE CLATTER OF MORNING BIRDSONG and a nasty grating noise. Lifting her head off the pillow, she rubbed her eyes. She was back in the Heifer House, in her own small bunkhouse bed. She could barely remember how she'd gotten there. It had been almost dawn before she and Mack parted ways. She'd tiptoed like a sneak-thief past the girls' room, slipping into the bunkhouse with her clothes rumpled and her hair in a bed-head tangle.

Dressing hastily in a pair of jeans and the wrinkled shirt from the day before, she shoved her feet into her shoes and staggered outside. Madeleine was rummaging around in the chuckwagon while Mack scraped out a black iron Dutch oven with an old tin spatula.

"Biscuits didn't rise," he grunted. "Have some dough. There's coffee, too."

Madeleine nudged another pot closer to the fire. "That's what you get for trying to cook without me. Don't know why you had to start so early."

Cat watched her students spill from the two bunkhouses in various states of grogginess. "Dora," she said. "Where's Dora?"

Mack cleared his throat and looked uncomfortable. "Ah, she's back at the barn. Vivian's showing her some stuff about the horses." He handed her an enamel cup of dark, hot coffee and a golden blob of heated dough.

She bit into the biscuit and washed it down with coffee. Mack didn't seem to want to look at her, or talk. She'd expected some shared smiles, the heady feeling of a secret kept. But he kept shifting his weight, clearing his throat, busying himself with the fire.

Great. She'd thought last night was something special. Obviously, he was embarrassed about it.

Not that it mattered. It was nothing but a fling.

He stopped fooling with the fire mid-poke and his gaze zeroed in on hers so strongly she wondered if she'd spoken aloud. He glanced around to make sure no one was looking and brought his finger to his lips and smiled.

Shh.

Her heart lifted, suddenly light as dandelion fluff with the small joy of sharing a secret. He went back to poking at the fire, and she went back to her biscuit, but the day had taken on a new shine.

"Sleep okay?" she asked Ed, doing her best to sound casual.

"Not really. Charles snores like a soldier," the old man said.

"That's right." Mack grinned across the fire at Ed. "He had the elk bugling, and it's only May." He made a whooping sound that was somewhere between a hollow cough and a yodel. Cat had never heard elk bugling, but she suspected it was a good imitation.

Charles shrugged off the joke with a laugh. Sitting cross-legged on the ground, he looked like a good-natured Buddha. "Where we headed today, trail boss?"

"Back to the canyon." Mack eyed the other students, who were lowering themselves onto the benches with varying degrees of stiffness. "You all up for it?"

"You bet," Ed grunted.

"We're rarin' to go," Emma said, almost falling onto the bench in her effort to sit down without bending her knees.

The girls finally turned up, providing a sprightly contrast to the old folks, and raced through breakfast. To Cat's surprise, the two of them deliberately chose to share her bench, and though they were too intent on eating to talk much, she felt as if she and Dora had somehow cleared the air.

Maybe her niece had just needed to get her anger out of her system. Cat resolved to listen today, to give her a sounding board. She wouldn't take anything personally or get defensive. She'd try to accept Dora for Dora, instead of trying to change her.

Both girls helped Maddie gather up the dirty dishes and load them into the chuckwagon, but the woman waved them away. "You go on and help with the horses," she said to Dora. "I've got all day to take care of this stuff."

Dora trotted over to Mack, who soon had her checking the knots that lashed their equipment to the pack horses while he tested cinches and adjusted bits on the riding horses.

"Ms. Crandall?" Viv was standing in front of Cat, looking uncertain. "Can I, um, talk to you for a minute?"

"Sure. I've been wanting to talk to you."

"Dora and I were talking yesterday."

Cat smiled. "I know. And I'm so glad. She needs a friend right now."

"She's really enjoying working with my dad on the horses."

"Yes, she is. Your father's a good guy." Cat hoped the warmth that rushed to her face didn't show.

"Yeah. But the horse thing—it doesn't really work for me."

Cat nodded. It was clear Viv was no cowgirl. She wore jeans, as they all did, but they were low-rise designer models sporting artful rips in the fabric and a splashy acid wash. Her top was a complicated, drapey knit number that emphasized her cute, youthful figure without looking slutty, and she wore a crystal-studded headband in her carefully-styled hair.

"I really like art. Drawing and stuff." The girl was a little motormouth, talking fast as if she was trying to make it through a long script in her allotted time with Cat. "I was wondering if I could work with you—with the other students, I mean. You wouldn't have to help me much or anything. I'd just kind of watch. Like auditing a class."

Cat paused. This was awkward. The price for the workshops was high, and she'd been cautioned to let the company know if any tagalongs joined the group. It was a money-making operation, after all, and they didn't want to let her services go for free.

But how could she turn down a teenager who was interested in what she had to offer? Viv looked so excited, twisting her body from side to side with her hands clasped in front of her as she waited for Cat's answer.

If only Dora was that eager to please.

"I guess we could find some equipment for you to use," Cat said. "I'm sure the others would be happy to loan you some materials." She was sure this was true. Paint and watercolor paper were expensive, but the older people would probably fall over each other in their eagerness to help a young person.

She eyed the horses, who were stamping and blowing in a long line along the fence. "The problem is the easels. Everybody brought their own, so there's no extra."

"Oh, that's okay." Viv's pretty face lit up in a smile. "Dora said I could use hers."

"But then what's she going to do?"

"She'll help my dad with the horses." Viv's grin widened. "We're trading places! Isn't that perfect? I mean, she loves horses and I love to paint, and we were each stuck doing the wrong job. This way we'll both have fun and my dad'll still have help."

Cat drew back. Dora wasn't going to paint?

She wasn't surprised at that decision. What surprised her was the sharp sense of loss she felt when she thought of the two of them working apart, rather than working together on their paintings. She wanted to help Dora. Teach her something. It wasn't about the painting; it was the togetherness she wanted.

"You'd better talk to your dad," she told Viv. Mack knew how she felt. He'd bail her out on this.

"Oh, he says it's okay." The girl danced in place. "He says I'm a whiner anyway." She grinned, as if her father had said she was beautiful or smart. "He seemed pretty happy about trading me for Dora. We decided last night."

"You and your dad cooked this up last night?" Cat narrowed her eyes. When would they have talked about it last night? He hadn't said anything to her about it when they were together.

"Well, Dora and I cooked it up. But Dad said okay."

"*When* last night?"

"After dinner."

The stab of loss was joined by an equally sharp jab of betrayal. Mack knew what this trip with Dora meant to her. How could he so carelessly take away the one bond she had with the girl, and then conveniently forget to mention it when they were together? It wasn't like they hadn't had time.

She shot him a dirty look but recovered when she realized Viv was still standing in front of her with a pleading expression on her face.

"Okay," she said. "Fine. But if Dora changes her mind, we'll find a way for both of you to paint." She smiled as a thought occurred to her. "You two are getting to be such good friends, you might want her to help you. Then your dad'll just have to handle everything on his own." She slid her eyes toward Mack, who seemed absorbed in the horses. She wondered if he was faking it, avoiding her gaze. "I'm sure he can manage. He's such a tough, self-sufficient guy."

He was going to be self-sufficient now, that was for sure. He'd messed with her relationship with her niece, then conveniently forgotten about it when he got a chance to get happy with her.

She shot him a glare and he turned as if he'd felt it burning into his back. Once again his eyes met hers, but this time there was no smile, no secret—just guilt. He knew damn well what he'd done.

She felt the bond between them snap, sharply as a broken stick, and just like that the day lost its shine.

Chapter 29

MACK FOLLOWED THE RIDERS AS THEY HEADED INTO the home stretch. They were strung out in single file, tipping and sagging in the saddle like a row of crooked fence posts. The day at the canyon had been long, and the route was the rockiest one on the ranch.

The horses lightened their step as they approached the corral, no doubt looking forward to burying their muzzles in the watering tank. Everybody was beat, including him, but the day had gone surprisingly well despite the tension between him and Cat.

She had a right to be angry. He should have talked to her before he approved the plan. And once he'd approved it, he probably should have told her about it before he'd—whatever they'd done last night. But he'd honestly forgotten. She'd looked so beautiful, and he'd felt—*bonded* to her somehow. He still did, in spite of her stony silence. It was impossible to explain, even to himself.

He'd worked all day to find a peace offering, knowing the one thing she wanted was a key to Dora's thoughts. He was pretty sure he'd succeeded in easing open at least a small break in the barrier the girl so resolutely kept closed. There were no easy answers, but at least they'd have an idea of where to start.

They. He needed to stop thinking that way. A week ago, he'd wondered if he was capable of real love for a woman. Now he knew that not only could he fall in love, but he could fall so hard his heart would shatter when this woman walked away.

A picture of Cat lying naked in his bed crossed his mind—her slim hips, the small but perfect breasts, the hair tumbled on the pillow. She might walk away, but that memory would stay with him for a lifetime.

Which meant he had no regrets.

"You going to help me with this or just stand there mooning over my aunt?" Dora asked. She was brushing Spanky, holding out his tail to one side as she detangled it.

"I'm helping."

"Go see her if you want." She combed through the tail with her fingers one last time and led the horse to his stall. "I can take care of the grooming."

"Nope. We're a team."

She grinned, and they worked in quiet unison for a while, grooming the horses and getting them fed and stabled. She was a good little horsewoman. He'd have to tell Cat how well she'd done.

She'd been cheerful, too. He was willing to bet her grief hadn't touched her all afternoon. Horses were good therapy, and the landscape here was healing. He knew that from experience.

"You can go relax a while, hon," he said as he shut the last stall. The horses were settled for the night, chewing their evening ration. He just needed to coil some rope and stow some saddles and he'd be done, too.

"Aunt Cat's probably already at the campfire," Dora said. "I could finish up."

"No, you go," he said. "I doubt she's speaking to me. She wasn't too happy about our arrangement."

Dora's brow creased in concern. "Viv said she was okay with it."

"Viv sees what she wants to see," he said. "Optimism runs in the family."

"Must be nice." She shoved her hands in her pockets and strolled off. It seemed like the day had transformed her. She'd changed from a sulky city girl to a bona fide cowgirl somewhere on the trail. As far as he was concerned, it was a change for the better.

"Come talk to her soon, though," she called over her shoulder. "You've got to make up before the barn dance. I *so* want to see you make her do the two-step."

He groaned. Tomorrow was mostly a day off for him. The students would be evaluating and reviewing the work they'd done so far, and then splitting up to paint scenes around the ranch—the barn, the horses, the ranch house itself.

He was looking forward to a day immersed in the real business of ranching—checking the herd in the north pasture, riding fence, taking care of a few small repairs around the place. What he wasn't looking forward to was the barn dance scheduled for the evening. Madeleine had hired some country band from town, and they were going to string chili pepper lights between the two bunkhouses and have a hoedown. A good time would be had by all—as long as you liked to dance.

"Come on, you said you know how to two-step," Dora urged.

"Yeah. My mom made me learn when I was six. Trust me, it's not going to be pretty."

As a matter-of-fact, it was going to be hell. His

mother had invited half the county to join them, including the Humboldts from out past Two Shot. Emily
Humboldt had been his best girl all through high school.
He could still picture the look of betrayal on her face
when he'd announced at a graduation party that he'd
filled his PRCA card and was going pro on the rodeo
circuit. Evidently, she'd expected a diamond to go with
her graduation tassel.

He'd run into her a few times since, and she'd seemed
friendly enough. But the barn dance setting reminded
him too much of the past, and there was a good chance
it would remind Emily, too.

He pitched the last saddle onto a sawhorse in the tack
room and headed for the fire pit. He'd planned on going
up to bed, avoiding a likely conflict with Cat. He'd
discovered during his marriage that it was best to let
tempers on both sides cool before revisiting an issue.

But Dora was right; they'd be thrown together at the
barn dance whether Cat wanted to see him or not, so he
might as well make nice now.

If she'd let him.

It didn't look promising. She was sitting alone on
the far side of the fire, hugging herself and staring
moodily into the flames. He ought to leave her to it
and count himself lucky for escaping another difficult
relationship—along with inevitable heartbreak. But
something about her dedication to Dora touched him.
How had she put it? *I love her like crazy—probably too
much*. That was something he could understand.

As he approached, Cat jerked to her feet and stalked
over to where the Delaneys were chatting about the
day's adventures. Okay, she didn't want to talk to him.

But he could talk to the Delaneys too, and she could hardly be rude in front of her clients.

He joined the small knot of artists and gave Cat a casual grin. "How'd my daughter do?"

He knew the answer. Viv had done great. She'd stayed on the fringes of the group at first, being careful not to take time away from the paying students, but her work was good enough to attract attention and the others had noticed. Cat had, too. She'd spent some time with Viv, explaining some of those art terms she was always dropping like small, incomprehensible verbal bombs into her lessons.

"She did well," Cat said.

He kept grinning and rolled one hand in a "keep going" gesture.

"Really well. You have a very talented daughter." She turned back to Abby and Emma, obviously hoping to resume their previous conversation and shut him out, but the women weren't playing her game.

"She's a sweet girl," Emma said, patting Mack's arm. "You did a good job raising her."

Abby nodded. "You sure did. Don't you think so, Cat?"

Cat nodded, her eyes darting around in search of an escape route.

"In fact, you probably want to talk to Cat about her future. Maybe Viv would like a career in art someday."

The two ladies wandered off, giving each other congratulatory winks. Mack wondered why they didn't just quit faking casual and high-five each other on their matchmaking success.

Chapter 30

CAT WATCHED THE OLD FOLKS GO, FEELING UTTERLY abandoned. They thought they were doing her a favor, matching her up with Mack. But after the way he'd betrayed her, she didn't even want to talk to him.

"Viv did fine," she said, and turned to go.

He put a hand on her shoulder and she stopped, trying to decide if she should shrug it off or spin and smack him. Unfortunately, her indecision allowed the warmth of his hand to seep into her skin, and she felt her heart soften in spite of herself.

"Viv's not the one I wanted to talk to you about," he said.

She turned. "Oh. You're going to tell me about your day with Dora?"

He nodded.

"I'm surprised she hasn't sworn you to secrecy."

"I wouldn't agree to that."

"Well, you agreed to everything else. You told her she could skip out on the workshop and mess around with horses all day. Thanks a lot, Mack. I told you she's what matters most to me. I wanted to spend the day with her. You knew that."

She shot him a glare that should have frozen him on the spot—although it was a challenge to freeze something as stunningly, ridiculously hot as this cowboy. He'd come straight over from the barn, and his chambray shirt was rumpled and flecked with hay. The sleeves were rolled up to his elbows, displaying ropy, muscular forearms, and a streak of dirt marred the faint stubble on his jaw.

Maybe he was right. Maybe things were too fancy in Chicago. Because she'd never seen a man so simply and viscerally masculine back East.

She shook her head. They were supposed to be talking about Dora. Maybe it wasn't all his fault they'd gotten sidetracked last night. She felt her anger easing and made one final effort to stoke up the heat.

"I'm trying to help her, and painting is my way in. It's the one thing we have in common. And you took that away."

"I didn't take it away. Dora didn't want to do it."

"She doesn't want to get up in the morning, either. She doesn't want to make nice with the other students. But she does it because she has to. She would have participated in the workshop, too."

"So you want to force her to? I thought you wanted her to be happy. And I can tell you, she was happier today than I've ever seen her."

She scraped the toe of her boot in the dirt, as if drawing a line he couldn't cross. "You knew what the girls were going to do. You *knew*."

She blinked fast. *Do not cry. Do not cry.*

"But you didn't tell me. You forgot all about it and let me be ambushed the next day. Meanwhile, you…" Her tongue felt thick and clumsy, her throat tight. "You helped yourself."

—◆◆◆—

Mack figured he'd better start talking before Cat defined what they'd done last night in terms he didn't want to hear.

"I really did forget," he said. "I wasn't playing you." His tongue seemed to have grown and his throat was tight. He knew what he wanted to say, but he couldn't get the words out. "I couldn't help myself."

Lame. Just lame.

She apparently thought so too, because she rolled her eyes. "Well, you obviously could help yourself to me."

He looked down at the toes of his boots and scuffed at the dirt. "That seems to come naturally."

Her frown tightened, and he waited for the storm to start. He had no excuse, and she was about to tear into him. This was the way every relationship he had ended.

The worst part of it was, he couldn't defend himself—because she was right. What he'd done had been wrong on so many levels he couldn't even count them.

"Look." He shoved his hands in his pockets and leaned against the corner of the bunkhouse. "I'm sorry."

Her lips twitched again. "You apologized last night, too."

"You think I apologized to get you into bed?"

She glanced right and left and he realized he'd spoken pretty loudly. Fortunately, nobody reacted. Although Abby and Em weren't far away, they were studiously keeping their eyes on each other. Probably pretending they couldn't hear so they could gather some juicy scuttlebutt.

"I meant what I said last night. I wasn't trying to manipulate you."

She stared at him for a moment and he braced

himself for a tongue-lashing. But to his surprise, she let out a laugh—a bubbling, overflowing, can't-help-it kind of laugh.

"This is ridiculous," she said. "It seems like our entire relationship has consisted of you apologizing to me. It's endless. You beat up my client. You seduce me in front of my niece. You give her permission to do exactly what I don't want her to do." The laugh trilled out again, floating through the night air, and several of the guests turned to look at them. "We alternate between having sex and apologizing."

He knew he shouldn't laugh with her. He shouldn't even smile. But he couldn't help it.

"Believe it or not, I'm actually trying to impress you," he said.

That made her laugh harder, in little bursts. She was holding her stomach. "That's what makes it so funny."

He tried to look insulted while she finished her fit of giggles, but it was tough not to join in. Finally, she got a grip on herself and looked up at him with shining eyes, her lips still quirked up at the corners.

Dang, she was gorgeous.

"I might have done something right today," he said cautiously.

That started the giggles again.

"No, seriously."

"Okay." She put one hand to her chest and sucked in a deep breath. "Look, you're a good person. You don't do anything out of meanness, and you don't lie. You protect the people you love. It's not that what you do isn't right. It's just—different. Different from anyone I know."

"Different from Ames Whitaker?"

"Very different."

"Is that such a bad thing?"

"I don't know." She giggled again. "Ask Trevor."

Now she had him laughing.

The storm of laughter finally cleared, leaving them both flushed and a little breathless.

"So what did you do right?" she asked.

"I got Dora talking," he said. "She told me some stuff that might help you figure out what's going on with her."

Cat glanced at the two older women, who were tilting toward them in their efforts to eavesdrop. She was surprised they hadn't used her laughter as an excuse to join them. Letting that goal trump their curiosity showed how determined they were to make the match.

But they wouldn't be able to resist much longer. She needed to remove temptation. She'd just consider it helping them through their recovery from terminal busybody-itis.

Grabbing Mack's arm, she towed him around the corner of the bunkhouse. He took full advantage of the move, maneuvering her against the wall so she was standing closer to him. That brought the scowl back.

"I just want to make sure we have privacy," she said. "I don't want to spread Dora's issues all over."

"I want to make sure we have privacy too." He looked down at her and thought about stealing that kiss again.

"Stop. This isn't some game." She shoved him away and he grudgingly took a step back.

"Okay. You're right." He probably shouldn't be teasing her. It was insensitive, considering how worried she was about her niece. But with her standing so close, it was hard to remember what he'd planned to talk to her about. All he could think to say was something like "please can we go back to bed," or "I want to rip that oversized shirt right off your tasty little body."

"Dora." He closed his eyes a second, wiping out the image of Cat naked in his bed and reorienting himself to the topic at hand. "She's angry with you, but mostly it's about her mother dying."

"Okay." She looked less than impressed.

"And…"

He suddenly realized how hard it was going to be to tell her what Dora had said. He'd been so glad to get to the bottom of the matter that he hadn't considered her feelings—just Dora's. Now he'd trapped himself into saying something that was bound to hurt her.

There was no way of putting it delicately. He was just going to have to spit it out.

"She resents you because she doesn't think it's fair," he said.

Cat wasn't going to let him off easy. "She doesn't think what's fair?"

"She doesn't think it's fair that her mother died. She thinks it should have been you."

Chapter 31

CAT STARED AT MACK FOR A MOMENT, ABSORBING HIS words, repeating them in her mind, wringing them of all the meaning she could.

She thinks it should have been you.

There was no surprise there. Nothing she didn't already know. Putting it into words made it sound stark and hurtful, but she'd sensed it long ago.

"Of course she does." She shrugged one shoulder. "Sometimes I feel the same way."

He blinked. "What?"

"It's just such lousy luck. Why did Edie have to get sick? Why couldn't it be someone who didn't have a child? It's natural for Dora to feel that way."

"I—I thought you'd be hurt."

She shook her head. "Not hurt. Just sad. She's lost so much." She scraped a line in the dirt with the toe of her boot. "So, that's all you've got?"

"Well, yeah," he said. "It took a lot to get that out of her, too. She kept saying she was fine, fine, fine. Typical female."

"Well, I guess that makes me atypical," she said. "Because I am most definitely not *fine*." She shoved off the wall, forcing him to either step back or let her slam into him.

He stepped back.

"I'm sorry." She raked her fingers through her hair.

"It's just that I know she hates me. I know she wishes I'd been the one to die instead of her mother. But that's a normal reaction to grief." She sighed. "I appreciate you trying, but there's something more there. She's flunking out of school. She'll barely speak to her father, or me. She's moody and sullen and we don't know what's going on in her head."

"She's a teenage girl. That's kind of normal."

"Not to this level it isn't."

"Well, if it's any help, she wasn't moody or sullen today. She was cheerful and helpful. She seemed happy most of the time, which is why I didn't bring up her mom until the last hour or so. Pushing her to talk doesn't get you anywhere. I hoped she'd bring it up, but she didn't. And when I brought it up, that's all she said."

"But she was happy?"

"With the horses, yeah. She enjoys that. And frankly, I think she was trying to shock me with that comment about you. Shock me, or hurt you. She must have known I'd tell you."

"Well, at least she was happy for a day. I've been worried her face would freeze in a permanent frown." Cat relaxed her own face, as if she was worried the same thing might happen to her. She gave Mack a tentative, heartbreaking half smile as she walked away. "I guess I should thank you for that. But we still haven't gotten to the root of the problem."

"Go find her," he said. "Talk to her. She's in a good mood for a change."

<center>~~~</center>

Cat found Dora in the kitchen, mustering up a snack for herself and Viv, dumping tortilla chips into a plastic bowl.

"Isn't that stuff for the dance tonight?"

"Aren't you supposed to be with your clients?" Dora scowled. "Quit telling me what to do."

Cat had hoped to start a casual conversation, but there was no hope of that. Folding her arms over her chest, she leaned against the counter.

"Come on, Dora. I'm not that bad. I brought you here because I thought you'd enjoy it. And you did enjoy it today, didn't you?"

"Yes, because I didn't have to do what you want."

"That's not what it's about."

"No?" Dora pitched her voice into a squeaky, nasal whine as she pulled a plastic tub of salsa from the refrigerator. "*You have to paint. You have to use your talent. You have to fulfill your amazing potential.*"

Cat decided to ignore the mockery and go for the heart of the message. "But I'm encouraging you, not telling you what to do. I'm sorry if it doesn't come across that way." She met Dora's eyes and tried to ignore the anger, resentment, and pure wrongheaded stubbornness she saw there. "I love you, hon. I just want what's best for you."

"You want me to be like you."

"No, I don't. I want you to be better than me." She cracked a crooked smile. "It shouldn't be too hard."

Dora wrenched open the salsa and the container tipped sideways, spilling a bright red streak on the counter. "I don't want to be anything like you."

Cat knew her niece was just spewing the anger that had built up from her mother's death. Maybe it was

cathartic for her. Maybe she could empty all her misery
and sorrow onto Cat and feel better. Cat was willing to
take it, but it wasn't easy.

"Dora, I know you miss your mom," she said. "Trust
me, I miss her too. And I'd have taken her place if I
could. I know you need her, and I know I'm a poor re-
placement. But I'm trying."

"You always *try*," Dora spat. "You always do the
right thing. Every day. All the time. My mom and I used
to make fun of you, you know that?" She grabbed the
end of a roll of paper towels and tugged, spinning a too-
long ribbon off the roll. Snapping it sideways, she tried
to tear it but only succeeded in unrolling more.

"Mom used to say you were all work and no play.
She said you didn't know how to live." She bunched
the towels in one hand and tore them off with the other.
"And then she was the one who died."

Cat reached for the wad of paper towels, wanting to
help, but Dora snatched them away.

"You would have been a good little cancer patient.
You would have had all the treatments—the ones she
wouldn't do." Dora was crying now as she scrubbed furiously at the streak of salsa. "You wouldn't have cared
if they hurt, or if they made you ugly."

"That was your mother's choice. They couldn't fix
her, you know." Cat put her hands on Dora's shoulders,
trying to stop the frantic scrubbing, but the girl shrugged
her off. "It only would have given her a few months."

"I know. Her choice. She could have lived longer, but
she was worried about being *ugly*." Dora slammed the wad
of paper towels into the sink and covered her eyes. "She
didn't want to live. But she had me! Why would she…"

She caught an escaping sob, sealing her lips shut and wiping away the tears. But when Cat put her arms around her, she let out a strangled cry and collapsed into sobs so visceral they were frightening. These weren't the dignified tears of a mourner at a funeral; these were the chest-heaving, shoulder-shaking tears of grief, raw and painful and heartbreakingly deep.

The heaves turned to shudders, the shudders to an occasional shiver. Cat let Dora collect herself, handing her a paper towel and stifling the urge to hand out platitudes.

Dora wiped her eyes and blew her nose noisily. "Never mind. It's stupid. It doesn't matter now anyway."

"Of course it matters, hon," Cat said. "Your mom loved you. She didn't want you to have to see her that way."

"Right." Dora pressed her lips together, refusing to succumb to tears again. "Because it wouldn't have been pretty." She turned to face Cat, her face pale with anger. "So I don't want to be an artist, okay? I don't want to make life all pretty and perfect." She grabbed the bowl, forgetting the salsa as she stormed out of the room. "There's nothing wrong with life being ugly and real. That's the way I want it."

―――

Mack was halfway through stringing the chili pepper light strings when a battered VW bus pulled up to the barn. Six men dressed head-to-toe in black stepped out and opened the back door. As they busied themselves hauling out large black cases, he saw the letters SWAT stencilled on the back of their shirts.

What the hell had Trevor told the cops?

"Can I help you?"

The biggest man set a case on the ground and turned. "We're the SWAT team."

Mack would have been alarmed, but the case was shaped suspiciously like a stand-up bass. Another man was unloading what appeared to be a guitar.

"And SWAT stands for..."

"Swing with a Twist," a smaller man said. He held a violin case, while his companions were pulling out various amplifiers and instruments. It looked like enough equipment to supply a philharmonic orchestra. "Little bit of big band, whole lot of country."

"Sounds great." Mack pitched in and helped them carry their supplies to a raised concrete foundation just beyond the bunkhouses. It had once been a small stable, but tonight it would serve as a stage.

The musicians and their helpers were soon hard at work, swarming over the makeshift stage and snaking orange electrical cords across the yard. Mack felt more in the way than anything, so he returned to his chores. The various artists were scattered around the grounds, absorbed in their paintings of various rustic buildings, fence posts, and views.

Musicians. Artists. Mack longed for the good old days, when all he had to deal with was cattle.

But the artists and musicians were the least of his problems. Gradually, the pasture by the barn began to fill with pickups and SUVs as neighbors arrived to join the festivities. He saw the Humboldts' big Ford diesel pull in, and he ducked into the barn. The longer he could put off this encounter the better.

He knew he should be playing host, but somehow the idea of talking to people seemed like torture.

Unless it was Cat. He missed her. And he'd probably keep on missing her while he watched her make nice with the neighbors and dance to the SWAT team. Because he couldn't go out there.

Not with Emily Humboldt on the premises. His relationship with Emily had been just like his relationship with Cat, but without the sex. One apology after another. And then he'd announced he was going pro on the rodeo circuit, without a clue that she was expecting a different kind of announcement.

He'd made the announcement at a graduation party, with the whole town present. He'd enumerated all the stops along the way, enthusiastically tracing out a road to the National Finals Rodeo that would take him all over the West, sometimes to more than one rodeo a day.

He'd thought she'd be happy for him. She was from a rodeo family, after all. He'd trained at her father's arena, and she'd cheered him on. But apparently, she'd expected things to stay that way, with only one real difference: she'd still be cheering him on, he'd still be hanging at her father's ranch, but she'd have a diamond on her finger.

Since then, he'd ridden in every arena in the West except the Humboldts'. He'd managed to steer clear of them even when he'd come home to visit. So his memory of Emily was still that shocked, sad face that had greeted his announcement.

It would have been easier if she'd been angry. He still felt bad about hurting her, but he hadn't wanted his life to end here on the ranch.

A half hour later he ran out of the busywork that let him stay in the barn. He'd reorganized the tack room, swept out the alleyway, and was straightening tools in the shop when a voice piped up behind him.

"Hi, Mack."

He turned to see Emily framed in the doorway, just as Cat had been a couple days ago. Her silhouette was sleek and neat, her shiny dark blonde hair spilling out from under a neatly creased Resistol, her jeans cupping her hips like a second skin.

"Long time no see." She stepped into the barn and sat down on a stack of hay bales by the door. "You look good."

She smiled, and to his surprise, he found himself smiling back. She was feminine in a big-boned, busty way, with high Scandinavian cheekbones and a generous mouth. He knew she still barrel raced at her dad's arena now and then, and the sport had given her the sinewy muscles of a born horsewoman.

"You do too." He was surprised to find he meant it.

She leaned back against the wall, a half smile tilting her lips, and considered him with an up-and-down appraisal. If a man looked at a woman that way, he'd be out of line. But it wasn't a sexual stare; it seemed more as if she was trying to figure out who he'd become in all the years since they'd seen each other.

"So are you done with rodeo?" she asked.

It was the question he'd dreaded. He'd been certain she would have settled down with someone by now and had a passel of kids. It was what she'd always wanted, but his mother said she'd stayed single all this time.

Surely she hadn't been waiting for him.

"I guess I am for a while," he said, treading carefully. "I need to stay here until we get the dude ranch going. Help out."

"That's good. I mean, for your mom." She cocked her head and watched him with narrowed eyes, like a snake watching a bird. He shuffled his feet, feeling as if they were suddenly three sizes too big. Clearing his throat, he struggled to think of something to say.

"I heard your marriage didn't work out," she said. "I'm so sorry."

He nodded, wondering where this conversation was going.

"I met your daughter, though. She's a beauty."

"Yeah." At least they could agree on one thing.

Silence settled over them, thick and awkward. He looked down at his feet, scraping a line in the dust, and then turned his attention back to the tools, fooling with a shovel and a posthole digger. He glanced at Emily, then quickly glanced away.

She laughed, her face relaxing into a wide, honest grin. "Don't worry, Mack. I'm not here to drag you off to a life of dinner parties and diaper-changing."

"Good. I mean…" He put his hands in his pockets, pulled them out, then hooked his thumbs in his belt loops. How could he make it clear to Emily that she still wasn't what he wanted—without being hopelessly rude? "Dinner parties aren't really my thing."

"I know." She stood, and he envied her ease and good humor. Emily had always been comfortable in her own skin. He didn't know why he hadn't stuck with her. Nor did he know why she didn't do anything for him now. She just wasn't his type.

She stepped toward him and touched his arm. He tensed, uneasy with the unexpected contact.

"There's nothing to worry about, Mack. I'm not here

to lure you into my lair. You did me a big favor when you walked away."

"Really?" He remembered the tears and recriminations, and the stony silence that followed.

"Really. Oh, I know I gave you a hard time about it. But I needed to step out on my own." Her eyes took on a happy glow. "I'm doing all the publicity work for the arena. Attendance is up almost fifty percent. And we were voted Best Small Town Rodeo by *Western Horseman* last year."

He nodded. "That's good."

"I was trying to define myself with a relationship, but I needed to cut loose and find myself. And I did." She swept off her hat and raked one hand through her hair. "So how about you? Did you find what you were looking for out there?"

He opened his mouth to answer, then simply shook his head. If Emily was looking for revenge, she'd found it. Here she was, confident and sure of herself, content with her place in the world, and he was still—what was he doing, anyway? Searching for something, that was for sure.

He just didn't know what the hell it was.

Chapter 32

NEIGHBORS AND BAND MEMBERS THRONGED AROUND the fire pit, working their way through plates of slow-cooked ribs, beans, and the inevitable biscuits. It was nearly dark before the SWAT team took the stage, tuning up with a series of squeaks and squawks that set Mack's teeth on edge.

He liked music well enough; it was dancing that made him nervous. His mother was already arranging the guests in two neat rows and teaching them the basic elements of country line dancing. Emily was front and center, hands on hips, confidently leading the group as the band started up a rousing up-tempo version of "San Antonio Rose." Madeleine called out the steps, clapping her hands.

"Kick one, two, and *kick* three, four. Spin and turn and clap! One, *two*, and three…"

The students dutifully spun and kicked, clapped and turned, following her lead. Gradually the mishmash of separate steps turned into a choreographed chorus line as everyone caught on and fell into matching rhythms. The students had hauled out their best cowboy duds for the occasion, but Cat was dressed as her sweet city self, in a glittery, loose-fitting top and a mass of sparkling beads draped around her neck. Bangles dangled at her wrists, and a pair of gypsy hoops hung from her earlobes, winking as they caught the firelight.

He'd gotten used to the simplicity of those big shirts she wore for painting and forgotten what an exotic, otherworldly creature she was. She hadn't dressed like this since that first day he'd seen her. Her jewelry swayed as she danced, and he knew if he stepped closer it would chime together with a faint gypsy jingle.

Her steps were more dutiful than graceful, and she certainly couldn't match Emily's enthusiasm. But Mack couldn't help watching her. It was that danged top, the way it skimmed her curves and draped over her hips. All he could think about was running his fingers over the silky smooth fabric, brushing the tips of her breasts, and watching her shiver in response.

But he wasn't about to join the line. Cowboys might dance in music videos, but those were barstool cowboys—Nashville types who wore the hat and boots as a costume on Saturday nights.

Ed was evidently happy to be a barstool cowboy. The old man was executing the steps with his trademark enthusiasm for all things Western, almost falling over as he lifted one foot to slap the side of his boot, then spun in a circle.

Cat flashed Mack a tight smile, but mostly she seemed preoccupied, staring straight ahead as she danced. It wasn't until the band started trading solos, riffing on the infectious melody of Stevie Ray Vaughan's "Honeybee," that she seemed to come alive. As the fiddle player careened up and down the scale, unreeling a tune that sounded more old-style blues than cowboy, she glanced up and down the line. She did one last shuffle and kick, then faded back into the shadows.

Impulsively, he strode through the crowd edging the

dance floor and went in search of her. He didn't have to look far before a glint of metal caught his eye, then a flash of pale skin. She'd backed into the darkness under the eaves of the Heifer House. Her eyes closed, she swayed with the beat, lost in the music and some sweet faraway dream.

Tilting her head back, she twisted her hands and stretched them over her head in a sinuous motion that echoed the grace of the fiddle player's fingers on the fretboard. There was almost no moon and a faint mist obscured the stars, so she was lit mostly by the remnants of firelight that cut through the darkness. Light flared up in her hair as she spun, then glanced off the curve of her swaying hip and lit the pale underside of one arm.

She obviously thought she was alone. A flash of firelight stroked her face and he realized her eyes were still closed, her lips slightly parted.

Caught by the lure of her body, he stepped closer. She seemed to sense him before he touched her, and her eyes opened lazily, like she was coming out of a deep sleep. She gave him that languid come-hither smile she'd given him the night before.

Sliding his arms around her waist, he pulled her to him and the two of them swayed like blades of grass teased by a shimmering breeze. Behind him, he could hear his mother, still calling out the line dance steps. He knew the others were slavishly following the routine, but Cat couldn't fall into line even if she'd wanted to. She'd never fit in out here, but for some reason she seemed to fit him.

Maybe that was the reason he'd never found a woman

he'd wanted to stay with. They were all too ready to
follow the leader. Cat moved to her own beat.

He tightened his arms around her and bent his
head, brushing her lips with his own. Without hesita-
tion, she let him in and the two of them slowed their
movements, shifting the energy that had set them
swaying to something a little more intimate and a lot
more potent.

The music stopped, the kiss ended, but she didn't pull
away. He looked down into her eyes, glistening in the
light from the fire, and thought maybe he'd found what
he was looking for after all.

Cat looked up at Mack and felt her heart dance a little
Riverdance jig against his chest. What was it about this
guy? She'd never had this kind of deep-down, unthink-
ing response to a man before. She could hardly quell
the urge to grab him by the hand and drag him off to the
Heifer House.

Judging from the warmth in his gaze, he was thinking
the same thing. She couldn't look at him and not touch
him, so she turned away.

"We'd better wait," she said. "I can't just walk away
from my students, you know."

"I don't see why not." Mack nodded to the front of
the stage, where the guests had taken a break from line
dancing and were enthusiastically clapping along with
the SWAT team version of "Li'l Liza Jane."

"I just can't."

She leaned back and he clasped his arms around her,
lacing his fingers at her waist. It felt good, having the

solid bulk of him behind her. What would it feel like to have a man like this backing her up every day?

Stifling, right? Restrictive. But hard as she tried to tell herself she didn't want to deal with a strong, possibly overbearing man, it just felt good.

They stood there on the perimeter of the crowd, watching the guests mingle with the neighbors. Madeleine had introduced Cat to most of them, and she reviewed their names and stories as she watched. Ed and Emma were chatting up Jodi Treadwell, a strikingly beautiful cowgirl who ran a therapy riding program north of town. Abby was deep in conversation with Nate Shawcross, another local rancher, while his wife Charlie danced with their adorable redheaded daughter. Another couple, Luke and Libby Rawlins, were sitting quietly by the fire, so content with each other's company they seemed oblivious to the rest of the crowd. Real estate agent Lacey Caldwell was pointing out the finer features of the ranch house to her husband Chase, who seemed far more interested in the barn.

Maddie was watching the shindig she'd set up with obvious delight. She was standing with Hank, and when the band struck up a new song she reached over and gave his hand a quick squeeze. Cat felt Mack stiffen, then sigh and relax. It had to be hard to see your mother fall for a man who wasn't your father, even if your father was gone and the man was as obviously devoted as Hank.

She scanned the crowd for a distraction.

"Who's that?" She pointed to an older man with a face that appeared to be worn by hard living rather than the weather. His hair was Ronald Reagan black and oily.

He was strolling up from the direction of the improvised parking lot with his hands in his pockets. It was an easy, casual posture, but Cat instinctively felt he was up to no good.

Mack tightened his grip on her. If his hackles had been raised before, they were bristling now.

"That's Ollie. Son of a bitch. I didn't think he'd have the nerve to come here."

"Your stepfather?"

"My mother's second husband. No father of mine." He grabbed her hand, practically dragging her past the fire toward the new arrival. They almost knocked over a couple of dancers in his haste.

"Ollie."

"Hey, son." The older man widened his lips in a phony smile.

"I'm not your son. What are you doing here?"

"Came to see your mother." The man's false bonhomie shifted to a tense, whining tone. "I got a right to see my ex-wife, don't I? I need to talk to her about some business."

"You don't have any business here but signing the divorce papers."

"Sure I do." The grimace widened into a grin, showing off two unsettling rows of unnaturally straight dentures. "I'm not signing any papers. I'm here to mend fences with your mother."

"That fence is beyond repair." Mack let go of Cat and grabbed the older man's arm, swinging him back the way he'd come.

Ollie pulled away, then gripped his arm with a wounded look. "That's Maddie's call, son."

"You call me son again and you'll be saying it

from the ground," Mack said, clenching his fists. "And stay away from my mother. You've done enough damage."

"Somebody had to take care of this place," Ollie said. "You weren't here. I did my best."

"You did your best to milk it for all the money you could get. And now you're trying to hang on, string things out. You need to sign the papers." Mack peered through the ground. "I saw Daniels here earlier. Maybe he's got the papers with him."

"Forget your lawyer," Ollie said. "Only person I'm talking to is your mother."

Cat edged away from Mack and Ollie. She sensed a showdown coming, and she wasn't sure she wanted to see Mack lose his temper and beat somebody up again. Although he did seem to have a knack for finding men who deserved it.

And she couldn't deny the thrill this relationship had brought her. For once, she felt as reckless and sexy on the inside as she looked on the outside. Despite her bohemian clothes and flyaway hair, she'd always been a little bit of a prude when it came to men. And to some extent, her love life had been stalled by her friendship with Ames. This wasn't the first time she'd used their friendship to avoid intimacy, but she vowed it would be the last.

She spent some time with her students, chatting with Ed and Emma and dancing a quick two-step with Charles, who proved to have the floating grace that so often makes big men good dancers. As the party started to wind down, the night air turned chilly and she went in search of Mack.

Edging through the crowd, she craned her neck to see if she could spot him or Ollie. As she neared the Bull Barn, she heard male voices and paused.

"They're not yours to sell."

Mack's voice. There was a note of desperation in it that chilled her heart. She shouldn't eavesdrop. His family issues were none of her business. But maybe she could help somehow.

Lightening her tread as much as she could, she crept closer to the barn. The two men were just inside the door.

"I'll talk to your mother about that."

"They're not yours to sell," Mack repeated. "So whatever deal you've got going, you need to cancel it and move on."

"Until those papers are signed, I'm still her husband."

Sensing he'd stepped over the line, Ollie backed up a step. Mack moved with him, one fist coming up fast. Ollie backed away just in time, then turned and fled for the parking lot. He beeped open a blue late-model Silverado and turned.

"I've been through the books. This place is shit, Boyd. Done." He climbed into the truck. "It'll take a miracle to save it. Your mother and her crazy dude ranch plans aren't going to do it." He slammed the door, then rolled down the window. "You might as well get back on the road. Rodeo's what you always wanted anyway."

"No." Mack straightened, then surged to his feet. "It's not what I wanted. Not without the ranch to back it up."

"Well, then you'd better keep on romancin' that little painter gal, 'cause there's no other way you're going to get folks to stay at this dump." He let out a cynical chuckle that made Cat's hackles rise. "Gives a whole new meaning to the phrase 'use it or lose it.'"

Mack grabbed the door handle and tugged furiously, slamming one foot against the truck in his effort to pull open the locked door. He nearly fell as Ollie rolled up the window and the truck surged forward, spinning out of the drive in a cloud of dust.

Cat backed away. Mack wouldn't want her to see his desperation, and he definitely wouldn't want her to hear what Ollie had said. Returning to the party, she eased into the line of dancers and picked up the steps as best she could, following Maddie's rhythmic calls.

"Kick one, two, and *kick* three, four."

Chapter 33

MACK SCANNED THE CROWD, SEARCHING FOR CAT'S willowy form among the dancers. Her pale grace should stand out like a heron in a hen coop, but he couldn't spot her. He could feel his world starting to spin again, and he needed a touchstone—something that grounded him.

She stepped out of the darkness and into the circle of light around the barn like the answer to a wish. "Hey. Where are you going?"

He scanned her face as she took his arm. She had so many smiles—the languid, sexy tilting of the lips, the wry, ironic twist, and this one—teasing, lighthearted, and filled with promise. That was just the smile he needed right now.

"I just wanted to take a break."

"Want company?"

He took her hand. "If the company's you, I do."

They didn't speak as they strolled through the barn doors into the warm, hay-scented darkness. He pulled her close and felt the world steady under his feet. He breathed in the scent of her hair, violets and roses, and let his hands skim over her hips.

He needed to take the next step with this woman, and that meant finding a way to tell her how he felt. But with his luck, somebody would come into the barn and overhear them.

"I know a place where nobody can find us," he said.

"Show me."

There was no pretending now, no false flirtation. She simply let him lead her to the back of the barn to the tack and feed room. Racks jutting from one wall held an assortment of saddles, while hooks draped with halters and bridles lined another. A row of metal bins below the hooks held grain and sweet feed, with various horse blankets neatly folded on top. Bales of yellow straw and bright green alfalfa hay were stacked against the other two walls.

The room smelled of clean leather and new straw—Mack's favorite scents other than the flowery fragrance of Cat herself. He could hear the high notes of the fiddle and the dull thud of bass coming through the walls. The only light came from a high window—a combination of cool moonlight and the warm glow of the fire. All he could see of Cat in the dimness was the sheen of her eyes and the light catching the colored stones she wore on a gold chain. Baubles and beads, gauze and lace—she was decked out like the queen. He loved the way she dressed, but he couldn't wait to get all those trappings off her and be with the real, unadorned Cat.

The scrape of the fiddle was interrupted by the whine of electric guitars. If he weren't here with Cat, he'd be out there with the rest of the revelers, standing just outside the circle, as he always had. He'd been an outsider all his life, looking for his own heart and never quite finding it here at the ranch, or out on the road. He'd never minded the loneliness of the road or the risks of the rodeo, because he'd had nothing to lose. He'd thought that made him free, but he was wrong. It only made him poor.

Not for long, though. His outsider status was about to change. He was going to stop looking for something vague and undefined and start making the most of what he had. Hopefully, the woman beside him would be part of that change.

He had four days to make that happen.

He grabbed a pair of clippers that hung by the hay bales and snipped the twine on one, then another, then another. As the bales broke open, he swept the loose hay to the floor. Grabbing two of the clean horse blankets, he spread them over the bed of straw.

"Hm," she said. "I think I'm about to have another Wild West experience."

Cat reached across the blanket and took Mack's hand. All her life, she'd settled for something—for a job in advertising instead of art; for an apartment instead of a home; for her lukewarm relationship with Ames instead of love. Once, just once, she was going to have the real thing.

They met in the middle of the blanket. Wrapping her arms around his neck, she pulled him to the ground until they were both sprawled on the clean blanket in the single square of light that slanted from the window.

She reached up and stroked that teasingly unkempt shock of hair that fell over his forehead, then swept her hand down the side of his face, tracing the shard of light that glossed his cheekbone, drifting down to the rough stubble of his cheek and stroking the line of his jaw. Closing her eyes, she did it again. She wanted to trace every curve and angle, memorize him so she'd know him in the dark—and so she wouldn't forget him when she was gone.

Because of course she was going. There was no question of that. They had four more days here at the ranch—four days to enjoy this surprising, surreal attraction of opposites. She ignored the pang of loss that shot through her at the thought of leaving him. It was ridiculous to even think about staying.

But staying in touch—that wasn't impossible, was it? She could come back sometime. Visit. She didn't have to say good-bye forever.

His next kiss was deeper and less playful. There was real feeling behind it—she knew that now. This wasn't a game or a rehearsal for the real thing; he'd let her into his life and trusted her with his heart.

She wanted to be worthy of that trust, which meant she couldn't hold back anymore. His hand brushed her breast and she twisted to press herself into his palm. Hooking one leg around his thigh, she pulled her hips to his and felt the hard evidence of his arousal. She closed her eyes and felt sparks flying from his touch. His fingers danced along her skin and the sparks grew to flames.

He pulled away and she squirmed, wanting more, as he pulled off her shirt and worked at her belt. He stripped her with the single-minded determination he brought to everything he did, and then applied the same commendable work ethic to his own clothes.

Laying a palm on his bare chest, she locked her elbow, holding him off for a second so she could look at him. She loved the way his muscles flowed and swelled, the practical economy of his movements. He was a working man, one who actually used his body, and every part of him served a purpose. The city boys she knew were nothing like him; they were just shells for their sophisticated brains and pretentious egos.

She was suddenly self-conscious. Her own body was hardly flabby, but she didn't use her muscles much. Her hips had a little spare padding, and her tummy had a slight roundness to it that suddenly seemed superfluous. She closed her eyes, feeling shy, and he pulled his hand away from her breast to cup her chin. When he didn't move, she opened her eyes to find him gazing intently into her own.

"What are you thinking?"

"Nothing." She tried for a careless smile, but it trembled at the edges. She pulsed her hips against him, hoping she could dodge the question and move on.

"No. Wait." He tilted her chin up, forcing her to meet his eyes. "You need to know some things."

"I already know." She smiled again. "The birds, the bees—it's okay, I get it."

"This isn't about that," he said. "It's about who you are." His eyes flicked over her body, taking in every slightly padded curve, and she felt heat rise to her face. "You have a beautiful body, Cat. It's what got me here. But what's keeping me is inside."

She bit her lip. He wasn't going to tell her that he loved her, was he? Because she wasn't ready for that. She didn't know what she was feeling, but she didn't want to define it; she just wanted to set it free.

He seemed to sense her discomfort, because he looked away, releasing his hold. "It's you," he said simply.

And then he was moving again, and she was moving with him, their bodies joining like two flames from the same fire. They caught and flared, ebbed to a quiet glow, then flickered to life again and the flames leaped and danced, reaching into the sky and lighting the whole world on fire.

Lying with him later, she remembered the way the embers in the fire pit glowed in the cool night. She felt that same soft heat in her own heart, and wondered if she was falling for him too.

It didn't matter. She'd just enjoy it while it lasted. He pulled her closer and she rested her head on his chest. They listened to the music, a slow song sung by the band's raspy tenor.

I'm crazy.

Crazy for feeling so lonely…

"Crazy," he muttered, echoing the song. His voice rumbled in her ear and that was all she wanted—just to hear him talk. She was learning that cowboys didn't have much to say, so she plumbed her mind for a question to get him going.

"Which is better—rodeo or ranching?" she asked.

Moving his hand in lazy circles on her back, he thought a moment and then the rumble started up again.

"Rodeo's a blast," he said. "Every ride's different. And you win or lose—it's one way or the other. You've got your answer in eight seconds, and it's not that hard to win. You just have to figure out which way the horse is going to buck. Long as you know what you're dealing with, you can ride it out. Ranching's a lot harder because there are so many ways to lose."

He paused and she knew he was thinking about his conversation with Ollie—and the fact that he might have lost without even getting a chance to try.

When he continued, she wasn't sure if he was talking to her or just thinking things through. "But you can always win somehow. There are always setbacks—droughts and heat waves, hard winters, money troubles—but the Boyds have always managed to hold on."

She let herself relax, breathing slow and deep with the rhythm of his heart. In spite of all the turmoil he'd had today, it still pounded with a slow, steady beat. She had a feeling his heart was as unchangeable as the land he lived on, and she wondered what would happen when she was gone.

She'd just be one of those setbacks. He'd struggle a while, but he'd find a way to win. And life on the ranch would go on.

She pictured herself months from now, sitting in her tiny apartment studio, staring at the brick wall outside her back window, listening to the chaotic sounds of the city. It would be a comfort to know that he was still here, his heart still beating steady.

She wasn't staying. Her life wasn't here. But lying there beside him, breathing in the comforting scents of leather and hay, she understood what it must be like to have a home like this and lose it. What had Ollie said back there in the firelight? *This place is done. It'll take a miracle to save it.*

Maybe she could be a part of that miracle.

Chapter 34

MACK LAY IN HIS DARK BEDROOM, WISHING HE WAS back in the barn with Cat. The party had wound down, and they'd risen reluctantly. Cat needed to check on Dora, and he didn't want Viv sleeping in the house without him there. He'd watched Trevor Maines drive away, but you never knew what a guy like that would do. Sure, his mother was in the house, but she had a lot going on.

So did he. The depth of his feelings for Cat had surprised him, and Ollie's warning had been a sharp and sudden blow. He needed to spend some time in the office tomorrow, go over the books. Find out just how bad things were.

The good news was that all this trouble put his priorities in perspective. He'd find a way to save the ranch, and he'd find a way to make Cat stay. Those were the two things that mattered, and he wasn't about to lose either one. He might have wasted his life on the backs of a hundred bucking broncs, but he'd learned one thing from rodeo: He was good at hanging on.

Closing his eyes, he ran through a half-dozen possible solutions in his head. He was pretty sure he had enough in his rodeo account to stave off the bank for a month or two and keep the cows in feed and veterinary care over the winter. Meanwhile, he'd study the books and find a way to make that side of the operation pay. And he'd encourage his mother to work at the dude ranch side of the business. That was the key.

Job one, though, was still to take care of the bird in the hand, and that was Cat and her students. If their experience worked out, he'd have some success to build on—and maybe he'd have Cat, too.

He was probably crazy to think she'd stay. She was a city girl who needed coffee shop lattes and art galleries. He couldn't offer her any of that. He couldn't offer her much of anything, given the ranch's precarious financial status. But he'd give her everything he had. Surely that counted for something.

He drifted off into a half sleep, thoughts of numbers and ranching plans giving way to memories of Cat lying in the moonlight. He heard the crunch of tires on gravel and figured a late-partying guest must just be leaving.

When a sharp noise snapped him awake, he shot upright. He had no idea what time it was, but the moonlight had dimmed and the crickets had hushed.

A slit of light edged the door. As he watched, it grew wider, and a crouching figure crept into the room.

Cat. He smiled in the darkness. He hadn't wanted to leave her, and he'd tried to talk her into coming back to the house with him. But she'd insisted that being together in the morning would look bad to her students. In reality, Emma and Abby would probably applaud if the two of them showed up to breakfast hot and disheveled with matching cases of bed-head.

He edged over, making room for her, as the door eased shut with a faint click. In the darkness that followed, he could only sense her presence by sound and scent. He could hear her shuffling cautiously forward, feeling her way. As she drew closer, he expected the sweet smell of violets, but she must have doused herself in some new perfume.

It wasn't good. He almost gagged at the combined assault of spices. It was some artificial scent, blended with something suspiciously like whiskey. He'd have to find a way to tell her this didn't work for him. Tomorrow, not tonight. He was doing his best to prove he could make it twenty-four hours without having to apologize.

He'd keep it positive. Tell her how much he loved her natural, flowery scent, and tell her not to cover it up. That was the way to do it.

He was getting good at this girl stuff.

The side of the bed sagged under her weight and he reached out to caress her. Making love in full dark was kind of a thrill. He didn't know if he'd be touching her breast, her hip, her belly…

His hand landed on something hairy and a low male scream shredded the silence, followed by a series of thumps and crashes as someone floundered across the room, desperate and graceless as a lobster on dry land. The overhead light flashed on.

Mack blinked in the bright light, then wished he hadn't.

Trevor Maines stood by the door with his hand on the switch, gaping at Mack with his mouth half-open. His normally sleek hair was standing up like a cock's comb, and his eyes were red-rimmed and bloodshot.

"What the hell?" Mack scrambled out of the bed, wishing he'd worn something more than boxers.

"Well." Trevor blinked owlishly a few times, then seemed to find his bearings and drew himself up to his usual erect posture. He always looked a little absurd with his flowing hair and oddly military bearing, but in his current condition the combination was ridiculous. "I shee you didn't washte any time moving into my room."

"News flash. Not your room."

Mack grabbed his jeans and sat back down to step into them. He zipped up fast, prepared for a fight. But the man before him looked more pitiful than evil. You couldn't hit a man when he was down, and Trevor had obviously had a rough night.

"I deshided to give you another shance." Trevor shook his head, as if repositioning his addled brains would help his muddled speech. "Nuther *shlance*. Nuther—nuther *opportunisy*. To redleem yourshelf."

Obviously, he'd chosen a bar over the police station and drowned his defeat in whiskey. Judging from the smell emanating from his pores, it hadn't been good whiskey, either. Mack wondered how the aristocratic Trevor had stooped low enough to drink Jeremiah Weed.

He stood a moment, swaying.

"Gotta shleep." He waved Mack away. "Move over."

"I'll do you one better. I'll move out." Mack gathered the few items he'd left on the nightstand, shoving them in his pockets while Trevor tipped over, landing with a solid *thunk* that nearly broke the box spring.

It was funny. With his shirt untucked and his hair in disarray, his speech slurred, and his aristocratic demeanor exchanged for a drunken stumble, the guy looked like any other bum off the street.

In fact, his new state fit him a little too well. The Richie Rich pretensions had always rung false to Mack, and he'd suspected the guy was exaggerating his wealth. But now his bullshit-ometer was clanging even more loudly.

He needed to get with Cat in the morning and find out what they really knew about this guy. But right now, he needed to find a place where he could keep an eye on things. Trevor was out cold, and there was nothing to do but let him sleep it off.

Closing the door behind himself, Mack glanced down the hallway. If Dora wasn't staying in the house, he could sleep in the extra bed in Viv's room. He looked over at his mother's door, wondering if he should wake her up and let her know the situation too. You couldn't be too careful.

But her door was wide open, and from his vantage point in the hallway, it was clear the bed was empty and hadn't been slept in. The old-fashioned chenille spread was as smooth and unlined as a newly groomed arena.

He winced. Hopefully Ollie hadn't returned to do whatever "business" he'd intended. Mack found it hard to believe his mother would fall for the guy's lines again, but if she'd done it once, she might do it again. He'd once taken Maddie's good sense for granted, but Ollie had changed all that.

He sighed. He wasn't about to chase after her. He was too afraid of what he might find. He might as well catch a few winks here, where he could still keep an eye on Trevor. If his mother turned up, he'd just get up and start the day early.

Standing at the window, he brushed the curtain aside and checked the parking lot beside the barn. Most of the vehicles were gone, as the guests had all gone

home. There were a few scattered pickups remaining—
probably guests who had been too drunk to drive.

He didn't see Ollie's Silverado. He'd have been able to
spot it, because the light in Hank's tiny apartment above
the barn was on, beaming a square of light right where the
vehicle had stood. As Mack watched, a shadow moved
across the lighted square on the bare ground. He couldn't
tell if it was a man or a woman, but somebody—or
somebodies—was awake in Hank's room.

Maybe his mother wasn't with Ollie. Maybe she
and Hank...

He didn't want to think about that. Collapsing onto
the bed, he closed his eyes and wished to God he was on
the back of a bronc. Then at least there'd be pickup men
to haul him to his feet and rodeo docs to dust him off and
patch him up. Here at the ranch, he could feel his grip
slipping, and there was nobody to catch him if he fell.

Chapter 35

CAT FELT LIKE ALL EYES WERE ON HER AS SHE EMERGED from the Heifer House in the morning. She wasn't sure anyone had seen her and Mack sneak off to the barn the night before, but she suspected Emma and Abby had been watching like a pair of matchmaking hawks.

And no wonder. She and Mack were better than a soap opera, fighting one minute and making love the next. She'd never had such a tumultuous relationship.

And she'd never felt more alive.

She slowed self-consciously, realizing she'd put a schoolgirl skip in her step. Hank and Maddie were bustling around the chuckwagon, finishing up breakfast preparations. Maddie handed her a tin plate loaded with fluffy scrambled eggs, home fries with onions and peppers, and two slabs of heaven-scented bacon. Hank gave her a nod and a smile. Funny, she'd never noticed that he was actually kind of a nice-looking man. Normally he just blended into the woodwork, but this morning he seemed more normal somehow.

She settled down on a bench and stretched her legs out while she tucked into her breakfast. It was a typical Wyoming summer morning, with a limitless blue sky and a faint breeze carrying the scent of sage and bits of birdsong. There was nothing to spoil her happiness; even Dora's issues seemed like a lighter load now that she knew what caused them.

She'd settled on a plan of action. A single, serious talk wasn't going to work with Dora. She simply needed to remind her niece, gently and continually, of all the ways her mother had loved her, all the things she'd done to prove it. Dora would heal. Cat would make sure of that.

She glanced around the circle, running a quick roll call in her mind. The three seniors were present and accounted for. Charles slouched on the far side of the fire, staring into the flames and shoveling food into his mouth as if he was afraid someone would take it away. Watching the lizard tattoo writhe as he lifted his fork to his mouth, Cat wondered again if he was an ex-con.

Mack was nowhere to be seen. He was probably in the barn, getting the horses ready for today's expedition. Cat was a little disappointed he hadn't joined her for breakfast, but that was all right. There were no strings attached to what had happened between them. There couldn't be.

Dora and Viv weren't around either, but Dora was probably helping Mack in the barn. And since the two girls had become inseparable, maybe Viv was helping too—or, more likely, standing around looking cute and talking a mile a minute. Cat smiled, thinking of how the girls had hit it off. Maybe she'd suggest that Art Treks do a camp for teenagers. She could see herself leading a summer painting excursion to Europe for high school students. Or one to Wyoming.

Actually, she wasn't sure she needed Art Treks backing her up. There were probably concerns she hadn't thought of yet—insurance, waivers, legal mumbo-jumbo—but she was also sure she could arrange a trip herself. As a freelance workshop facilitator and tour guide, she'd be able to pick her own locations and write her own lessons. And she might make enough to quit Trainer and Crock.

Scraping up the last of her potatoes, she brushed a few crumbs from her shirt as she rose. She'd worn one of her thrift shop painting shirts today, a pink Etienne Aigner that came nearly to her knees. It was already decorated with a few wayward paint stains and hung open over a gray long-sleeved jersey she'd layered with a fitted navy MoMA T-shirt. It looked like the day would be a cool one, but riding could get warm and layers could easily be shed.

She thought about all the layers she'd shed the night before and shivered. She'd never given as much to a man as she'd given to Mack—not in all her life.

She was going to have to be more careful.

"I'm going to go check on the horses," she said.

"Make sure you check that cowboy too," Emma said. "Check him *out*." She gave Cat an exaggerated wink.

"She already did that," Abby said. "But if I was her, I'd do it again."

Cat did her best to smile past her embarrassment and set out for the barn. It was a beautiful morning, with a faint breeze stroking the grass and the sky the impossible blue of a robin's egg. Three of the horses were already lined up at the hitching rail, and Mack was leading another from the barn.

"Need help?" she asked. "Or do you have all you need?"

"Nope, I'm fine." He draped the horse's reins over the rail and swung an arm around her, pulling her close for a kiss. It felt good, like they were a couple. She decided to let herself enjoy that feeling for a while.

"Tired, though," he said. "I was up all night keeping an eye on Trevor."

She whirled. "*Trevor?*"

"Came back last night. Damn near crawled into bed with me. Said he was going to give us another chance. Generous of him, but he was drunk as a skunk."

Cat stood at the rail, unsure what to say or even what to feel. She'd been worried about what would happen if Trevor went to the police. His return should be good news. But having him back made her uneasy.

"Don't worry," Mack said. "He left early this morning. Stumbled out of here around dawn."

She glanced around the barn. "Isn't Dora helping you this morning?"

"Not yet." He shrugged. "You know how teenagers are about mornings."

She felt a slight stab of worry—or was it defensiveness? "Dora's always been an early riser."

"Well, maybe my daughter's giving her a crash course in teenage vices, like sleeping in till noon," he said. "She was an early riser too, until she hit fourteen or so."

Cat watched him load cases and supplies onto the patient Spanky. He looked like he had everything under control, but Dora had promised to help. Cat had come to terms with the idea that her niece didn't want to paint, but she wasn't going to let the girl snooze the day away.

"I'll get her."

She jogged up the stairs to Viv's bedroom and rapped on the door.

No answer.

"Dora? Viv?"

Still no answer.

She cracked open the door and peered inside. The bed by the window was in total disarray, with covers flung over the footboard and a pillow on the floor. But the other bed was neatly made, with pillows plumped at the head and placed at artistic angles.

Cat couldn't picture Dora getting up and making the bed. She'd never angle the pillows with that kind of care—especially not when her friend had simply flung the covers off. Maybe she'd slept in the Heifer House.

She felt a twinge of unease. She should know, shouldn't she? She'd been thinking Ross wasn't taking proper care of Dora, but was she doing any better?

Mack had everything ready for today's trip. He just needed to gather up the artists, which was about as much fun as herding cats.

He was learning more than he wanted to know about the artistic temperament. Even Cat, who was organized and responsible, could be driven to slack-jawed distraction by a certain slant of light or raptured away by a gracefully gnarled tree. In some ways he enjoyed it. It made him see the land in a new way.

He sauntered over to the fire pit, checking the landscape for stragglers. Like yearling calves, artists had a tendency to wander off, but feeding time generally brought them home. Right now they were clustered around the chuckwagon, with Cat at the center of the group.

Cat. He couldn't help picturing her the night before, sprawled in the hay, naked in his arms. But as he approached the group, he realized something was wrong. Her voice was high-pitched and shrill.

"Has anyone seen her? Talked to her?" She swiveled to face his daughter. "Viv, she must have said something. Think!"

He couldn't help bristling at the way she was haranguing his daughter. But when he caught sight of Viv's worried face, he realized something more than an art lecture was going on.

"I don't know," she said. "I mean, she's been having a rough time. Her mom, you know?"

A sympathetic murmur rose from the group.

"But she never said a word about going anywhere, I swear." Viv crossed her heart with a pointed index finger in a gesture she'd used since childhood.

"Are you sure? You two have been so close." Cat was glaring at Viv as if she could see straight to her soul. "You need to tell me the truth."

Viv blinked fast. "I don't know anything. I really don't."

His daughter looked so hurt Mack wanted to hug her—or hurt somebody. He pushed through the group to confront Cat. "She swore, okay? Viv doesn't lie."

"I wasn't—I just…" Now it was Cat who was blinking. Women were falling apart all around him, all because his supposed assistant had gone off on her own without telling anyone. "Dora's missing. Just gone. I'm worried, Mack."

"She probably stormed off on her own, like she did that first day," he said. "She doesn't exactly toe the line, you know?"

"No. She took her clothes." Cat's worried eyes looked

enormous in her pale, drawn face. "We have to start a search." She turned to Mack. "Where could she go from here?"

"Nowhere," he said. "You know how far it is to town. And it's not like she could hitchhike. She'd have to get a ride."

He hadn't thought Cat could get any paler, but she looked like she was going to faint.

"Trevor," she said. "She must have gone with him."

"She'd never do that," Viv said. "She couldn't stand him."

"Then he made her go somehow." She grabbed Mack's arm. "We'll have to call the police."

For a moment everything receded as if he was looking through the wrong end of a telescope. He remembered the stench of whiskey that had emanated from Trevor the night before, and the way his skin had crawled at the man's touch.

He didn't see how Trevor could have taken Dora. He'd heard the guy leave. But he'd thought Dora was in Viv's room, so once the guy left the house he'd assumed both girls were safe.

"I'll call the police," he said. "We'll get the state cops to put out an APB."

He tried to slow the whirling in his mind and think. Where would Trevor go? East of the ranch was a long stretch of featureless highway that led to Casper. West was the Wind River Canyon, and a trackless wilderness that was a frequent destination for desperadoes, runaways, and folks with dark secrets.

He headed for the house—and the phone—at a run.

Chapter 36

CAT SAT AT THE KITCHEN TABLE, PINNED TO HER CHAIR by the sympathetic gaze of Madeleine Boyd. She was forcing down a cup of tea and wondering how long she'd have to sit there before she could start pacing again.

"The police will be here any minute," Madeleine said. Hank, who was sitting beside her, nodded solemnly.

"Any minute?" Cat tilted her wrist to look at her watch for the fifth time in a minute. "It's been half an hour." She'd given them a description of the Lexus and they'd promised to put out an APB, whatever that was. But she could tell the operator wasn't taking her seriously. There'd been a series of questions obviously designed to see if Dora was a runaway, and the woman had seemed skeptical of Cat's assurances that her niece would never set out on her own.

Fortunately, she hadn't had to mention that Dora's mother had just died, that she'd been having trouble in school, or that she'd been sulky and rebellious since she'd arrived. All those things pointed to a possible runaway, but she was sure Trevor had something to do with this. Dora wouldn't just run off.

If only she'd listened to Mack. If only she'd stopped fussing about her precious career and kept her niece safe. If anything happened to Dora because of her negligence, she'd never forgive herself.

"I can't just *sit* here." Cat shook off Maddie's calming hand and shot to her feet. "I need to do something."

"There's not much you can do. And the police will do everything they can."

Cat knew she was right. The police *would* do everything they could—but it was precious little, and they wouldn't have to do it if Cat hadn't failed as a guardian. She ran through the events of last night in her head and felt like kicking herself. She'd left Dora and Viv to themselves. She'd told herself she was giving the girls a chance to bond, but the truth was she was relieved to shed her responsibilities and get some time alone with Mack.

She'd assumed the girls were having a pajama party, painting their nails, and playing truth or dare while she got busy with the ranch's handsome wrangler. But Viv said they'd turned in early, tired from their long day. Viv had slept in her room, and Dora had headed for the Heifer House.

That was the last anyone saw of her. Unlike the bed in Viv's room, her bunk was mussed as if it had been slept in, but she'd been up and out of bed before anyone saw her. Abby and Emma hadn't been lying when they said they slept like the dead, and Cat had slept the heavy, dreamless sleep of the sated.

The front door slammed. Cat leaped to her feet but slumped back into the chair when Viv ran into the room carrying a laptop.

"You have to see this." She set the laptop on the table and pointed triumphantly to the screen.

Facebook. A photo of Dora beamed from the top. It was the photo Cat had found in the fire. If Dora didn't like the photo, why would she use it online?

Cat didn't use the service herself. She knew she

should; it would be a good way to promote her work. But it cut into valuable painting time, so she'd never paid much attention to it. "This is Dora's page?"

"She has 534 friends," Viv said, as if that proved something.

"Good for her," Maddie said. "Popular."

"There's, like, no way she can know all these people. And look." Viv hit a button and scrolled through a list of contacts, with thumbnail pictures beside each name.

When she stopped scrolling, Cat's gaze immediately zoomed in on one picture in particular—and blanched. It looked like a typical high school yearbook photo from the nineties. The subject, a blond teenager with an angular jaw, faced the camera with his chin tilted slightly upward, giving him a supercilious air. The boy looked no more than eighteen, but there was no mistaking who it was.

She gasped. "That's Trevor Maines."

"Yup. Or at least, it was." Viv clicked on the picture to enlarge it.

"That has to be over ten years old," Cat said. "He's practically a teenager."

"I know." Viv clicked back to Dora's page. "And look. Dora tells everything she's doing. Everywhere she's going. Including here."

Cat grabbed the laptop with both hands and stared at the entries. Sure enough, Dora detailed her every move. From home in LA to the airport to Denver to the ranch. There were even links to the Art Treks site.

"He's posing as somebody younger online," Viv said. "He's stalking Dora. And he followed her here."

"Mack has to see this." Cat scrolled down the page,

noting some flirty status updates from Dora. There were lots of commenters, but she didn't see Trevor among them. Still, Viv was right. Trevor was "following" Dora. And not just in the virtual world.

Suddenly everything made sense. "The picture," she said. "The burned picture. It was Trevor. He must have printed it off his computer, and he burned it so we wouldn't find it."

Panic scrambled her brain. She needed Mack. He'd know what to do. He always knew when it came to Dora.

Shoving her chair back so hard it hit the wall, she ran past Viv and out the door.

Mack was stabling the last of the packhorses when Cat and Viv ran into the barn. He'd left Rembrandt saddled and ready, just in case they needed to mount a wilderness search. Normally, he could track just about anything, but between the Art Trekkers and the party the ranch was one big mass of footprints and tire tracks. And Trevor's head start made it unlikely Mack would be able to catch him on the highway. The state police were far better equipped to find the silver Lexus somewhere on the highways and back roads of Wyoming.

Ed, Abby, and Emma were gathered over by the hay bales, their faces drawn with worry.

"I just wish I could *do* something," Ed kept muttering. Emma would pat his arm every time he said it. Mack suspected he said it a lot. With all Ed's high spirits, the limitations that came with age had to be frustrating.

"Mack, look." Cat burst into the barn carrying the laptop he'd given Viv for Christmas. Her normally glowing skin was pasty, and her pretty eyes were red-rimmed with dark circles around them. Behind her, Viv looked equally stressed.

"Viv found Dora's Facebook page."

"She was on it last night, and she left it open," Viv said. "Guess who she's friends with."

He took one look at the screen and felt his stomach bottom out. Trevor Maines.

"He's friends with Dora?"

Viv nodded.

"Maybe she's just done that since she got here," he said.

"Nope." Vivian set the laptop down on top of the cooler by the barn door. "See, if I click 'see friendship' it says how long they've been friends. It's been over a year."

"Can you find his page?"

Viv typed in "Trevor Maines" and found a page for something called "The Maines Event." She clicked that one and brought up a page about fashion.

"He said he was a fashion photographer," Cat said. "At least that much was true."

"Yeah, but look at the models." Mack pointed at a photo that had been added just two weeks earlier. It was a teenaged girl, clad skimpily in shorts and a torn T-shirt. She was giving the camera a pouty, sultry look that didn't suit her obvious youth.

Vivian clicked a link and brought up a blog, also called "The Maines Event." It boasted more photos of young girls, introduced to the viewer with names like "Bambi" and "Lola." The accompanying text gushed over their "waifish" and "childlike" qualities.

It made Mack's blood run cold. The photos were

oddly clinical, the girls posing stiffly in come-hither poses against crushed velvet backdrops reminiscent of seventies-era yearbook photos.

He glanced up at Cat and swallowed the urge to say "I told you so." It wasn't necessary. She looked devastated.

"Maybe he took her for revenge," Viv said. "He was pretty pissed at you, Dad."

"Then why doesn't he take his revenge on me?"

"Are you kidding? You flattened him."

Mack stared at the screen, his stomach churning with anger and dread. Putting an arm around Cat's shoulders, he pulled her close, but she stiffened and moved away.

"We'll find her," he said. "I swear we'll find her. And when we do—well, revenge works both ways."

Chapter 37

CAT AND VIV HUNCHED OVER THE COMPUTER, EXPLORING Trevor's website.

"Dora's not into this fashion crap." Cat winced, realizing Viv probably was. "Why would she have become Trevor's 'friend' in the first place?"

Viv was scrolling rapidly through the blog. "He posts coupons sometimes, and advice on makeup and stuff. Every girl clicks on that stuff once in a while—even Dora. And he has buttons right there to 'like' his Facebook page, and once she does, it's easy for him to get her to 'friend' him. And look how many friends she has. I mean, she must just friend everybody."

"Was he having any conversations with Dora on Facebook?" Cat asked.

Viv shook her head. "I couldn't find any comments from him or anything. Not for the past few months, anyway. He's probably just lurking."

"Lurking?"

"Reading posts, but lying low. Not commenting. Then people forget you're there."

Mack strode in the barn door. "How do you know about this stuff?" he demanded.

Viv rolled her eyes. "I'm smack-dab in the middle of the Facebook demographic, Dad. I have to know about this stuff. Would you rather I *didn't* know about lurkers?"

"Guess not."

Ed toddled into the barn, moving stiffly from his days in the saddle. "You seen Charles?" he asked. "Me and the ladies haven't seen him all day."

Cat met Mack's eyes and saw her own worries reflected there.

"Do you think…"

"I don't know what to think anymore," Mack said. "Did anyone see him at breakfast?"

Cat opened and closed her mouth a few times before she managed to answer. "He was there. But he left as soon as I said Dora was missing. Do you think…"

She didn't have to finish. The idea that Charles could be in cahoots with Trevor struck them all speechless.

"He wouldn't," Abby said. "He's a good guy." She ducked her head, and her plump face flushed scarlet. Maybe Cat wasn't the only one who was enjoying something more than the scenery at the Boyd Dude Ranch.

Emma looked up into Abby's flushed face. "You're not *involved* with him, are you?"

"Not really," Abby muttered. "Well, maybe a little. And, Mom, you liked him. You know how nice he was. You said he was a gentle giant."

"We don't really know him, though," Emma said. "And that tattoo…"

"Exactly." Ed had folded his arms across his chest and thrown his shoulders back. "Why would a good guy have a tattoo like that? I think he's been in prison, or maybe a gang."

The light dimmed as a hulking shadow filled the barn's doorway.

"Nope. Not a gang." The light returned to normal as

Charles stepped inside. Fishing a wallet out of his back pocket, he flipped it open to reveal a brass shield.

Cat and Viv were openly gaping at the man, and Mack wasn't doing much better. "You're a cop?"

"FAM." He snapped the wallet closed and took in their blank looks. "Federal Air Marshall."

All three of them goggled at him. He grinned, then let out a chuckle and turned to Ed. "Surprise."

"Oh." Ed waved a hand vaguely in the air. "I thought it might be something like that. Didn't want to give you away. You're undercover, right?"

"I prefer to call it camouflage." Charles shoved the wallet back in his pocket with his lizard-bedecked hand. "It helps to blend in with the bad guys."

"So what can you do?" Cat quickly caught him up with what they'd found and showed him the website. "This is Trevor's website. He came back last night, but he's gone now—and so is Dora. We think he—he…" She couldn't go on.

"We think he took her," Viv said.

Charles studied the screen a moment.

"You might be right," he said. "That guy's been putting my back up the whole trip."

"I don't want to be right," Cat murmured. Mack put an arm around her. She thought about shrugging it off, but this was one of those times when it felt good to be taken care of—even if he couldn't solve the problem.

"You got any info on him?" Charles asked.

"I can check the forms," Cat said. "But the company doesn't do background checks." She looked sheepish. "I didn't even know peoples' ages. He probably lied anyway."

"He flew here, right?"

She nodded.

"Whose computer is this?"

Viv raised her hand like a school student. "Mine."

"Mind if I use it to check a few things?"

Viv shook her head quickly. "Go for it."

"We'll check NCIC, see if he has a record. See if there have been any similar episodes. We'll…"

"NCIC?" Mack asked.

"National Criminal Information Center."

"See?" Abby punched the air. "Told you he was one of the good guys. We'll have that jerk roped and hog-tied in no time." She winked at Cat. "And then you two can ride off into the sunset like in one of those old movies."

She was talking to Mack and Cat, but she glanced over at Charles as she said it and the two of them exchanged knowing smiles. There was definitely something going on there. And they probably had a better chance at a happy ending than he and Cat did. Right now, it seemed like the two of them were riding off into a thunderstorm, not a sunset.

Charles was clearly more at home on a computer than he was in the saddle. He played the keyboard like a piano, filing a form on one federal database, then killing time while he waited for a response by uncovering a LinkedIn profile that outlined Trevor's career as an employee of the State of New York. In real life, Maines was nothing but a petty bureaucrat who distributed recycling containers and oversaw the sorting of paper from plastic.

"Nothing on NCIC," Charles said. "Guy doesn't have a record."

"Well, that's something. So what do we do now?"

Charles tapped the keyboard a few times and brought up a new profile. This one was topped by the same image of the young Trevor Maines that Viv had found in Dora's sketchbook.

"Match.com?" Abby shoved her way to the front of the crowd circling the computer. "Boy, you federal agents have access to everything."

Charles ducked his head. "I'm not really performing in an official capacity right now."

"What? You mean…"

Ed slapped his knee. "Looking for love on the Internet, hey? I've heard that works pretty well."

Emma shoved an elbow in her husband's ribs and he winced.

"I travel a lot," Charles mumbled. "Hard to meet women."

"That's what vacations are for," Abby said. She simpered, and Mack cringed—but Charles just smiled.

———※———

The crunch of tires on the driveway led them all to the door to see a dark blue cruiser with the logo of the State of Wyoming on the side. Just the sight of the officer's neat uniform made Cat feel like things were under control. Charles was good. This was better.

The fact that the trooper was a manly six foot something and built like a beefcake model didn't hurt. And she had to admit it was nice to see a man with a crease in his pants.

Mack and Viv had emerged from the barn with her, but the cop focused on Cat immediately. Resting one elbow on the roof of the car, he took off his mirrored sunglasses, revealing soulful brown eyes in a square, honest face.

"I understand you have a missing person." He whipped a small notebook out of his shirt pocket, along with a pencil. The man exuded an air of competence, and Cat felt suddenly fluttery and weak.

"My niece."

"There's a good chance she was abducted or lured off." Mack stepped up with a photo of Trevor that Charles had printed off the computer in the ranch office. "By this man."

"And who is he?" The trooper lifted one brow toward Mack, and Cat finally recovered from her girlie state to feel the hostility simmering in the air.

"A guest on the ranch."

"And you're accusing your guest of kidnapping because…"

"Because I caught him in the girls' room last night. And I've seen how he looked at Dora. Since the two of them are missing at the same time, it's obvious." Mack shifted impatiently. "We found a website where he posts pictures of teen girls. Trust me, he's trouble."

"He's the driver on the Lexus you called in?"

Mack nodded. "A silver Lexus SUV. A rental."

"And you say you…" The trooper looked down at his notes. "Caught him in the girls' room?"

Mack nodded. "I chased him off, but he turned up again last night. Drunk."

"And he left this morning?" The trooper frowned. "Was he sober enough to drive?"

"Wasn't my day to watch him," Mack said.

"Sounds like it should have been."

Cat glanced from the trooper to the cowboy. She sensed something more than a cop/constituent relationship here. She sensed a pissing contest. It was masculine, petty, and probably not very productive.

"I can't believe he managed to get out of the house," Mack said. "He was drunk as a skunk."

"Maybe he was faking it," Cat said. "I'll bet you anything he planned this. Came back for her." She almost choked as the thought occurred to her. "Viv's right. He's probably getting revenge."

"So this is my fault?"

"It's not your fault Trevor's got an ego the size of Texas." She turned to the cop. "Do you need the picture?"

He took it from her hand, his fingers brushing hers. Was that deliberate? "Why don't we go in the house?" Those big brown eyes seemed to speak of something way beyond reviewing the evidence. Could the guy possibly be trying to pick her up?

"You can tell me more about your niece," he continued. "I need a detailed description, plus likes and dislikes, places she might go."

She balked, unwilling to go in the house and talk about things they already knew. "Don't you need to send out the picture? And wouldn't it be better if you were out there looking for the Lexus?"

He didn't look pleased. Ego again. Men didn't like having their expertise questioned.

"We'll get to all that," he said. "Let's go on in, and we'll talk."

Mack watched Stan Brownfield walk away with Cat. He needed the man's help—or at least, he needed his radio and the cooperation of his coworkers. Brownfield himself he had no use for at all.

"Who is he?" Charles asked.

"State cop," Mack said.

"I figured that out. But you know him, and you don't like him. Who is he?"

"Local guy," Mack said. "I went to school with him."

"Let's see." Emma placed her index finger on her chin and looked thoughtfully skyward. "Quarterback, I'll bet. Big man on campus. Got all the girls and wronged every one of 'em."

Mack barked out a bitter laugh. "You must have gone to high school in Grady too."

"No," she said. "But I know the type. And we're not going to let him take your girl."

"She's not my girl," Mack said. "Not even close. Not after this."

He strode out to the hitching post, where Rembrandt was waiting patiently.

Mules were better company than women anyway. He always thought better around animals, and he needed to find a way to help Dora.

"Sorry, buddy." He lifted the headstall over the long ears, cupping his hand to take the bit as the animal released it. "Left you in the hot sun, didn't I? We'll get you back in the barn."

It was obvious that his tracking skills weren't going to help find Dora. And Brownfield had all the resources when it came to finding the Lexus.

But Mack knew Dora. The two of them had talked all

day on the trail, hitting topics ranging from the nausea-inducing smarminess of Justin Bieber to the soul-numbing boredom brought on by the James Fenimore Cooper novel she had to read over the summer. Had Dora dropped any hints as to where she might go? They'd talked about food, music, trucks…

Trucks.

He felt his heart flutter with a surge of excitement. Slamming Rembrandt's stall door with a bang that made the normally placid mule let out a startled honk, he headed for the back of the barn and checked a row of hooks that were screwed onto a two-by-four nailed to the inside wall. Bundles of keys hung on four of the five hooks. The fifth was empty.

Swearing under his breath, he exited the back door and jogged to the machine shop. Half of the rickety old building housed excess bales of hay, keeping them out of the weather. The other side housed the ranch pickup, a 1954 International held together with duct tape, barbed wire, and rust. Dora had caught sight of it when he'd sent her for extra bales and asked if it ran.

It did.

Sliding the wooden bolt aside, he swung open the wide shed door.

The truck was gone.

He never thought he'd be so happy to have a vehicle stolen. He didn't know how Dora had managed to start the balky engine and take off without anyone noticing— especially Hank, whose bathroom window looked out over the shed.

But of course, Hank had been busy last night. Mack

shuddered and shoved that thought aside. His own worries would have to wait. He needed to find Dora.

Hopefully she'd just gone joyriding, or taken off to get a break from the group. The thought of calling Brownfield flashed across his mind. The old pickup would be easy to spot, with its rattletrap tailgate and dented side door.

But she couldn't have gone far. The truck ran, but just barely. Once Dora hit the hills, she'd be lucky to make thirty miles an hour. If she headed west, there was no way she'd make it over the pass. And if she went east, there was a good chance the truck would break down on the way. It needed a new water pump, and he was pretty sure the fuel filter was clogged.

He headed back to the ranch office. Cat was sitting in the battered office chair with her arms crossed over her chest, staring at the phone.

"Come on," he said. "Let's go get her."

She gave him an annoyed glare and returned her gaze to the phone. "She's been gone too long, Mack. I have to wait for the cops to call."

"Mom'll answer from the house. Trust me, she'll be on that phone before you can so much as twitch. And I've got my cell." He tossed the keys to his Ford in the air and caught them. "Meanwhile, we're going to find Dora. She's not with Trevor. Come on. I'll fill you in on the way."

Chapter 38

CAT SAT STIFFLY IN THE PASSENGER SEAT OF MACK'S pickup, scanning the roadside, peering down turnoffs, searching for any sign of the old pickup. She'd called the police again, and a woman there had promised to relay a description of the pickup to Officer Brownfield. But Mack seemed determined to make his own search, and doing something—anything—felt better than sitting at the ranch waiting for the phone to ring.

She felt a little guilty about leaving her students behind. They'd paid a fortune for this trip, and today they hadn't done a lick of painting. Everyone seemed to understand, but they were hardly getting their money's worth.

But she was reordering her priorities, putting Dora on top. If she'd done that sooner, she wouldn't have fooled around with Mack and none of this would have happened.

She listened to the throaty roar of the engine while she watched the fence posts flick past.

"She'd head for Casper," Mack said. "She's not stupid, and there's nothing north of here but high plains."

"There's Yellowstone."

"She'd have to cross three hundred miles of nothing before she even got close. Dora might love the outdoors, but she's a city girl born and raised. Don't you think she'll head for town?"

"Probably," Cat said. "She'd need breakfast, for one thing."

They were entering a no-man's-land of battered warehouses and galvanized Quonset huts that apparently marked the outskirts of Casper.

"What's her favorite fast food?" Mack asked.

"She doesn't eat that kind of thing. Edie wouldn't let her."

"Sometimes that just makes it taste better."

"You'd think so. But that was one thing she and her mom agreed on. What they both loved was diner food. They used to try the meatloaf every time. Edie said they were taking the meatloaf tour of the world and they'd write a book someday."

Mack shook his head. "I knew she was a weird kid."

Mack slowed as they passed a fifties-style diner with red and chrome trim, scanning the cars and trucks in the lot. There were lots of pickups, but none as disreputable as the ranch truck.

"Looks like a meatloaf kind of place," he observed.

"It's almost eleven." Cat scanned the parking lot. "She's probably long gone."

"Not if she stopped." He grinned. "The truck vapor-locks. If she shut the engine down for any reason, it would be a good half hour before it would start up again. Most people would give up before that." He nodded toward the map pocket in the door. "Grab that map and we'll make a plan."

Cat ignored him, hiking herself up in her seat and craning her neck to stare at the truck stop they'd just passed. "What color did you say the truck was?"

"Rust, mostly. But it used to be blue."

"I think I saw it."

He braked hard and crossed a lane of traffic, careening off the exit like a NASCAR driver heading into the final turn. Cat grabbed the door handle as they spun onto a service road, then slid into the dirt lot behind the truck stop. He eased past a line of Kenworths and Peterbilts. Sure enough, the old International was parked at the back of the lot.

Cat wouldn't have guessed that the thing would even start, much less handle highway driving. It looked more suited to a junkyard than a parking lot. Dora was lucky it hadn't shaken apart on her before she'd left the driveway.

Tumbling out of Mack's pickup, she peered in the International's side window and saw Dora's backpack perched in the passenger seat. She jiggled the door. Locked. At least the kid had that much sense.

"Let's try the mini-mart." Mack grabbed her hand and hauled her toward the entrance to the small store, with signs in the plate glass windows advertising beer and soft drinks. The other side of the low concrete building was a restaurant.

"There's no rush." Cat tugged her hand away. "She's not going anywhere without the truck."

"Unless she hitches a ride."

"Oh, shit." She stepped up her pace. "She's not that stupid. Is she? You don't think she's that stupid, do you?"

An electronic cuckoo-bell sounded as Mack opened the swinging glass door. Standing on the dirty black doormat, Cat scanned the racks and shelves, taking in a seemingly endless selection of trucker hats and tourist T-shirts.

After searching up and down aisles packed with cans of Chef Boyardee and Alpo Prime Cuts, bags of Doritos and cellophane-wrapped Twinkies, she followed Mack through a scuffed entryway into the attached restaurant, searching for that halo of blonde frizz.

The counter stools looked like a seated police lineup, with the suspects ranging from seedy to shady to downright disreputable. Some crouched over coffee, watching the reflections in the grill's stainless steel backsplash as if they expected the cops to arrive at any moment and take their meth supply. Others hunched over blue plate specials, sawing at chicken fried steaks drowned in lumpy creamed gravy.

No Dora.

The booths hosted a more companionable lot—an overweight couple who probably divided the driving as well as the wide slice of pie they were working on; a group of bearded men who looked like they'd sworn off showering until the Cubs won the World Series; and a rowdy group of twenty-something boys scanning the crowd for babes. One of them shot Cat a wink and a leer, but Mack stepped up close behind her and the winker was suddenly engrossed in the scenery outside the glass window.

"She's not here." Cat hugged herself, staving off panic. "You don't really think she'd hitch a ride, do you?"

"I think she's smarter than that," he said. "But who knows? I didn't think she was unhappy enough to run off, either."

A chubby young waitress with black curls cascading from a checkered headband reached behind Cat to snatch up two menus from a holder on the wall.

"Two?"

She didn't wait for an answer, just led them to a cracked vinyl booth.

"Special's chicken fried steak," she chattered. "Cream gravy, mashed, and peas. Pie's extra." She looked up at the ceiling as she recited the varieties. "Apple, banana cream, pecan…"

"I'm just looking for my niece." Cat knew interrupting was rude, but who knew how long the list of pies might be? "Have you seen a teenaged girl in here? A little blonde, curly hair? Kind of frizzy?"

"Yeah. I saw her." The waitress slapped the menus on a table still streaked with the damp tracks of a dirty dishcloth.

Cat remained standing, one hand on Mack's arm. "You saw her?"

"Yeah." She made an impatient gesture toward the booth. "Here you go."

"I'm sorry. We're not eating," Cat said.

"Okay, then." The waitress scooped up the menus and started for the kitchen.

"Wait. Sorry. I just need to know when you saw her." Cat touched the waitress's shoulder and the woman whirled to face her.

"Look, we get lots of girls coming through here, okay?" She jutted her chin as if daring Cat to question her further. "And I got lots of work to do."

"Just tell me if she left. Who she went with."

The waitress glanced right, then left, like a trapped animal. "I didn't see anything."

"But…" Cat was struggling with the urge to give the waitress a kick in the shins, but a strong hand gripped her arm and lowered her into the booth. Mack slid in beside her, blocking her escape.

"Two coffees."

"We don't have time for this," Cat hissed. "We just need to know…"

"We're taking the time." He nodded toward the waitress, who was stalking around the side of the counter. "And try to treat her like a human being. Are you Chicago folks always this rude to the help?"

"No." Cat looked down at her lap, suddenly ashamed. "I'm sorry. I'm just so worried."

The waitress returned with two thick ceramic mugs and a glass coffee pot. Mack gave her a friendly grin.

"Thanks, Belle."

Cat glanced from the waitress to the cowboy, wondering how they knew each other, but no sign of recognition passed between them. Then she caught sight of the girl's plastic name tag.

"Belle, I'm sorry I was so abrupt," she said. "It's just that I'm worried about my niece."

The woman gave her a quick nod, then turned her attention back to Mack. It figured. Throw that good-looking cowboy into a crowd and women glommed on like magnets. Maybe it was the hat. Or the jeans.

Maybe it was the ten-dollar bill he was sliding across the table.

"So that blonde…" He let the question trail off, as if he didn't really care about the answer.

"She was in here almost an hour." The suddenly smiling Belle poured their coffees, lifting the pot with a flourish as the dark liquid streamed into the cup. Steam rose in fragrant swirls, making Cat realize she hadn't had anything to eat or drink since her breakfast had been cut short. "She didn't hardly eat a thing, so I kind of ran her out." A slight defensiveness entered her tone. "Can't hold a table with customers waiting, can I? We're here to do business, not run a charity for runaways."

"She's not…" Cat realized she was getting rude and defensive again. Dora *was* a runaway, after all. That was precisely the issue. "So did she leave?"

"Don't know. One of the guys tried to get her to go with him, thought she was—you know." The woman lifted her painted eyebrows, and Cat realized she had a lot to learn about truck stops. "But she told him off." She smiled again, displaying a crooked eyetooth. "Sassy little thing."

Cat bristled. "How could he have thought she'd have anything to do with him? She's not…"

Mack's hand settled over hers and pressed down. Hard. Looking at the waitress, Cat realized there was a good chance she had her own trucker waiting for her at home.

"Belle," hollered a bearded man from a neighboring booth. "You gonna gab all day? Need a fill-up over here."

"I got it, I got it. Hold your horses." Belle started toward the bearded man, then turned back to Cat. "I saw her out there, crossing the road." She pointed out the window and Cat eyed the uneven expanse of macadam that led to the highway. Cars flashed by at eighty miles an hour, along with eighteen-wheelers that rattled the windows as they bounced over the cracked concrete.

The waitress quirked her painted lips in a humorless smile. "Don't see any grease spots in the road, so I reckon she made it."

Chapter 39

MACK GRIPPED CAT'S HAND IN HIS AS HE WAITED FOR A break in traffic. A tractor trailer hurtled past, stirring up a swirl of dust and blowing back his hair.

"Come on." He dragged her after him, almost pulling her over as he ran. She'd kept up with him in every way at the ranch, and he'd forgotten she was so much shorter than he was. She was doing her best, though, and didn't complain as they clambered over the Jersey walls that divided the two streams of traffic. If she managed to keep up, they wouldn't become grease spots on the highway either.

By the time they reached the far side of the road, he felt as if he'd swum a particularly tumultuous river. Glancing up and down the row of buildings bordering the highway, he spotted a chipped sign that read "Auto Repair and Restoration" and took a sharp right.

The building beneath it needed some repair and restoration itself. A low stucco box, it was painted a hideous shade of mustard yellow broken only by long jagged cracks in the concrete. The broken glass in the door was mended with a few crooked strips of masking tape, while the missing panes in the window beside it had simply been replaced by plywood.

A skidding, rattling noise greeted their arrival, and a figure scooted out from under a car. It appeared to be a man, but it was hard to tell through the black grime that

coated him head to toe. He was so skinny and jug-eared—
and so ancient—that Mack wondered if this was the place
where the term "grease monkey" had been coined.

"Help ya?" Man or monkey, he wasn't about to rise
from the wheeled creeper he lay on. Propping himself
up on one elbow, he regarded both of them with blue
eyes that were bright as crystal in the grime smudging
his face. If she hadn't been so worried about Dora, Cat
would have laughed. Resting his head on one elbow,
the mechanic looked like another ironic interpretation
of Manet's snowy-skinned Olympia.

He smiled, exposing false teeth nearly as bright as his
eyes. "I can fix most anything."

"How 'bout an International Harvester pickup?"

"Well, isn't that something." He smacked his thigh.
"I haven't seen an International in months, and you're
the second one today."

The man struggled to rise, but what was evidently a
bum hip had him thrashing on the floor like a grounded
trout until Mack offered him a hand and helped him on
his feet. Cat wondered what he did when nobody was
around to help. From the look of him, he probably slept
on the creeper.

"Somebody brought one in earlier?"

"Didn't bring it in. Couldn't. Little girl came in,
wanted me to go over to the diner and look at one. Felt
like a heel sending her away, but she said it didn't run
and I can't travel these days." He punched his hip as if
he could smack something back into place. "Crossing
that road's taking your life in your hands, 'specially
when you can't move so fast."

"Where did she go?" Cat asked.

The man shrugged. "Don't know. Didn't pay attention." He looked suddenly stricken, and for a moment Cat thought his hip had gone out or something. "Little thing's not in trouble, is she? She seemed okay."

"Was she on her own?"

"Yup." He ran his hands over the sparse strands of hair on his bald head and grimaced. "All alone. I should have called someone. Got her some help. But she lit out of here like somebody was chasing her."

"And you didn't see which way she went."

He shook his head, staring ruefully down at the smudged concrete floor. "Didn't see. Sorry."

Mack took Cat's hand as they exited the garage. Once again, he was taking care of things, helping her out of a jam.

She tried not to feel irritated—with him or herself. This was his world. It was only natural he'd be the one solving the problems. It wasn't a reflection on her intelligence or capabilities.

But she couldn't help feeling useless.

They stood in the hard bright sunshine outside the garage. The light reflecting off the mustard-colored stucco bathed Mack in a golden glow that made him look like the hero of some long-ago Western. He squinted, looking up and down the highway, and those rugged crow's-feet bracketed his dark eyes.

"She has to be on foot," she said. "I really don't think she'd hitchhike."

"Let's hope you're right. We'll cruise the service road, search all the parking lots. She can't have gotten far. It's not much of a town."

"That's what worries me," Cat said. "I mean, you don't even have real cops here."

"I thought you were all impressed with Officer Brownfield."

She laughed. "Are you kidding?" She shot him a disbelieving stare. "He was an idiot. Did you not notice he was totally coming on to me?" She snorted. "Real professional."

His smile was clearly relieved. Had he really thought she'd fallen for Officer Brownfield's knight-in-shining-armor act?

They braved the rushing cars and trucks again, scampering across the highway at the first sign of a break in the northbound traffic, then scrambling over the concrete barrier to wait for a southbound truck to pass. The wind from its passing buffeted Cat, tossing her hair around her face and throwing dust in her face. Coughing, she followed Mack at a dead run across the road.

"Need anything to drink?" he asked.

She shook her head, stretching her stride to keep pace with his long legs. "I'm fine. Let's just find her."

They'd just rounded the corner of the truck stop when she spied a tiny figure perched on the running board of the played-out ranch pickup.

"Dora!" She nearly fell as she tugged her hand from Mack's and dashed across the lot. Dropping down beside her decidedly bedraggled niece, she choked out, "Honey, where have you been?"

"No place." Dora, slouched on the running board with her elbows on her knees, scanned the broken-down buildings that surrounded the parking lot, scowling. "Bumfuck, Wyoming. That's where."

Cat put her hand to her chest and took a breath,

hoping to suck in some sanity with the clear sunlit air. She'd been thinking the entire drive about what she'd say if they found Dora, how she'd handle the situation now that she knew just how desperate the girl was. To take off like this, head out into the middle of nowhere— she had to be terribly unhappy.

"What were you doing, hon?"

Dora shrugged. "Nothing."

"Well, that's good news," Mack said. "Your aunt thought you might have taken up hooking at the truck stop. Glad to hear you didn't throw yourself to the Bubbas."

Cat started to protest, then swallowed her anger. Mack's joking tone had charmed Dora into a faint but perceptible smile. Maybe she should stop the lecturing and the advising, the analyzing and the counseling. None of that was working.

Maybe she should follow Mack's lead and lighten up.

"You at least need some new clothes if you're going to change careers," she said. "They have some nice trucker caps in there. I'm thinking these Wyoming guys will go for anything that says 'John Deere' on it."

Dora and Mack both stared at her for a moment, their mouths slack with surprise. Then Dora let out a little laugh.

"I thought about that," she said. "But I didn't know if I'd have any money left after I fixed your damn truck. I sure as hell don't want one that says 'International' on it. What the hell kind of brand is that, anyway? Can't you buy an American truck?"

"It *is* American. The full name is International Harvester."

Dora scowled. "That explains it. It's not a truck; it's fucking farm equipment."

"Exactly," Mack said. "It's not made for highway driving. How are you planning to get it back where you found it?"

"Oh." She looked stricken, and Cat wondered if this was the first time she'd realized how much trouble she'd caused. "I can pay to have it towed if you want. I mean, my dad can pay."

"Your dad didn't drive it to death," he said.

Dora stared down at the gravel lot. "I could do some extra work."

"Like what?"

Dora thought a while. "I'm good at braiding manes and tails," she said.

Mack laughed. "Great. That's just what I need—a pack string gussied up like show horses."

Dora gave him a thin smile that spread into something genuine when he smiled back.

"Let's just see if it'll start," he said.

"It won't. I tried, like, four hundred times."

"Maybe that's the problem. How long's it been since you tried?"

She shrugged. "Half an hour? Maybe a little more?"

"Okay." He gave her a devilish grin. "How 'bout this? If I get it started, right here, right now, you braid all the horses' manes and tails."

"Okay." The way Dora jumped on the deal, it was pretty clear she loved braiding manes.

"You ready to go home?" Cat asked as Mack climbed into the truck.

"Home?" Dora's eyes widened, and Cat wondered just how bad things were back in LA with her dad.

"Back to the ranch, I mean." She felt her face

reddening. She'd been there a week, and she was calling it home. What did that say about the life she'd carved out in Chicago?

Dora looked at her like she'd grown wings and a tail. "You're not going to yell at me?"

"No. I'm just glad we found you."

"You're not going to lecture me?"

"No. Well, maybe later." Cat gave her niece a crooked smile and threw an arm around her shoulder. "But for now, let's just go back. Did you eat?"

Dora nodded. "I had the meatloaf."

Cat felt tears heat the back of her eyes, but she blinked them back as the truck shuddered, hiccupped, and roared to life.

"It just has to sit a while," Mack told Dora. "If you'd just eaten your meatloaf and tried again, you'd be to the border by now."

He stepped out of the driver's seat and gestured for Dora to get in.

"You want me to drive it?"

"You got it out here," Mack said. "You can get it home." He turned to Cat. "I'll call the cops and tell 'em to stop looking."

He reached up and pressed his hat down firmly on his head and strode off to his truck.

Cat watched him go. She couldn't blame him for being angry with Dora. Hell, she was angry with Dora. But the kid looked exhausted.

"I'll drive," she said.

Dora climbed in the passenger seat while Cat scanned the controls on the truck and tried out the gear shift.

"You called the cops?" Dora said.

"Of course we did." Cat pulled out of the lot and made a sharp right, then cruised onto the entrance ramp. Once they were on the highway and up to speed, she turned back to Dora.

"We thought Trevor kidnapped you."

"Trevor? Why?"

Cat watched Dora from the corner of her eye, searching for the telltale signs of a lying teenager. She knew from her own adolescence how good girls were at covering up things, like a trip to the mall when they'd said they were going to the library, or a meeting with a boyfriend when they were supposed to be at a friend's house. But Dora's posture was relaxed as it could be under the circumstances, and her eyes were clear and guileless.

"We found him on your Facebook."

"Trevor?"

Cat slanted another look at Dora. "You really don't know, do you?"

"Know *what?*"

"Do you remember a fashion site called 'The Maines Event'?"

It took a moment, but recognition finally dawned on Dora's face. "Oh, yeah. They show all kinds of skank clothes. I got a coupon there for some lip gloss a long time ago. What does that have to do with—*oh*. That's his last name, isn't it?"

Cat nodded. "He's been your Facebook friend ever since you got that coupon. He knew you were coming here. He followed you."

Dora clasped her thin arms around herself and bent over like she was going to throw up on the dashboard. "Ugh. Are you kidding me?"

"No. Of course, they probably can't do anything about it."

"Who, the police?"

"Right. Because your Facebook profile says you're twenty years old."

"Oh," Dora said. They rode in silence for a good half hour before she spoke again.

"I'm in trouble, aren't I?"

Cat shook her head. "No."

"I'm not?"

"No. I'm not going to punish you, Dora. That's not my place. You keep reminding me I'm not your mother. Well, you're right. I'm not. All I'm going to ask you to do when we get back is take down that Facebook page. I want you to do it while I'm watching, as soon as we get home."

Dora fidgeted, twirling a strand of blonde hair around one finger. "Okay. Right away?"

Cat nodded.

"But don't you have a class to teach?"

"Yes, but you come first," Cat said firmly. "You always come first."

Chapter 40

MADDIE SLOTTED THE LAST OF THE LUNCH PLATES IN the dish drainer and dried her hands. Mack had called to say he'd be home in a half hour with Cat and Dora.

She pulled out an old Junior League cookbook and flipped through it, looking for new recipes. She was good at chuckwagon cooking, but the fare was a little limited. She needed to make something new, something impressive. The Art Treks group would only be there for three more days, and she wanted to make sure they raved about the food.

Three more days. Then Cat would be gone, and Mack would be impossible. Maddie's plan had backfired like an old jalopy with a busted carburetor. She'd hoped for sparks between her son and the leader of the trip, but she hadn't expected those sparks to turn into flames.

Worse yet, Mack was planning to audit the ranch books once the dudes were gone. She'd told him they were in trouble, but she hadn't told him just how bad things really were. Ollie had taken her for everything she had, and then some. She'd been ashamed to talk about it, but the day of reckoning was coming closer and closer.

She was still staring at the cookbook, pretending to read recipes but really just staring, when Hank walked in.

"I need to talk to you," he said in his rusty, seldom-used rasp.

"Now?"

"It's as good a time as any."

She followed him to the table, where he proceeded to stare down at the table for a good five minutes, apparently trying to work up the courage to speak.

She could hardly stand to watch him, he was so uneasy and awkward. She'd come to know him better in the past months, better probably than anyone had ever known him. She knew he was a good man, an honorable one. She knew he loved her.

She wished she'd known it sooner. Maybe if she'd known how Hank felt, she wouldn't have been so quick to marry Ollie. But Hank and John Boyd had been like brothers, so he'd never said a word.

That was probably half the reason for the awkward silences between them. She'd gone to him for comfort after the dance—a stupid thing to do, seeking comfort from a man who had no more manners than a bull calf. He'd sat with her on the sagging sofa in the little sitting room in his apartment in the barn, sat there and held her hand and stared at the wall. Never said a word. Never touched her, past the hand-holding. She'd finally slumped over onto his shoulder and fallen asleep, and he'd still been there when she woke up. Still staring at the wall.

And now here he was, sitting and staring again. But this time he was staring right at her.

She shoved her chair back and stood.

"Wait," he said.

"I'm done waiting. I've got work to do." She turned sideways on the chair, ready to rise. "You're a slow man, Hank. Slow to talk, slow to act."

He nodded, as if mulling what she'd said over in his

head. She figured they were done talking, and whatever he had to say would remain unsaid, like everything else that had ever passed through that hard head of his. But then he cleared his throat and fixed her with those pale eyes, pinning her in place.

"You ought to find yourself a man," he said.

Now she did shove the chair back—shoved it until it slammed into the wall behind her.

"A man? You think I need a man?" She prided herself on self-control, but she couldn't help raising her voice. "I've been married twice, Hank. Once to the best man in the world, and once to the worst. What is it you think I ought to do now? Go into town and see if I can find myself another crook like Ollie? Or should I look on the Internet?"

She heaved to her feet and walked over to the sink. She'd already polished the kitchen till it gleamed, but she grabbed a bottle of spray cleaner anyway, along with a dishcloth. She squirted the counter beside the sink and started scrubbing as if her life depended on it.

She heard Hank push his chair back, but she refused to turn around. He'd go now, like he always did. Amazing how a man who never opened his mouth could end up saying something so tactless.

She should find herself a man. That was crazy.

But he didn't leave. He stepped up behind her. Took the spray bottle. Took the dishrag.

Next thing she knew he was taking her. And kissing her like a crazy man.

He might not talk much, but he could sure express himself.

Finally he pulled away, leaving her breathless. Her

hair had come down from the tidy bun she always pinned to the back of her head, and her lips felt hot and bruised. She backed into the counter and stared at Hank, at this man she knew so well and didn't know at all.

"Why didn't you do that last night?"

"You were upset," he said. "I didn't want to take advantage."

"Well, you should have."

"You wouldn't have known I was serious. You would have thought you'd started it."

"I was *trying* to start something."

"I want you to know it's me starting it."

She stared out the kitchen window. "I hope Cat's giving that little girl what-for," she said. "If Mack had taken a truck at that age, I'd have tanned his hide."

"Quit trying to change the subject," Hank said. "Don't put me off."

She shook her head. "You're a fine one to talk about putting people off."

"Last night would have been wrong and you know it," he said. "I was just savin' you from yourself. You didn't know what the hell you were doing."

She squeezed the rim of the sink so hard she thought the porcelain might crack in her grip, but she didn't turn around. Rock solid ranch wives didn't cry in front of the ranch hands.

But Hank was more than a ranch hand. He was part of the ranch, as much a part as the barn and the pasture. Maybe that was why she'd wanted him last night. She was trying to hold onto the place, but everything was slipping through her grasp. Hank seemed like the only thing in her world that would never change.

"I know Ollie hurt you, Maddie. I shouldn't have let it happen."

"He broke every promise that mattered."

"I know he did."

"But you've never broken a promise in your life, have you?"

He looked away. "Only one."

She shot him a questioning glance.

"When John died, he made me promise to take care of you. And I didn't do a very good job of it."

"I wouldn't let you."

He stepped up to her and took both her hands in his. "I'm not a ladies' man," he said. "I don't know how to sweet-talk anybody. Why, if we… you know… I'm not sure I'd know how. But you could give me a chance."

Madeleine laughed, her heavy heart buoying up with the sweet ridiculousness of Hank's courting methods. "I suspect you'll figure it out. And I've had enough of sweet-talking."

"Then give me a chance."

She looked long and hard at those pale honest eyes in his work-worn face, the lines fanning out from the corners from all the sunny days he'd collected working at the Boyd ranch. She'd known him most of her life, but she was starting to see she'd never really known him at all.

But she trusted him.

"I thought you believed a woman should have back-bone," she said.

"I do." He kept his eyes steady on hers. "And I don't know any woman's got more spine than you."

"I was a fool." Those pale eyes saw too much. "I listened to Ollie's sweet-talking and I believed every word he said. John never was much for words, and I guess I was hungry to hear them. Vanity, that's what it was. I was no smarter than a teenaged girl."

"He was a con man. He knew what he was doing."

"John would have seen right through his foolishness. He would have been ashamed to see me fall for it. I always wonder if he's watching, wondering where the hell my good sense went."

"If he's watching, he's proud of you."

"Proud of me? I almost lost the ranch, Hank. He's rolling in his grave."

"But you didn't lose it. Ollie wanted you to. He set his sights on it, and he knew your every weakness, and mine too. He thought he had it, but you stood up to him. You threw him out." He pushed his chair back and stood. "That took backbone."

"I suppose." She wiped her hands on the soft cotton of her apron. Hank was fooling with his hat, and she wondered which would wear out first, the hat or the apron.

"I thought we were goners." He set the hat on the table, crown down, and stood. "If Ollie'd had his way the place would be sold by now, cut up into lots. I'd be out looking for work, and I don't know where you'd be. Mack would be on the road again, with no place to call home. But you stood up to him, and you won."

She nodded, staring out the window as he stepped up behind her and put his hands on her shoulders.

"I knew John better than anybody but you. And I know he'd be proud of you. I'm proud of you."

He turned her gently, forcing her to face him. He slid his hands down her arms and folded her hands in his. Then he leaned in and pressed his lips to hers.

She might have backbone, but Hank Slay had elo-
quence. She never would have guessed such a quiet man
had so much inside of him.

"All right, Hank," she said. "I'll give you a chance."

He smiled, those eyes crinkling up at the corners,
and she wondered if she'd ever seen him smile before.
Maybe, when a favorite mare had foaled or a day of
branding had gone particularly well. But never like this.
Never anything like this. The man just lit up, and she felt
an answering light in herself, deep down where she kept
her secrets hidden, under the bluster and the busyness.

She smiled back.

"You're an extraordinary woman, Maddie Boyd. I'd
do just about anything for you."

She wasn't sure if Hank Slay was the ranch's elder
sage or its holy fool. But she did know one thing for
sure, and it surprised the hell out of her.

The man had actually said a five-syllable word.

Chapter 41

MACK WATCHED DORA TIE RIBBONS ON THE BRAIDED mane of the pudgy little roan. She'd come from her chat with Cat about Facebook etiquette with her sullen facade pulled back into place, and had been silent all day long.

"We need to talk," he said.

"I already talked to Aunt Cat," she said. "She made me shut down my Facebook account."

"Well, now you have to talk to me."

"What, are you my dad now?" She curled her lip. "I already have one, you know. And I didn't realize your relationship had progressed that far."

"It hasn't." Mack slouched against the barn wall and folded his arms over his chest. "She has no idea I'm talking to you."

"Then I don't have to listen."

"I thought you didn't let her tell you what to do."

She tossed her golden hair, a gesture that might have been impressive if it hadn't just set the frizzy halo to bobbing. "I don't."

"Well, you should." He shifted his shoulders, rubbing his back against the rough wood. "And you should treat her better, too."

"Why? She's not my mother."

He straightened and pinned her with a hard stare. He wasn't about to argue with her; this was non-negotiable, so he made it short and sweet. "Your aunt is one of the few people in the world who really cares about you. And you treat her like shit. She deserves better."

Dora looked outraged. "What, are you in love with her or something?"

"Yes." The conviction in his voice surprised him as much as it did her. "She's the best person I know."

Dora's fingers clutched at the horse's mane so hard that the normally sleepy Spanky stamped his foot and took a step sideways. "But she's always telling me what to do. And she doesn't understand me. Not one bit."

"You think my mother understands a damn thing about me? Think again," he said. "And she bosses me like a prison guard. But I know she'd do anything for me. Just like Cat would for you."

He started walking away. He'd had his say, but he couldn't resist tossing a final sally over his shoulder. "If I were her, I'd give up on you."

Dora was still clinging to the horse's neck, and he saw a look of panic cross her pretty face. He'd thrown his loop, and it had landed dead center. He just needed to tighten the rope.

"Since she's not out here now, trying to talk to you, I'm thinking maybe she already did."

~~~

Cat was packing up a few last-minute supplies in the Heifer House's front room when Dora found her. Though her back was turned, she knew that light step. It was more hesitant than usual. Cautious.

Either that, or this was some kind of ambush.

It didn't matter. This morning's events had worn her

out as far as the Dora situation was concerned. She felt like she'd failed, but to her surprise she didn't feel like making amends for it.

Because success wasn't really possible. Dora would never get over what had happened. She'd always bear the imprint of her mother's death—every time she visited a hospital. Every time she painted a picture—if she ever did that again.

Things didn't go back to normal after such a cataclysmic event. They changed. Hopefully one day doing the things that reminded Dora of her mother would feel sweet to her. Right now, the wound was too raw.

Cat was starting to feel like she was making it worse. They were both dealing with the situation as best they could, but for both of them, that meant not very well. Maybe someone could make this easier for Dora, but that someone wasn't Cat.

She slid brushes into the pockets of a canvas carryall one after another, arranging them by size and type. Damn, she was tired. She just wanted to go curl up on her lumpy mattress and zone out for a while, but she'd dodged too many of her responsibilities already. If her students hadn't been so sympathetic, they probably would have called the company and complained. They definitely weren't getting their money's worth.

She tested the spring of a sable brush with her thumb, thinking about Chicago. She'd be going back there soon, back to her old job, back to a life that didn't include cowboys or horses or making love under the stars. A life where you could barely see the sky, where you never set foot on grass that wasn't manicured and mown.

Even with all the disasters, she'd fallen for the Boyd

Dude Ranch. Fallen for the wide-open landscape, the light, the sunsets, the moody skies. Fallen for Mack.

"I came to say I'm sorry," Dora said from behind her.

"Sorry?" Cat blinked at her niece, struggling to step out of the swamp of depression she'd wandered into.

"I wanted to ask about my mom."

Cat sighed. "You know she loved you, don't you? Your mom loved you more than anything."

Dora swallowed and nodded, looking down at her hands.

"She didn't want to leave you," Cat said.

"I know." Dora sat down on the doorsill and gazed sadly out at the plains rolling off into the distance. "I wouldn't have wanted her to suffer. It's just…"

Cat swung the bag over her shoulder and leaned against the door frame. "Is that what you think? That she didn't want to suffer?"

Dora shrugged. "Well, yeah." She hugged her knees to her chest. "Who'd want to suffer?"

"It wasn't about her," Cat said. "It was never about her, not once she had you." She looked down at her niece and saw a sheen of tears in her gray eyes. "She didn't want *you* to suffer."

Dora rested her chin on her knees. "You think?"

"I know," Cat said. "She wanted things to be pretty and perfect for *you*, honey. Not for herself."

Dora seemed lost in thought for a while. Finally, she straightened her legs out and looked up at Cat.

"How come my mom stopped painting and stuff?"

Cat thought a moment. She'd always figured Edie was simply too busy having fun to take the time to paint. But there was more to it than that. Somewhere along the way, she'd lost the urge to create. She hadn't had the drive to find her own starry night after she married and had Dora.

"Do you think it was because of me?"

Cat floundered for an answer. She didn't want Dora blaming herself for anything. She herself had always blamed Ross and all the distractions he'd put in her path. But Edie had painted a little bit, up until she had her baby girl.

Suddenly, Cat knew the answer. The right answer, which thankfully was the answer Dora needed to hear. She dropped down to sit beside the girl.

"Yes, hon. It was because of you."

Dora bit her bottom lip. "I'm sorry."

"You don't have anything to be sorry for. Edie and I were both driven to be creative. We were just the same. Looking for that one thing, the creation that would define us, make us whole."

"Your starry night."

"Exactly." So Dora had been listening.

"Well, Edie found hers." She was talking as much to herself as she was to Dora. "And once you find it, maybe you don't have to work so hard anymore. Maybe you've given the world something so special, you don't have to try anymore."

Dora looked mystified. "What was it? I never saw it. Was it really good?"

"It was great." Cat smiled. "It was *you*, honey. You're the best thing Edie ever did. You were everything she ever wanted." She reached over and patted Dora's leg, looking away to hide the tears standing in her eyes. "You were her masterpiece."

The two of them sat in silence for a while, watching a meadowlark flit up from a fence post with a sharp cry. Cat thought of Ted, of what he'd said when she left.

Once I married Joyce, had the kids, it turned out this was enough.

He was talking about family. About finding something with real meaning, creating something that really mattered.

Maybe all along she'd been searching for the wrong thing.

She blinked back her tears and looked back at her niece. Dora's gray eyes scanned her face, as if searching out her feelings.

"What's the matter?"

"Nothing." Cat smiled. "I'm fine."

"No, what? I want to know," the girl said. "You're always worried about what's bothering me. I want to know what's wrong with you."

Cat huffed out a short laugh. "You already know what's wrong with me. I don't know how to live, remember?"

"That's not true." Dora fidgeted, but she kept her eyes on Cat. "Mom was wrong."

Cat shook her head. "No, honey. Your mom…"

"Yes. You're a better person than Mom was. You do the right thing, every time. You take care of everybody else, and you do it so well nobody notices. *I* didn't notice." Her hands twisted in her lap as she talked. For the first time since the funeral, she looked more sad than angry. "I'm really sorry I took off. And I'm sorry about what I said. It's not your fault Mom died, and I'm—I'm glad you're here."

Dora swiped the back of one hand over her eyes, and Cat realized she was crying. "I just really miss her.

She was my mom, and it's so not fair." She ducked her head and clutched a handful of hair in each hand, staring down at the ground. "So not fair."

Cat patted her shoulder, lost for words. Dora's thin back was heaving with sobs.

"I'm sorry I ran away," she said in a tiny, broken voice. "And I'm so, so sorry I was mean to you. And I'm sorry you can't stay here, forever and ever, because I know you want to."

"I don't want that," Cat said, patting her back. "I'm fine in Chicago."

"No, you're not," Dora said. "You hate doing that stupid job, in that stupid city. You're just too nice to say so." She sat up, sniffling. "You should stay here and paint every day, and marry Mack." Tugging herself away from Cat, she sat up, blinking as if she'd just awakened from sleep. "That's what you should do. You could marry him, and then you could stay on the ranch and paint. It would be perfect."

Cat laughed, wiping her own eyes. They'd only leaked a little, but Dora's ridiculous solution to her life dilemmas had chased the tears away in a heartbeat. "I can't marry Mack," she said. "I barely know him."

"Yes, you do. And he loves you," Dora said. "He told me, and I barely even asked. He'd marry you, I know he would. And then you could stay here forever. He'd take care of you."

"It's not that simple, honey."

"It *is* simple," Dora said. "The ranch will always be here."

"We don't know that for sure."

Cat remembered the conversation she'd overheard

between Mack and his stepfather. If the bank took the ranch, Mack would be set adrift. The land would be chopped up and houses built on the little flat parcels of land that would mean nothing without the grander whole. Eventually the mountains would fade into the background, the golden glow on the grass would fade, and life here would end up like life everywhere else— hectic, workaday, and mind-numbingly ordinary.

She bent down and gave her niece a quick, warm squeeze. "There is no forever. Not even here." She was blinking back tears again, and she wasn't sure she'd succeed this time. "Not even for Mack. And a girl's got to take care of herself."

Cat stood, channeling all her energy into a desperate effort to suppress the tears that were burning behind her eyes. She didn't know what was wrong with her, but she was about to have a meltdown. Maybe it was relief at finding the real Dora buried under all those layers of grief. Or maybe it was something else. Whatever it was, it wasn't going to stay inside her.

"I need to go," she said to Dora. "I'll—I'll be right back."

She fled the room, leaving a mystified Dora behind her. Blindly, she floundered down the hallway and out of the Heifer House. Nobody was around, which was a good thing because the tears were flowing freely now. She put her head down and power walked to the cabin, figuring it was her best bet for being alone.

She sank down on the front step, grateful for the overgrown half-dead lilac bush that shielded the corner of the porch from view. Dropping her head into her lap, she let all the emotions she'd held so tightly at bay through the past day out into the light.

Her shoulders shook with sobs, and a harsh animal sound escaped from somewhere deep inside her. She let it form into words.

There is no forever.

And she wanted forever. Forever with Mack. She loved him, and that was one thing that would never change.

She remembered watching him walk away at the truck stop, how he'd squared his shoulders and tugged at the brim of his hat. She'd felt a pang of loss then, and the same feeling was overwhelming her now. She'd be leaving soon, leaving him behind, and she'd probably never see him again.

But she needed him. He'd helped her find Dora, literally and figuratively, and she was starting to think he'd helped her find herself, too. She'd been here two weeks, and she'd become a new person, more alive and in tune with the world than she'd ever been before. Alive, and in love. And in a few days, she'd lose him.

She hid her face in her hands and let herself cry.

Chapter 42

MACK PITCHED HIMSELF INTO THE OLD LEATHER OFFICE chair, waving away the puff of dust that rose from the cushion. He'd definitely neglected the business side of ranching for too long.

Turning on the ancient desktop computer, he pulled out an old-fashioned ledger as the machine hummed to life. His mother had never really mastered the computer bookkeeping system he'd started for her, so she noted everything in the ledger and he caught up as best he could whenever he was around.

He flipped the big book open, scanning page after page of familiar handwriting. The early pages were in his father's neat block penmanship; the later ones in his mother's slanted chicken-scratch.

He flipped one page, then another, and suddenly the handwriting changed. This had to mark Ollie's tenure. In some lapse caused by grief or blind love, his mother had handed the books over to Ollie. Mack knew they'd be a mess, but he'd have to put them together as best he could. He'd need to inventory supplies and equipment, try and match things up, figure out just what Ollie had stolen and what he'd left behind.

He puzzled over the cryptic entries for a while, then gave up and grabbed a stack of unopened mail his mother had leaned up against the monitor. It was time to face the music—and the unpaid bills.

The first envelope was for the new liability insurance his mother had taken out to cover the dude ranch. It was a big chunk of change, but the next installment didn't come due until spring and by then they'd hopefully have calves on the ground to sell. The bred heifers up in the north pasture were about all the assets the ranch had left, but if all went well they'd pay off the mortgage installment, the insurance, and whatever else the dudes didn't pay for.

He picked up another envelope. It was handwritten, with a local return address.

Sullivan Ranch.

Well, that was odd. He didn't much like Sullivan, who treated his hands badly and his livestock worse. The man was all about the money. Mack doubted a communication from him could possibly be good news.

Sullivan's chicken-scratch was even harder to decipher than Maddie's, and Mack had to scan the letter several times to make sense of it. Something about missing cattle, and numbers not matching a bill of sale. He flipped to the second page. It was a bill of sale all right, and Mack recognized Ollie's handwriting from the ledgers. He scanned the form for half a second, then swore and shoved the chair back from the desk so hard it careened across the rough wooden floor and slammed into the wall.

Barely noticing the impact, Mack slumped forward and put his head in his hands.

Ollie had sold the herd. Sullivan claimed he'd bought them, and there were several head missing. He wanted Mack to make it right, but Mack didn't have his money.

Ollie did.

Mack didn't have anything.

Cat almost groaned aloud at the sound of approaching footsteps on the dirt path to the cabin. Hastily wiping her tear-streaked face with the back of her hands, she smoothed her hair and pasted on a smile. She had a feeling it wasn't very convincing, but it would have to do.

What little smile she'd been able to muster faltered when she saw Mack's face. The lines on either side of his mouth were deeper than usual, and the creases at the corners of his eyes that normally looked outdoorsy and kind of sexy simply made him look exhausted tonight. He looked like he'd just heard about a death, or some kind of terrible disaster.

"What's wrong?" She jerked to her feet. "Is Viv okay? Maddie?"

"They're fine." He brushed past her almost rudely, stepping inside the cabin. She was pretty sure he'd have shut the door on her if Maddie hadn't force-fed him on manners all his life. As it was, he kept his back to her when she followed him inside. His hands were shoved in his pockets and he was staring straight ahead through the window, as if he was watching the grass grow.

"What's wrong?" she repeated. "Did Trevor press charges?"

"No. But if he did, at least I'd have a jail cell to live in. The way things are going, I won't have much else. Neither will my mom. Or Viv."

She put her hands on his shoulders and kneaded the tense muscles. "Tell me."

He turned to face her and she wrapped her arms

around him. He held her, reluctantly at first, but when she rested her head on his chest she felt him relax and he pulled her close.

"I don't want to drag you into this," he whispered into her hair.

"You're not dragging me," she said. "I'm coming along of my own free will."

He held her a moment, then let her go and turned away. "Ollie sold the cattle. Sold them and took the money. I was counting on that cash from the calves to cover bills in the spring. Without it, there's no way we can hang on to the ranch."

She followed his gaze through the window to the land beyond. It didn't look like much from here—just a broad expanse of rough grass dotted with sagebrush and rocks. But she knew it was everything to Mack.

"Did Ollie have a right to sell them?"

Mack shrugged. "No, but it won't matter. It'll end up in court. Sullivan's a litigious bastard, and we can't afford a lawyer."

"But we saw the cows," she said. "Cattle. Whatever. They were in your pasture. You showed them to us just the other day."

He nodded. "Sullivan's counted them, though, which means he probably rounded them up. He says three are missing. He says I owe him for that." He let out a mirthless huff of laughter that almost broke her heart.

"Maybe he didn't take them yet."

"Maybe." He looked dubious.

"Possession is nine-tenths of the law, right?"

"Maybe." He scratched his head and grimaced. "We're grasping at straws here, but maybe."

She ran her hands up his arms and nested her fingers in the hair at the back of his neck. "Can you do anything about it now?" she asked.

He gazed out at the darkening plain. "Not really. I'll need to ride up there in the morning. But it's a rocky trail. I shouldn't do it in this light."

"I know something we can do in the dark." She gave him a smile and laced her fingers around his neck. "And I bet it would take your mind off your troubles."

Hiking herself up on her toes, she brought her lips to his.

For once, kissing Mack wasn't everything she hoped for. Sure, it was long. It was deep. It was passionate. But somehow, it was infused with sadness. She was pretty sure he was kissing her good-bye.

And she wasn't ready for that. Wasn't ready for it at all. She remembered Dora's words.

He loves you. He told me. It's simple.

It *was* simple. All her previous relationships had been tangled and complex, wrapped up in power struggles, half-truths, and doubts. But this one was simple.

She loved him. He loved her. All she had to do was make him see that no matter what happened, they belonged together.

Their lifestyles didn't. Their occupations didn't. But the two of them, as people, belonged to each other.

She deepened the kiss and tugged him closer, pressing her body to his. His body responded instantly, like always, but she could tell his mind was pulling away even as his arms held her close.

"Let it go," she whispered. "Just for now. Let it go, and be here with me."

"I don't have anything to offer you," he said. "No ranch. No future."

"How about your heart?"

He gave her a sad smile. "You already have that."

"That's all I want." She breathed deep, savoring the now-familiar scent of him. "That's all I need."

—⁓—

Mack couldn't help admiring the view as Cat straightened her arms and let her head fall back, her hair trailing down her back. She pulled him off-balance in a slow sideways spin smiling into his eyes. When she dropped down on the overstuffed sofa he fell like a half-sawn tree, catching himself on one knee before he crushed her against the cushions.

Falling into Cat felt inevitable, like giving in to an irresistible force he'd been fighting far too long. He let himself relax, savoring the warmth of her body against his. She was soft where he was hard, giving where he held firm. She answered something inside him, filled his empty places. Together the two of them made something whole. How was he ever going to let her go?

Sprawled beneath him, she tilted her pretty face up and gave him a sweet come-hither smile. Her lids dropped sleepily over her eyes until he could just see a glimmer of blue through the dark fringe of her lashes. In the dim light, her skin looked pale as moonlight, her lips rich and red, and he couldn't help tasting them. They were soft and berry-sweet, warm as sunshine, pure as the blue sky. They tasted like home.

A stab of regret pierced his heart so sharply he drew

in a quick, stunned breath. She was leaving in two days. He might never see her again.

"Let it go," she murmured against his cheek. "Let it go and just be here *now*."

He kissed her again, letting all his feelings for her flow through his lips into hers, from his hands to her body. He let go, like she'd said. Once he stopped resisting, love rushed in a torrent from his heart to hers, unstoppable. Letting loose the feelings that had ached inside him for so long made him feel light, warm, and free. Old wounds were closing, breaks mending, and his heart surged strong and steady with life and love.

She paused and pulled away, and their eyes met in a gaze that was totally unguarded, open, and unafraid. He was sure he'd never shared himself so completely with another person as he did in that moment.

When she kissed him again, the tide had changed and she was doing the giving. She filled him up, bringing every nerve and cell to life and making him whole in a way that would sustain him no matter what happened. He was about to tumble into a maelstrom of disaster, about to lose everything he had, but this moment was magic and nobody—nobody—could take it away.

He felt her move against him and his body answered instinctively, calling and responding over and over. Wrapping her legs around his waist, she pulled him close with her heels pressing against the back pockets of his jeans.

She twisted and writhed beneath him and he responded without thinking, kissing and licking, caressing and stroking. Her shirt was gone, her bra swept away like all the other barriers, and still he couldn't get close enough. She'd unbuttoned his shirt at some point, and now he shrugged it off, fighting a brief battle with the fabric before tossing it to the floor. His jeans followed, then hers. There was a crash as he kicked something over, but instead of stopping to see if he'd broken something he kicked it again and returned to Cat, only Cat. She was all that mattered in his world right now. Maybe she was all that had ever mattered.

She was so soft, so warm, so open and ready for him. When he slid inside her it was like coming home, and he realized he *was* home. There would always be a fire burning for him here, a light shining in the dark. The ranch and everything else he'd built his life on might fade away or fail, but this love was forever.

Letting her warmth surround him and fill him, he let go of the world and all its complications and lost himself in the simple, instinctive ecstasy of love.

When he lifted his head Cat's eyes were closed, her lips parted in rapt bliss. She opened her eyes just a little and there was that look again, honest and pure and giving. She knew what he was feeling.

He knew she felt it too.

Cat felt her body softening and warming, an odd, heady relaxation taking over her limbs as a sweet, hot pleasure opened at the heart of her like a fern unfurling in sunlight. Looking up at Mack, she saw his eyes go dim and lose their focus, and then she lost herself in him and gave herself, body and soul, to the force that was pulling them together.

Love caught her like a warm wind and lifted her out

of her life, out of the ordinary world. She floated, rising and spinning, swirling and soaring, until it set her down gently and she came blinking back to life.

Mack stroked the side of her face and kissed her again. This time there was an aching tenderness in his touch that almost broke her heart.

It was like the kiss they'd started with—he was saying good-bye. This man who felt like he'd lost everything was giving her everything she'd ever wanted—love, tenderness, passion. His heart.

It was more than she'd ever had from any man. And it was more than enough. She'd take it home, and she'd treasure it. And somehow, someday, they'd find a way to keep it.

Chapter 43

CAT LEANED AGAINST THE SIDE OF THE CHUCKWAGON, sipping coffee from a thick porcelain cup and watching the sun rise on a blessedly normal day. Her niece was safe. Better yet, Dora seemed to have found her old self buried under the layers of her grief. And today, the group would get back on schedule. There were two days left in the workshop. Two days to redeem herself to her students.

She blew the steam from her cup and swore to herself she'd make these days count. She was still dizzy from the night before and felt like there'd been some kind of seismic shift in her heart, but she'd have to figure out her personal life later. Right now, she had a job to do.

So did Mack, fortunately. He'd ridden up at dawn to check the north pasture and discovered he had cattle to care for after all. He was still worried, but he'd decided to deal with Sullivan later in the day. Right now, he agreed they needed to do the best for the students. The horses were saddled and ready. They just had to get breakfast out of the way.

Emma traipsed out of the Heifer House in a pink velour robe. Ed followed in a blue bathrobe, with striped pajama pants poking out of the bottom. Cat had just started to pour them some coffee when she heard the thudding tattoo of hooves in the distance.

Turning, she watched a dust cloud rise on the horizon as a rider approached.

She thought of all the old black-and-white Westerns she'd seen. A rider thundering up to a ranch always meant trouble—outlaws, maybe, or rustlers.

She squinted, watching the rider approach. The horse and rider were silhouetted against the rising sun, so she couldn't make out the specifics at first. But as the rider approached, she made out a slim figure with a pouf of golden hair that bounced with every stride.

Dora.

Cat frowned. Mack had encouraged Dora to go riding when classes weren't in session, but he'd told her not to go alone. And Cat was sure he wouldn't want his horses worked that hard. As the girl approached, she could see the animal's eyes rolling in panic, and its sides were slicked with sweat. He galloped nearly to the fire pit before Dora skidded him to a stop.

"Cattle." Dora spun the horse and pointed north. "That way. Trucks."

Cat couldn't help smiling. Dora tried to be cool about the excitement of ranch life, but clearly the sight of actual cattle had been too much for her.

"It's a ranch, hon," she told her niece. "They've got cows."

"But they're loading them up," Dora said. "Stealing them." The horse bobbed his head, clearly picking up on his rider's excitement. "Rustlers!"

"Are there injuns, too?" Ed asked, grinning. "Maybe a wagon train? Did John Wayne show up? Always wanted to meet the Duke."

"I'm not kidding. I heard Mack saying there were

cows up there, and I wanted to see. But there are trucks too, and men unloading horses. I think they're going to steal Mack's cows!"

Mack approached from the barn where he'd been saddling horses. He was already frowning, eyeing the exhausted horse. "Dora, were you out by yourself?"

"No, Viv was with me. She stayed up there. They're stealing your cows!" She struggled to catch her breath. "Up in the pasture. There are big trucks—tractor trailers. And horse trailers. Viv says they're getting ready for a roundup."

"There a name on these trucks?"

"Sullivan Land and Cattle Company."

"I should have known," he muttered. "They figure they can get away with it while we're busy with the dudes."

"Hah!" Dora spun her horse again, obviously reveling in her part in the drama. "They didn't figure it was the dudes that would catch 'em."

Mack set off for the barn, his long legs making short work of the rugged path, then stopped and turned to Cat. "It won't be much of a delay. The horses are tacked up and ready. I should be back by the time breakfast's done."

The students milled around, spooning scrambled eggs from tin plates and plowing through a plateful of bacon as Maddie churned out more and more food. Dora was trotting after Mack, determined to be a part of the upcoming drama.

"I'll be right back," she called over her shoulder.

Abby paced by the fire, obviously agitated. "I can't believe this," she muttered. "Really can't believe it."

"I'm sorry," Cat said. "I can't believe how many

things have gone wrong." She took a deep breath. "I'm sure the company will refund at least part of your fee."

"It's not that." Abby shoved her hands in her pockets and kicked at the dirt. "It's that dirtbag stealing Mack's cattle. We ought to do something."

"I'm sure Mack can handle it."

He'd handled everything else, including her. She wished there was some way she could help him, but the best bet seemed to be staying here, holding down the home fort.

She did her best to make small talk, keeping one eye on the trail to watch for his return. But the cloud of dust that finally appeared in the distance cleared to reveal a single rider. Dora, again approaching at top speed.

"Aunt Cat." She pulled up the horse and let it dance in place. If possible, she was even more breathless and excited than she'd been earlier. "You have to come. Viv's hurt, and Mack's really, really pissed, and he went on up there, and they have, like, I don't know how many men up there. I'm scared he'll get in a fight. You have to come."

"Viv's hurt?"

"She fell, I think. I don't know. She's resting now, but she was on the ground when we found her. I think something's broken. And Mack…"

Cat couldn't even imagine Mack's fury. Viv had probably just had a riding accident, but if he thought the Sullivans had caused it, there was no telling what he'd do.

"We need to go up there. I think he'll listen to you."

Cat took off for the barn at a run.

—◦◦◦—

Dora led Cat along a meandering trail that headed into the hills on the north end of the ranch. It was an uphill climb, but Rembrandt made it look easy. As hoofbeats approached from behind, Cat tugged him to a stop, but he danced like a racehorse at the starting line.

It was Ed, mounted on Bucky. He was hardly dressed in his usual Western wear. Cat did a quick double take.

"Your bathrobe doesn't go with your boots."

"I know, dammit." He looked down at his feet, where his striped pajama bottoms were a mass of wrinkled cotton tucked into his boot-tops. "But slippers aren't safe for riding."

Cat did another double take when another horse and rider crested the hill, and then several more. Evidently the whole class had decided to go along for the ride.

"What are you guys doing up here? This could be dangerous."

"I know," Ed said. "You think I'd miss it?"

"There was no stopping him," Emma said. She was right behind him. Their outfits matched.

Abby was next in line. "I told him me and Charles should come, but do you think he'd wait for us? Nope." She shook her head. "Stubborn old man."

"Hey, show some respect for your daddy."

Cat scanned the line. Despite her annoyance, she could barely suppress a giggle. Evidently no one had taken time to change. Only Maddie, trailing the line on a white mare that matched her pale face, was dressed for riding.

"Maddie," Cat said. "You don't need to deal with this."

"It's my problem. I'll see it through." She gestured

toward the barn. "Hank's coming too. He just had to saddle up."

At least they had one experienced rider coming. Cat started to tell the rest to turn around and head home, but their eager faces and bright eyes made her pause. They were having a good time. Maybe it wasn't what they'd signed on for, but she could hardly refuse to take them where they wanted to go—pajamas and all.

"Come on, Aunt Cat," Dora called. She'd stopped her horse beside a rocky outcropping just below the crest of the hill. Viv sat on the rock, holding onto her horse's reins with one hand and clutching her knee with the other. Cat urged Rembrandt into the surprisingly speedy trot that seemed to be his fastest gait. She slid out of the saddle when they reached Viv.

"What happened, hon?"

"They ran me off." The pain was obviously at war with a generous helping of anger. "We heard them first. They were shouting, and I heard the truck doors slamming. I knew something was going on, so I said we should go home, but Dora wouldn't listen. She rode up ahead. I couldn't stop her."

As if to illustrate her impulsiveness, Dora clicked to her horse and kicked it into a gallop, cresting the hill before Cat could get out so much as a squeak.

Viv rocked slightly, still clutching her knee. It was obvious she was in pain. "One of the guys rode up and I told him to get off our land." Tears sprang to her eyes. "He took his reins and whapped Booger in the face. Booger reared and I fell. I got back on and made it this far, but I can't ride, so I told Dora to go ahead." She clutched her knee tighter. "It hurts so much."

"Let me see."

Viv pulled away. "It'll be all right. Just go get my dad. I'm afraid he'll do something dumb. You know how he is."

Cat nodded, remembering Trevor's bloodied face.

"I told him I just fell, but he knows I ride better than that. He's so mad. If he confronts those guys…"

Cat remembered the Sullivans from the dance—big men, quiet, with hard eyes.

"It's just over that ridge," Viv said. "The cattle are spread out in the valley, but they were unloading horses, and they had the trucks parked at the loading chute."

Cat looked down at the injured girl as the rest of the class approached. "Somebody has to stay with her."

"I'll be fine," Viv said. "You need all the riders you can get. Just go. All of you."

Chapter 44

CAT PULLED UP AT THE TOP OF THE HILL TO SURVEY the situation, motioning for the rest of the riders to stop. A rolling pasture spread out before them, cloaked in golden grass and dotted with rocky outcroppings.

The cattle were milling around outside a rickety wooden corral, lowing their distress. A livestock truck was backed up to a loading chute, and several mounted men hovered at the edge of the herd. She couldn't tell who was who at this distance, but she was sure Mack was down there.

If she had any sense, she'd round up her students and take them back to the ranch. She was sure foiling cattle rustlers was hardly an Art Treks–approved activity. This was probably the end of her new teaching career, but surprisingly, she didn't care. What mattered was the ranch. And Mack. Mack mattered most of all.

She'd wished for a chance to help him the way he'd helped her, and it looked like this was it. She was no cowgirl, but there had to be a way to keep those animals from getting on that truck. She'd gather the students together and work out a plan.

Ed pulled up beside her and she turned to speak to him, but he took one look at the situation and kicked Bucky into a gallop. She gripped her saddle horn and watched him careen down the slope, wondering not if, but when he'd tumble off the horse and break his neck.

Then Emma passed her, and Abby and Charles. Only Maddie stopped.

"Where's Hank?" Cat asked.

Maddie glanced behind her. "He must be having trouble," she said. "I don't know what's keeping him."

"Go back and see. We need him, Maddie. If Viv can ride, maybe you can take her with you."

Reluctantly, Maddie turned her horse and headed back. Cat set off after the rest of the class, wondering how she'd stop this sure disaster. If she could catch up and pass them, she could regain some control. But Rembrandt laid his ears back and flat-out refused to step up into a trot.

"Come on, buddy." She nudged him again and rocked forward in the saddle. He turned and gave her a look that clearly said she wasn't the boss of him, then bent to crop the grass.

She pulled the reins and he jerked his head up.

"Don't make me kick you," she said.

He took one step, then another. When she finally got to the gate, everyone was hushed, listening to Mack's conversation with a short, portly man with a bristling mustache she recognized from the hoedown. Sullivan.

"Ollie wasn't authorized to sell them," Mack was saying. "I'm sorry. It's a misunderstanding."

"That's something you'll have to work out with your father," Sullivan said.

"He's not my father, and the sale's off."

"Can't stop what's already happened." The heavy man rested one arm on the saddle horn, then crossed the other on top. "They're my cattle. Bought and paid for."

"We were never paid."

"Your father was."

Cat flinched, expecting the worst, but Mack simply stayed rigid in the saddle.

"Stepfather," he said. Judging from his tone, the word was synonymous with *maggot*. "And again—not his cattle to sell. You got robbed, Sullivan." His horse took a step toward Sullivan. "Now get off my land."

Mack's eyes were fixed on Sullivan, so he hadn't seen the cowboys ease toward the herd. It wasn't until the cattle began to surge toward the truck and the first heifer clanged her hooves against the metal ramp that he looked up. Another followed it, and another. Mack had been right; they were Zen cattle. They strode up the ramp and into the hot, dark truck as placidly as they did everything else.

Cat urged Rembrandt through the gate. Despite what had happened with Trevor, she didn't think Mack solved every problem with his fists. But in this case, she wouldn't blame him.

There was a flurry of movement behind her, a quick rustle as the students drew closer. Ed, of course, wasn't satisfied with staying behind. He pulled up alongside her.

"They're taking the cattle," Cat said.

"No they're not." Ed narrowed his eyes, scanning the herd. Rising up to stand in his stirrups, he reached up and pressed his hat to his head. The pajamas were still bunched around his boot-tops as he pitched back into the saddle and kicked the horse—hard. His robe flapped behind him as he rocketed into the pasture with a whoop worthy of Geronimo.

"Git along," he hollered. "Git along, you doggies, you."

The slow ride home gave Maddie plenty of time to worry. Her granddaughter had barely been able to climb into the saddle, and it was obvious her knee was hurting her. Back in the pasture, Mack was arguing, perhaps fighting, with the Sullivans. The students were mixed up in the whole thing too, so the dude ranch project was now officially a bust. She'd won everybody over with her cooking, and they'd been a good-natured group. But now they were actually in danger. That couldn't be good.

Don't borrow trouble, she told herself. She'd always believed in following her instincts, doing her best, and letting the future sort itself out. Of course, that hadn't worked out too well for her. That attitude had let her ignore the niggling doubts that tickled the back of her mind when she'd pledged herself to Ollie. Maybe she needed to look ahead more often.

Looking ahead right now wasn't doing her any good. There was no sign of Hank on the long stretch of trail leading to the ranch, and the place looked deserted except for a few vehicles parked in the pullout. Mack's pickup, the International, the old Continental John had bought Maddie for trips to town, and one other car—or no, not a car. An SUV.

She squinted as they plodded closer. A silver SUV. Her stomach twisted. Trevor was back.

Viv saw it at the same instant. "That guy's back. The pervert." She clicked to her horse and he broke into a swaying trot. Maddie could see the girl was clenching her teeth against the pain in her leg, but nothing would slow Viv down once she got a burr under her saddle. Maddie nudged her own horse up to speed and followed.

As they pulled up to the hitching rail, the late-afternoon sun slanted through the big double doors of the barn. Anyone else would have seen a tidy, well-kept stable, but Maddie noticed an open cooler, the sack of grain slashed open and spilling onto the floor, and a bottle of beer, smashed into pieces, lying in a pool of amber liquid. There was still no sign of Hank.

She ran for the house.

Crossing the porch in two steps, she ran inside. She swung the door closed softly and rested her back against it, catching her breath. The house was ominously silent.

She could wait for Mack. She could call the police. But then there was a sound from the kitchen, a clink of china like a teacup on a saucer. It was hardly a gunshot, but she was so tense it cut through the silence like a bullet.

Hank. If something happened to him, that future she was planning would be bleak indeed. Her mind racing, she stood up on tiptoe and lifted her grandfather's Remington from its place of honor over the door. Tucking it under her arm, she edged over to the kitchen door and peered inside.

Hank had his back to her. She'd always liked the back view of a cowboy, the muscles they got from riding and roping, and she was beginning to appreciate Hank's muscles more than most. Right now his backside was wrapped up like a present, with her apron strings tied in a big old bow just above it.

He turned and she saw that he held a plate full of artfully arranged shortbread in one hand and a teapot in the other. The frilly apron around his waist was at odds with his rugged face and battered boots. He didn't notice her standing there with the gun; his eyes were fixed on the dining nook where Trevor sat sipping from a china cup.

"So," he said in his gravelly, seldom-used voice. "Tell me about those supermodels."

The crunch of gravel from out front made Maddie lower the gun and glance out the window. A dark State of Wyoming cruiser pulled into the drive, and Officer Brownfield stepped out. Maddie quietly returned to the door to let him in.

The state trooper's boots thudded on the floor, distracting Trevor from an elaborate story about Victoria's Secret Angels. His eyes widened when he saw the cop.

"Mr. Maines, you're under arrest." Brownfield strode to the table and jerked the man out of his chair. "You have the right to remain silent…"

Trevor jerked in his grasp. "I told you, I didn't do anything. That girl ran away. You have no right to harass me this way. I'm calling my lawyer. I'm calling the governor."

"You can call anybody you want." Brownfield gave Trevor a jerk of his own. "We know you didn't take the girl. But Hank here called us when he found you here, messing around in the barn. There's a bag of rat poison in the barn and another one in your car. Poisoning livestock's serious business in this state, pilgrim." He cleared his throat. "You have the right to remain silent…"

Maddie looked at Hank in wonder as the trooper droned on. "You kept him here. You served him tea."

Hank nodded. "People will do just about anything for a taste of your shortbread, Maddie." He looked down at the apron, a rueful grimace on his face. "And I'd do just about anything for you."

—◊—

Mack's mind was racing as he stared down Sullivan, who was mounted on a tall bay gelding decked out in a showy silver-mounted bridle. He wished this was the old West. He wished he had a peacemaker. Hell, if he'd been the gun-toting type this might never have happened. He'd have killed his stepfather before the man could touch his mother—shot him down like the varmint he was.

The cloud of dust he'd raised when he approached Sullivan was clearing, drifting away in the hot summer air. He could feel his future floating away with it, scattering like dust, settling over the hallowed ground of his fathers to mix with the soil and be forgotten.

Sullivan's jaw was set, and his men were jostling the herd forward. One stubborn heifer had paused at the bottom of the ramp, spooked by some shadow or maybe just distracted by a glint of sun. In any case, the bottleneck at the front of the chute was jammed, and the other cattle were beginning to mill and low. A few turned back and Sullivan's riders slapped their hats on their thighs to urge them back on track. One man let out a shrill yip.

Mack scanned the herd. If Viv were still here, the two of them could probably drive the cattle away from the truck, at least for a while. But he couldn't take his eyes off Sullivan. Holding eye contact seemed essential, somehow, as if nothing could happen as long as he held the other man's gaze. The moment drew out, the sun heated, and Mack felt sweat dampening the back of his neck.

A sudden flurry of hooves sounded behind him. He

snapped his head up to see five horses burst into the valley, galloping at top speed, charting a crazy, zigzag course for the very center of the herd. In the lead was Ed, clad in baggy pants and a loose striped shirt. Some kind of white cape was billowing out behind him, and his horse seemed to be trying to outrun this mystery pursuer. The other students were strung out behind him, controlling their mounts with varying degrees of success.

"Git along, you doggies!"

Ed plowed past Sullivan's men and exploded into the center of the herd, his horse rearing up on his hind legs and screaming out a protest at the unexpected excitement. Mack clutched his chest as Ed grappled with the saddle horn, then stood in his stirrups and waved his hat. Hell, he was wearing *pajamas*. And that was the old man's bathrobe billowing behind him, a waving white flag that meant anything but surrender.

The cattle were panicked, lowing in terror, the whites of their eyes showing as they grimaced with fear. They began to circle, mill, and spin with Ed at their center. Bucky's front hooves hit the ground once, then twice, before he reared up again and Ed slipped backward. The old man hauled on the reins and the horse ducked his head against the bit, then toppled sideways. Horse and man disappeared in the center of the circling herd.

"Git along," hollered another voice. Abby. She was heading toward her father at a dead run. She must think she could drive the cattle away, but she'd only make things worse. Mack saw Ed's horse rise and run off, but he couldn't see the old man through the milling herd of cattle.

Mack nudged Spanky into action, trying to work his

way to Ed as Dora passed him, with Emma and Abby close behind. The little girl was bent over her horse's neck like a jockey. Everyone and everything seemed to be going ninety miles an hour. Emma's horse was out of control. Charles was clinging to his saddle horn as if he was prepared for an impromptu bronc ride.

But Rembrandt, with Cat on board, picked his way sedately through the cattle and made his way to Ed, unmoved by the chaos around him.

As the dust cleared, Mack saw Ed crouching on the ground, clutching his hat with both hands as if it could somehow save him. Mack sucked in his breath as Cat steered Rembrandt toward him.

For a second, Mack thought the mule was going to walk right over the old man, but he stepped carefully over him and planted his feet, standing firm as the herd broke in two and flowed around him. A chunky little heifer ran into him from behind, but the big mule laid his ears back and let out a bray of protest, holding his ground. As soon as the herd passed, Cat swung from the saddle, letting the reins dangle as she knelt beside Ed.

Wiping sweat from his forehead, Mack blinked twice, then swung into action. Circling to the back of the herd, he positioned himself in the flight zone and urged them forward with a wave of his hat. As he headed for Cat, she waved him away.

"Ed's okay," she hollered. "He's all right."

"Go get them sons-a-bitches," the old man quavered. He was clutching his hat to his stomach. "I'll be there in a minute."

Mack whirled his horse and took off after the herd. He could count on Rembrandt and he could count on Cat.

That left him free to get the cattle away from Sullivan's riders and out of reach. Cat was right; possession was nine-tenths of the law, and he wasn't going to let even one more animal into that trailer.

He needn't have worried. The old trail horses, miraculously, had caught the excitement and were performing like seasoned cutting horses. Rookie riders clung to saddles as the horses circled, spun, bucked, and pranced, and the cattle, confused by the chaos, scattered in panic. Mack pulled Spanky to a stop and watched the herd stampede for the hills.

He'd never seen anything so beautiful in his life. And behind them all was Cat, helping Ed rise as Rembrandt stood with his four legs planted like a show horse squared for a halter class, protecting the man who knelt beneath him.

Chapter 45

CAT HELPED ED OVER TO THE GATE, WHERE HE LEANED on a post and caught his breath.

"You okay?" she asked.

"Okay?" The old man grinned. "I'm better'n okay. That was the most fun I ever had in my life, and it's been a fun life." He chuckled. "Course, I thought it was about over when that horse reared up."

"I thought so too," she said. "Are you sure you're all right?"

"Sure." He patted her shoulder. "You go talk to that man of yours."

She didn't bother to correct him. Mack was her man—at least for now. Swinging up onto Rembrandt's back, she walked him over to where Mack was resting his arms on the saddle horn, talking to Sullivan.

"They're my cattle," the man said, narrowing his eyes. "I bought 'em fair and square."

"From a con man," Mack said. "Look, I can sympathize, but he didn't own them and he didn't have a right to sell them. You can take it up with him, but if you come out here and load up those critters, I'll have you in jail for rustling."

Cat couldn't help adding her two cents. "Those cattle are all Maddie has left. You wouldn't leave a widow woman without any means of support, would you? I thought you cowboys had some kind of honor code."

Sullivan worked his mouth as if something tasted bad, then looked down at his saddle horn. When he met Mack's eyes again, some of the hardness had gone from his gaze. "I paid for 'em," he said, but it was more a whine than a challenge.

"I'll help you run down the bastard and we'll string him up in court," Mack said.

Sullivan nodded and took the hand Mack offered. The two men shook and shared a nod, and the deal was done.

"You've got quite a crew there." Sullivan watched the students scamper around the pasture, struggling to get their overexcited horses to go after the cattle. It was the first time Cat had seen the man smile.

"Dudes." Mack grinned and glanced over at Cat. "Can't live with 'em, can't shoot 'em."

———————

Mack smiled to see how proudly Ed sat in the saddle, riding back to the ranch at the head of the posse that had foiled the rustlers. He was John Wayne, Henry Fonda, and Glenn Ford all rolled into one pajama-clad hero.

Mack felt fairly heroic himself, for the first time in ages. More than that, he felt hopeful. His cattle were scattered, but they were still his cattle. His daughter was injured, but she'd managed to hike herself up into the saddle and there didn't seem to be any permanent damage done. And despite the unscheduled mayhem, the students were chattering with excitement.

And Cat had risen to the occasion like a champion. She'd faced the emergency head-on, stayed steady and focused, and taken the whole thing in stride. She'd behaved like a seasoned ranch hand—or a ranch wife.

Wife. Maybe that was too much to hope for. She had goals and dreams that ranged way beyond this patch of Wyoming land, and he didn't want her to give up who she was. Still, there might be a way…

A plan flashed into his head, an idea that might let him and Cat have everything they wanted—including each other. He'd barely begun to work it out when they crested the hill.

As the ranch came into view, what should have been a triumphant homecoming turned into yet another disaster.

—∾—

Cat gasped as the ranch came into view and she saw the cruiser parked in the turnout. There was no sign of Maddie or Hank, and her gut twisted with dread. In the excitement of the cattle scattering and the students breaking for the hills, she'd forgotten that Maddie had gone back for Hank and never returned. Something had happened. And generally, when the police were involved, that something wasn't good.

She wanted to slide off her saddle and run for the ranch house, but Mack and Viv had more at stake than she did.

"Go," she told Mack. "I'll see to the horses. Dora will help."

Dora nodded and edged her mount up to take the lead. She'd become a capable cowgirl in the twelve days they'd spent at the ranch, replacing her sulky, troubled demeanor with a new confidence.

The students had learned as much about horsemanship as they had about painting—maybe more, given today's advanced exercises. She barely had to prompt them to pull the animals up to the corral fence and loop the reins over the top rail.

"Go on up to the house, Aunt Cat." Dora slid from the saddle and grabbed Ed's mount. "I'll get these guys taken care of."

"We'll help," Abby said. Cat started to protest, then realized that by "we" she was referring to herself and Charles. For once, Ed seemed willing to do the sensible thing and toddle off to the Bull Barn so Emma could see to his bumps and bruises.

"You sure you don't need help?" Cat was torn. She wanted to do right by her students, but she needed to know what was going on inside the silent ranch house.

"You go on," Abby said. "Just come out here quick as you can and tell us what the hell's going on. Inquiring minds are dying to know."

Cat was starting up the steps when the front door opened and Officer Brownfield strode out, his face set in a grim scowl and his hand on his sidearm. His beefy hand gripped the biceps of none other than Trevor Maines, who glanced at Cat, then shifted his eyes away quickly. There was a flat, cold hatred in his eyes that gave her a sudden shiver despite the warm summer sun.

Backing up against the porch rail, she watched the trooper frog-march Trevor to a cruiser and shove him inside. She wondered why policemen always pushed the perp's head down to keep him from hitting it on the car roof when they so obviously wanted to give it a good crack against the chrome.

Maddie came out and stood in the doorway, Hank standing behind her.

"Hank," Cat said. "I was worried about you."

He blushed scarlet and started fiddling with his hat, circling it one way, then another. "I came back and he was here," he said. "Guess he came back for revenge or something. Had a sack of rat poison, and he was getting ready to mix it in the feed when I found him. Broke into the beer cooler, too."

"I pretended I didn't know what he was doing. Invited him in for tea while I called the cops. They'll put him away for a while. We take livestock poisoning damn serious around here."

He flushed more deeply and the hat spun faster. Maddie chuckled.

"I come back and found the two of them chatting over as nice a plate of shortbread as you'll ever see." She jostled Hank affectionately. "This one had laid out a plate of cookies nice as you please, and brewed a fine pot of Earl Grey. I didn't know he had it in him."

"Least I didn't have to make conversation," Hank said. "The man does go on."

Cat couldn't help laughing. "I'd say you've shown dedication above the call of duty," she said.

"I'd say so too." Maddie beamed, and Cat realized there was more than duty between her hostess and the hired man. "Way above."

"Told you I'd do anything." Hank gave Maddie one of those rare smiles that lit up his face. "Guess now you know it's true."

Chapter 46

CAT WOKE EARLY THE NEXT MORNING—EARLY AND alone. They'd all stayed up late the night before, hashing and rehashing the roundup and the details of Trevor's arrest. Dora was thrilled to have been the one who caught the "rustlers." Ed was thinking about "gettin' him some cattle" and moving out West permanently. Emma and Abby were trying to talk him down from his Wild West euphoria, but without much luck.

And Mack—Mack was very quiet. He seemed to have something on his mind, and she could feel his eyes on her whenever he was near. But every time she caught him staring, he looked away. Maybe because today was the last day of classes. Tomorrow would be her last official day at the ranch.

But this was the last day with the students, and she needed to get things started.

"We've spent a lot of time learning how to look, how to see, and how to translate that onto paper," she said once she'd gathered the students around the chuckwagon. "But today we're going to put all that together and learn how to feel."

She paced the edge of the fire pit. "Don't just paint what's on the surface. You don't always have to paint what you see. Take reality and make it your own."

Make it your own. She couldn't even do that with her own life. She'd be going back to Chicago the day after tomorrow, and she felt like she was taking a trip to a far country. It was as if the ranch had become her reality, and everything before it had been a dream.

She wondered if Van Gogh had felt that way about St. Remy, where he'd painted his *Starry Night*. She was starting to think that she'd found her own—that ultimate expression of herself. The problem was, she didn't think it was a painting.

It was a place. It was a way of life.

She turned toward the students and hesitated. She'd learned so much in the past week. The most important parts of it weren't part of the curriculum, but she wanted to pass it on.

Because being an artist didn't just mean learning to paint. Being an artist was about knowing your heart and being able to show the world all that it held. That's what Ames did, and that's why he'd been so success- ful. He painted from the heart. It wasn't much of a heart, but he was honest about what was in it, and that touched people.

She'd always believed she'd succeed if she worked hard enough, but you had to live hard enough, too. It was the time she'd spent with Mack, with Dora, with Maddie and all the rest of them that had made her see what mattered.

She could hardly tell her students that, though. She knew how they'd react—the knowing glances, the in- dulgent smiles. They'd think the relationship with Mack had gone straight to her head.

But though she couldn't tell them, maybe she could show them.

"We're going to the canyon today. There are a million

things to paint, and I'm not going to pick one for you. Find what speaks to you. Take everything you've learned here and put it in a painting. Paint what you want, how you want."

Charles put his hand up, hesitantly, like a student who couldn't quite understand what the teacher was saying.

"Are we still using the limited palette?"

Cat smiled. "No. You use whatever colors you want. Whatever colors you *feel*. That's what it's about today."

The ride out was uncharacteristically quiet. Everyone seemed to be lost in their own thoughts, and instead of the usual banter there was only the creak of saddle leather and the slow plodding of the horse's hooves. After yesterday's excitement, today seemed like a dream.

They'd seen the canyon before, but it still evoked a long breath of wonder from everyone in the crew. It was as if a great fissure had been cut in the earth, a jagged scar that revealed the complicated underpinnings of the seemingly placid prairie. Layers of silt and clay and sandstone revealed the beginnings and endings of worlds, eras that had been all and everything to whatever creatures roamed the surface before it was submerged under the next world, and the next and the next.

The sun did its best to light the canyon, making the wildflowers that clung to its sides glow against the dull rock. But shadows took over halfway down, shrouding the craggy depths in mystery. Only the river that had created the deep gash in the earth managed to catch the light, its mirror-bright surface reflecting the sky in a slice of rippling silver.

They pulled up their horses at the edge and drank in the view. Even Ed had nothing to say.

Finally Cat cleared her throat. "Well, this looks good," she said.

Always a poet.

While the students set off in search of inspiration, Mack strung a coil of rope around a circle of trees to turn a small clearing into a makeshift corral. The horses milled inside, browsing on the greenery and nuzzling each other. After unloading everyone's equipment, he settled down as usual, finding a comfortable log in a spot laced with dappled shade. Tippy sat at his feet, flinging her head back to beg for more attention whenever he stopped absently rubbing her shoulders.

Dora stood at the edge of the corral, the sun turning her hair into a flaxen crown.

"Aunt Cat? Do you want to go together?"

Cat smiled, feeling a little guilty. Getting Dora to paint had been an all-important mission through most of the trip, yet today she hadn't even noticed that her niece had brought supplies for herself as well as Viv.

"That's okay," Cat said. "You can go with Viv if you want. I—I don't think I'd be much company."

Dora nodded. "I guess you need some time to yourself."

Cat remembered what Mack had said when Dora had first arrived. *It's all about them, and it's all about drama.* Dora had grown up on this trip. Cat didn't need to hover around her anymore.

She watched the two girls set off, falling instantly into lively conversation, and checked to see that everyone else was happy. Emma and Ed had headed north with Abby, while Charles set off on the trail that led into the canyon's shadowy depths. Cat was tempted to watch over them, to dart from one group to another and help everyone with technique, but she'd told them they'd be on their own. Besides, Dora was right—she needed some time to herself.

Slinging her bag over one shoulder and her collapsible easel over the other, she set off in the opposite direction from the others, scanning the canyon as she went, looking for a scene that spoke to her. She hadn't thought too much about what she wanted to paint, so she was open to anything: a close-up portrait of a flower, a long view of the canyon, or a forest scene.

But when she came to the right place, she recognized it right away. As she set up the easel, she felt something rise in her chest, a lightness that seemed to make the world around her a little brighter.

She'd have to get that into the painting somehow.

———

Mack knew he should announce himself. He felt like a stalker, or maybe a voyeur, standing behind Cat and watching her paint. But he loved the way she became totally engrossed in what she was doing, the way she moved like a sleepwalking ballerina, the way she took on a new grace and beauty when she did what she loved. Even Tippy seemed to understand Cat shouldn't be interrupted; she hung back with Mack rather than doing her usual enthusiastic meet-and-greet.

Cat was painting the canyon. The foreground of the painting was a rock that jutted out into the drop-off a few feet from where she stood. Below it, seemingly bottomless depths were shrouded by mist struck by sunlight. On the far side of the canyon, huge pines lined a rock wall; above them stretched layer on layer of rock—red, yellow, and gray—and above that a thin crust of grass and a few tortured trees.

Above that was the horizon and a sky lit with delicate pink hints of dawn. It was clear the sun was rising behind the viewer, and a shaft of light slanted through the mists and lit a small tree that was clinging to a crack in the canyon's layers of rock. He knew without being told that the little tree was the real subject of the painting. It was struggling into the light, holding tight to a narrow cleft in the rock but reaching and straining for the life-giving rays of the sun. One yearning root snaked out to the edge of the rock, like a toe testing cold water.

He'd never been much for academic interpretations, symbolism and imagery, all the intellectual claptrap that got in the way of just sitting back and enjoying a book or a painting or a piece of music. But he knew without even thinking that the tree was more than a tree. He wondered if it was Dora, or him, or Cat herself.

Maybe it was all three. Or everyone, doing their best to grow in whatever poor soil they were given, reaching for the light in everything they did.

He looked at the scene itself. He'd seen it a hundred times, maybe a thousand, but he'd never noticed that tree. He'd never seen the light look quite like that, either.

"It's dawn," he said without thinking.

She whirled, giving him a strict schoolteacher-squint as she held her brush in the air like a weapon. He'd better be careful or she'd paint him to death.

"What?" She blinked as if she'd been asleep for a hundred years, and he had to resist the urge to go to her and kiss the cobwebs away.

"You're painting sunrise." He nodded toward the far side of the canyon. "You changed the light."

"I know." She cocked her head and looked at the painting with a critical squint. "I didn't realize it till I got halfway through. That's how I feel, I guess. Like everything's just beginning."

She backed away from the painting and the two of them stood together, soaking it in. Tippy nudged her hand and she petted the dog's head without looking.

"It's good," he said. "Amazing. It looks like you just stopped time—like everything's about to change at this exact second."

Cat turned to him smiling, fully awake now, fully in the moment. She reached for him and he took her in his arms, looking down at her and feeling that mysterious tug, that pain in his heart.

"It is," she said. "And somehow, it's going to change for the better." She rested her head on his chest. "I just know it is."

Chapter 47

CAT LEANED THE LAST PAINTING UP AGAINST THE WALL of the front parlor and took a step backward. She should be looking at brushstrokes and composition, color and value—things the students had learned from her over the course of the workshop.

But instead she saw the other things they'd learned—less tangible things. She saw that Ed had painted Emma and Emma had painted Ed. Their figures didn't take up the whole canvas, but somehow they became the focal points of their landscapes. She saw that Dora had painted a loose, impressionistic view of the prairie meeting the sky—a painting that was full of open space and possibility. She saw that Viv had worked much more tightly, preserving a view of the canyon as if she wanted to hold it still forever, put it in a frame so it would never change.

Abby had turned a wall of rock into a bold abstract piece, and Charles had done the same with a tumble of river rocks. Their paintings were so similar they could have been done by the same hand. Hmm. Interesting.

She stood by the window, looking out at the scrubby ground surrounding the house. Little birds were hopping from branch to branch in the spent lilac bushes by the front door, chattering like a roomful of gossips. She remembered how bleak the ranch had seemed when she got there. Now it seemed uniquely alive, not just with the birds but with the breezes, the sunshine, the sweet scent of sage.

She thought of Modigliani as she had when she'd first arrived. Picasso, burning his drawings. Van Gogh, freezing in that stark, simple room. No matter what their circumstances, they'd been able to find the beauty in their world, to see it and show it by putting their hearts into their paintings. They'd made the world their own.

But this world would never be hers. She was going back to Chicago. If Art Treks kept her on, she'd keep spending her vacations as a teacher, always in a new location. Italy. Scotland. France.

Those places had glittered for her when she'd started this journey. That had been her goal—to travel, to see new places.

But now she didn't even want to leave the ranch. She wasn't done, she realized. There was more here to paint. More to see, every day. The sun always came up on something new here, every day a bright new promise.

She'd thought the place held nothing for her. She'd expected to miss all the excitement of the city, but the truth was, there was nothing for her to miss. She wasn't sociable enough to enjoy the parties and gallery openings. She wasn't rich enough to take advantage of the restaurants and shows.

And the truth was, she dreaded going back to the concrete and brick, the square city blocks and angular buildings. She'd fallen in love with the winding roads of the West, the curves of the landscape, the way the clouds drifted aimlessly in the endless sky.

She looked up as the students filed into the room. Tonight was her last chance to make sure their Art Treks experience stuck with them. She'd been determined from the start to give these people their money's worth. Everything had gone wrong, but she knew they'd learned a lot. They'd made connections with each other, and every person you loved helped you see the world in a new light.

Wasn't that what really mattered?

She knew she needed a plan, but her mind had gone blank. She'd asked the students to come prepared, so at least she knew how to start. They'd been told to explain why they chose the subject they did, and how their painting evolved from their experiences on the trip.

She watched them arrange themselves as they always did—Emma and Ed on the sofa, Abby sitting stiffly in an overstuffed armchair. The two girls were behind the sofa, resting their elbows on the leather cushions.

She didn't know where Mack was. Maybe his office. He'd said something about needing to use the computer, so he was probably working on the ranch's financial issues again.

She wished he was here, but life had to go on. Even when you wanted it to stop. Even when you found a perfect moment with the perfect man, the real world kept on spinning.

Charles came in and perched on the arm of the sofa near Abby, and Cat could swear the air in the room changed. Maybe somebody had gotten something out of this trip. And judging from Abby's shy smile, it was a very good thing.

She'd let the students start, and she'd take it from there. She'd learned as much from these people as they had from her.

"Ed, would you like to start?"

The old man cleared his throat. "Well, I didn't

know quite what to do today. You didn't give us much direction."

Cat felt a tug of fear in her gut. Why was she still hoping this would work out? She'd failed these people. Nobody came on this trip to learn how to see inside themselves. They just wanted to learn to paint, and she'd taught them so little.

"So I didn't quite know what to paint. I mean, usually there was a lake, or a tree, or something, you know? Emma saw some flowers she liked, so we stopped, and then I tried to think about composition, like you showed us. And I asked myself what was the focal point of this scene, like you said."

Well, at least someone had learned something. She'd talked about focal points the first day.

Ed held up a painting of his wife standing at her easel in a sea of wildflowers. The painting was promising, but not quite finished. "And I decided it was Emma. She's been my focal point for fifty years. I guess she still is, even with all this pretty land to look at."

Emma turned her own painting around. She'd painted flowers, but in her painting they had been plucked out of the meadow and bunched in an old, gnarled hand.

"I'd have gotten more done if she hadn't made me hold the flowers," Ed groused.

"I wanted you in the picture too. I was remembering that time we went camping."

He snorted. "I took her up to the Adirondacks, made her sleep in a tent and eat Vienna sausage out of the can. And all she remembers is that I gave her a bunch of weeds I picked along the trail."

"These are perfect," Cat said. "You couldn't have done the lesson better."

"But they're not finished," Ed said.

"But you caught what matters, and you can finish up the details later. It's not what's in front of you that matters. It's how it makes you feel. These are wonderful."

Ed and Emma beamed as she turned to Abby. "Abby? What did you paint?"

The woman started blushing even before she spoke. Her voice shook a little as she stood up and showed an abstract painting done in warm shades of brown and blue with touches of red. It was the colors and composition that mattered, but Cat recognized the wall of the canyon, with its layered streaks of rock.

"I liked what you said the other day about form versus representation," she said. "I know most everybody picked something pretty to paint, like the flowers, but I wanted to do something different. I saw the rocks, and, I don't know." She ducked her head. "They were so ordinary they were beautiful."

"I did the same thing." Charles turned his painting around to show an abstract depiction of some round river rocks. He, too, had concentrated more on color and texture than form, and his painting was surprisingly successful. "I don't think something has to be pretty to make a beautiful painting. You just have to look a little closer."

Cat looked from one painting to the other. "Did you two work together?"

"Nope." Abby looked uncomfortable, as if she'd been accused of cheating. "We were on opposite sides of the canyon. I was near the top, and it looks like he went down to the river."

"We just think alike." Charles moved over to sit on the arm of Abby's chair. The two of them put their heads together and it was clear they'd found their own focal points.

"Viv?" Cat gave the girl a smile of encouragement. "Our most improved student, by the way. I can't believe how good you've gotten. You have real talent."

Viv glowed as she shyly turned her painting around. She'd climbed down to the river and done a study of rocks and trees and flowing water. It was meticulously detailed, with every blade of grass defined.

"Lots of detail," Cat said.

"I wanted to save it." Vivian blushed. "Hold onto it, just exactly as it is now. Dad says things are going to be okay, but I was thinking about losing this place, and I—don't want to. That's what I like about painting. You can hold onto things."

She glanced at Dora, who turned her own painting over. It was similar to the one she'd torn up the first day—a long view of the canyon, with the river glowing at the bottom.

"That's beautiful," Ed said. Emma nodded.

"I like the way it fades out," Viv said. "Just turns into a blur, so you can't really see the horizon. It's like the river goes on forever."

"I guess I wanted to say that we don't know what the future holds," Dora said. "But we keep going—like the river."

"What about your future?" Ed asked. "Are you staying with Cat? That father of yours isn't looking after you too well."

Cat sucked in a quick breath. She hadn't asked Dora

yet if she wanted to stay with her. That was a personal conversation, one she'd been trying to get the nerve to start. Now Ed had laid it out in front of everyone, and he'd insulted Dora's dad. She waited for the fireworks to start, but Dora only shrugged.

"Not right away," she said. "I think I need to look after my dad for a while. I'll visit Cat a lot, though. If she'll let me."

"Of course I will, hon. I was going to ask you to—well, we'll talk about it later."

"I'd come visit a lot more often if you lived here."

Cat felt like every eye in the room was watching her, and she glanced around for an escape route. "Um, I don't know—I…"

"You know how you always say my mom didn't fulfill her purpose?" Dora said.

"I was wrong about that, hon."

"I know." Dora flailed a careless hand, waving away the issue. "But you know, you aren't fulfilling yours. You ought to be a mom. You're always taking care of people. You should marry Mack and live here and raise a bunch of kids and paint."

Ignoring Cat's red-faced embarrassment, she turned to the rest of the students. "Don't you all think that's what she should do? She has this sucky job back in Chicago, and a shitty little apartment. And they're crazy about each other. It's okay with you, right, Viv?"

Viv shrugged. "Sure. Whatever makes him happy. She's better than Emilio, that's for sure."

At least Mack wasn't in the room to hear Dora's crazy ideas. Much as she wanted her time on the ranch to last forever, Cat knew it was a ridiculous idea. She and Mack had known each other for all of two weeks, and however powerful her feelings had become, it just wasn't realistic to think his were the same.

She cleared her throat, as if that could erase the awkwardness of the moment, and shifted into teacher mode. "I'm glad you all had such a good time," she said. "Now tomorrow…"

"Hey, wait," said a deep voice from the doorway. "You forgot something."

Mack strode into the room carrying her painting, and she felt herself color as brightly as any dawn sky. She couldn't explain why her own painting made her uneasy, but she'd left it behind on purpose. Every time she looked at it, she felt like she was the little tree she'd painted, clinging to a shelf of rock for dear life, resisting the pull of the shadowy depths of the canyon. She hadn't wanted to dissect the feeling behind the painting with all these people watching. Heck, she hadn't even wanted to think about it herself. That's why she'd left it back in the Heifer House.

As Mack held it up for everyone to see, she felt naked and off-balance. She certainly couldn't present an intelligent analysis of her technique. Oddly, she couldn't really remember painting it.

She looked at the group—Ed and Emma holding hands on the sofa, their daughter beside them, talking to Charles. These people were her friends. So why did she feel so exposed?

Chapter 48

CHARLES LOOKED AT THE PAINTING AND SHOOK HIS head. "That's fantastic," he said.

Emma nodded. "Beautiful. The way you caught the light. The way the tree looks so fragile."

Cat glanced at their faces. The admiration was real.

"It's about being on the edge," she said. The feeling she'd had when she painted it came back to her—a sort of trance, where the whorls and currents inside her mattered as much as the breeze rattling the sagebrush and the sun warming the rocks. "The tree's clinging to the edge of the rock, trying to reach for the sun. I suppose the canyon is the unknown, with all those shadows." She glanced at Mack. "It's dawn, a new day, and everything is about to change."

As she looked at the painting, it drew her in. It was good that it disturbed her. Good that it made her uneasy. She'd told everyone they should paint what was in their hearts, and she'd done just that.

It was the best thing she'd ever painted.

"*I'm* about to change," she said.

A long silence followed. Everyone was looking at the painting, and she shifted nervously.

"Well, that's about it," she said. "The shuttle will be here at 9:00, so we'll have our usual seven a.m. breakfast. I hope you all enjoyed your Art Trek and you'll tell your friends about your time here." She cringed internally, but the speech was scripted, a requirement of the job. "You'll be receiving an evaluation form in the mail, and the company would like you to give them your honest opinion of what we do right and what we could do better."

She felt like she'd just walked over that cliff, sealing her fate. Even if the students tried to be kind, they were likely to reveal some of the disasters that had plagued the Art Trek. She really hadn't been in control—not from day one.

She jerked her head up as Ed began clapping his hands. Emma joined in, then Abby and Charles. As she stood there blinking in surprise, the ovation continued.

"Well," she said when the applause faded. "You're— you're very kind. I'm sorry that things didn't go smoother. We missed a couple days, and..." She blinked back tears.

"Smooth is boring," Ed said. "I like the bumpy parts of the ride."

"Me too," Abby said. "This was the best vacation we ever took. Usually Dad takes us to these stuffy hotels, with everybody bowing and scraping. It's awful. Nobody really talks to you, but you know they go home and talk *about* you. Here we felt like part of the family."

"And we learned a lot," Emma said.

"That's great," Cat said. "Thank you. I guess everyone got something out of the workshop, then."

"Even me," Mack said. "I got something out of it too."

Cat hoped he'd gotten something out of it. She hoped he and Maddie would get that contract. Maybe they would, since the students were so pleased.

"I got you," he said. "At least, I hope I did."

Cat froze, and everything around her seemed to freeze with her. How long had the birds been silent? A moment ago they'd been chattering in the bushes. Now the hush was eerie. The room was suddenly a tableaux in a painting, a character study of a drawing room soiree. Everyone was smiling expectantly; everyone was watching her. She felt like they expected her to reveal a hat and whip out a rabbit, or produce scarves from her sleeves.

She wasn't ready for this. She was still sorting out her life, trying to figure out where she was going.

"Let me show you something." He fished a folded sheaf of papers from his back pocket and handed them to her. She flipped through them. They were printouts from the Internet.

"Equine Excursions in Provence" read the first one. The second showed reproductions of Van Gogh paintings alongside photographs of their subjects: the Chateau d'Auvers, the hospital at St. Remy, the Langlois Bridge. Another showed riders threading in single file through the breathtaking landscape of southern France.

She looked up at Mack and blinked.

"I found a guest house we could rent by the week," he said. "It's got room for us and eight students, plus a stable for horses. I've found two outfits we could rent riding horses from. They don't have packhorses, but the country's not that rough. We could take the supplies in a wagon."

"In France?"

"They have openings in December. I don't have much to do around here that time of year." He grinned at

Maddie, who had come to stand in the doorway. "Hank and Mom could take care of the place."

"So you're saying…"

"I'm saying we could set up our own Art Trek," he said. "I'll take care of transportation and logistics. You take care of the art side of things."

"I'd go," Ed said. "You just let me know. You need a deposit?"

Cat stared at him, openmouthed.

"I'd go too." Charles glanced at the woman beside him. "If Abby went."

"I talked to a lawyer in town about a contract," Mack said. "For a partnership. We could host classes at the ranch in the summer and fall, travel in the winter."

"A lawyer? A partnership?"

"Or a minister and a marriage. Your choice." Smiling, he knelt at her feet. "I'm asking you to stay, Cat. I'm asking you to marry me."

She knew she had her mouth hanging open like an idiot, but she couldn't wrap her head around what he was proposing.

Proposing.

She felt like the tree again, poised on the edge of a precipice. But this time, she wanted to let go. There was no fear in falling when you had a safe place to land.

But was it really safe? Or was that wishful thinking? Anything could happen. She'd known Mack all of two weeks. How could she leave behind the life she'd worked so hard to build—leave it for a man? Edie had done that, and she'd barely painted anything since.

But she'd changed for a man who didn't care about her work—a man who thought only of himself. Mack had just proven that he cared about Cat's interests as well as his own. They'd be partners. She'd help with ranching, and he'd help with workshops.

And what was she leaving behind? A city of glass and concrete. It wouldn't be much of a sacrifice to trade the hard-edged world of Chicago for the open spaces and big skies of the Boyd Ranch.

Mack was still kneeling at her feet. "Step off the edge, Cat. Take a chance."

"I—I don't know," she said. "I don't know what I should do."

"What do you want to do?" he asked.

In a heartbeat, she realized that was the one question she could answer. She wanted to go back up to the cabin and sink into bed with him, bury herself in the sight and scent of him, and forget everything. When they were together, she had everything she'd ever wanted.

She knew where she belonged.

"I want to stay," she whispered. "I want to stay, and in December I want to go to France."

"Good." He swung her around, grinning, and swept her into his arms. "You can find that starry night for real."

"I think I already did."

He stood. "Is that a yes?"

"Yes." It came out in a whisper, but she'd never meant anything so sincerely in her life.

He bent to kiss her. For a second she looked sideways at the students, but they were suddenly all captivated by Emma's painting, exclaiming over some detail in the flowers she'd painted.

Nobody was watching. She tipped up onto her toes and met his lips, and suddenly the birds were singing again. She could feel the still air starting to move, the breezes clearing the room and bringing in sunshine and sage scent and warmth. She was in the center of her universe, the place where she belonged, and for once the future looked like a smooth road rather than a struggle.

She put her arms around Mack's neck and deepened the kiss. She'd forgotten there was anyone else in the room until the clapping began again.

When the kiss broke, she turned to see the group standing by the sofa, grinning and clapping. Dora and Viv had joined them, and Maddie and Hank stood in the doorway.

"Hey, look," Mack said. "We got a standing ovation."

And he kissed her again.

Acknowledgments

The image of the lone cowboy riding the range in solitude is at the heart of Western classics like *Shane*, *Unforgiven*, and *High Noon*.

But though I like to think I'm "cowboy tough," I could never have made it through the past year without the help of my friends. It takes a village to create a cowboy, and that village is Cheyenne, Wyoming. I'm lucky to live there, and I'm grateful for all the support my books receive from our uniquely Western community.

I could fill another book with all the people who deserve my thanks, but I'll have to limit myself to a few. I'd like to thank Colette Auclair for the rants, Cie Patterson for the eggs Benedict, and Laura Macomber for the martinis.

Writers need other writers, and I'd like to thank Mary Gilgannon for the Mexican lunches, the Cheyenne Area Writers Group and my Saturday friends for always being there, and Carolyn Brown for being the best long-distance friend a cowgirl ever had.

Writers need a backup team, and I have one of the best. My agent, Elaine English, has been an understanding friend through this difficult year, as has my editor Deb Werksman. I'm also grateful to Danielle Jackson, Dominique Raccah, and all my Sourcebooks sisters for their support.

I was raised to be a writer by a family of readers,

thanks to my parents Don and Betty Smyth and my sister Carolyn.

But most of all, I want to thank my husband Scrape McCauley for being tougher than any cowboy and standing by me through the hard times. You are the best man I know and I love you beyond words.

Cowboy Crazy

by Joanne Kennedy

———

Sparks fly when sexy cowboys collide with determined heroines in a West filled with quirky characters and sizzling romance. Acclaimed for delivering "a fresh take on the traditional contemporary Western," Joanne Kennedy's books might just be your next great discovery!

From stable to boardroom...

Sarah Landon's Ivy League scholarship transforms her from a wide-eyed country girl into a poised professional. Until she's assigned to do damage control with the boss's rebellious brother Lane, who's the burr in everybody's saddle. He's determined to save his community from oil drilling, and she's not going back to the ranch she left forever. Spurs will shine in this saucy romp about ranchers and roots, redemption and second chances.

———

Praise for **Tall, Dark and Cowboy***:*

"Another steamy, suspenseful offering from the popular Kennedy." —*Booklist*

"A sassy and sexy wild ride that is more fun than a wild hootenanny!" —*The Romance Reviews*, 5 stars

For more Joanne Kennedy, visit:

www.sourcebooks.com

Tall, Dark and Cowboy

by Joanne Kennedy

—⁓⁓—

She's looking for an old friend...

In the wake of a nasty divorce, Lacey Bradford heads for
Wyoming where she's sure her old friend will take her in.
But her high school pal Chase Caldwell is no longer the
gangly boy who would follow her anywhere. For one thing,
he's now incredibly buff and handsome, but that's not all
that's changed...

What she finds is one hot cowboy...

Chase has been through tough times and is less than thrilled
to see the girl who once broke his heart. But try as he might
to resist her, while Lacey's putting her life back together, he's
finding new ways to be part of it.

—⁓⁓—

Praise for Cowboy Fever:

"HOT, HOT, HOT...with more twists and turns than a
buckin' bull at a world class rodeo, lots of sizzlin' sex,
and characters so real you'll swear they live down the
road!" —Carolyn Brown, *New York Times* and *USA
Today* bestselling author of *Red's Hot Cowboy*

www.sourcebooks.com

Just a Cowboy and His Baby

by Carolyn Brown

———————

She's got her eyes on the prize...

Gemma O'Donnell wasn't the first woman to win the ProRodeo buckle for bronc riding, but she was darn well going to be the second. What she didn't count on was her main competition sweeping her off her feet.

He'll do whatever it takes to win...

Trace Coleman isn't really after a title—he needs the cash prize to buy his dream ranch. But one sexy, determined cowgirl keeps getting in his way. In his effort to take her out of the running, he risks losing both the title—and his heart.

They're both in for a little surprise...

Everybody's world is turned upside down when a pint-size bundle of joy gets dropped right into Trace's lap... and suddenly all the stakes are higher.

———————

"Brown is a superstar...Full-throttle
fun."—*Wendy's Minding Spot*

For more Carolyn Brown, visit:

www.sourcebooks.com

One Hot Cowboy Wedding

by Carolyn Brown

~~~

A marriage made in Vegas...

Hunky cowboy Ace Riley wasn't planning on settling down, but his family had other plans for him... The only way to save his hide, and his playboy lifestyle, is to discreetly marry his best friend, Jasmine King.

Can't possibly last...

Feisty city-girl Jasmine was just helping out her friend—that is, until their first kiss stirs up a whole mess of trouble, and suddenly discretion is thrown to wind.

One hot cowboy, one riled up woman...
And they'll be married for a year, like it or not!

~~~

Praise for Carolyn Brown's Spikes & Spurs series:

"An old-fashioned love story told well...A delight." —*RT Book Reviews*, 4 Stars

"Tender and passionate love scenes... endearing and quirky characters...an absolutely adorable story." —*The Romance Studio*

For more Carolyn Brown, visit:

www.sourcebooks.com

Jesse

by C.H. Admirand

Loneliness will take a man places…

Jesse Garahan has plenty of Irish charm, but having had his heart demolished twice, he's sworn off women forever. Until the fateful day he meets Danielle Brockway and her tiny daughter on their way to their new home in Pleasure, Texas.

But there may be places he doesn't want to go…

Fiercely protective of her little girl, Danielle isn't about to let Jesse get anywhere close enough to hurt either of them, no matter how much longing she sees in his eyes…

Praise for **Dylan***:*

"Readers will be left panting."
—*RT Book Reviews*, 4½ Stars

For more C.H. Admirand, visit:

www.sourcebooks.com

About the Author

Joanne Kennedy is the author of five Western contemporary romances: *Cowboy Crazy; Tall, Dark and Cowboy*; *Cowboy Fever*; *One Fine Cowboy* (nominated for a RITA award for best single title contemporary); and *Cowboy Trouble*. A transplanted Easterner, she ran away from home to the West at the advanced age of thirty-two and was delighted to discover that cowboys are real and chaps are leather pants with no seat.

At various times, she dabbled in horse training, chicken farming, organic gardening, and bridezilla wrangling at a department store wedding registry. Themes that have remained constant throughout her life are Jack Russell terriers, a tendency to confuse fiction with real life, and a stubborn belief in romance that led to multiple dysfunctional relationships with inappropriate men before she finally got it right.

Now older and hopefully wiser, she lives in Cheyenne, Wyoming, with two dogs and a retired fighter pilot. The dogs are relatively well-behaved.

Joanne loves to hear from readers and can be reached through her website, *www.joannekennedybooks.com*.